Prep For Doom

Band of Dystopian
Authors & Fans

Prep For Doom

Managing Editor: ER Arroyo
Story Development: Sara Benedict, Jon Messenger, Cheer Papworth
Content Editing: Sara Benedict
Copy Editing: Maia Driver

Table of Contents

PROLOGUE: *The Gift*

by Caroline A. Gill

Bursting open, the thin, wooden door slammed against the wall and cracked in half.

"Get down!" a man yelled.

Chaos erupted in the large classroom. Five armed rebels ran in, sweeping chairs to the side, looking for any resistance.

One jumped onto the teacher's desk. The intruders were masked with black scarves across their noses. They stunk like burnt food and blood.

"What's happening? Who are you? What's going on?" Questions filled the air. Most of the girls were screaming. Three students jumped out the only window, falling to the ground outside like dung from an elephant.

Dede Afi John held her ground and her breath. With a sinking feeling in her stomach, she knew exactly who these men were. Nigeria was not far enough away for any girl to be safe. Fresh out of nightmares, straight from the newspaper headlines: these were the rebel warriors of Wayo Wahala. Dede knew why they had come.

"Quiet! All of you, quiet now!" one of the men yelled. "We are soldiers. Nothing bad will happen to you." He looked hard at the school girls, hugging each other tight, and tried to persuade them. "You have nothing to fear. We are here to help you." His red shirt said otherwise. Red was the color of death. His voice was not kind.

A feeling of foreboding fell across her heart. Dede gulped but kept silent. Her wide, brown eyes knew the truth, though, and she couldn't hide that.

"You, there," one of the men called to her, returning her stare. "What's your name, girl?" In the time it took for her to blink, he aimed his rifle at her head. In shock, she watched his face, every fear in her gone wild. *I am nothing to this man,* she thought. *Nothing.* Stunned, the tall, high cheek-boned girl stood still as death.

"D—Dede Afi, my name. That's my name," she spit out finally.

"You will follow us in a straight march, you and your friends. No talking or I use this." He fondly stroked his gun barrel like a pet snake.

Dede wanted to refuse and spit in his face. She wished she had been one of the girls who had jumped out the window and ran. A classmate behind her started crying. Two men moved through the crowd. Within seconds they reached the howling girl, throwing her onto the floor, forcing her mouth shut. Harsh hands wound thick tape around the girl's bleeding lips. Then the two men hauled the bound girl upright like prey ready to be gutted. Dede had a choice to make.

Bowing her head slightly, she stumbled at first. These men spoke of peace and aimed weapons of war. Dede knew only one thing mattered now. Resolutely, she set herself one simple task: *I have to keep Yaa, Afua, and Ato safe.* Carefully, she wrapped her arms around her friends and they hurried out the broken door.

"There will be an opportunity to run. And I will take it," she vowed in a whisper. "Be ready."

"Who are they, Dede?" Ato mumbled. The four of them held hands, shuffling with the thirty other girls into the courtyard. "Who are these soldiers? Are they our Black Stars?"

Dede said nothing as one of the guards glared at her group. There were no black star patches on any of the men. These men were not soldiers of Ghana. There was no honor in these men, only fear and guns. And they would not keep their word—there was no protection for Dede or any of the girls at Bawku Technical Institute. "No, we are alone. No one in Bawku knows we are in danger," Dede murmured.

Huddling closer, Yaa began to cry. It hit them all. They were in bad trouble. Guns were everywhere. Men were yelling. Behind them, shots rang out. Dede jumped. That was the side of the school where the boys from her class had been taken. Worse, no one stopped or hid at the terrible sound. The rebels who pushed her friends down the hallway didn't flinch.

Outside, orange dirt was everywhere, clay in the buildings, in the courtyard, in the walls, and on their cheeks. One by one, the girls were forced to lay in the dust. One by one, their heads were covered in coarse burlap yam bags. The harsh fabric scratched their faces. Thankfully, there were little gaps in the weave which Dede could see through. It was almost bearable. Then, wide and heavy, the boot of a man pushed on Dede's back, cracking her spine. She cried out in pain as breath left her lungs.

The man yelled out, "You will be silent." A hush fell across their panic. The entire courtyard smelled of fear and piss. "When I tell you, line up by the front gate and board the waiting buses. You will not alert anyone or this gun and the guns of my friends will finish what we have started. You need none of this education. We are here to help you find your true place. We will take care of you from now on."

Tears fell sideways across Dede's nose and down to the hot ground. "My life is over," she whispered. And she knew it was true.

All Dede had ever wanted was to be an engineer. She had always known how the world fit together. Even as a child she could find the swiftest answer to any puzzle. As her bare feet touched the hot rubber of the first bus step, Dede knew the puzzle she had understood her whole life was broken into pieces forever. There was no escape.

Near the back of the old bus, Yaa and Afua sat together. They clung to each other like mona monkeys in the dark of night. Dede found a seat right behind them.

At the front of the bus, there was a sudden commotion as some girls tried to run away. Gunshots rang out. The red-orange sand became redder.

Dede gasped at the callous men, at their indifference to pain and murder. After that—after they killed a girl for trying to escape—the bus loaded past capacity very quickly. Because of the harmattan dry heat wave, it was terribly hot already in February. Soon, the interior of the vehicle already stank with fear and sweat.

Dede held Ato's hand. Fearful, she chewed on her bottom lip. The windows were sealed shut and covered in black fabric. The heat was awful.

"Hush," Dede whispered as Ato sobbed, in spite of her own tears. "Hush, dear. Our parents will find us." She spoke the words without believing them.

Three buses had been loaded with girls in Bawku, Ghana. By the time they reached Dapaong, there was one.

Scared as they all were, there was nothing to be done as the gunmen lined them up in the shadow of the large vehicle.

Forced to pee by the side of the road, they were pushed and jeered at like cattle. Dede's generous heart went numb. Boarding the cursed bus again, it was all she could do to gulp the cooler desert air before she was shoved back inside. The girls were again imprisoned.

Ato sniffled and cried. Dede nudged her friend. "Stop. Ato, stop," she whispered over and over. Finally, as the bus turned northward and the sun began to lower, the interior cooled down bit by bit. All the girls collapsed into a troubled slumber, scared out of their minds, adrift in the desert on their way to the hands of terrible men.

The bus stopped later that evening for the men to gather in a circle outside, singing their traditional songs, clapping and rejoicing in their victory. Shouts of congratulations filled the desert sky. Howling boasts and jokes sounded like the yelping of hyenas to each crying child.

One girl, Abigail Adwoa, tried to sneak out the back of the bus while their captors celebrated. She was caught. The man who had abducted Dede and her friends took his gun and hit Abigail in the forehead. She fell, bleeding from her ears and nose. Then he shot her. Straight in the head. He didn't even flinch at the blood and brain that splattered the side of the bus.

"He shot her!" Yaa cried.

"Shush!" Ato said, "At least it wasn't us."

Afua did not even react. Instead, she shut down, turned her gaze away, and closed her eyes.

Dede understood. She too had run out of tears. Constant fear had drained her. It was the same man who had said that he would not harm them. That he was there to help. Dede felt an anger rush through her, and then despair. "Our lives are worthless." Dede let that hard truth sink in.

The bus continued on in silence. Dede's head kept wobbling as she leaned on Ato's shoulder, until finally she slept.

In her dream, the sun was rising, brand new, orange as a boiled cassava. Momma and Da were laughing in the kitchen. Little Kaakyire ate toasted sorghum cereal and threw some of the mash at the wall. Anan and Num fought over a blue head scarf. That last morning had been loud and noisy. More chaos than Dede ever wanted. In her dream though, the ruckus became the sounds of angels playing.

I miss you so much, she thought.

Then, Dede remembered that Manu and Mensa had stormed through the room, grabbing some dried bananas and a bit of water. Her brothers laughed and joked. Manu kept spinning his basketball around like one of those fancy professional players from America, the Harlem Globetrotters. He swore daily he was going to join them. "I am gonna be famous with the ladies!" he would boast and then swagger about like a cock rooster until the whole family laughed.

An unmarked package sat on their kitchen table, taking up almost a quarter of the space. Da had remarked when he found it on the doorstep, "Who would have sent us such a large present?" As the Honorable Chief Executive of Bawku Municipal, village leader of the Black Stars, Da sometimes got gifts, but this was enormous.

After everyone had eaten, Anan eagerly tore it open. Inside was a beautiful gift, fit for a king! Hundreds of chocolate bars, enough for the whole village! Ghana grew most of the cocoa for the whole world's supply, but no one had actually tasted a real piece of candy. It cost almost a week's salary to purchase one.

"What? Who would send us such a treasure?" Da looked mystified.

Num didn't wait one second. She dove straight at the box and took a bar. Tearing open the wrapper, her face melted in bliss faster than the chocolate could ever have dissolved on her tongue. "Oh my!" Dede's little sister purred. "It's so very lovely." Eagerly, everyone grabbed two bars.

"We will save some for our neighbors," Da said with a grin. "I will give these treats out to everyone I meet. Today is a good day!"

Dede had replied, "It is the water that loves you that enters your pot. Such a beautiful present!"

They all giggled.

In her dream, Dede remembered how she had looked at the chocolates that morning. Dede really wanted to eat one right then, but she wanted to share them as well. So, happily, she stuffed two in her school sweater pocket to share with her friends at lunchtime.

The Afi John family was always generous. The surprise box of sweets would be no exception. The delicious candy would be gone before sunset.

With a wave, Da took the box and most of the chocolates with him as he left for work. First, he hustled her older brothers off to paint the interior of the Bawku Episcopal Church. It was good money. It would mean school for Anan and Num, better opportunities for all. Dede watched her father walk out the door, watched her mother turn to make some agbeli cake. While still dreaming, Dede could have sworn her mother looked right at her, eye to eye, before resuming cooking in the kitchen.

"Momma? Momma, I love you," the stolen girl murmured in her sleep. Dede wanted to rush into her mother's arms. But they were gone, like everything else.

Abruptly, the terrible bus that carried her away from family and home slammed to a stop.

Dede was thrown forward, hitting her head on the seat in front of her. It was pitch black outside, well past midnight.

"Where are we?" Ato asked, yawning and clinging to Dede's hand.

Their brutal kidnappers forced all the girls off the bus. Afua and Yaa were ahead of Dede and Ato. One of the gunmen gestured to the left. Dede and Ato went to where he pointed. When you stand in hell, does it matter where? Ato's hand felt slippery and weak.

At least we have each other, Dede thought gratefully. Really, Dede had little hope that anyone would be able to find them. She didn't even know where they were. Everything she could see was foreign, even some of the plants. The sun was rising to her left, so they were heading east. *East to Nigeria*, Dede thought but didn't say the words out loud, *straight into the terrible unknown.*

A rough hand lifted her chin. Fierce, dead eyes peered into hers, examining her face, ears, and hands. A man wearing jeans and a gold chain inspected her mouth and feet, as well. He examined the students like they were yearling cows at auction. His prying hands moved on to Ato, who whimpered at his touch. Ten strangers gathered near the bus, all men. They spoke loudly in an unfamiliar dialect, their voices haggling, "Twelve dollars!" And then, "No! Fourteen dollars!"

None of the men looked at the line of sweaty, scared, barefoot girls. Dede leaned back in line so she could see Yaa. Afua just stood there looking at the red sand, her gaze as empty as the dull clay that surrounded them. Yaa's wide eyes were full of life as she returned Dede's gaze. There was nothing to be done there, in the desert, surrounded by armed men. Dede shook her head. Yaa turned away. They would have to wait for a better opportunity.

With no warning, five students were separated from the main group. Gun barrels forced the rest of the girls back on the bus, the only shelter they had left. Dede knew one of the five miserable captives left behind. "Godspeed, Leelah. Godspeed you home," Dede whispered. No one would ever find Leelah.

Again, the bus filled with the militants and their worn prisoners. Opening his front shirt pocket, the man who had stood in their Bawku classroom yesterday and promised them all that he would take care of them, that same devil, now had a grin on his face and a wad of cash between his fingers. Dede was reminded of her mother's saying: *A child breaks the shell of a snail, not the shell of a tortoise.* It was easy for a bully to destroy a weak person. *I must grow strong. Fear cannot rule me. That man, these Wayo Wahala, they will pay for their arrogance!* Dede swore it to herself, to her ancestors, and to every star in the sky.

Carelessly, the gloating leader stuffed the money in his shirt while ordering the driver onward. “Go,” the smiling man commanded. “Hurry, my brother.”

Trundling along, the vehicle blew heavy diesel fumes that choked most of the rear passengers. The captives didn't even have the energy to vomit from the thick exhaust. On they went, grateful for relief from the heat of the hard February sun. Dede began to count the jolts of the bus.

Then, Dede's hand brushed against her school sweater. In her pocket, she felt the wrappers of the surprise chocolate. She had forgotten all about the treats. “Oh, no. They've melted,” she mourned. Hunger demanded she eat the spoiled candies anyway. It was odd though, how in moments of crisis, it was the little things that made her sad.

Next to her, Ato was miserable. She was hot and whiny. Once the tears ran out, Ato cried to herself in a low, keening sound. “Ato, hush.” The noise she made was loud enough that one of the armed men stood up in the front and glared at her. Taking two fingers, he pantomimed that his hand was a pistol. With it, he shot them both in the head with imaginary bullets. Dede shrunk down in her seat, pulling her weepy friend with her. Silence was demanded. Life meant that little.

Dede shared one candy bar with little Ato. Hungry as she was, Dede tossed the other bar to Yaa. Her friends smiled for the first time in a day, even Afua. Eagerly, the four girls licked all the melted chocolate off the inside. For a while afterward, Dede made a tiny paper plane with the wrapper.

The long hours of the bus ride were not pleasant, especially once the sun rose again. Mosquitos were everywhere, feasting on the frightened girls. Dede didn’t know if it was the heat, her hunger, or the buzzing insects, but her head ached. More pain than she had ever felt, the feeling spiraled through her, landing in her stomach. She felt queasy, even though they had been given no food. The urge to vomit surged. Finally, the men passed around six bottles of water. All the students shared, careful not to spill any of the precious liquid. The last bottle was nearly empty by the time Dede and Ato touched it. Quickly, they sipped the remaining liquid, grateful to have even a drop.

A couple more hours passed before the brakes squealed. Up front, the thick, black, rubber doors opened. The guards laughed, bragging, “We have returned. We did it!” The black-masked men were all happy, congratulating each other. Two bounded off the bus. Dede wanted to run.

Gesturing with their guns, the leader said, “Get off now. You. Off!”

One by one, the girls crept past his leonine gaze and into the open air. Dede hugged Ato tightly, though her muscles ached with every movement. "My friend," she whispered, "always." Ato took a deep breath, closed her eyes, and stopped her crying. Clasping hands, they were lined up with the other girls and marched into a nearby building. Dede and Ato held each other tight as they struggled to keep their balance.

Above the door, the sign read "Arwa's Farmers Marketplace."

Dede nudged Ato. "It's a market, Ato! Maybe we will get some food, little bird." She whispered to the smaller girl, who looked sickly. Even the thought of food made Dede's stomach churn and squeeze tight, a tortoise withdrawn deep in its shell. Her mouth watered despite the nausea.

All the fingers are not the same. Each has its own purpose. I must do what I can with the opportunity I am given. Dede kept that thought close to her heart as the girls stumbled into a red clay courtyard. Three unfamiliar men pushed the group of captive girls forward until they formed two lines.

"Welcome to the marketplace!" one very loud man yelled, quieting everyone. He did not speak to the girls. He addressed the crowd, "We welcome you, true believers in a United Nigeria. We are the mighty hand that punishes wrongs. We will push the West out of Nigeria!" Loud applause and echoing followed his words. "We are Wayo Wahala! We are the fighters of the true nation! We sell the women of the Gold and Black Stars. You must show them the true path. I will sell them here in the market. We will fight for our freedom with this money!"

A huge crowd was gathered in the courtyard. A crowd of thousands of strange, armed, menacing fighters. They looked at the dirty, exhausted, and frightened girls with the eyes of acquisition. In numb shock, Dede listened to the announcer's words.

And then the bidding began.

It was over quickly. Unbelievably, Dede was purchased for 2200 naira or fourteen U.S. dollars. Ato was smaller and had red, tear-streaked cheeks so she was cheaper. Each of Dede's friends sold for twelve dollars. They were sold for less than the price of a pair of jeans. Dede couldn't believe it. Rough hands grabbed the girls, pulling Dede away from the last bit of home she had. Almost immediately, her three lifelong friends were taken away in different directions, scattered among the gigantic crowd, lost to each other.

Dede felt very hot, like the sun had exploded inside of her. In rage, she screamed out their names, "Afua! Yaa! At—" A heavy hand slapped her face, knocking her to the ground. Two hard kicks to her side and Dede fell silent as blood from her nose bloomed across the sand.

Her head ached so much. Her heart was broken. Dede was completely alone. Hard fingers pulled her upright and poked her forward into a waiting, rusty Jeep. It felt like each place the man touched her immediately bruised. Some food would probably help, but the melted chocolate was all she had had for more than twenty four hours. Dizzy, Dede didn't understand most of what happened around her. Afua, Yaa, and Ato were gone.

A voice growled behind her, demanding obedience, "Sit! Girl, you are nothing but a slave. A woman's place is at the feet of a man, serving him. You will obey me. There is no question, you will. You are a Black Star mona monkey. You are Anto—no one. Nothing of value."

Dede's legs collapsed.

Slumped against the vehicle, it was hard to think. A few duffel bags landed near her. "Worthless woman," the gruff voice snickered. "Pick those up and pack them in the back, next to the water, Anto. You can drink one bottle only."

Struggling to rise, Dede bit her lip.

Why am I so dizzy? she wondered as she grabbed the bags and dragged them to the open trunk. The sight of the case of water made her want to cry. *I am so thirsty,* she thought. Desire made her rip a hole in the plastic. "W—water." Her lips moved over the word like a prayer. Opening the bottle, the kidnapped girl sipped when she wanted to gulp. Dede cried when she wanted to scream. Everything was upside down.

Overhead, the merciless heat of the harmattan sun beat down on her short hair. A black scarf was thrown at her. Putting it on was the real death, she knew that. It was their hair covering, the Wayo Wahala. Wearing it meant giving in. But there was no point in fighting. There was nowhere to run. Not when her life was worth so little to these people. Death, rape, or slavery? Was one better than the other? Placing the headdress of a slave over her hair, Dede was lost.

Standing in the exact same spot that Dede had been sold, the man in the red shirt yelled, "Hallo?"

Then he shot his gun into the air to grab the crowd's attention. "Hallo. Listen! We brothers of Wayo Wahala, we demand to be heard." Another man aimed a camera at the speaker, recording his words. "I am using this opportunity to send this message to the African King in Nigeria and the rest of the rulers in the Western world. We are ready to fight. We will use these girls, these children, as a shield if your armies come against us.

"We are determined. We will be victorious. Our goal is the freedom of the African man. Down with the arrogance of the West. Down with their colonies! Down with the rich, fat lions who rule on the sand thrones! No one has freed the stupid girls from Chibok. No one has freed the girls of Bawku, Ghana. No one can. Our path is great! Victory is ours!"

Dede wanted to cry. Her family would hear this mad man. His evil words would break their hearts. *I am a slave.* Dede couldn't bear the idea. A fit of coughing overcame her for a moment. She wiped her mouth with the back of her hand. The loss her family would feel when the news reached them, it would be a deep, cutting, unending pain. She would never see them again.

As the victorious man shouted on his arrogant message, Dede felt unusually sick. She ran to the corner and vomited up bile even though her stomach was empty. Even from where she stood, the girl could not escape the words that rolled across the crowd:

"So don't worry, all parents of Bawku and Chibok girls. Your children will convert to our cause or they will be strapped with the bombs of victory and we will return them home to you. More than two hundred girls have joined us in the last few days. Our way is just. I am Atta Djidi. I tell you this: We will win!"

The crowd roared its approval, guns firing randomly into the air.

Suddenly, somewhere from within the Arwa market, a loud commotion erupted.

It seemed like a thousand voices started shouting all at once. Men poured out of the shaded hall, running past Dede in the courtyard. She heard cries of confusion, panicked cries of plague, sickness, and fear. She heard all the words but didn't understand. Until someone said the word 'Bawku.'

Two men pointed at her and ran up. With great effort, Dede stood tall, matching their stares and examination until one of them slapped her cheek, knocking her to the ground. "Stop that!" he ordered. Rudeness would be punished. Pride had no place in a slave.

Dede silently vowed then and there to fight the river of hate that had swept her friends and family away. *I will never be an engineer*, she thought, *That was stolen from me. But my mother would never allow her daughter to walk in shame. Honor is not in the things that are done to me, but in what I do.* Pride? That was the least of her problems.

"You are from Bawku? Yes?" a man older than her father yelled at her. His remaining teeth were yellow and ground down. Blackheads were scattered like crumbs across his nose. Bits of bread and sauce marked his chin. "The bus, the girls, all from Bawku?" he insisted.

Dede nodded. "Yes," she said slowly, not understanding.

A flash of fear rode across the strangers' faces. Dede looked at the men, her cheeks red from each time they had hit her. "Why? What has happened in Bawku?"

No one answered.

Their leader, the man in the red shirt approached, looked her in the face, turning her head side to side. "She is fine. She is good," he finally said with certainty. "There is no need to worry. Our friends have struck the fat lions of Bawku down. We have stolen the last of the worthy. The girls can join Wayo Wahala or die."

Turning away from Dede Afi, he walked to the middle of the courtyard where everyone could hear him. With great solemnity, he talked to the upset crowd. "Calm down. It is nothing for us to fear. Our rebellion is heard. Our friends have destroyed Bawku. We took the only innocent children with us. We will raise them correctly. Wayo Wahala will show the world the true path!"

Across the courtyard, Dede saw Afua huddled near a group of men. She spotted little Ato and dear Yaa as well. The three girls whom she had played with and loved her whole life, her best friends, were still in this place. *For this little moment, I am with my friends!* She comforted herself. *And this moment is all I have.* Standing submissively by the man who had purchased her life and blood, Dede was filled with a strange hope.

Dede worried about her family. She wondered what happened to her home, to Bawku. Sneaking closer to the groups of men, finally she heard the truth.

"Bodies everywhere, they said."

"Streets full of dead. Only a handful left alive!" More urgent whispers, bits of knowledge, and gossip floating on their words.

"Distance will protect us. The town of Bawku was Black Star only."

"They paid the price."

"Stronger men would not have died."

Dede's heart trembled. *Dead. All dead.* The captive girl tried to understand the words. *How can this be? In my home town? In Bawku?*

What happened? Tears rolled down her cheeks, salty and warm. *Why? Momma? Nan? Mansu? And Da?* Dede had trouble breathing. She became delirious with grief.

To the west, the sun began to set. Sometime later, she thought, *At least they will never know this sorrow, what has happened to me. For that mercy, I am glad.*

Her eyesight dimmed for a moment. She pushed her tears away on the back of her wrist. Over where Afua was standing, Dede saw her friend wipe her hand across her wan face. Yaa looked weak as well.

Dede thought back across the terror of the last thirty six hours. Everything that happened that last morning at her home, every detail stood out. What had been different?

Sweat broke across her forehead. "It is so hot," she whispered. Coughing once into the horrible black scarf that marked the end of all of her dreams, Dede felt dizzy. A shooting pain went up her leg. Another muscle spasm gripped her side. "It is so hard to see," Dede complained to the uncaring men. But she was nothing to them, less than a dog: she was a girl.

After wiping the sweat and tears from her eyes, Dede saw blood smeared across her arm. Violent red drops marked her clothes. *Not tears! I am not crying tears.* A part of her knew, then. A part of her understood. She coughed into the black fabric, turning her scarf brilliant red.

Dede blinked ten times to clear her vision. She watched her captured schoolmates. Standing as a witness to the awful mess of twisted politics, Dede felt only a deep and true love for her friends.

For a brief moment, Dede's gaze took in the shining of the first stars, their light faintly glimmering. They were always there but only became visible as the sun fell into the vast ocean. The most beautiful things were always saved 'til the end.

Abruptly, all the militants in the Arwa market got out their knives and sat. They all faced the south, land of their oppressors. Their terrible machine guns laid next to their heads while the fanatics clapped their hands and chanted strange rituals. With fierce devotion or complete ignorance, the fighters performed their thanks, bowing down to the tear-soaked earth, bonding the Wayo Wahala terrorists together.

Dede took three deep breaths, exhaling wide and far, and then she walked through the rows of celebrating men. She fought a terrible pain with every step. Her eyes were full of Yaa, full of little Ato standing against the far wall. Blood fell from her tear ducts. Liquid burst from her eardrums, trickling down her neck. Dede's gaze stayed wide.

When she reached the middle of the courtyard, Dede was surrounded by hundreds of militants in every direction. Their voices were raised in joy, devoted to their cause with every breath they took.

Reaching in her pocket, her fingertips sought the comfort of her last bit of home, the chocolate wrapper. It crinkled in her sweating hand.

Then Dede started coughing.

ONE: *Lethal Inception*
by TK Carter

Peter Franklin Donalds Headquarters – Four Months Later

Michael stared at the white tile floor and ran his tongue along his top teeth as he shook his head. "You want me to get it, Mom?"

Dr. Karen Phelan jiggled the key in the locked laboratory door and huffed. "That's enough out of you."

He shrugged and adjusted his backpack as he rolled his eyes to the camera monitoring them from the ceiling. He raised a middle finger and ran it up and down the bridge of his nose, then blew a kiss to the security guards behind the lens. He smirked and leaned against the wall while contemplating his next hack that would send the fat bastards on another wild goose chase. His dirty blonde curls draped across his forehead and provided just enough camouflage for his scanning eyes.

His mother bucked away from the door and handed the keys to her husband and Michael's father, Dr. Steven Phelan. "Here. You do it."

Steven slipped the key in and pushed the door open without revealing his grin. "It helps if you use the right key, Karen."

She scowled and tugged on Michael's shirt. "Inside…now." Michael entered the same lab that once intrigued him but now bored the pants off him. His parents spent most of his life in this sterile, worthless room perfecting their social awkwardness and amounting to nothing more than aging biology students. His mother pressed her hand against his back and guided him through the lab, around the tables, and into the tiny office in the back that she shared with Steven. "Here we are, again, Michael." She did that nostril flare thing that drove Michael nuts.

He let his backpack drop to his mother's office chair and muttered, "Home sweet home."

She put her hands on her hips. "Hey, this is all on you, pal." She looked at Steven. "Think it's safe to leave him in here?"

His father waved her off. "PFD's security is way too sophisticated. He can't hack it."

Michael clenched his jaw to prevent a smile from forming. He threw up his hands and sighed. "He's right, Mom. I've tried. I can't crack it." He slammed himself into his father's leather chair and kicked his feet up on the desk.

She eyed him and chewed on her bottom lip. "Stay off the internet, Michael. I mean it. Get that English homework done before ten, or your laptop is mine. And put your feet down." She stomped into the lab and powered up the computer systems.

Steven sighed and looked at Michael. "You really screwed up this time, boy. You better listen to her today, because she's mad enough to let them arrest you. Got it?"

Michael shrugged and slid his feet off the desk. "It wasn't that big of a deal."

"Hacking into the school grading system and altering final grades is a big deal, Michael. Again. It's still a big deal. Just like it was at every *other* high school that's expelled you in the last three years." He sighed and rubbed his head as he hitched a thumb over his shoulder. "I gotta get in there. Just...keep it legal today, okay?"

Michael sighed heavily and waved at his dad's retreating back. He craned his neck and watched him walk to the coat rack, don his lab coat, and settle into his workstation just out of sight. Michael's mouth twitched with the grin he'd suppressed as he slid around the desk and grabbed his backpack. One of the conditions his mother negotiated during his expulsion conference was that Michael would be given an opportunity to homeschool until they could make other arrangements. Once a week, Michael and Karen met with the principal, turned in his work, and retrieved his next week's lesson plan. Michael wished he'd been kicked out of school years ago; this was cake. But, he had to look miserable to Karen, or she'd have him enrolled in a new school regardless of the nearing last day for summer break.

He slammed the textbook and notebook on the desk and looked up to glare at Karen for good measure. She flared her nostrils and returned her focus to the lame research she and Steven so proudly fawned over. Michael swore to his friends that his parents were really virgins, and he was conceived in a petri dish. Some days he believed it himself. He curled over the English book and tapped his pen against the desk.

Steven yelled, "*Michael.*"

He looked up and tossed the pen onto the desk as he pulled the book into his lap and leaned back in the chair. His leg bounced with anticipation as the computer on the desk smugly stood guard over his twitching fingers. Michael glanced at his parents then slid the keyboard tray into position. He placed the textbook over his hands and stared at the pages while his fingers worked the keys below. He shifted his eyes in time to see Karen walking toward the office. A quick Ctrl-Alt-Del locked the computer screen, which thankfully was out of sight of parental observation. He cleared his throat and shifted in his seat as she neared the door but stopped just outside. She studied the dry-erase board mounted on the wall next to the opened office door and popped the lid off a marker. She made a few notes, replaced the lid with a palm slap, and glanced at Michael. She pointed at the book in his lap then spun on her heels, her lab coat swaying behind her like an angelic cape. Saint Karen Phelan—using all her heavenly powers for good to thwart the powers of evil bacteria. The eternal good girl. Michael scowled and unlocked the computer again.

His first attempt at hacking the security room produced no results. He tilted his head and smirked. *They've upped their game since our last encounter*, he thought as he started round two. The thrill of the chase quickened his heart rate and he had to suppress a celebratory hand clap when the security room monitors blipped onto his screen. He chuckled as he shook his head and sighed with victory. He almost felt sorry for the poor bastards on duty that day. It wasn't personal—just a cat-and-mouse game with a bored, under-stimulated teenager too smart for sentence structure or solving for x.

The laboratory telephone rang its shrill request for communication. Michael's startled knees hit the keyboard tray and launched the textbook onto the floor. He scrambled to pick up the book and lock the computer screen before his mother answered the phone that hung next to the dry erase board outside the office.

"This is Dr. Phelan." She paused and braced herself against the doorframe. She gasped, "*What*? But how?" Michael studied her paling face and strained to hear her muffled words. "Sweet Jesus, okay, let me think. How long ago?" She turned to the clock over the door and swallowed hard. She shook her head. "That's too much time. That's..." Her eyes fell to Michael's as the weight of the call draped across her shoulders. She turned her back to her son and snapped her fingers at Steven. She waved frantically to come to her, tilted her mouth away from the phone and said, "It's AVHF."

"And?" Steven shrugged and twirled his finger.

"It's out, Steven."

"Out? Out where?" His face screwed in confusion.

"Here!"

He took a step back and rubbed his head. "That's impossible," he whispered, the bewilderment etching new features in his face. "How long? How long has it been out?"

Karen nodded to the person speaking on the phone. "Yes, I understand. We'll get right on it." She hung up the phone and buried her hands in her hair. "Twelve hours, give or take."

"Okay, okay, CDC is probably already working on containment. We'll... Karen, listen to me, now. We've got the vaccine, so we just need to get busy, 'kay?"

She looked at him slowly and nodded. "Right. Right..." She stumbled toward her workstation.

Steven stepped into the office with Michael. "Something pretty serious just went down. Don't worry, we can handle it, but just...just lay low in here, okay?"

"What's AVHF, Dad?"

Steven winced and shook his head. "I don't have time to get into it right now, but please just do what I ask. No smart-mouthing, no pen-tapping. Just be as quiet as you can while we do our thing."

Michael nodded and watched his father close the door, something he never did. Michael racked his brain trying to remember the details he'd chosen to ignore while his parents participated in cryptic shop talk at the dinner table. When he thought their line of work was interesting, he tried to crack the code. When he decided they were both lab geeks, he tuned them out. *AVHF... AVHF...* He slipped his hands onto the keyboard and used the closed door to his advantage.

Hacking into his parents' lab notes had never been much of a challenge. They used the same passwords for email, bank accounts, and thankfully, their lab notes. He scanned recent notes and found nothing of interest, so he backed up six months and scanned the notes until the acronym flashed. He scrolled up and read words that chilled his blood. "*Viral... high mortality rate... airborne... death within twenty-four hours of exposure.*"

He whispered, "And this shit's out?"

Slamming desk drawers and shouting erupted in the lab. Steven shouted at his wife, "Karen, will you please stop?" Michael rolled the chair away from the desk and strained to hear.

"The vaccinations are gone, Steven."

"Did you look…"

"I looked everywhere, Steven. They're gone!"

The loud clicking of angry fingers working a keyboard filtered under the door and into the office. "Jesus…where are the files?"

Karen Phelan stormed into the office with sheer panic and hatred brewing in her eyes. "What have you done, Michael? Where is it?"

Michael's eyes bulged as he looked from his enraged mother to his disbelieving father. "Do what? I didn't do anything?"

"Where's the file, *Michael?*" She spat his name. "This is no high school game. This is *life* and *death*. Where's the file?"

Michael looked at his father. "I…I don't know what she's talking about."

"Look at his face, Karen. He's clueless. And he doesn't even know about the vaccinations."

"You have thirty seconds to replace that vaccination file, or so help me…"

"I didn't do anything, Mom! I didn't take your stupid files!"

She flared her nostrils and backed away from the desk. "Well, they're gone." She pushed past Steven and slammed the mouse at a different workstation to boot a different computer. "The *research* is gone, the *vaccinations* are gone. Everything—*gone*."

Steven walked around the desk and grabbed Michael by the shirt. "Did you take those files?"

Tears pricked Michael's eyes as he stared into his father's wild eyes. "Dad, I swear I don't know what you're talking about. I know I screwed around before, but this time it's not me."

Steven released his grip and glanced at the computer screen holding the Phelans' research notes. He pointed at the screen. "Really? You're caught red-handed, Michael. Put the files back. I can't tell you how serious this is."

Michael whispered, "I know. I know how serious. I read the notes. Just now, I mean. Dad, I didn't take the files, I promise. Did you…did you create a vaccine for AVHF?"

Steven walked to the door. "You've got one minute. Put them back." He slammed the door.

Michael swallowed the lump in his throat and took a deep breath. He turned the chair and tried to shake off the looks of hatred from his parents as he processed what they'd said: There was a file, it's not there now, and that's bad.

Vaccination file. That's what his mother had called it. AVHF... outbreak... death after twenty-four hours... vaccine. *Someone stole the vaccine*?

In the lower left hand corner, a black shadow caught Michael's eye as it slid from one camera angle into the next. He leaned over the keyboard tray and squinted to make out the details. They'd slipped out of the security office, but they weren't in any uniform Michael had seen before. Realization washed over him as three men in black riot gear slipped into the last camera frame right outside the Phelan's lab. Michael's shout of warning to his parents was drowned out as the men burst through the lab door and shouted orders at the Phelans. Michael slid under the desk and tried to calm his pounding heart and rapid breath so he could hear.

"Get down! Get down, now!"

Steven Phelan shouted, "Jesus, guns? Karen, do it!"

Karen screamed, "Was it you? Are you in on it? You can't do this! We have to—"

A shot rang out followed by a wretched moan by Michael's father. "Oh god, oh god, no. Karen."

Another shot ended Steven's mourning and made an orphan out of Michael. He buried his face in his elbow and squeezed his eyes shut.

"Clear."

"Clear, here."

"Grab the lady. I'll get Dr. Phelan. Stax, watch the hallway and put Gridley on standby to wipe the security tape."

"We could put them in the office." Panic raced through Michael's body. He eyed the small, rectangular window near the ceiling and knew he'd never make it without being seen.

"Nah, it's supposed to look like they ran. They'll be found in there. Come on. Clock's ticking."

Michael stifled the whimpers clawing at his throat as he envisioned his dead parents being discarded like yesterday's trash. Dead parents. Looks of hatred. They died thinking he betrayed them over some stupid hack job that never happened. The last look from his mother seared into his mind—her wild eyes, disgusted. His peacekeeping father, the man who championed him and confided behind Karen's back that Michael would probably end up being the top computer wizard for NASA or something. Dead. Uncertain if his son had committed the ultimate hack at his expense. Witness to his wife's murder just seconds before the gun leveled at him.

Scuffing boots returned to the lab floor. "We gotta clean up this blood."

"Report in and tell them phase two is complete. We ditch the riot gear, suit up like PFD security, and wait for further orders."

"'Kay, that's got it. With eight minutes to spare. Tell Gridley he's good to wipe the security tape. It'll be like they never showed up today."

Michael's mouth went dry. He stood right in front of the security camera this morning and flipped off the guards. They had to have infiltrated the security office after the Phelans arrived for work, or they'd have known Michael was in the lab. He'd have to wipe the recording before they found out, before they found him. Michael shoved his grief deep into the caverns of his soul and felt the tip of revenge prick his fingertips. A swell of rage brewed in his chest as all the pieces fell into place. Missing vaccinations and files, outbreak, dead scientists, assassins fabricating their exodus…the outbreak was no accident, and this was a cover up.

He waited for the laboratory door to close and slid from under the desk. Out of habit, he glanced through the window to see his parents' whereabouts and winced. He bit his trembling lip and swiped his eyes with his sleeve. He moaned as he looked at a picture of his parents on the desk, a picture that he'd never noticed before. He slid the frame into his backpack and centered the keyboard over his lap. The clock in the room grew louder and louder with each passing second. He was faster, smarter, and more familiar with back-dooring the security system than whoever this Gridley fellow was, and Michael had some reckoning to do. He started with the most obvious camera—camera six—just outside of the lab. His fingers flew across the keyboard as sweat weaved through his curls. "C'mon, c'mon, c'mon." Lines of records populated the screen, and Michael scrolled through screen after screen of stored footage from the camera. He slowed the scroll as he neared the date stamp beginning at midnight. The files were divided into four-hour increments.

12:00-3:59 a.m.

Page end.

He slammed the page down key and shoved his palms into his eyes.

The recordings from 4:00-7:59 a.m. and 8:00 on were gone. Michael felt the tickle of the crosshairs that just fell on his head.

He shoved his things into his backpack and scanned the office for evidence of his presence that morning. He flipped the pack around to zip it and stared into the portrait faces of his parents. Back when they thought he was a wholesome kid with a cute fascination for computers. Back when he thought they were nothing more than washed up biology majors creating the next big hand sanitizer. Before they accused him of virtual genocide. Before they were murdered and hidden from him forever.

He couldn't save them, but he could save the data.

His nostrils flared as he slammed the backpack onto the floor and guided the keyboard tray over his lap. Michael logged into his online file storage site, encrypted the keystrokes and enabled security alerts for possible breach while he hacked into his parents' backup history. He flipped screens to the live security monitors to see if his death squad was en route, but no one approached. He returned to the lab backup, cracked the security measures, and waited for the files to load. He switched screens and saw on camera one, near the front of the building, two men in black riot gear running down the hallway.

Michael's heart pounded, his breath whistling through his teeth. "Oh god, oh god..." He rocked as he watched the lab data slowly populating one line at a time. Years of research data, lab notes, trials, and findings combined in one-day increments over at least five years.

He watched the men advance from camera two to camera three as the data from the current year slowly appeared on the screen. February, March, April, May...June. Michael sighed and picked a random day to open and scan.

He clicked on the file, the box opened—no files. He went back a month—no files.

The men advanced into camera four, and Michael knew if he didn't leave now, he would never leave alive. He enabled a deleted data recovery option and held his breath as he watched the green bar press closer toward completion. He opened Outlook on Steven's machine and started a new email. He scanned the saved contacts until he found one with CDC as the company and selected the name.

Subject: READ IMMEDIATELY

This is Michael Phelan. My parents are dead and their research destroyed. The link below will hopefully contain what you need to stop this thing if it uploads before they catch me. If I survive, I'll come to you.

The data recovery box flashed on screen saying, "Data recovery completed." Michael clicked on the box and found the research files. He clicked on the file from the day before, selected, "Restore" and changed the output location to the online site. He clicked, "upload" and flipped to the security screen. Camera six showed two men motioning to each other as they planned to enter the lab. Michael squeezed his eyes shut and clutched his backpack to his chest. The file was six percent uploaded with an estimated time of four minutes remaining. Michael copied the link to the website and pasted it into the body of the email he drafted as the door to the lab slammed open and the men stomped across the floor. His shaking hands struggled with the mouse, and tears blinded him. He blinked hard and let them wash the keyboard below.

The doorknob turned slowly. Michael inched the mouse toward "send" and moaned when the men slid the door open slowly like a cat toying with its prey. The upload file glowed green with twenty-seven percent completed. He tried to steady his hand and dragged the mouse back across the screen to send the email.

"What are you doing, son?"

Michael wiped his eyes and cleared his throat. His voice cracked, "Research."

"Aren't we clever?" The larger of the two men raised a middle finger and ran it up and down the bridge of his nose then blew a kiss at Michael. "Very clever, indeed."

Thirty percent completed.

Michael right clicked the security camera hack from the taskbar and ended transmission hoping to clear some bandwidth for the upload. "Nice gun."

"You're going to have to come with us."

"I can't leave, sir. My parents will be back any minute to pick me up." Thirty-four percent.

The other man scoffed and started around the desk. "Let's see your research." Michael flinched and hit the show desktop function.

"Sorry, I was just logging off."

The first man nodded and said, "Yes, you were." He yanked the power strip out of the outlet, and the computer went black.

I never hit send. He stared at the black screen and his reflection. Screens like the one in front of him always represented a lifeline, a way out. A place to escape when the world around him was unsatisfactory. Yet the vulnerability of the machine was that it relied on the power strip. Unplugged, it was just a black box showing the reflection of a boy with a gun slowly inching its way toward his head. He squeezed his eyes shut and thought of his parents—their life's blood was poured into their work then splattered across the lab floor. He'd lived his short life in front of his computer and any second now, his blood would spray across his father's.

He lowered his head and stared again into the picture faces of his parents. They dragged him to the Grand Canyon on a family vacation three years earlier—the last family vacation they took thanks to Michael's deviant online behavior and their demanding jobs. The nerds. The lab geeks. The social know-nothings. They knew what he thought of them, and they never once corrected him. Never tried to change his opinion. They'd made a vaccine to stop a deadly disease; Michael changed grades in high school Biology for fifty bucks a person so football players could be eligible to play next year. Judging by the statistics in his parents' research, all but two of those players would be dead in a few days, and the unspent money was hidden in a video game case in Michael's room. And, the heroes of the day, the Phelans, were dead.

A blast of air hit his forehead from the air conditioning vent above. He envisioned his mother's ghost clawing through the vent to smooth his hair and touch his face one last time. An apologetic caress from the other side admitting that she knew he hadn't betrayed them. A tear slipped from his face and dripped down onto hers in the picture—the last tear she would wipe away.

He heard the second hand pounding away the last few moments of his life followed by a round entering the chamber of the gun next to his head. "Say hi to your folks for us."

He never heard the shot.

TWO: *Siren*
by Megan White

"Claire!" Her name was roared from outside the room in which she was standing. Rushing out, she came face to face with Logan.

With hands folded across his chest, he looked her square in the eyes. He was pissed. "How long have you been here?" It wasn't a question; he knew the answer.

She pushed past him, not caring what else he had to say. "I don't have time for this, Logan. I have fifteen patients and god only knows how many more on the way."

"Eighteen hours," he spat back, following her to her next room. "How are you supposed to help anyone if you're a zombie?"

"What am I supposed to do, let these people suffer because I'm a little sleepy?" She swirled around to face him head-on. "I don't know when you lost your compassion, but you might want to rethink your career choice." But that was a lie. She knew exactly when he lost his desire to help others. It was when he joined that stupid conspiracy website. Not only was Logan Claire's boss, he was also her ex. He called himself a prepper. To her, it was the dumbest idea imaginable. They were in the middle of one of the biggest cities in the world, packed in like sardines. She knew he could prep all he wanted, it wouldn't do any good.

Blocking her way into the next room, Logan demanded her undivided attention. "You can either go home willingly, or I will have you written up for insubordination. I need you healthy and alert and you are far from that right now."

Claire clenched her next patient's file, furious that he would threaten her. "You have got to be kidding me."

"I don't joke, Claire."

She looked at him with fire in her eyes. The Logan she had fallen in love with two years ago was gone. His once neatly combed and styled black hair was a curtain of matted curls that stuck to the sides of his face, evidence that he had failed to shower—again. He didn't look like a doctor, he looked like a shut-in who was forced to deal with the rest of mankind, and his attitude reflected it.

"What's your choice?" He pushed her to answer.

Shoving the file she held into his chest, she stepped close to him. With her lips pressed to his ear, she whispered, "Go to hell." And the saddest part was she meant it. She felt betrayed by him in the strangest way. That prepping site took Logan from her and created a paranoid monster. She wanted her Logan back, wherever he was hiding.

Without chancing another look back, Claire grabbed her bag from behind the nurses' station and headed for the double doors that separated the ER from the outside world. Her anxiety that was nonexistent inside those protective walls returned the moment she breathed in the fresh air. The hospital was her safe place. In the outside world, she wasn't a brilliant doctor who helped save lives; she was just Claire, a young woman who felt like she was stumbling through life with a blindfold on.

The walk to the parking garage was always a time she used to reflect on her day. That day had started out like any other. It wasn't quiet by any means, it was Manhattan after all, but by midday, they were swamped with unknown, flu-like cases. It was, by far, the worst flu outbreak she had ever seen. She knew where she was truly needed, and a few hours' rest was all it would take to bring her back to life.

With a sigh, she cranked up her Beetle and turned the radio to an earsplitting volume hoping that the noise would drown out her thoughts. Only, she couldn't find what she needed. Channel after channel gave another report of what she already knew.

'Worst flu outbreak in years,' 'Outbreak of the century,' 'Hospitals overrun by mysterious illness.'

"That's the way to keep the public calm!" she screamed into the emptiness of her car. She knew it was reports like those that caused people with a simple cold to flock into her ER and take up beds that were needed for the truly ill. For the first time in eighteen hours, Claire wanted nothing more than a hot shower and her warm bed.

When she pulled into the congested traffic of lower Manhattan, she began to count the minutes until she could hop in the shower and wash the day away. At every block she was stopped at a red light, and every light seemed to take hours. Twenty minutes later, she was home, ready to get some sleep so she could get back to her patients.

Claire shared her tiny apartment with her younger sister, Haylee,

Haylee's daughter, Emma, and occasionally, Logan. Though the nights that Logan stayed over were no more, and no one was happier about that than her sister. It had been them against the world since their parents died. Killed in a car accident when Claire was sixteen, their deaths forced Claire to grow up far too fast. Their deaths were the reason Claire chose to work in the emergency room.

At sixteen, Claire made a promise to ensure that Haylee would be taken care of, and she had yet to break that promise. Foster home after foster home, Haylee was Claire's only priority. Emma came along when Haylee was only eighteen, and she instantly became Claire's heart.

"Hey girl," Haylee's bright smile greeted her the minute she walked through the door. God, did she love that girl. "Asshole got the rest of his stuff and left you a note on the counter."

Okay, maybe not as much love as I thought.

Exhausted, Claire let her bag drop to the floor with a thud. "What does it say?"

"How am I supposed to know? I'm not a snoop."

Not a snoop. Claire repeated Haylee's words to herself and then laughed, her eyes rolling so far back in her head that she feared they were stuck. "Really now?"

"Fine," Haylee huffed as she walked into the kitchen where she snatched the note from the counter and feigned reading. "It says here that we're all going to die."

"Geeze." Claire wanted to scream at the top of her lungs. Her once brilliant boyfriend had turned into a conspiracy nut. Scaring her sister and her niece with his crazy theories about mass deaths was one of the reasons she had to leave him. If he wasn't screaming about Big Brother's video surveillance or cell-phone tapping, he was spouting off about how the government was trying to poison the population.

"I need a shower." Claire sighed as she turned from the kitchen, leaving Logan's note untouched.

"Sounds like a good plan." Haylee snickered as she shoved an Oreo in her mouth. "'Cause you smell like vomit."

"Haylee!"

"Just speaking the truth."

Ignoring her, Claire looked around for her bundle of energy, Emma. "Where's my baby girl?" It wasn't like her not to run into Claire's arms the second she walked through the door. "In bed," Haylee said around the cookie in her mouth. "She came home from school early with a mild fever and has been sleeping ever since."

Claire's heart lodged itself in her throat. "Sick?" She turned for the hall and stared at Emma's closed door. All the patients she saw that day flashed in rapid succession through her mind. Emma couldn't be sick, she tried to reassure herself. Not like them, no.

"It's just a little fever," Haylee said as she grabbed Claire's shoulder. "There's nothing to worry about." But Claire wasn't so sure. She knew bringing illnesses home with her was a hazard of the job; because of what she did for a living, she could cause her family to become sick.

"After I scrub this yuck off me," Claire looked her sister dead in the eyes, daring her to disagree. "I will be checking on her." Haylee knew when it came to Emma, Claire didn't play.

Running into the bathroom, Claire turned the water to the highest temperature she could stand and soaped her body until her skin felt raw. If Emma wasn't like the other patients she had seen that day, the last thing she wanted was to make her ill.

Within five minutes, she was scrubbed red, wrapped in a towel, and headed to Emma. What hit her the moment she opened the door would be burned into her memory for the rest of her life.

Emma, tiny little Emma, laid on her side, red from fever, soaked in sweat. Running to her side, Claire placed her hand on her head and cursed when the burn met her palm.

"Haylee!" Claire shouted before turning to Emma to whisper, "Emma, sweetie." Claire had seen it a dozen times that day: patients would come in with a mild fever only to quickly deteriorate.

She felt Haylee come up behind her and stop. "What's wrong?" Her casual tone grated Claire's nerves. Claire couldn't turn away from Emma, not even to address her sister. "We need to get her to the hospital, now."

"For what?" Haylee's dismissive tone was like nails on a chalkboard as she continued, "It's just a little fever. If we take her to that germ-infested place then she will get sick."

"Look at her," Claire screamed as she pulled to her feet. "She has more than a little fever."

Haylee's eyes grew wide with panic. "You don't think it's what everyone's been talking about, do you?"

Claire didn't want to scare her, even as her own heart was breaking, but she knew the truth. Emma was sick, sicker than she had ever been, and she needed medical attention. "Get her in the car and I'll be right down."

But when Claire finished dressing and made it back to Emma's room to pack a bag, Haylee was standing over Emma, frozen and expressionless.

"Haylee," she spoke her sister's name softly. "What are you doing?" Claire wanted to scream at her to move, but she had seen that face more times than she could count. Haylee was frozen with fear. Yes, Claire had seen that expression on every loved one's face that knew death was near, but Emma was not going to die, she reassured herself, *not on my watch*.

"The News," Haylee's voice cracked with emotion. "They said people were dying from this."

God, did she hate the news. "Some have, yes, but that doesn't mean Emma even has it. We don't even know what it is."

Emma didn't have time for Claire to talk her mother off the ledge. Pushing Haylee out of the way, she wrapped Emma in her blanket and stood. "Are you going to stand there all night or come with us?"

With Emma limp in Claire's arms, her condition truly hit home. Within the few minutes it took her to get dressed, Emma's fever had risen. She tried to tell herself that it wasn't possible, but she knew better. All night, she had seen patient after patient deteriorate right before her eyes.

Placing Emma in her car-seat, Claire turned to Haylee. "Sit in the back with her." Even though Emma wasn't conscious, Claire didn't want her to be alone. She didn't want her to ever be alone.

Racing down the still-crowded streets of Manhattan, Claire did her best to keep her mind off the worst.

Kids get sick. It's normal. A little fluid and maybe some IV antibiotics and she'd be all better—laughing and running around like her usual self.

"What do you think it is?" Haylee asked, stiff in the seat next to Emma.

Claire's fingers wrapped around the steering-wheel with white-knuckle force as she looked at Emma through her rearview. "We don't know." None of the tests she'd run that day came back conclusive. Whatever they were dealing with, it had never been seen before. Claire knew there was nothing that she could say that would ease Haylee's worries, and she didn't want to lie.

In a perfect world, Claire could shut off her emotions and be the doctor. Emma wouldn't be her niece, she would be a patient. Claire knew Emma needed that from her; she needed a doctor with a level head.

Haylee and Emma were Claire's life. They were all she had, and Claire would be damned if a little bug took either of them away from her.

"How are you feeling?" It was a question that should have already been asked. It was a line that was ingrained into Claire's vocabulary, utilized any time a family member brought a sick patient into her ER.

"Fine." But it was obvious Haylee was far from fine.

Nodding at her, Claire tried her best to smile. "You don't seem symptomatic." Though she knew that didn't mean much with whatever the illness was. A healthy individual could change in a matter of hours.

Turning into the ER parking lot, Claire pointed to the side door that read, "Employees Only." "Here," she said as she handed Haylee her badge. "Go in through there and ask for Logan. He should be on the floor."

"What if he's not?"

"Then tell a nurse you're my sister." Claire huffed out in frustration. "Just get her in there and I'll meet you after I park."

"Okay." With stiff movements, Haylee bent down and pulled Emma from her seat and headed for the door.

Slamming on the gas, Claire peeled away from the staff entrance and slid her tiny car into the first parking spot she could find. Leaping from the car, she sprinted, with newfound energy, through the parking garage that she had left less than an hour ago.

Bursting through the doors of the ER, Claire raced straight toward the triage desk. "Where's Emma Calloway?" she all but screamed at Sloan, the only nurse in sight.

"Are you back on shift?" Sloan asked with a tilted head.

"No." Claire tried her best to catch her breath. "My niece, where is she?"

Sloan tossed her ebony black hair behind her shoulder, turned to her computer, and began to type out a series of commands. "Room 207." She barely got the words out before Claire took off.

The ER at New York Presbyterian was huge—a maze of corridors and rooms were laid out before her. It seemed like no matter how fast she ran, time was against her.

"Claire!" A strong hand wrapped around her arm, stopping her in her tracks, "what are you doing back here?"

"I don't have time for your crazy." Claire yanked her arm free of Logan's grasp. "Emma's sick."

"Shit." Logan's chest visually deflated. "You don't think?"

"Yes, I do." She replied quickly as she turned away and continued her race down the hall.

"We can't help her. You know that," Logan said, easily keeping pace with her.

"Either you can help me," Claire snarled at him as she continued her race to Emma, "or you can get the hell out of my way."

He stopped dead. "You shouldn't have come back, Claire. You'd have known that if you read my note."

Grabbing the door to room 207, she turned to face him. "If you can't keep your opinions to yourself, stay away from this room. The last thing Haylee needs is something else to worry about."

"What are her stats?" Claire asked the minute she pushed through the door and saw the familiar smiling face of Cindy, a brand new, fresh-out-of-college RN.

"Temp is 104.1. BP is 136/98, respirations shallow at 6 BMP."

Haylee was at Claire's side in a flash, needing her to decode all the medical jargon. "What does that mean?" she asked with tears swimming in her eyes.

"That she's sick," Claire answered as vaguely as she could. "I'm going to insert a line, give her a fever reducer, and draw some blood," Cindy quickly addressed Haylee, then looked to Claire for approval.

"Stat rush on those labs," Claire ordered, even though she knew exactly what they would say…nothing.

"You got it, doc."

Cindy was a tiny thing at just five feet, but she was a fire-cracker that never stopped moving. If anyone needed something, she'd have it done and returned faster than anyone else on staff. Claire knew, if nothing else, they were lucky she was their nurse.

It wasn't until Cindy was gone that Haylee collapsed in the chair closest to Emma. "You have to save her," she cried out to Claire. "She's all I have."

Walking to her sister, Claire grabbed Haylee's hand and made a promise no doctor should ever make, "I will do whatever it takes to save her."

Just then, a knock sounded on the door. "Claire?" Sloan popped her head inside. "Can I see you outside for a minute?"

"Sure," she answered her, then stood and looked to Haylee who had yet to take her eyes off sleeping Emma. "I'll be back in a second, okay?" But Haylee didn't say a word or move a muscle; Claire knew her sister was lost.

"What is it?" Claire asked the five foot seven beauty that was Sloan, after closing the door behind her.

Claire watched as Sloan's face fell. "Nine of your patients from today are gone."

"What do you mean gone?" It was a dumb question. Claire knew exactly what Sloan meant. They were dead. The patients that exhibited the same symptoms as Emma were dead.

"They all bled out." Sloan shook her head as if she was trying to dislodge a haunting memory. "You did everything you could."

Slumping against the cement wall, Claire's face fell into her hands. "Did I?" she asked, knowing that she hadn't done everything in her power to save them. How could she when she didn't know what she was saving them from?

"We can't fight something if we have no idea what it is," Sloan said softly.

"How is this even possible?" Claire's breath left her lungs in a rush. "How can no one know a damn thing?" Feeling defeated, Claire turned away from Sloan. "Thanks for letting me know." But even to her, her voice sounded hollow.

Claire walked back into the room where her angel rested, sat in a chair, and waited for the results that would either brighten her little world or crash it into eternal darkness. It was the waiting that was agonizing. To her, it seemed like hours passed before another knock came, but when it did, Cindy didn't have to say a word. "No." Claire shook her head in denial.

"I'm so sorry," Cindy whispered as she handed Claire the labs, which confirmed her worst fear, Unknown Pathogen. Rec' Quarantine. "We're going to have to isolate her."

Claire's entire body began to shake with rage. "I'm not leaving her." The mere thought outraged her. She refused to leave Emma alone, not when she was fighting for her life, not ever.

"Claire?" Haylee spoke her name so softly she almost missed it. "I don't feel so—" She was cut off by retching.

"No." Claire looked to Haylee as her head began to swim and her heart clenched in her chest. *No.*

Running to her side, Claire grabbed the trash can and placed it in front of her sister. "Cindy," she called to the nurse who stood frozen beside her. "Get me another bed—now."

Grabbing Haylee in her arms, Claire lowered her into a chair, and then went to Emma's bed. She couldn't care less what hospital protocol was. She wasn't separating them. Leaning down, Claire unlocked the wheels to Emma's bed and pushed it against the wall.

Haylee looked up from the wastebasket with tears streaming down her cheeks. "What's happening?"

For the first time since she was sixteen years old, Claire felt useless. She couldn't fix this.

"I have the bed," Cindy called from the other side of the door.

"Bring it in," Claire said, hoping Cindy would hear. "Push it right against Emma's," she instructed when the door opened to Cindy pushing in a bed three times her size, "IV, anti-nausea, fever check. Maybe we can stop this thing in its tracks." Claire added after Cindy locked the new bed in place.

"If speed is what you need…" Cindy smiled.

"Then you're my girl." Claire tried to smile back.

"Lock it down." A man's voice boomed from just outside the room. "Lock the entire place down."

At the sound of the man's order, Claire's heart began to beat so fast that she feared it would break right through her sternum. She looked to Cindy for answers only to see the same panic she felt reflected back at her.

"Get her set up." Claire nodded to where Haylee remained slumped in her chair. "I'll try to see what's going on."

Not waiting on a reply, Claire pushed through the door, and what awaited her she swore could only exist in the movies. Dozens of people in white HAZMAT suits swarmed the halls, slamming doors and shouting orders.

Grabbing the nearest man in white by the arm, Claire spun him to face her. "What's going on?" she asked with authority ringing in her voice.

"Quarantine, ma'am," the man answered, sounding bored.

"Doctor Calloway," Claire corrected him.

"Like I said, Doctor Calloway, we are closing down this hospital. No one in or out."

Dropping his arm, Claire looked at him in disgust. She knew there were sick patients needing to get in, loved ones waiting to see their family members. "On whose orders?"

"The CDCs," he replied. "Get back to your patients, Doctor Calloway." And just like that, he was gone, back to shouting orders.

"What's going on?" Cindy asked the second Claire made it back into the room.

"Quarantine," Claire mumbled, slowly becoming numb to the world around her.

"Just Emma and Haylee?" Cindy asked, looking to both of them and then to the door.

"No." Claire gulped against the ball that lodged itself in her throat. "The entire hospital."

"You can't be serious."

With her legs no longer able to bear her weight, Claire collapsed into a chair.

"I have everything set up." Claire could hear Cindy say from somewhere far off, "I'm going to see what's going on out there."

Hours passed whilst Claire remained frozen in her chair. There wasn't anything she could do besides watch helplessly while Emma's and Haylee's vitals continued to worsen.

Not being able to stand waiting any longer, Claire kissed them both and left the room on a mission to find someone, anyone, who could give her some answers.

Stepping into the hall, Claire entered a sea of white. Masked men and women cluttered the halls as they dashed back and forth.

"Miss?" one called out. Choosing to ignore him, she continued on down the hall. "Miss!" He raised his voice when Claire refused to stop. "You need to get back into your room." A strong hand landed on her shoulder, stopping her cold.

"I'm a doctor." She shrugged off his restraining grip. "I can help."

"I assure you, ma'am, there's nothing you can do to help. We have everything under control."

Leveling him with a stare that should've burst him into flames, Claire stepped closer. "I have been with these patients for days. I can help."

"Days?" He took a step back. "And you feel fine?"

"That depends on what your definition of fine is," she answered sarcastically.

"No symptoms: fever, nausea—"

"No," she cut him off mid-sentence.

"What room are you in?"

"I'm with my niece and sister in room 207."

"And you're feeling fine?" he repeated himself.

"Yes," she answered with a huff. "Are you going to let me help or not?"

"All staff on duty are being tested." He looked her over with a shrewd eye. "Go back to your room and I will send someone in for you shortly."

Reluctantly, Claire returned to her room, and within five minutes of sitting, the same man she spoke to at the beginning of the lockdown came in unannounced.

"Doctor Calloway?" he asked in an official tone.

"Yes." Claire nodded as she stood.

"No, have a seat." He stepped to her with his hand pushed away from his body. "I'll only be a second. May I see your arm?"

"May I ask what you're testing me for?" she asked, mimicking his monotone.

He blew out a breath in what could only have been annoyance and shook his head.

"Do you see that little girl in that bed?" Claire pointed to her four-year-old niece who lay in bed—the only evidence of her life being the monitors that continued to beep a steady rhythm. "And the woman next to her? They are all I have. I need to know what they're up against."

He looked from Emma and then back to Claire. "Unknown Airborne Viral Hemorrhagic Fever." He said with a bowed head.

Claire's breath left her lungs in a rush. "Airborne?" She shook her head, not wanting to believe him.

With a solemn nod, he looked back at Emma. "Yes."

She didn't feel it when he stuck her to draw her blood, nor did she notice when he left. There were only two things on her mind, the two halves of her heart who were fighting for their lives a few feet away.

"How are you doing?" Cindy whispered through a barely cracked door, her head only slightly poked through.

"Okay," she lied, "and you?"

"I'll be fine," Cindy answered with a smile as she lifted her arm. "Actually, more than fine." She placed her hands on her hips and a smug smile took over her face. "Seems like this bug don't want none of this."

Claire's chin hit the floor. "You're immune?"

"That's what they're telling me," Cindy beamed. "It also means nothing can stand in the way of my helping Emma or Haylee."

Emma's once steady heartbeat began to accelerate, snapping Claire back into reality.

"Emma." Fear gripped her as she raced to Emma's side only to freeze when she saw the blood begin to pour from Emma's nose and mouth. "She's hemorrhaging." Claire's heart dropped as the words left her dry lips. Monitors started to sound one right after the other. Emma's tiny heart was racing—her breathing so shallow the monitor hardly registered it. "What is her temperature?" Claire yelled.

"It's 105," Cindy shouted back, ready to take her next order as it came.

Claire froze when she saw a flicker of movement from Emma's once motionless body. It was quick, lightning fast, but Claire knew good and well what was happening.

"Get me some Lorazepam," Claire ordered to Cindy. Emma was seizing. The screaming of monitors continued to blare as Claire watched Emma jerk a second, and then a third time, only to soon be taken over by violent convulsions. *Where the hell was Cindy!*

"Here," Cindy yelled as she came sliding into the room with a hand full of syringes. Grabbing the first one, Claire shoved the tip of the needle into Emma's IV line and slowly administered the first dose, praying that it would stop the convulsions.

"It's not working," Claire yelled over the alarms that were sounding all around them.

"Her heart!" Cindy shouted, causing Claire to zero in on Emma's heart monitor.

"Get the crash cart." Claire demanded as she clasped her hands together over Emma's tiny chest and began compressions.

"Here are the paddles." Cindy pulled Claire's hands from Emma's chest and shoved the paddles of the defibrillator into her shaking palms.

After Emma's tiny heart beat one last time, Claire screamed the words she had said so many times before, "Clear." She slammed the paddles to Emma's chest and waited to hear the sound of her beating heart. She cried out when the monitor continued to scream that her Emma was gone. "Clear," she yelled out, shocking Emma's heart again and again. "No!" *She's not dead.* Claire refused to believe it. *She can't be...*

"Claire, she's gone." Logan's voice sounded in her ear, "You did everything you could."

"No." She fought against his hold; she wouldn't let him keep her from saving Emma.

"You've been going at it for ten minutes!" Logan yelled over her screams. "She's gone, Claire."

"She can't be." Claire's knees gave way and she was met with the cold, unforgiving cement floor. The last thing she saw before the darkness consumed her was Emma, covered in blood, dead in her bed.

* * *

"Doctor Calloway," someone whispered. "Miss Calloway?"

No. She tried to refuse the voice that beckoned her to wake into a consciousness that she couldn't bear. In the darkness, there was no pain, no loss. In the darkness, Emma wasn't dead.

"Claire," her name was spoken close to her ear. "We're running out of time."

"No," she mumbled.

"Claire, we need your help. We need you to wake up."

"Emma." Her niece's name left her lips in a sob. *She needed my help*, Claire thought, *and I failed her*.

"Haylee needs you now."

At the sound of her sister's name, she shot up in bed, and she looked over the room. She saw the familiar features of a hospital room—sterile and cold, but there was no Haylee. "Where is she?" Claire asked as she tried to stand, only to be shoved back down by a man covered head-to-toe in a white plastic suit.

"Please, Miss Calloway, give yourself a minute before standing. You took a nasty fall."

"I don't have time." She sneered at the masked man. "Where's Haylee?"

"Haylee is in stable condition, for now."

She knew that voice—it was Cindy. With her eyes locked on the tiny blonde, Claire begged, "Where?"

"Please," Cindy's hand came to rest over hers, "Listen to what these men have to say."

Is she crazy? Claire thought. *They didn't have time, Haylee didn't have time.*

A man wearing only a respirator mask and dressed in a tailored black suit stepped in front of her. "It seems that you are immune to this horrific illness, Miss Calloway." He spoke in the same authoritative tone as the CDC workers. "We need your help."

"What can I possibly do to help you? I couldn't even save my own niece." Claire turned away from the newcomer.

"With skill, no, you can't. It's your blood that will save her—your antibodies," he corrected, trying to get her attention. "If we can figure out how you're immune, we could save millions. You could save millions."

"You want to use me as a lab rat?" she asked, turning to face him and spearing him with a death glare.

"Us." Cindy stepped forward. "They want to use us. We are of no use here. You could save Haylee if you come with us."

"Think of your niece, Miss Calloway." The man wearing the respirator mask stepped in front of Cindy. "Would she want you to sit back and let her mother die?"

"Don't you dare." If she could have spit fire, the entire room would've been engulfed in flames. *How dare he use her niece's death to coerce her?*

"There are thousands of children just like Emma who will die if we don't find some type of cure."

"Saving lives is what we do, Claire." Cindy smiled next to the man dressed in black.

With eyes shut tight, Claire nodded, knowing Cindy was right. "I need to say goodbye to my sister first."

"We don't have time for that, ma'am."

"Then you'll make time." She scowled at the man. "Because I'm not going anywhere with you until I see her."

His eyes narrowed as he looked Claire over. "Take her to her sister," he ordered a man in white who simply nodded his compliance.

She followed him silently down the dimly lit hall of the ER until he stopped just outside of room 207. She wasn't sure what she expected to see when she opened the door, but it was the empty bed where Emma once slept that ripped her to shreds. Emma was gone.

"Would you like me to grab you some water?" the man asked from the doorway.

"Please," she answered quietly, willing to agree to just about anything to have a minute alone with her sister.

He closed the door with a nod, leaving her to say her goodbyes.

Claire slumped to her knees beside Haylee's bed. "I'm so sorry." A sob shook her body as guilt consumed her.

"Claire?" She jumped at the sound of Logan's voice. "You're not sick?" He ran to her with open arms.

"What are you doing here?" Shocked, Claire took a step back, refusing his embrace, still furious at the man she once loved.

"I'm here for you, babe. We have to go." He grabbed her arm in a tight hold. "You have no idea what we're dealing with."

"Actually, I do." She planted her feet where they were. "It's AVHF."

"That's not what I mean." Logan's hands dove into his hair. "These men, you have no idea how dangerous they are. We have to go." He grabbed her arm and tugged just to be jerked back when she refused to move.

"You can't leave." She pointed to the man in the HAZMAT suit making his way toward them.

"Yes, I can." He held up a white card with the letters PFD stamped on the front.

"What's that supposed to mean?" Claire asked as she squinted at the tiny index card.

He flipped it over to reveal the word, Immune, on the back.

"You're immune?" Claire asked with suspicion lacing her voice, knowing that neither she nor Cindy was given a card.

"Yes, and we have to go—now." He started for the door.

"I'm not going anywhere, and neither should you. You could help people. Don't you get that?" She knew the old Logan would have jumped at the opportunity to be the hero, but this new Logan, he was another man entirely.

"Miss Calloway," the CDC agent spoke with concern as he stepped between her and Logan, "are you ready to go?"

Logan pushed the man aside and stepped toward her with rage in his eyes. "She's not going anywhere with you." Logan grabbed Claire around the neck and pulled her to him, but no sooner than Logan's hand touched her, did three men cloaked in white swarm the small room. With military-like precision, they had Logan on the ground.

"Miss Calloway." The first CDC agent extended his hand to her, ignoring the mess of men writhing on the floor in front of him. "Are you ready to go?" he repeated himself.

"Y-yes," Claire trembled as she looked from Logan to the man reaching for her. Placing her hand in his, she allowed him to guide her from the room.

"When you learn the truth," Logan yelled, "come find me!"

"Where's Cindy?" Claire asked, trying her best to push the thought of Logan to the furthest part of her mind as possible.

"She's already gone," he answered her quickly. "There's a car waiting outside." He stopped just short of the exit and pointed to a black SUV that had the same insignia painted on it as the card Logan had: PFD.

As she neared the truck, the man dressed in the perfectly tailored suit, whom she had seen when she woke in the hospital bed, stepped from the passenger side and opened the back door. "Please, Miss Calloway." He motioned to the back seat. "We don't have much time."

She swallowed against the lump in her throat as she saw a second man, dressed similarly to the first, waiting in the driver's seat. As she sat in the back of the SUV, and the door shut behind her, all the crazy Logan spouted about the government flooded into her mind. Who are these people? She couldn't help but ask herself.

"PFD, as in the pharmaceutical company?" she spoke up from the back of the SUV, remembering the logo on the front of Logan's immunity card. "Is that why you came for the immune?"

"We're here to help put a stop to this virus," Man in Black number one deflected her question, "that's all you need to know."

"Do you have names?" Claire asked suspiciously.

"You can call me Commander Sawyer."

"And I'm Lieutenant Edwards," the driver added with a wink in his rearview.

As they continued to drive south out of the city, Claire's heart began to race. "Where are we going?"

"A safe haven," henchman number two, Lieutenant Edwards, answered with finality.

There was something about them that didn't sit well with her. She wanted to blame it on Logan's crazy conspiracy theories, but there had to be more.

"Commander Sawyer," a brash male voice sounded over the SUVs speakers, "Do you have subject 001?"

Claire couldn't help but scoff at the fact she was being referred to as "Subject 001."

"Yes sir, en route."

Silence once again took over the small space, adding to her discomfort.

"We don't have much farther to go." Sawyer turned in his seat and smiled.

"I really have to use the restroom." Claire knew, if she had any chance to escape, it was then or never.

"You can go when we get to our destination," GI Joe number one answered her harshly.

"I don't think you understand. I haven't used the bathroom in eight hours. There is no holding it."

"Are you feeling sick?" Sawyer turned to face her with concern in his eyes.

"No," she assured him, "but if you don't find somewhere to stop, I will use the seat."

"I'm stopping, Sawyer. The last thing I want to do tonight is clean the seats."

"You have five minutes," Sawyer instructed as they pulled into a gas station just outside Chinatown.

Claire had five minutes to plan her escape, and she could only hope that the bathroom had some way to the outside.

Racing to the safety of the gas station, she found the bathroom and thanked the gods for the window above the sink. Climbing onto the porcelain sink, she shimmied through the tiny window and dropped the six feet into a dark alley.

With nowhere to go, and what seemed like two military men on her heels, she pulled out her cellphone and dialed the only person she could—Logan.

"Claire?" Logan answered on the first ring. "Are you okay?"

"No," she panted into the phone, "I'm not okay. I'm in an alley, running from GI Joe one and two."

"Where are you? I'm coming to get you."

She looked around until she saw a street sign. "Just outside Chinatown on Park Row," she replied quickly.

"So they were right," Logan breathed into the phone.

"Who was right about what?"

"Staten Island."

"What? I'm nowhere near Staten Island," she snorted, mentally raising Logan's crazy level a bit higher.

"Stay in the shadows and start working your way north. I will find you."

As instructed, Claire started north, staying in the shadows when she could. To her, it felt like hours were passing when she knew it was only minutes. With every noise she heard, her mind raced and her body tensed. But it wasn't until the sound of screeching tires sliced through the eerie silence of the night that her breath caught in her throat.

Looking up, she froze as a white van slid sideways, stopping inches from her feet. Before she could scream, before she could run, the side door slid open and a masked man hauled her inside.

"There's my girl," Logan crooned from the front seat of the van as the man that grabbed her strapped her to the seat.

"What the hell is going on?" Claire screamed as she tried to fight against his hold.

"We need you, baby." Logan turned in his seat, face red, sweat dripping from his brow.

"Logan," she spoke his name as calmly as her nerves would allow, "you're sick. We need to get you to the hospital." But how was he sick? He had a card that said he was immune.

"They can't help me," he coughed out, the violent heaves racking his body. "It's you I need."

What? Panic overtook her as she began to pull at her restraints.

"Start the line," Logan ordered the masked man. "Don't worry, baby," he smiled as he looked her over, "you won't feel a thing."

"Why are you doing this?" Claire began to thrash in her chair as she tried to fight off the man with the needle.

"You thought I was crazy." Logan laughed through hacking coughs. "You never listened to me, but you can never say I didn't try to warn you."

"Warn me about what?" Claire hoped that if she kept him talking, he would change his mind. He had to change his mind.

"This was all planned—the virus, the deaths…everything."

Without warning, the pinch of a needle bit into her arm, and she yelled out from the sudden pain.

"Don't fight it, Claire," Logan spoke in a soothing tone. "Like you said, you're going to save lives."

"How'd you know?" She hadn't told him she was immune.

"Do you think I'm an idiot?" he snorted, sounding insulted. "You have been tirelessly working with infected patients without a single symptom. If you hadn't come back to the hospital, if you would have just stayed home like I told you, all of this would have been done and over with hours ago."

"I loved you," Claire whispered out as fatigue started to take over.

"And I had to find someone immune." Logan smiled back at her. "What better candidate than the woman who once loved me?"

"No." Claire's mind drifted to Haylee who was alone and dying in a hospital bed.

What felt like a weight was placed on her chest, and with every breath she took, the pressure increased.

"It won't be long now," she heard Logan mumble.

"Do we need all of it?"

The world started to blur for Claire. It tilted on its axis as she watched her blood travel down the thin tube connected to her arm.

"Every last drop."

A scream sounded from far off, a screech? Lights flashed, blinding lights that made her wonder if she was back at the hospital.

Cracks of thunder exploded through the van, followed by what she thought was rain.

How is it raining inside?

Claire tried to force her eyes to open, to focus, to fight the pull of sleep.

"Get that out of her arm!" she heard someone scream.

"Sawyer?" she asked, but he didn't hear her. Nothing could be heard in the darkness that pulled her under. No light, no sound, no pain. It was a place void of all emotion. It wasn't death that was hard for her; death was easy; death was painless; death was letting go.

* * *

"Claire?"

The light called to her like a Siren on the ocean, but she fought it, refused to answer its call. The darkness was where she wanted to be.

"Claire?" Her name was spoken by a familiar voice. "You're okay. You can wake up now."

Claire knew there was no use fighting the light. The darkness was gone, and with it, so went the numbness that swaddled her in its protective hold.

Upon opening her eyes, Claire saw a face beaming down over her, but it wasn't the face she wanted to see.

"Cindy?"

THREE: *Unsafe Haven*
by Casey L. Bond

The long shift at the bakery had taken its toll on Lexia. She wrapped a loaf of bread in wax paper and sat it on the step in the alley just outside the back door. Double checking her pocket to make sure she had grabbed her keys, she walked quickly past shops and businesses lining the busy streets to the subway station and descended to the underground world of eccentricity. In nine stops, she could emerge into the light again. While waiting on her train, she popped her earbuds in and cranked her iPod's volume up.

She stretched her tired back and fingers. With a sharp mind and fast hands, she'd always performed tasks quickly. Not only had it been a necessity at such a busy workplace, it had meant her survival. Her mom had passed away three years ago and the life insurance money, combined with the money she earned by working was enough to keep her alive. With it, she was able to pay rent, buy food, and even splurge on thrift-store gems once in a while if she was careful. Making money stretch was an art form.

The subway train was late, according to the digital clock on her iPod's display. *Come on.*

At sixteen, she lied about her age. Every piece of identification lied for her. They said she was eighteen, old enough to work and live on her own. The concerned looks for her said that some questioned her affirmation. But no one cared enough to bother her. She was making it. Maybe they asked themselves, "Why ruin a good thing?" She would be eighteen soon enough and most people didn't want to meddle, or didn't care enough to take action.

She could hear the train approaching, even over the music on her iPod. She waited for it to stop and the doors to open. Passengers flowed out of the cars. She and the mass of people around her pushed their way inside just before the beeping sound signaled the closing doors behind her back.

No seats were empty. She didn't need one anyway. Holding tight to a metal pole that was anchored at the ceiling and floor, she let the rocking rhythm soothe her tired legs. Lexia couldn't hear much going on. But her light brown eyes took it all in. Some folks in her car looked frazzled and tired. Others impatient. No one looked happy or even content.

An older woman with fuzzy blue hair coughed into her hands and then clutched her handbag as if she was about to be mugged.

To her left, almost pressing up against her side, a middle-aged business man, wearing what looked like a designer suit and too much cologne, sneezed into his perfectly pressed, white handkerchief. She told herself she was just being paranoid.

All she'd heard at the bakery during her shift was about the truck that wrecked a few days ago, and how people were falling ill all over the city because of some virus. The patrons of the bakery who were still well had been ordering bread and cakes as if tonight might be their last supper—literally.

It was kind of like the pandemonium a snow-storm caused in the aisles that had bread and milk: chaos and empty shelves.

The train stopped at another station and then pulled away again. Two more stops and she'd be able to get out of the metal car.

Her cell vibrated in her pocket so she pulled it out, ignoring the coughs and sneezes around her, and swiped her finger across the screen.

It was a text from her friend Mary, who also worked at the bakery.

DID YOU KNOW THAT GIO AND TONY WENT HOME SICK TODAY? THEY'RE BOTH IN THE HOSPITAL NOW.

Great. She'd worked this morning right alongside Giovanni. He hadn't looked well at all. She noticed his absence in the afternoon, but was so busy she couldn't allow herself time to dwell on it.

She typed a reply. THAT'S AWFUL :(

It only took Mary a second to respond.

DO U THINK IT'S THAT VIRUS FROM NEWS? PEOPLE ARE DYING NOW!

Lex looked around the train. NO. PROB JUS A COLD.

RIGHT. That was all the reply Mary gave. Lexia bet she moved on to another friend who would discuss the possibility of an apocalyptic scenario. The girl read too many books. Lex shook her head briefly and shoved her phone back into her pocket.

Her stop was fast approaching, so she moved closer to the doors. When they opened, she made her way out of the underground. It was three blocks of sidewalk lined with cabs on one side and shops on the other. Her building wasn't anything special. Just brick, mortar, and glass. It was non-descript but functional—a shelter from the street. She climbed the three flights of stairs to her tiny one-bedroom.

Looking over her shoulder, she quickly unlocked the three deadbolts and the lock on the door handle. She shuddered. Maybe her dad's paranoia had rubbed off on her after all. She pushed that thought out of her mind as she stepped over the threshold. It took her less than two minutes to drop her stuff on the tiny folding table standing by the door, and head to the shower to wash the lingering smell of sugar and dough off her skin.

That night, she began to chill. Lexia didn't own a thermometer, but she didn't need one. It was obvious that she had a fever. With the fever came a headache so severe that any sliver of light was too much for her to bear. She stumbled across the floor and barely made it to the bathroom before vomiting up what she believed was every tiny speck of food she'd eaten that day and maybe the day before.

Vomiting's friend diarrhea came to visit her and actually spent the night. But those kinds of sleep-overs were the worst kind.

By morning, Lexia was weak. Every single muscle fiber in her body ached. She didn't want to move. She didn't want to open her eyes.

When she did peel herself off the couch for yet another bathroom excursion, she saw that those eyes were bloodshot. It was disturbing as hell.

Lexia touched the tender, swollen skin around her face, her mouth gaped open at herself in the mirror, a strand of drying saliva stretching from lip to lip like an errant spider web.

That was when she collapsed. Her legs were no longer able hold her weight. Soon, her lungs were unable to expand with the life-giving oxygen she needed. She fell asleep to the fluttering and pecking sounds of the pigeons that always perched on her windowsill, oblivious to anything but the hope of their next crumb.

* * *

Lexia stared at the door. Someone was outside—a very angry someone. They were beating on the wood like they wanted to splinter it, jerking the door handle so hard she feared that the entire thing might tear off its hinges. The warped wood would only last so long and the longer she watched the peeling paint curls shimmy and shake under the beating they were taking, the more worried she became that the person on the other side of that door would soon burst into her living room.

She was afraid.

She bit her thumbnail and curled into a ball on the sofa, making herself as tiny as possible.

The furious pounding continued.

Dramatic? Maybe. But she'd survived the virus and was trying to survive the apocalypse. She'd earned dramatic.

The wild beating that the old door was taking proved its strength. Some paint chips weren't as stubborn. The weak ones floated to the floor, delicate as feathers on the wind.

Finally, she heard an exasperated huff from behind the door just before something heavy fell against it. Lexia presumed it was a body. *Didn't matter. She wasn't going outside. Uh-uh. Not for anyone or anything.* No. Lexia was staying put. It was safer that way.

When her father was taken away, Lex had been forced to drop out of ninth grade. She got a fake I.D. and a job. Before the bakery, she'd taken any odd job offered, some that paid almost nothing. But every little bit helped and somehow she'd made it. She'd often gone to bed hungry, cried more times than she could count or remember, and lost track of almost all of her friends.

Lex stared at her phone. Nine-one-one wasn't an option anymore. There was no one else she could count on. She'd tried texting, calling, e-mailing Mary. No response. Mary was either holed up too…or dead. Probably the latter. A tear fell onto her cheek.

Then, the thing outside her door made a noise—a familiar tone that she hadn't heard in so long that it literally broke her heart.

"L-L-Lex."

She jumped from the couch, running across the cold, bare floor, and fumbled to release every deadbolt that separated them. When she opened the door, he fell inside.

"Dad?" The word left her mouth in a whisper. But she recovered her voice. She extended her fingertips toward him. Was he real? When he looked up at her and extended a hand for help, she eased hers into his and squeezed, pulling him upright. "What are you doing here?"

She hadn't paid her bills this month, hadn't worked since she got sick. But her water still ran, the electricity was still on, and her cell and television still worked. No one was worried about delinquent accounts when everything around them was collapsing, rotting. It made sense that her dad had escaped. Everyone was dropping like flies. They couldn't have the staff to cover the asylums.

"No g-guards. I left. Home is safe," he asserted.

Grabbing his elbow, she helped him up with a grunt. Gregorio De Santis stood just inside the doorway, looking shiftily around the small apartment. He turned to the door, glancing between it and Lex. "'s not safe."

Lexia glanced to the still wide-open door, moved over to it and closed it, twisting all of the dead bolts until they couldn't twist any more.

Her dad nodded. "'s not safe."

He always said that. He'd been saying it for years. It was a nervous tic, part of a multi-word diagnosis that at the same time fit him perfectly and yet couldn't quite pin him down. It didn't matter what they labeled him. Lexia's dad had lost part of his mind.

Lexia watched her father nervously pace around the room. He had nothing but the clothes on his back. He eyed the perfectly intact, but old windows as if they were broken, with shards gouging into the air at precarious angles.

She took him in. It had been almost a year since she had seen him. He was too thin. His hair was completely gray, too. The strands of dark brown had been hanging on for dear life last time she'd seen him. Amazing how much could change in three hundred sixty five days. But then again, so much had changed in just the past couple of weeks.

"'s not safe," he muttered, pointing at the window and looking at her with fear-widened eyes.

"Do you need your box? Can you make it safe, Dad?"

He nodded. So, she went to the tiny closet beside the bathroom and began removing all of the crap she'd piled upon the box. The box held all the things he would have wanted her to keep. All but the newspaper clippings—they ended up in the garbage. At one time, he'd plastered them haphazardly all over every inch of wall surface. Some were even taped to the ceiling; the tiny squares of adhesive still peppered the plaster in places when she'd left the house for the last time.

Lexia hefted the small cardboard rectangle and carried it to the card table, setting it down gently. There'd been times when she'd gotten angry with him for going crazy, for being hauled away from her when she needed him most. More than once, she'd considered chucking the box out the window.

Her father wrung his hands. The tension didn't last long. He dove into the box, sorting at a feverish pace until his hands hit pay dirt.

Oh, no, she thought, wishing she'd taken that item out of the box. She could have used it for herself and avoided this entire scenario. But, how was she to know her dad would bust out of the crazy house and come knocking.

Greg held up the almost-full roll of aluminum foil like he was lady freaking liberty, wearing a cheek-splitting grin.

Lexia let one side of her mouth tip upward as he went to work covering her only view of the outside world. She wasn't sure what exactly he thought the foil would do for them. Block the aliens from spying on them? Prevent the intrusion of the government spies he thought were everywhere? Or maybe he used it to make himself feel a sense of peace, or safety. If it helped him with that, she could live with foil-covered windows—at least for a while.

She didn't have much food left in the cupboards and the fridge was bare, too. It wasn't like she could run down to the corner store anymore. So, she'd made what she did have stretch really far. Since she'd gotten ill, Lexia hadn't had much of an appetite anyway. But now, she had her father to feed, too. She would have to figure out a way to get some food.

There was always raiding the other apartment units for food that may have been left behind. But the thought of smelling the rot of the dead turned her stomach into mush.

There had to be another way. And Lexia vowed to find it.

Using her cell phone, she began to search online forums within Little Italy. Maybe someone had set up a market of sorts, to exchange things or goods. Maybe someone was offering food for those who didn't have it. Churches and charities usually did that, during emergencies.

She searched while Greg worked. Eventually, he had claimed much of the wall-space, having brought a gallon-sized Zip-Lock bag of his own, stuffed full with clippings. They were all about the virus, the government, and how its release—down to the vehicle accident that had caused it all—had been planned and unleashed upon the population.

Lexia believed in the principle of Occam's razor. The simplest solution was usually correct. The truck carrying the virus had been driven by a human being. Human beings often made mistakes. Therefore, the accident had been caused by human error. There was no government conspiracy involvement, no corporation funding and facilitating the spread of the disease, as some of the articles alleged. This was just fuel for his crazy fire, as far as Lexia was concerned. And that was a fire she wished would burn its way out.

She wanted her dad back. She wanted to be a normal sixteen year old, maybe even finish high school and look ahead to college. But as she looked around the room at all the bold-face type and tin foil staring back at her, Lexia knew that college was no longer an option.

The pair settled down eventually that night—at least, Lexia thought it was night—and fell into a deep sleep.

They should have taken turns or shifts to keep watch.

* * *

Lexia sat up in her bed, clutching her blankets to her chest. She silently cursed herself. Of course there was noise in the apartment. Her dad was back.

Her heart beat wildly and she panted from the start. She lay back down and rearranged her pillow, nestling back into the warmth of the bed beneath her.

Greg was snoring softly from the couch. She listened to the rhythm and let her eyes drift closed.

Something in the other room struck the floor with a loud thunk and then rolled until it hit her door.

Her eyes popped open. She could see the object blocking the small amount of light under the door's clearance.

Crunching noises came from across the apartment's tiny space, echoing loudly. That was not Greg. He was still sawing logs.

Careful not to make noise, Lexia eased back her covers and put her bare feet to the floor and rushed across the bedroom. She pulled the handle of the small chest of drawers beside her bed and felt for her handgun.

When the cool metal was in her grip, she eased it out and flipped the safety off, holding the pistol so that its barrel pointed at the floor in front of her. One thing her paranoid dad did teach her before getting carted off was how to handle a gun, and handle herself in dangerous situations.

More shuffling from the other room. It was getting louder. How was her dad sleeping through this? She knew he was okay because his snoring was so insanely loud. And she was grateful he hadn't been harmed. If she worked quickly, neither of them would be.

She slipped into the darkness, ready to confront the intruder head-on.

Sort of. Her heart was pounding, her palms were sweaty, and her breathing—it definitely wasn't loud and steady like dear ol' dad's.

Lexia reached out, feeling along the wall until her fingers found the light switch to her right. Mentally she counted down in order to psych herself up.

Three.

Two…

ONE!

She flipped the switch and was immediately blinded. On a positive note, so was the intruder.

"Dad!"

He snorted and sat up.

"Dad. Someone's in here! I can't see!"

As her vision returned and color took form, she saw a writhing mass of men. One was her dad. The other was…Angelo?

Angelo Gallo. The bane of her existence in high school.

"Dad! Stop!"

She pulled her father's elbow until she caught his attention. "'s not safe!"

"No! Dad, stop. I know him!" Greg stopped pounding the young man and sat up on his knees, still straddling Angelo's legs to restrain him.

"What in the world are you doing here, Angel?" Internally, she snorted a little. He was anything but an angel.

The young man shoved at Greg, who wouldn't relent. "Get off me, old man!"

For a second, Lexia thought that Greg might start trying to kill him again. Those last two words ignited a fire in her dad's eyes: *old man*.

"Dad, please get off him. Check the doors. Make sure they're safe." That last word had gotten his attention. Greg nodded and climbed off the young man's legs, rushing to the door and checking the locks in triplicate.

She offered a hand to Angel, but he just sneered at it, wiping his bloodied lip with the back of his hand.

His dark hair was shaggy and too long. He hadn't had a haircut in a while. But it looked good on him. Lexia thought that just about anything would look good on him. He was just that guy: the hot Italian that other guys buddied up with and girls batted eyelashes at. In school, it had been almost ridiculous. "The Italian Stallion," he'd named himself. *Nice.*

Working at the bakery, she'd seen him at least once a week. She'd seen many classmates come through their doors. No one ratted her out. Somehow, they'd understood her predicament and kept their lips zipped.

"Explain," she ordered.

"Put the gun down, Lexia."

She shivered. Just hearing her name on his lips was almost enough to undo her. She lowered the gun.

"I'm not gonna hurt you. I wouldn't do that."

She rolled her eyes and looked at her dad, who nodded, patting his side. He always carried when he was home. *Stupid boy*. He'd been lucky. If Greg hadn't been sleeping so soundly, he would have more holes in his body than Swiss cheese.

Lexia returned her pistol to its proper place and then returned, shrugging on a sweater. One man, one boy were staring each other down, her dad standing guard at the door.

That wasn't how Angel had come in, though. And, unlike his namesake, he hadn't flown. He'd climbed the rickety fire escape and eased up her window. It didn't lock. None of them did. But her dad's aluminum foil was quite loud when disturbed. It had let her know that someone was there.

Maybe Greg wasn't quite so crazy after all.

Greg's voice startled her.

Greg was muttering under his breath. "'s not safe. 's not safe. 's not safe." Over and over…and over.

Angel was just staring at him. What had been an angry, dark look had faded into understanding and wariness.

Great, she thought.

"Sit, Angel. You better explain why you broke into my apartment in the middle of the night." She glanced out the now-open window to make sure it was still dark outside. Yep. Still night.

He huffed and drew his dark brows down as he settled uncomfortably onto the edge of her couch. "I needed some stuff."

"You could have knocked and asked me for it."

He ran his fingers through his hair. "You wouldn't have given it to me."

"Maybe. Maybe not. But you don't just climb through someone's window in the middle of the night."

Signature smirk in place, Angel replied, "Romeo did it."

Heat surged into her cheeks. "You're not Romeo, Angel. What did you need?"

He swallowed. "I need the gas masks and some supplies I thought your dad might have left behind. I didn't know he was here."

"You came into my home to rob me. I almost shot you. Do you even get that?"

He coughed. "Yeah. I get it. I'm not stupid, Lexia."

"Are you sick?" She glanced from her dad, who still stood near the door glaring at their exchange, back to Angel.

"Not anymore."

Her brows rose along with her curiosity. "You got sick? You survived?"

"Yeah. So did you."

"How did you know that?"

Angel glanced at her just for a moment; his cheeks turned the slightest shade of pink. "I just know."

"Well that's not creepy," Lexia responded. She didn't know what to think of that admission. "Tell me or I won't help you."

"I've been checking on you, okay? I saw you through the window."

"You climbed the fire escape?" The very thought of the height made her stomach turn flip-flops. It turned them faster because Angel had been keeping an eye on her.

"Hey, why do you need the gear, anyway?"

Angel pulled his iPad out of the inside of his pocket and glared at Greg. "You cracked it, man!" He ran his hand through his hair.

Greg didn't flinch, just stared him down until Angel relented and looked away. Lexia made a mental note never to challenge her dad to a staring contest. *Holy crap. He was intense. And a little scary when provoked.*

Angel began punching a web address into the browser. A site began to load, albeit slowly. *Prep for Doom*.

"What's *Prep for Doom*?"

Angel smiled. "It may be a ticket out of this hell hole."

"What do you mean?" Lexia sat down beside him and watched his fingers swipe the screen as he scrolled down the posts until he found what he'd been searching for.

"Look," he looked up at her. She could see his desperation. "According to these guys, there's this safe haven on Staten Island. It's stocked with food and supplies. And there aren't dead people everywhere." He blew out a harsh breath. "I know you've been holed up in here, but Lex, you have to be running out of food. And there are dead bodies everywhere. If we thought the virus was bad, who knows what diseases can be caused from all of the rotting bodies. They're everywhere. No one moves them. No one wants to touch them. The stench alone..." Angel cringed.

Lexia couldn't imagine what was going on outside. But from what Angel said it was horrific.

"How did you learn about this site?"

A full-on blush made Angel's cheeks glow. "Look, I know I'm not what you'd probably consider a survivalist, but I agree with a lot of the things these guys have to say. I've been hovering around in the forum for a while. I got an invitation to join," he shrugged. "So, I joined."

He got an invitation to join a group that was prepping for the apocalypse? That wasn't weird or anything, Lexia thought. Angel was strong. He was athletic. But he wasn't one of these guys who left the city streets to go hiking or anything.

"Have you checked out the safe zone or heard from anyone who actually made it there?"

Angel shook his head. "No."

She knew he wondered the same thing she did. Were they all dead now? Or, could some of them have made it?

Lexia rolled the thought of a safe zone around in her mind. It would be weird to live with strangers. But, they might be safer there. They would have food and water, shelter...

"'s not safe," Greg shouted, abruptly interrupting her thoughts.

Angel looked at him and asked, "What's not safe?"

"'s not safe," Greg ground out. Lexia's dad started pacing, pointing frantically at his articles on the wall. She stood and walked over to where he had stopped, pointing like a dog who was signaling his master.

The article he was fixated on read, "PFD Conspiracy: The Truth Behind the Lies."

"Peter Franklin Donalds," she mouthed, studying the simple, diamond-shaped logo emblazoned with the company's initials.

"'s not safe, L-L-Lex."

He begged her with his eyes. Greg was scared. He was always paranoid, but not usually genuinely afraid.

Lexia swallowed and turned back to Angel, who was watching them curiously.

"I've heard of Peter Franklin Donalds. The reporter, Amy Savino, has talked about them. I don't watch television that often, since we only have one station and it's all news all the time, but I have heard of this, Dad."

"'s not safe."

She smiled and grabbed his hand, giving him a comforting squeeze. "It's okay. We're safe here."

Angel stood up. "So, I guess I should go. I'm gonna at least check it out, Lex." Lexia almost laughed when he ticked his head back toward the window. Shredded silver strands of foil hung off the edge. The rest of it was crumpled where the two panes met.

She looked to her dad. "Do you want to go with him? To Staten Island, Dad?"

He shook his head in a vehement no. "'s not safe."

Part of her wanted to hug her father. Something in her gut said that Staten Island was bad news. Maybe it wasn't safe there. Maybe someone had played some sort of a sick joke on people. Or perhaps, everything the anonymous person posted was true.

She mentally kicked herself. She was sounding more paranoid than her dad. But he wouldn't make it. She knew it. He was comfortable in their apartment. He felt safer there—with aluminum foil-covered windows, a few old handguns and walls plastered with newspaper clippings—than he would feel anywhere else.

Lexia would have to find food. But, they could make it. They could stay inside, stay safe.

"Can we give him a few things, Dad?"

He looked from her to Angel and scowled. Lexia knew he was still angry that Angel had broken in with the intention of stealing what he needed. But this was survival. Wasn't everyone doing what they had to do instead of what was proper? Wasn't she about to steal food if she had to?

"Dad, we're staying put. Let's help him out. Maybe he'll come back and tell us if it's safe. Right, Angel?"

"Yeah! I'll come back for you," Angel agreed quickly. Angel was many things, but he wasn't a liar. He would come back for them. And that alone was enough to ask her dad to help.

"See," she begged her dad.

Greg seemed to mull it over for a long moment. He finally nodded.

"What do you need?" Lexia asked. She had Greg's blessing to help Angel out.

Angel left through the apartment's window—his choice, not hers—with a gas mask, a couple of maps, her old pink backpack, a spare flashlight, and one of her dad's revolvers. That would leave them with three. Her Dad had refused to give him any bullets, insisting that it wasn't safe. He didn't trust Angel, not that Angel had given him a reason to.

Angel didn't say thank you. He didn't hug her or promise her anything. When he slipped out the window his dark brown eyes said he would be back. And she hoped he was able to keep his promise, hoped he would make it to the safe zone, and then hurry back to her.

She sighed, watching him climb down the fire escape, retracing the steps he'd taken to get to her. Turning around, Lexia watched her father work diligently to recover the disturbed window.

The whole world was disturbed. Now Greg just fit in with everyone else.

* * *

Lexia hadn't heard anything from Angel. He should have been there and back in a day. Maybe he'd gotten hurt or into some sort of trouble. The thought made her stomach hurt.

There was a tiny sliver of aluminum foil peeled up on the corner of one of the window panes. She could see that it was daylight. It was bright, almost promising. Maybe Angel would come today.

Her dad was another story. He hadn't eaten in a day, shaking his head, saying his usual garbled phrase…repeatedly.

If something didn't give soon, she might lose her mind.

An hour ago, he'd gone into her room and closed the door before she could question him about what in the world he was doing. Sometimes, he needed to be alone. Since he wouldn't leave the apartment, he'd barricade himself behind closed doors.

Lexia's knuckles rapped against the cool wood. "Dad?"

No answer.

"Greg?"

Nothing.

Then she heard the worst sound in the entire world.

Her dad had begun vomiting. She could hear him stumble toward her tiny bathroom, hear the splatter across the tiles that said he hadn't quite reached the toilet.

"N-n-NO! L-Lex! 's not safe!" he roared, just before retching again.

But it was safe. She'd already gone through it. She would see him through this, too. Lexia thought for a second about how to get the door open. She had no idea how to take it off the hinges, or how to pick a lock. Brute force was her only option. Time for Louie.

Louie was her Louisville Slugger. Made of thick, solid wood, Louie was a good option. She lined the bat up with the door handle and took a couple of practice whacks before finally swinging it down in a heavy arc.

A few swings and loud cracks later, the handle broke and the door swung open.

Emotions warred in her father's face. Greg was simultaneously relieved and afraid that Lexia was with him. She helped move him toward the toilet, positioning him for what was going to be a long day.

Thank goodness she still had cleaner under the sink.

* * *

He'd had a headache and his face looked flushed. Those were the first signs. She'd dismissed them. Everyone got headaches once in a while. When the vomiting started, she knew, but thought he would pull through. When blood filled his vomit, it became clear that he was in trouble.

Greg was now snoring softly on the couch. His eyes were vampiric now. Bruises covered every inch of his skin, capillaries and veins had busted in the middle of the storm that had struck such a physically strong man down. *How can the tiniest of organisms still cause such mayhem*, she thought.

Lexia peeled back a little more of the foil along the corner of the window. It was pitch black outside. But someone still living nearby had their television on. Freaking Amy Savino. If she could, she might stab that woman with a spoon. Lex was tired of hearing only her and her conspiracy theories. She was making things worse, not better!

Her father's chest rattled and then the gurgling began to pour from his lungs. He blinked awake, too tired to lift his head off the pillow beneath it.

His red eyes pleaded with her, but for what?

"L-Lex?"

She left her perch by the window and knelt beside him, grasping his hand in hers.

"Yeah, Dad?"

He whimpered, causing a shiver to run down her spine. Greg began to speak, his mouth forming a red bubble of saliva within his lips. It popped.

Lexia watched him. He squinted his eyes, face tormented, but no tears came out. His body had no fluid to spare. A silent scream.

He clutched her hand to the point of breaking the fragile bones within. But she didn't let on. She gripped his hand tighter.

"It's okay. I know you're in pain, but it'll be okay. I made it, so you'll make it, too."

He shook his head slightly and closed his eyes. Greg's breaths became labored, the sound echoing through the room, drowning out all other noises inside or out.

Lexia held his hand and listened to the death rattle rumble in his chest. She sat on the bare floor beside him until they both nodded off, unable to resist the enticing lull of sleep.

When she awoke, Lexia wished she'd been stronger, had been able to stay awake. Her father's hand was cold in hers. His chest did not rise or fall. The terrible rattling sound was gone. And, so was her father.

She eased her hand out of his eventually, moving to the sink to do the dishes. Her hands. They needed to do something.

She scrubbed everything in sight—every countertop, every appliance. The windows.

They needed to be clean. When she looked from their light-blocking foil covering back to her father, who lay dead on her couch, it hit her. And she exploded.

Ripping each and every shred of foil off the panes and sill, she raged against the stupid silver false security, of the unfairness of survival, and the pain of having just lost her father…again.

She cried and thought of smashing everything with Louie, but changed her mind. Lexia had a better idea. Blowing her nose into yet another tissue, she began making a mental packing list. She was going to Staten Island. If Angel was there, and if it was safe, she could stay there. She could survive.

An hour later, her black backpack was stuffed full of everything she thought she might possibly need. Two handguns were tucked into inside pockets and one warmed the small of her back. Her boots were laced.

With one look back at her father, who just looked as though he'd fallen asleep, she released the locks that held her in. A gust of wind rattled the newspaper clippings lining her walls.

She silenced them by slamming the door shut behind her and stepping out into the hallway, into the stairwell, and then into the alley that ran alongside her building. Lexia eyeballed the fire escape. It was the same one that Angel had scaled to break in, the same one from which he left.

It was smart to move at night. She had dressed in dark clothes and would blend in with the shadows.

She could do this.

It could work.

Everything was still. No cars on the road. No subway trains. The only movement came from other shadows that lurked in the darkness—like her, and the bicycle that almost ran her over, its rider cursing her a blue streak as he corrected himself.

Rats scurried along behind dumpsters and the wind blew her hair into a tangled mess. But she kept walking, keeping close to the sides of the buildings. Eventually, the sun was rising and the birds were chirping happily.

It was a long walk to New Jersey, but, she'd made it. When she stopped to catch her breath and check things out, the sun was high in the sky, warming her skin and the pavement surrounding her. The Goethals Bridge stood just ahead. It was the only way on and off of Staten Island now. She'd read that little tidbit briefly while Angel had scrolled through the posts on that weird website. *Prep for Doom*.

Well, the bridge that she kept closing in on looked like the gate of doom. It was menacing. If an inanimate object could be frightening, this piece of architecture fit the bill.

All she could think of was her father—the fear in his eyes when he looked at the Peter Franklin Donalds logo, the obsession with clipping even the oldest of newspapers until only slivers of black and white print were left in his lap or in heaps on the floor.

His words. Above all, she heard his words in her mind.

“’s *not safe.*”

FOUR: *HAZMAT*
by Jon Messenger

The dust was thick in the basement. Terrance Lenape didn't make it down there much anymore. For a while, he had been in the basement almost every day, building or organizing. Like everything else since he retired, his interest seemed to wane after a while.

Floor-to-ceiling baker's racks lined the walls and were placed seemingly haphazardly through the center of the unfinished room. Rows of canned goods stood out on one, their labels all meticulously turned forward. Another held dry goods while another held toiletries. It was well organized but abandoned, as another flight of fancy struck Terry.

Lilly teased him constantly about the basement, accusing him of wasting all that money and time, that there were a hundred other better things that he could have done with his retirement. Terry frowned as he looked at the solemn room. It didn't seem like such a waste anymore. He clenched the paper in his hand, wrinkling and creasing it in his grip.

He heard footsteps in the kitchen and the basement door flew open, flooding the rickety wooden steps with light. "You down there, Terry?" Lilly asked nervously.

"Yeah," he replied, "just seeing what we had."

"The news is running another story on the outbreak."

He took another look around their storage room—prepper pantry, as Lilly fondly referred to it—before pulling the string on the light bulb.

Terry hurried up the steps, cringing at every creak of the wooden staircase. The stairs, like everything in the basement, had been on his "to-do" list for years but somehow never seemed all that important.

"It looks like it's spreading," she said, from her spot on the couch. "I feel like we should be doing something."

"Like what?"

"Like share our supplies. We have a ton. Isn't that what the stupid prepper group was all about, helping everyone else during the apocalypse?"

"Prep for Doom isn't stupid," Terry said, holding up the crumpled piece of paper in his hand. "They're the only reason we know about the safe zone on Staten Island."

"Then we should be telling other people about it," Lilly replied, climbing slowly to her feet. Her black hair was streaked with gray and new wrinkles had appeared at the corners of her eyes. "If we're not going to share the food we've got, the least we can do is tell people where to go."

"How many people would you like to tell?" he argued, raising the same valid points he'd raised at least a dozen times before. "Staten Island has a population of around five hundred thousand. How many live in New York City alone? Eight million or so? You know the New Yorkers already know about the safe zone. They're already going to be overwhelmed without us inviting more people from Jersey to head up that way."

"Maybe we shouldn't go then. I saw on the TV, the reporter said everyone should just stay in their homes."

Terry huffed. "How long do you think our food will last? People have been looting some of the other neighborhoods. It's only a matter of time before they come here, too."

Lilly changed the channel to another news station. A myriad of depressing images flashed across the screen and Terry had to look away.

"We can't stay here," he said, more calmly. "We don't have anything with which to defend ourselves. We're not going to be able to keep people out."

She turned toward him, her blue eyes stern but full of compassion for her nervous husband. "Maybe we should have got a gun. All the prepper shows always showed them with guns."

"Lilly, I'm a retired high school chemistry teacher. You make quilts. What do we know about guns? If we got one, we'd probably just wind up shooting each other on accident."

He took her hand. She slipped her fingers into his and gave his hand a squeeze.

"I still say we go to Staten Island. We have those old Army protective suits and gas masks. That should keep us safe while we drive up there."

Lilly looked around her living room, so full of character and life. Cross-stitched pictures hung on the walls, dangling over family portraits taken decades ago of a much younger, skinnier, and vibrant couple. She hated to leave it; Terry could see it on her face. Her expression seemed to sag with disappointment, knowing she couldn't take it all with her.

"Okay," she whispered.

* * *

Packing didn't take long. They stuffed changes of clothes into a suitcase and filled an old backpack with some canned goods and bags of homemade trail mix. A few bottles of water filled out the bag.

Placing the bags next to the side door leading to the garage, they walked downstairs together, into the gloomy basement. Terry turned on the light, though he didn't really need it. The meager light streaming through the narrow windows was enough to find the plastic bin near the back. He pulled off the masking tape from the edges and lifted the lid. Inside was a pair of matching olive green MOPP suits. They slipped on the pants and jackets over their clothes, pulling an uncomfortable elastic string from the back of the jacket, under their crotch, before connecting it to a hook in the front. Terry would have never been able to put on the protective suit, with all its pieces, had it not been for the same Prep for Doom group that got him started on the basement.

They pulled on the heavy rubber boots over their tennis shoes, feeling awkward as they did. They made his feet wider and longer than they had been before, making it uncomfortable to walk. The only things remaining in the bin were the rubber gloves and the gas masks, complete with hoods the color of muddy water.

Terry slipped his over his head, pulling the elastic straps in the back to tighten it around his face. He dropped the hood into place and turned toward Lilly, who had to stifle a laugh at the sight.

"Your turn," he said, though his voice was hard to hear through the mask.

She slipped hers over her head, mimicking Terry as she tightened the straps in the back. As she raised her head and smoothed back the hood, he could see the eyepieces fogging.

"I can't see anything," she said, lifting the mask from her chin and wiping the inside. "Is this supposed to happen?"

"You need to clear the mask," he explained. "Here. Put the mask back down and blow out as hard as you can when I tell you."

She went through the steps until a tight seal was formed around her face. The fogging stopped, though he could see her shoulders moving with each labored breath. He had to admit that breathing with the gas mask was far more difficult than without. He hoped they didn't have to do anything too strenuous while wearing all this gear, since he wasn't sure his old body could handle the effort.

"I feel ridiculous," she complained.

"You look ridiculous," he countered, "but this isn't about looking good. Come on, let's get on the gloves."

He had to tilt his head nearly all the way down just to find the gloves. Everything was a bit more difficult with a mask on his face. He slipped the gloves on. Almost immediately, he could feel his hands sweating. The gloves didn't breathe at all.

Shambling as best they could, they climbed the stairs back to the main floor and collected their bags. Glancing one final time over his shoulder, Terry said a silent farewell to their house. He hoped he'd see it again.

Walking into the garage, he loaded their suitcase and backpack into the backseat. He climbed behind the wheel, feeling clunky as he did so. His gloved hands didn't grip the steering wheel very well and the boots made pressing only one pedal at a time fairly difficult. Eventually he slipped the keys into the ignition and started the car. With a push of the garage door opener, light flooded the garage.

He backed out slowly, unsure what they'd find behind them. As the car rolled onto the street and Terry shifted into drive, he was surprised by the sight around him. Their neighborhood looked completely unchanged. A bike was abandoned on the neighbor's lawn. Lights glowed from living rooms where families gathered around the television. Had it not been for what they were watching, it would have been easy to mistake the scene for one of familial tranquility.

After seeing so many horrific scenes from around the world—of bodies being piled in the streets and hospitals completely overwhelmed, to the point that the sick and the dying were sharing gurneys in the hallways—he expected something worse. Seeing a level of normalcy in their neighborhood was unsettling.

They drove out of town in silence, Terry's mind ablaze with a million questions, the least of which was how, logistically, they'd make it all the way to Goethals Bridge by car. The freeways would be packed bumper to bumper with people trying to get out of the cities. He didn't even want to think about the Turnpike.

He glanced over at Lilly and saw a different emotion reflected in her eyes. Noticing his stare, she quickly looked out the window, where she watched the subdivisions roll by. She didn't care about the supposed Staten

Island safe zone. The news had recommended they stay in their house, but if it hadn't been the recommendation of the news, she would have found another way to try to convince him. He knew that she would have stayed, boarding up the windows and doors if need be. It had been her life during all the long years of Terry's teaching, until he was finally able to retire and they both started drawing Social Security checks. Neighbors had come and gone; they had watched children be born, grow, and move out, all from their front porch while sipping on a glass of tea.

Terry sighed, though the sound of it was lost in his mask. Reaching out, he took her hand. It felt alien, with two thick rubber gloves between them, but she glanced back all the same, her eyes glistening through the plastic lenses. He couldn't tell if she was smiling, but he assumed she was.

* * *

The easiest way to Elizabeth, the town outside the Goethals Bridge, was I-78 East to the Turnpike, but even as they approached the first on-ramp to I-78, they knew it wasn't a good choice. Cars were backed up nearly two miles from the entryway, a never-ending single-file line of brake lights stretching as far as they could see. A second muddled row of cars sat at a stop beside those entering the freeway, drivers who thought merging at the last moment would be a quicker option. With I-78 at a dead stop, however, no one moved, causing more and more congestion.

Lilly drummed her gloved fingers on the console. "I thought everyone would be driving away from New York, but they all look like they're heading toward it. How many preppers were on that silly website?"

Terry shook his head as he watched the never-ending line of taillights. "Not this many. Someone must have leaked the location."

"Well, we're not going to make it using the interstate. Do you know another way?"

Terry sighed and drove around the gridlock, choosing instead to stick to back roads. The route wouldn't get them all the way to Elizabeth, but they'd be moving, which was a far cry more than they would be doing on the interstate.

Once they were well past the traffic, Terry pulled over to the shoulder and turned on his hazard lights. They blinked a steady cadence as he reached into the back seat, retrieving an old, battered atlas. He didn't own a smart phone or a GPS. Finding the map of New Jersey, he let his fingers trace some of the numbered State Highways that would get them closer to where they needed to be.

Cars passed them as they sat on the shoulder, some slowing to gawk at the two people in drab olive MOPP suits. Terry tried his best to ignore them, but he felt the same creeping sensation he'd felt when the gaggle approached them earlier, as though being in the masks made them targets for those who would take from people who were unable to defend themselves.

The car rocked gently as each vehicle passed, the wind pressure shaking their Oldsmobile. He dropped the atlas onto the back seat as a semi passed them, violently rattling their car.

Terry frowned as he turned off his hazards and turned on his left blinker. Waiting for a gap, he merged into traffic and continued driving east.

Traffic moved slowly but steadily forward. It wasn't more than twenty miles to the bridge, but it would take hours by car, longer by foot, since neither he nor Lilly were in all that great of shape. He had once been an athlete and she a cheerleader in their prime, but their prime had passed by long ago. The paunch around his waist was a result of too little exercise and too much home cooking. Though he'd never admit it to his wife, she suffered the same affliction.

"What's that?" Lilly asked, pointing ahead of them.

Terry couldn't see well around the SUV in front of them, but he could see smoke rising above the vehicles. In a cascade of lights, cars slowly applied their brakes and rolled to a stop.

The driver's door on the SUV swung open and a man climbed out onto the running boards, staring over the traffic in front of him. He shook his head slowly before disappearing back into the vehicle. Glancing in his rear view mirror, Terry saw others climbing out of their cars before throwing their hands up in disgust.

Curious, Terry unbuckled his seatbelt.

"What are you doing?" Lilly asked, surprised.

"I'm going to see what's causing the traffic jam."

She shook her head. "Just stay in the car. It'll clear up soon enough."

"You don't believe that any more than I do. If it's a bad accident; we may not be able to keep going this way." As he reached for his door handle, she grabbed his arm. He paused and patted her hand affectionately before opening his door and climbing out.

He immediately saw why everyone wore a look of disgust. Less than a quarter mile ahead, a semi had jackknifed before flipping onto its side. It blocked the whole road, even covering the gravely shoulders. A few four-wheel drive trucks and SUVs were rolling through the sloped grass on either side but most vehicles were turning around and driving back the way they came.

He leaned down and looked into their car. "Jackknifed semi," he said blankly.

"Can we go around?" she asked.

Terry laughed, though the sound was flat and mechanical through the mask. "Not in this old clunker. Our best bet is to—"

"Hey," a man yelled from one of the cars behind them. The chemistry teacher rose from his half crouch and glanced over his shoulder. A man in a plain t-shirt was standing beside the car behind them. "What's with the get up?"

Another car had pulled beside them, originally turning around but suddenly interested in Terry.

"I asked you a question," the guy said when Terry didn't answer.

"Get in the car," Lilly said, watching the scene unfold through the back window. "Just ignore him and get in the car."

"There's nowhere to go," Terry muttered, though he was sure she didn't hear him.

"Why are you wearing all that?" the man behind him asked, pointing at him threateningly. "You know something we don't?"

Terry stepped to the car's back door and pulled it open, though his gaze never left the inquisitor. Reaching in, he grabbed the backpack and slung it over his shoulder.

"Get out of the car," he said, making sure Lilly could hear him.

"No, you get in. Let's just drive away from here."

The second car had turned itself at an angle, blocking the westbound shoulder.

"There's nowhere to go," he said louder this time. "Just get out."

He stole a glance over his shoulder toward the trees just off the road. With the heavy backpack over his shoulder, he grabbed the handle to their suitcase and slowly pulled it from the car.

"Are you deaf?" the abrasive man asked as he approached. "How about you take off that suit?"

Terry hefted the suitcase. Filled just with clothes, it was light, but its hard plastic exterior still gave it some girth.

"Terry?" Lilly asked nervously as the angry man drew nearer.

"Get out of the damn car, Lilly!" Terry yelled as he threw the suitcase at the man.

Caught by surprise, the man didn't raise his arms as the hard plastic crashed into his face. He collapsed as the latch on the suitcase sprang open, spilling clothes all over the road.

Terry turned and ran around the car, grabbing Lilly's hand as she slowly climbed out of the passenger's side. He pulled her down the incline and into the woods, ignoring the slew of profanity that chased after them.

* * *

"Stop," Lilly said for the tenth time. Her breathing was labored and her shoulders heaved and fell with every weary breath. "I need to stop."

Terry didn't argue. It was almost impossible to get a lungful of air while wearing the gas mask. All he wanted to do was pull it off his face and suck in a few deep breaths, but he didn't dare. He still remembered the blood seeping from the man's nose and knew that was only the start. The piles of bodies unceremoniously forgotten on the newscast were where it ended.

The backpack slid from his shoulders as he came to a stop. He dropped it heavily onto the ground. His back and shoulders ached from the exertion. He wasn't used to carrying an extra forty pounds under the best of circumstances, and running through the woods in protective gear definitely didn't qualify as "best of circumstances."

He slumped against the tree and rested his hands on his knees. The sweat that had been pooling in his gloves now felt like a lake. As he straightened his back to work out a side stitch and raised his hands over his head, sweat ran freely down his arms.

Lilly hadn't moved since they stopped. She had fixed him with an intense stare that he couldn't properly read.

"Are you okay?" he asked.

For a moment, she was silent. Then she cleared her throat. "I need to pee."

He was caught off guard but glanced around anyway, to make sure no one was watching. The woods were empty; they had lost their pursuers long ago, if the men had even decided to enter the woods in the first place. "Then go pee."

She placed her hands on her hips. "And just what, drop my pants out here?"

"That's the general idea, darling," he replied with a chuckle.

"What's the point of all this protective equipment if we can just take it off whenever?"

"It keeps us from getting the virus on us," he explained. "It's airborne, you know. Technically, it could get in you through a cut on your skin if you weren't careful."

"Is that true?" she asked nervously.

"I'm not a biology teacher but that's why you keep a bandage on a cut, to keep out dirt and germs."

She hesitated, despite the fact that he could now tell she needed to use the bathroom. "Well, not to sound crude, but as soon as I drop my pants and underwear, I'm exposing a delicate area to the air. You don't think I could get sick that way, do you?"

Terry blushed, knowing his wife was turning a deep shade of scarlet underneath it all. "I think that falls into the same category as getting an STD by sitting on a toilet seat. I think you'll be okay."

Satisfied, she walked around the back of the tree. He heard snaps being undone and zippers being lowered. After an eternity of her undressing, she finally started relieving herself.

"What about when we need to eat?" she asked while otherwise preoccupied.

"What about it?" he asked.

"We're going to have to take off our masks to eat. Isn't that going to expose us to whatever's out there?"

Terry paused, unsure how to reply. He had gleaned as much information as possible from the *Prep for Doom* site and what news he could watch before they left, but some questions were never answered. He didn't know how widespread the disease had become. It was airborne, but that usually meant it passed from person to person at a distance, rather than through bodily fluids.

"We should be okay, so long as we eat away from other people, like out here in the woods," he finally replied.

"You paused," she said, as she pulled up her jeans. "That's what you do when you're just making up an answer."

"I'm not making it up," he said, though he knew she was right.

She didn't argue as she stepped around the tree. "Ready to go, old man? You sure you can handle that backpack alone?"

"After you, you old battle-axe," he chided.

* * *

They ran into a hiking trail a short while later, one that ran between subdivisions, all the while butting up against the backs of privacy fences. It was deserted and quiet, though he was sure people eyed them warily from the windows of the houses they passed.

The trail was well maintained, with larger rocks having been pushed to the side, forming a sort of perimeter as they walked.

After a couple hours of hiking, Terry could feel the pain in his knee flaring. He chose a spot between subdivisions, an area where the trail flitted between the trees and was concealed from sight of most of the houses nearby. He smacked his lips as much as he could and felt his dry tongue scraping across the roof of his mouth. His lips were parched, despite the moisture trapped underneath his mask and hood.

"I need to rest and we both need to eat and drink something," he said.

She didn't argue as he sat down on one of the paver stones lining the trail. She sat down across from him and watched as he unzipped the bag. He pulled out a bottle of water and unscrewed the lid. Grabbing the filter on his mask, he stared into her eyes.

"Here goes nothing."

He pulled the mask off in a single movement, not bothering to loosen the rubber straps. He gulped air into his lungs like he was a deep-sea diver, surfacing after an eternity underwater. The air was cool and fresh, rejuvenating him with every breath. There was a crispness in the summer air that was a mixture of blooming flowers and damp leaves. He couldn't remember the New Jersey air ever smelling nicer.

"I think we're safe," he said and Lilly quickly followed suit.

As she closed her eyes and took deep breaths, Terry chuckled to himself. She opened one eye and arched an eyebrow. "What's so funny?"

"You have a line all the way around your face from the mask."

"You didn't happen to bring a mirror in that survival kit, did you? Because you may want to take a look at yourself before you start teasing someone else."

He stopped laughing but the grin never left his face. He took a long drink from the bottle, draining half of it before handing it to Lilly. As she drank, he withdrew a couple granola bars. It wasn't a satisfying lunch, but it stopped the rumbling in his stomach.

"What do you think Staten Island will be like?" Lilly asked between mouthfuls of food.

Terry shrugged. "They'll probably have some guards, so the sick people can't get in. The website said they had food, water, and shelter, so it can't be all bad."

"And they're just letting anyone in?" She sounded skeptical.

"I would assume they're letting in people who aren't sick, for starters. If the news is true, that cuts out a big part of the population. After that, yeah, I do think they're taking anyone who can make it there."

She glanced over her shoulder, as though suddenly interested in the nondescript trees around them. He knew her mannerisms well, after nearly forty years of marriage.

"What are you thinking about?"

She shook her head and raised a hand to her face, wiping her eyes. "I'm just thinking about all the people that aren't going to make it to the safe zone. There have got to be thousands of people who are sick right now, who don't have these suits or food or water. People who are just scared to death, hiding in their homes, waiting to die. It's terrible."

"Millions," Terry corrected.

She frowned at him. "That entire exchange and all you took away was my underestimation."

He shrugged as he pulled his gloves back on. He picked up his mask and started loosening the straps once more.

"Just a little longer," she sighed.

"We need to get going. It's going to be a long walk to Goethals Bridge."

They gathered their belongings and started following the trail once more. It would take nearly a full day of walking before they got to the town of Elizabeth. That was assuming his knee held up to walking nearly ten miles in one day.

The trail wound farther and longer than Terry had expected. He stole glances between the houses they passed but could see only empty streets. No one was walking around. No kids were playing. There weren't even any cars driving away. It was deathly quiet.

As they came around a blind curve in the path, they saw a man standing perfectly still up ahead. Terry placed a hand protectively in front of Lilly, pulling her behind him. Their feet scraped in the gravel and the man turned his head sharply toward them.

Terry stifled a cry of surprise when he caught sight of the man's face. His dark hair was unkempt and matted to his head from sweat. He absently wiped his nose on the back of his arm, leaving a streak of blood stretching across his face. His eyes were bloodshot, run through from corner to corner with bright red veins. There were tracks on his cheeks, however faint, that told Terry blood had once seeped from the man's eyes.

The man took a halted step toward them, clutching his stomach as though in pain. "Help me," he moaned.

"Come on, Lilly," Terry said. "Just turn around slowly and let's go back the way we came."

Lilly nodded and took a step backward. The man raised his hand, begging them to stop, as he appeared crestfallen. "Please, please help me."

"We don't have anything for you," Terry said sternly, though he immediately regretted speaking. He shouldn't have acknowledged the man at all.

"I'll take anything," the man groaned, clutching his stomach again. He took a staggering step toward them, wincing as he moved. "Food, water, anything."

"I'm sorry," Terry said, following Lilly's lead and walking away.

"Those suits," the man said feverishly. "They can keep me safe, stop me from getting sicker."

Terry shook his head. "You're already infected. The suit won't do anything for you now."

"You can't just leave me here," the man sobbed quietly, doubling over where he stood.

"I'm really sorry," Terry said, turning away and walking briskly to catch up to Lilly.

"You can't leave me here!" the man yelled as he ran toward them with a surprising burst of speed.

Terry turned abruptly but the man knocked him from his feet with a strong forearm. Terry tumbled backward, tripping over a large rock, and falling into the grass. From his position, he watched in horror as the man jumped on Lilly's back, clawing at her gas mask.

"Give me the mask!" the man yelled, spittle flecked with spots of red blood flying from his lips.

The man slipped his fingers under her chin and pulled the mask forward, breaking the tight seal around her skin. She screamed in fear, a noise that vaulted Terry into action. His hands closed over a rock as he stood and he rushed toward his wife. The infected stranger and Lilly turned quickly in a circle as she tried to dislodge the crazed man. As the stranger turned toward Terry, he swung the rock as hard as he could, smashing it into the man's face. The man slumped to the ground, releasing Lilly.

"He nearly pulled off my mask," she said, panicked and seemingly oblivious to the bloody mess that remained of the infected man's face. "He broke my seal and breathed right on me. Oh God, Terry, he breathed on me. The disease is airborne and he—"

"Shh," Terry said. He helped her fix her mask before holding her close, hushing her every time she started talking. He was glad for the layers of the MOPP suit. She couldn't feel his racing heart or hear the panic in his voice.

* * *

They stopped early for the night, only a couple more miles down the road. The hiking trail had ended and they were forced to follow the asphalt. There were a lot of parked cars lining either side, but they were all abandoned. Still, they walked far off the road and out of sight before setting up a makeshift camp.

Lilly's eyes were still wide with fear and she rocked slightly. She clutched her legs through her protective gear, refusing to remove her gloves or mask even as Terry passed out food and water.

"You need to eat," he said.

She shook her head. "He breathed right on me. I could feel his breath across the back of my neck. What if I'm sick?"

Terry knelt before her and pulled off his mask. With a free hand, he brushed the sweaty salt and pepper hair off his forehead. "You're not going to get sick. You'll be fine, I promise."

"How can you know?" she said curtly.

He took her hands and gave them a squeeze. "This thing is like the flu. Every flu season, you're exposed to the virus hundreds of times a day but you're not sick every day. It takes all the right circumstances for you to get sick. He might have breathed on you, but you're going to be fine."

She nodded and pulled off her mask with a shaking hand. Nervously, she took the food from Terry and started eating her dry granola bar, washing it down with swigs of water.

"We lost the sleeping bags with the car," Terry explained, "but it's a warm night, so it shouldn't be that bad to sleep under the stars. Just like when we were first dating, huh?"

She gave him a weak smile but she wasn't sufficiently distracted from the chance of getting sick.

Terry's smile faded and he lay down on the grass. "I'll wake you in a few hours. We'll get moving again when it's dark. It's less likely people will make a scene about our suits late at night."

She nodded morosely before laying down as well. She rolled away from him, showing her back. Terry was pretty sure she didn't fall asleep, but he tried his best to close his eyes and get some rest before they had to start again.

* * *

A soft beeping woke him. Terry pushed the button on the side of the watch, turning off the incessant alarm. It was nearly pitch black around them. Lights from nearby towns hadn't reached the middle of the field where they slept.

He stood, feeling the aches and pains of sleeping on the hard ground. He was too old to go camping, something he had given up when they were both still in their thirties. He was a far bigger fan now of memory foam mattresses.

Lilly was still asleep and he had to shake her shoulder a few times before she gave a soft moan. She rolled toward him and covered her eyes, as though blocking out a bright light that wasn't there.

"Are you okay?" he asked, his stomach turning in knots as she tried in vain to sit up.

"My head is killing me," she moaned. "It feels like someone stuck a knife in my eye."

He rubbed her back as he chewed on the inside of his lip. "It's just stress. It's been a really tough day on both of us and we did more exercising in the past twenty-four hours than we did the past ten years combined. You just need a good night's rest, something we can get on Staten Island."

She nodded, but the effort seemed to hurt her head even worse. Slipping a hand under her arm, he helped her to her feet. She stood unsteadily, unable to assist him as he slipped her gas mask back into place. As he tightened the straps on the back of her head, she winced.

"Sorry, darling," he said as he pulled down the plastic hood. "Let me carry your water and the backpack, okay?"

She didn't put up much of an argument and leaned on him when he offered his arm for support.

It was dark on the road but he didn't risk pulling out a flashlight. It seemed that the outbreak had brought out the worst in people and he didn't want to draw any more attention to them than absolutely necessary. They still had nearly six miles to go to the bridge, which would take them a couple hours if they could maintain a decent pace. He glanced over nervously toward Lilly, wondering if she'd be able to keep up. Her head clearly still hurt and even in the darkness he could see her rubbing her stomach.

There were a lot of things he wanted to say to set her mind at ease, but didn't want to spoil the nighttime stillness. They seemed content to walk in silence. He knew she was worried; to a certain degree, he was, too. He had to remind himself of every disease scare he'd lived through: H1N1, Ebola, and countless others he could barely remember. Whenever the media started scaring people about the illness, every symptom seemed like the disease. Someone sneezed and immediately assumed it was Ebola.

Lilly coughed into her mask, a strangely hollow sound. He gripped her arm tighter, keeping her upright and walking even as she cringed from the effort.

* * *

The city of Elizabeth was pretty well illuminated as they walked into its limits. Lilly struggled to breathe through the bulky mask. She had tried to take it off a few times during the past couple of hours but he had managed to keep her covered.

Her face was screwed up in anguish as she nearly doubled over and he was forced to stop until it passed. As she finally caught her breath, she looked up at him apologetically. Her eyes were bloodshot and she blinked furiously as though they were bothering her.

"I'm really not feeling well," she muttered. She wasn't standing upright anymore, walking now with a constant stoop as her stomach cramped. "I think I'm going to be sick."

Her stomach wasn't the only one upset, though Terry's wasn't because of illness. His insides were doing somersaults as he glanced at his wife.

"Let's find you a bathroom," he said, glad that the hood concealed the quiver in his voice.

The streets were startlingly empty. He peered through a few shop windows and knocked on some doors, but no one answered. Grasping the doors, he jiggled the handles, trying to find one unlocked. Finding a bench, Lilly sat down and rested her head in her hands.

With a sigh, he turned back toward his wife. She had lowered her hands to her knees and her breathing was ragged, as though she were about to be physically ill.

"I need to find a bathroom," she said between breaths.

She pulled off her mask suddenly and hurried behind a row of bushes. Terry could hear her retching as she puked whatever contents had remained in her stomach. It sounded violent and each break was filled with her miserable sobs.

Terry's heart pounded in his chest. He broke the seal on his mask so that he could wipe away the tears welling in his eyes. When the vomiting stopped, he quickly replaced his mask and cleared away the lump in his throat.

She staggered from behind the bushes and he took her arm for support. He could feel the heat radiating from her skin, even through the MOPP jacket. "Are you okay?"

Looking up at him pleadingly, she shook her head. "That infected man on the trail—"

"Has nothing to do with this," he interrupted. "It's the flu."

"Terry," she said, placing her hand over his.

"Or a cold. Or allergies."

"Terry," she said a little sterner.

"Or malaria!" Terry said, pulling his hand away. "You're sick but you'll get better. We've just got to get to Staten Island and then you'll get all the treatment you need to get better."

She looked at him, tears dropping from the corners of her eyes, but she nodded without argument. Terry could feel the heated flush in his face and he bit his lip until he tasted blood.

Together, they continued their trek to Goethals Bridge.

* * *

The sun was rising as they stood in line on the bridge. Not as many people offered strange looks for their protective suits. There were lots of others, some in the orange bubble suits and others in the thin white medical garb, with plastic face guards. People talked quietly amongst themselves, though rarely did groups intermingle. Most people just kept to themselves as they shuffled toward the large concrete walls that blocked their view of the camp within Staten Island.

Dark clad guards in body armor and gas masks stood guard on either side of the single entrance onto the island, machine guns slung low across their chests. Despite the loaded weapons, they cordially waved people forward, shuffling the long line of refugees toward the military-style tents on the other side.

Terry pulled Lilly upright as they walked between the concrete barriers, trying to keep the illusion that she was still healthy. They entered a narrowing passage between two chain-link fences, topped with concertina wire. The passage funneled them toward a tent, outside of which another group of armed guards stood.

A sign at the end of the passage ordered them to stop and wait to be called forward. As they waited their turn, they saw people receiving finger-prick blood tests, the machines into which they were fed offering immediate results of infected versus healthy.

The man in front of them stepped forward and slipped his finger into the outstretched box. He winced as the needle pierced the tip of his finger. He withdrew his hand, rubbing it as he waited for the results. He tried striking up a conversation with the guard, but the black-armored man had nothing to say.

The light on top of the testing box turned red and the guard gestured toward a pair of other guards who came and grasped the man by his upper arms. The man squirmed but their grip was vice-like.

"I'm not sick," he yelled as they pulled him out of line. "It was a mistake! You made a mistake!"

Terry didn't see where they took him because Lilly nearly collapsed against him. She was shaking violently. As he slipped an arm around her waist, she tried to pull away, stepping backward away from the testing station.

"I can't do this," she muttered. "We need to go."

The guard at the testing station waved them forward.

"We're safe," Terry whispered. "Everything's fine."

"Everything's not fine," she hissed. "I'm sick and they're going to know. They're going to take me away. Please, Terry, let's just go."

The guard waved them forward emphatically and the people in line behind them started to complain.

"You saw what they did," she moaned. "That's going to be me."

Tears streamed down her face, marring her pale skin with faint pink tracks.

He pulled her close and slipped his hand behind her back. He held her tightly to him as he supported her. "It'll be fine, it'll be fine. Look, I'll go first, okay?"

He pulled off his glove and placed his index finger into the box. He felt the sting of a needle piercing the tip of his finger and a welling of blood. A second later, the meter turned green. The security guard looked at him before gesturing toward the gap in the Jersey barriers.

"Welcome to Staten Island," the security guard said, his voice muffled by the respirator. "You won't have a need for the HAZMAT suit once you get inside."

Terry stepped past but hesitated, turning to wait as Lilly hesitantly approached the guard. The man repeated his instructions to her. Her hands were visibly shaking as she pulled the rubber glove off her hand. Her skin was deathly pale and she had trouble lining up her index finger with the hole in the box.

She looked pleadingly at Terry as she inserted her finger. Within the tent, a guard was calling Terry forward, but he refused to go until Lilly was by his side.

A fresh set of tears streamed down Lilly's face, though it was hard to see through her mask. Her shoulders shook with each sob. She didn't even look down as the light on the testing box turned to red.

"Terry," she said, as the guard called the others forward to take her away.

"No," Terry said. "You made a mistake. Test her again."

"Sir," the guard said sternly, "you need to step away." The guard clenched his rifle tightly, his finger dancing around the trigger.

The men grabbed Lilly and started pulling her away.

"Let her go!" Terry yelled, rushing forward. "You made a mistake!"

The guard at the testing station stepped into his path. Reflexively, he lashed out, catching the guard in the face. The guard's mask fell askew as he fell to the ground. Terry was running toward Lilly, reaching for her hand, when the world went still around him.

They say you don't hear the shot that kills you. It wasn't true. All Terry heard was the gunshot. What he couldn't hear was the rest of the world. The guard yelled at him but no words came out. From the corner of his eye, he could see Lilly crying behind the plastic faceplate of her

HAZMAT suit, but her words were silent screams.

When the pain blossomed in his stomach—stretching from his gut all the way to his spine—the sounds of the world came crashing back to him like an implosion. His knees went weak. Despite his outstretched hand, Lilly seemed to get further and further away. He dropped to his knees before tilting and collapsing onto the ground.

His vision was blurry but he could see Lilly being pushed to her knees a few feet in front of him. He tried to call out for them to stop, but he couldn't seem to catch his breath. One of the guards drew a pistol and pointed it at her. Terry sobbed as the guard pulled the trigger and Lilly pitched forward onto the asphalt.

He suddenly felt exceptionally tired and his eyes fluttered closed.

FIVE: *Existing*
by Cameo Renae

Sixteen-year-old Kiana Reed shrieked as a speeding car crashed through the storefront of a small electronic shop across the street. Glass exploded and screams erupted from passersby. Some ran in to help the injured while others fled with stolen goods folded within their arms.

She sat, watching the events unfold from her bedroom window of their third-floor apartment, where every crack and crevice had been sealed under dense layers of duct tape to keep out contaminants.

She then noticed her neighbor, Mrs. Lee, dashing toward her car with David, her five-year-old son, in her arms. Panic brimmed as David glanced up and his weak, crimson eyes met hers. Trails of blood streamed from his nose and ears.

Helpless, Kiana pressed her clammy palms tightly against the window; the disturbing sight of the boy she babysat caused tears to erupt and spill down her cheeks. David's mother wailed, pleading with him to hold on as she buckled him into the seat. They were probably headed to the hospital.

As their car disappeared down the street, Kiana pulled the curtain shut, temporarily veiling the madness below. She wiped the tears from her face and headed toward her dad's room, hoping he had more information on the virus.

During the last few days, the rioting and looting were worsening, and with each passing day, fewer people roamed the streets. Little did they know, in their blind desperations, they were infecting each other.

Since news of the outbreak—following the first related death—Neil Reed, Kiana's father, had been glued to his computers. He was a computer geek—a tech by day and gamer by night. His brown hair was a disheveled mess, as was his room, buried under empty Coke cans and Twix wrappers.

Kiana heard the story countless times of how her dad was arrested at thirteen. He was charged for hacking into a banking system, transferring money into his mom's account, and then sending a virus, hoping it would cover his tracks. What he didn't know was that he crashed the system.

They were poor at the time, and he only did it so his mom could have a happy birthday. Just once. But her birthday was far from happy when law enforcement came knocking on their door. Neil was banned from using a computer until he was eighteen, given strict warnings, and kept under close watch.

At the age of nineteen, Neil met a girl. He thought they were in love, but things changed when she became pregnant. Six months after she gave birth, she left, claiming she wasn't ready to be a parent. Neil wasn't ready either, but despite his situation, he made it work and his daughter became his life.

Kiana peeked into his room. "Dad, it's getting bad out there. I think we should leave soon. People are going mad. They're breaking into stores and running off with stuff. What if they break into our place?"

"I'll make sure we're safe. We'll leave soon, but first we need a plan and I'm working on it. Right now, it's safer here. Why don't you go and check the seals on the doors and windows again?"

"I have. One gazillion times. They are completely secured under layers and layers of duct tape. No contaminants can get in or out."

"That's good, sweetheart," he said robotically, glancing between his four computer screens. He suddenly turned up the volume on his television as a reporter, Amy Savino, of WNMN news started speaking. She appeared distressed and seemed to think there was some kind of conspiracy behind everyone getting sick. She also mentioned the name Peter Franklin Donalds.

As her rant continued, Neil began typing, quickly pulling up information on the company. His first two screens were zipping with information.

"How can you read all of that?" Kiana questioned, amazed at her dad's computer skills.

"My brain is hardwired for it," he muttered, then paused and glanced back at her with a grin.

"Not surprised. And you better not think of hacking that company. I don't want the government busting down our door and dragging us away," she sighed, rolling her eyes. With one hand, she attempted to swipe a bunch of cans and wrappers from his desk into a trash can below.

"Right now, we're the least of the government's problems. And I'm not hacking, just gathering information."

"Have you found anything new?" Kiana stood next to her dad, her mind whirling, wondering if they would be survivors or statistics.

"The CDC hasn't released any new information about the virus, but it's spreading quickly. I have a few connections saying hundreds have been flooding the hospitals with early signs. Rumor is...they're all dead within one day."

"One day?" Kiana shrieked. "Are you serious?"

"*Dead* serious." He took a swig of Coke. "No pun intended."

There was a ding on the computer. A message. Neil clicked it and photos instantly popped up on the screen.

The first was the corpse of a man lying on a gurney. His crimson eyes were wide open, and his mouth and chest were stained with blood like he'd vomited it up. Dark bluish-purple veins were visible beneath his pallid skin.

At the bottom of the picture were words:

Name: Undisclosed

Time of death: 5:42 a.m. - 23 hours after the presumed time of infection.

Cause of death: Unknown

Location: Mount Sinai, NY

The next was of a woman. She looked young, possibly in her twenties. Her eyes were closed, but her long blonde hair was glued to the side of her pale face from dried blood. It had been flowing from her eyes, ears, and nose.

Name: Undisclosed

Time of death: 7:14 p.m. - Time of infection unknown. Under investigation.

Cause of death: Possible AVHF

Location: Riverside Methodist Hospital, Columbus, OH

"Oh my God." Kiana's hands clasped tightly over her mouth. "It *is* spreading."

Neil quickly collapsed the message and turned toward his daughter. "I'm so sorry, Kiana. I didn't mean for you to see that."

"It's fine," she answered. But inside, she was shaking. "Who's sending you all of this information?"

"Inside sources from an online group that has members all over the country. It looks like the photos were taken by cell phones, probably from members working in those hospitals. These are only a few of the hundreds who've been infected. Soon it will be thousands."

"They die of bleeding?" Kiana's voice trembled, her thoughts instantly turned to David. A pang of uncertainty twisted her gut, and her heart ached as she thought of the pain his family was enduring, fearing the outcome.

"Yes, bleeding is the biggest manifestation of the virus. Complications from blood loss are usually the root cause of death," he answered sadly.

Kiana shook her head; tears pooled and then spilled from her eyes. "David, the kid two doors down, was bleeding from his nose and ears. His eyes were bright red just like that man in the picture." She was trying to hold in her emotions, but the past few days of chaos were wearing on her. "He's going to die, isn't he?"

Neil shook his head and replied, "I don't know."

Death loomed all around them, but for now they were safe. A mere speck in a tiny sealed apartment, directly in the middle of terror. The virus was merciless. It didn't have an ounce of compassion or hesitation in taking innocent lives, including children.

"I'm so sorry," Neil sighed, holding his arms open to his daughter. Kiana walked into his embrace.

"Do they have a cure?"

"Not yet, but I'm sure they're working on it. In the meantime, I'm securing a safe place for us to stay and wait this out. Somewhere we can survive until the madness passes, or until they do find a cure."

"Have you found a place yet?"

"A couple of sources mentioned a few safe zones across the state. The largest is on Staten Island and another *secret* bunker in Kingston. There are also smaller places being set up closer to us, but the problem is...they're smaller. That means fewer resources, which could be a significant problem. I've just learned that the PFD pharmaceutical company is the same group that set up the safe zone on Staten Island. I don't know, but it sounds fishy to me." His fingers flew across the keyboard, pulling up more information.

Kiana noticed an open chat box on his *private* screen, with messages from PFD 117.

"Is that someone who works for the pharmaceutical company—PFD?" she questioned, directing her finger to the name on the screen.

"No, but it's funny they both have the same initials. PFD 117 is an old friend of mine. He's a member of Prep for Doom, a secret organization in charge of the bunker in Kingston. They've been planning for the apocalypse for years now and have a large facility with everything needed to wait it out. This *friend* of mine is working on the inside of the bunker and said they have a considerable amount of supplies, food, and reserves. But it's private, and only select people are given the location."

Kiana looked sadly into her dad's eyes. "Will we be able to get in?"

"That's what I'm working on, sweetheart. I'm trying to ensure a space for us."

"What about the safe zone on Staten Island?"

"Personally, I think Staten Island is too much of a risk. Something tells me the reporter is on to something. It's just strange that the pharmaceutical company is running the safe zone. They are claiming to have food, shelter, and all the amenities, but it's heavily guarded and the only way in is through Goethals Bridge. There seems to be a checkpoint, and I'm sure they'll be screening each person to make sure they aren't infected. The pharmaceutical company will have every immune person in its clutches. I know it seems like the perfect place for shelter, but something just seems to scream *guinea pig* to me."

"Then again, you could be overthinking things. You tend to be a bit presumptuous," Kiana giggled.

"It's my job to overthink and be presumptuous, especially with a sixteen-year-old," he answered, kissing her forehead. "I couldn't care less about the legalities and investigations behind the outbreak. My goal is to gather enough information to keep you safe. I'll leave the pharmaceutical company, CDC, government, and whoever the hell else is involved in this mess, to hash it all out amongst themselves. Hopefully they'll find answers and a cure in the process."

"Thanks, Dad. You're the best," Kiana chimed, hugging his neck.

"You're the only good thing I have in this godforsaken world, and I would never take you to a place with questionable risks. Besides, Kingston is closer…although, it might take half a day to get there by foot unless we find transportation."

"That's what you get for buying that old beater." Kiana rolled her eyes. "I told you to invest in the *newer* truck."

"You did. But that old beater ran for nine good months, and I didn't have to make payments on it. It's the reason you have that new iPhone, so don't knock her. Her engine just happened to blow at the worst imaginable time."

"Yeah," Kiana exhaled. "Well, I better go scrounge up some lunch. Your brain will need more than Coke and Twix to run on."

"You should also recheck our gear and packs to make sure they're set.

If things get any worse, we might have to leave sooner than later."

"I don't think we can survive any longer than a day here. It's hotter than hell, and I feel like I—I can't breathe." Kiana grabbed her neck and rolled her eyes back, choking and gasping for air.

"Not funny." Neil shook his head, unamused. "Remember, don't run the outside AC. Use your portable fan."

"My fan just circulates hot air," she huffed. "I give us a day to survive here before we suffocate."

"That's all I need. Just give me a day."

"Promise?"

"Promise," Neil said, reassuring her.

"Fine," she sighed. Kiana knew if anyone could get them to safety, it was her dad.

Before she left the room, his attention was already turned back to the screens, his fingers zooming over his keyboard. She smiled, shook her head, and then walked out.

Kiana threw together some peanut butter and jelly sandwiches to avoid the use of the stove. When they finished lunch, she made her way to the bathroom. She couldn't shake the images on her dad's computer screen, or the look of David's little blood-covered face. They were on constant replay through her mind, and as much as she tried, she couldn't shut it off. Overwhelmed, she pressed her back against the door and slid to the ground, hugging her knees and weeping.

After she gathered herself, she washed her face and leaned in close to the mirror to examine her eyes. They weren't bloodshot like the others with the virus, but they were tinged with pink from crying.

Next, she headed into her bedroom to check their gear. Their protective suits and masks were neatly laid out, making them easily accessible. They'd practiced putting them on countless times to make sure everything could be secured quickly and adequately.

Then she re-checked the contents of their packs, assuring they had everything needed to survive for a few days. In her pack, Kiana included a few photos and some of her favorite books to help get her through the tough times. There was no doubt they were coming.

As she walked past her dad's room, she smiled. Because of him, they had answers. And although they were horrifying, they put periods to most of the question marks so they could move on to more important things, like survival.

As soon as the first person was diagnosed with the virus, Neil was notified. That's when he began to seal their apartment, making sure no contaminants could get in.

He was part of the world's finest network of computer specialists and apocalypse preppers. Nerds and hackers who could crack codes, build walls, send viruses, and virtually make themselves invisible to whomever they wanted, including the government. They were secretly preparing for the apocalypse, and it was finally upon them. Not in the form of zombies, which many of them suspected, but as a fatal and highly contagious virus with no known cure.

The group was proving to be proficient. With a few touches of buttons, members in critical areas managed to secure and connect secret information to associates around the country. Neil was one of them.

It was nine o'clock when Kiana finally lay down on the couch in their living room. The light from her dad's room seemed to offer a bit of peace. Her mind was reeling with the day's events, but somehow, she managed to fall asleep.

* * *

It was still dark when Kiana was shaken and jolted awake.

"Get up. We have to leave…now." Her dad's voice was quiet yet demanding. Knowing he meant business, she didn't hesitate. She jumped up and headed straight for the bedroom.

"What time is it?" she breathed.

"Around two in the morning," he whispered.

"What's going on?"

"There were gunshots and screams in the building. It could have been on our floor."

"What if they're still out there when we leave?" Kiana's pulse began to race.

"We aren't going out the front door. We're taking the escape ladder down the side of the building."

"You're kidding, right? That rusted old thing? With our gear and masks on?"

"We'll go slow. I'll even tie a rope around you, in case you fall."

"I'm not worried about falling. I'm concerned about who else will be on the ground when we get there. You know, like the crazy people with the guns or the infected?"

Neil hesitated. "Here," he said taking hold of her hand and placing a cold metal object in it.

She immediately pushed it back at him. "No way. I don't even know how to use a gun."

"It's just in case. You probably won't even need to use it," he whispered softly. "But if we come into a situation where our lives are jeopardized, all you have to do is aim and pull the trigger."

"Dad—"

"I need you to be strong. We have a long way to go, and there are a lot of sick people out there who couldn't give a damn about us."

"Fine," Kiana sighed, reluctantly taking the small revolver and placing it on the bed while she dressed. She knew he was right.

The Personal Protective Equipment made her feel like she was preparing for a secret op. Everything her dad bought was black: long-sleeved shirts, vests, gloves, boots, and gas masks. Her father insisted on the gas masks because he didn't trust the simple medical masks. It was another risk he wasn't willing to take.

As Kiana secured the gun in her pocket, a thundering boom in the hallway made them freeze. Then, a loud scream from a neighbor pierced the darkness.

"Who is it?" Kiana whispered, tightly gripping her dad's arm.

"I don't know, but we need to move," he urged.

In the dark, they quickly made their way into the living room where Neil began peeling away layers of duct tape around the sliding door. As he did, Kiana pressed her ear against the front door. The hallway had gone silent, and she wondered what was more horrifying—the screaming or the silence?

"Kiana," her dad whispered loudly, making her jump.

He motioned her to follow as he disappeared outside onto the balcony. To the right, against the brick wall, was an escape ladder that led down to the ground. It was thin and badly rusted, and he prayed it would hold them both. Glancing over the railing to confirm the alleyway was clear, Neil signaled for Kiana to go first.

"Take your time," he said, encouraging her. "There's no need to rush. Just make sure your grip and footing are secure before you take your next step. Okay?"

"Okay," Kiana responded.

"You've got this," he said, helping her over the railing. He tied a small rope around her waist, and then secured it around his. "Slow and steady."

Grasping the rungs was easier than it appeared. Kiana began to descend while Neil followed directly after. Halfway down, distressed screams reverberated against the buildings, making Kiana and Neil freeze on the ladder, blending into the darkness.

Running down the alleyway was a couple wearing white medical masks. The woman tripped and tumbled to the ground.

"I can't do this anymore," she bellowed, then began incessantly coughing. She leaned forward, throwing her mask off, and began vomiting.

"Shit," the man cursed. He stepped behind the woman, holding damp hair from her pasty face. When she lifted her head, the streetlight illuminated blood running down her chin onto her light colored clothes. "Help! Somebody help," he shouted. But his pleas filled barren streets. "Hold on, honey."

Kiana moved slightly, tensing the rope.

"Don't move," Neil whispered loudly between his teeth.

But he didn't need to worry. Kiana was frozen. Fear had gripped every inch of her as she watched the virus claiming another victim.

The screeching of tires and sounds of roaring engines echoed from an adjacent street. Soon, two cars pulled into the alleyway.

"Help us, please!" the man bellowed, holding the woman's convulsing body in his arms.

A white lowrider passed right by the pleading man.

He extended his arm to the second vehicle.

A red car, with airbrushed flames and skulls on the sides, came to a screeching halt. The driver rolled down his window; his face was concealed behind a dark gas mask that had two round circles for eyes. A long black hose, resembling an elephant, extended from the bottom of the mask and disappeared into his chest, which must have housed the filter.

"Please help us. My wife is sick," the man cried, desperation embedded in the deep lines on his forehead.

"Yeah, sure. We'll help you," the driver said in a gruff voice.

"Thank you," the man replied. "Thank you so much."

The driver twisted his head back and gave a nod. Then, the rear window rolled down and a long black shotgun barrel emerged. Within a split second, gunfire blasted and echoed through the alleyway as if a bomb had been detonated.

When the firing ceased, the man and woman lay lifeless, riddled with bullet holes. The pavement was puddled with blood. The driver swung open his door, stepped out, and began dumping a bottle of liquid over them. He then lit a match and tossed it. Raging flames engulfed the bodies in an inferno.

"There's your help," the driver laughed. "I did you a damn favor." He turned back to the passenger. "Effing infected walking around trying to kill us all."

"Let's get the hell outta here man," the passenger urged.

The driver tossed the empty bottle into the flames, then jumped back into the car and sped off.

"Kiana, we need to go," Neil coaxed. When she didn't respond, he stepped down toward her. "Kiana. Move. Now." His voice was desperate and filled with urgency.

After a moment, she responded and slowly climbed down. As soon as their feet touched the ground Kiana turned and fell into her dad's arms.

"They killed them," she sobbed "They only wanted help, and they killed them."

"I know, sweetheart. A lot has changed out here. We need to be extra careful." He placed his hands on the sides of her mask and lifted her face to meet his. "I need you to be strong, and do whatever it takes to survive."

She nodded, blinking the tears away.

Neil pulled his cell phone from his pocket and brought up a map while Kiana untied the rope from their waists. Shortly after, a message from PFD 117 popped up. It was an address.

"Is that the location of the bunker?" Kiana questioned.

"Yes," he replied, punching in the address to route them. "If we move fast enough, we might be able to get there before noon."

"You lead, I'll follow."

She was trying hard to hold herself together, but her heart and mind were reeling with the horrors she'd just witnessed. She knew the outside world was going to be bad, but she never expected it to be monstrous. How could people be so cruel?

Her safe, simplistic life was forever changed in the moment they stepped outside of their apartment into the real world. She knew she had to be strong, not only for herself, but for her dad. She wanted to save him and get him to the bunker, just as much as he wished to do the same for her.

Sirens blared in the distance.

"Stay close," Neil whispered.

"I will."

Quickly and silently, they slipped into the barren streets, away from the burning bodies.

They stayed in the shadows, zigzagging through dark alleyways and side streets, trying to avoid contact with anyone. Knowing the sun would be rising in a few hours, they pushed on.

Kiana remained directly behind her dad and never complained. She was a pretty tough kid, growing up and learning to deal with feminine things on her own. Although Neil didn't voice it as much as he should have, he was very proud of her.

Neil's mind replayed the horrors of the murdered couple. It was beyond him how twisted and evil people became when faced with death.

How many innocent lives were already infected? How many were at home dying? How many parents were watching their children suffer?

No one had suspected a fatal pandemic to hit, silently and swiftly spreading. The fear of waking up with a fever, knowing it could be the virus taking hundreds, if not thousands, or even hundreds of thousands of lives, was a reality. A horror. An invisible and violent death with no preference and no cure.

Because Neil tried to steer clear of the heavier population, it wasn't until eleven in the morning that they'd traveled two-thirds of the way. The sun was high in the sky, slowing them tremendously. The heat was getting to Kiana, but screams and gunfire a few blocks away kept Neil pushing.

"Dad," Kiana groaned. "I need water."

"You can't take your mask off out here."

"I can't go anymore. I'll pass out if we keep this up. I need to take a break," she pleaded. Her mouth and throat were parched, her head was throbbing, her muscles were cramping, and she felt nauseated. All signs of heat stroke.

Neil didn't want to stop until they reached the safety of the bunker, but after seeing his daughter's flustered face, he decided to find a place to rest. Down an alleyway was a small Mom & Pop shop with a "Closed" sign hanging from the window. From his pack, Neil pulled a little pouch with some tools in it. Within minutes, he had broken in.

After locking the door behind them, they made their way toward the back and found a small, empty storage room. Neil turned on the light, closed the door, and sealed it quickly with a few layers of duct tape.

"We'll rest here for a bit. Drink some water and try to take a nap."

Kiana peeled off her mask and drank most of her water before cuddling up into a ball on the floor and immediately passing out. Neil stayed up and rerouted their current position. They were so close to the bunker. In less than a few hours, they could be safe.

After letting Kiana nap for a few hours, Neil finally woke her.

"Hey, we need to get moving."

"Alright," Kiana yawned. After finishing her water, she reattached her mask. "How much further is it?"

"Not much. Just a few hours away."

As they headed back out of the alley and rounded a corner, Neil's arm flew back, halting Kiana. He stood, frozen, a few feet away from a red car painted with skulls and flames. Behind it was the white lowrider, and leaning against it were three men, two of whom were involved in the murder.

All three horrifying masks turned toward them.

"Dad?" Kiana's voice trembled.

"It's okay," he answered.

He reached back and took her by the hand, tucking his phone into his pocket. His heart beat against his chest as he placed his fingers around his Glock 26, filled with jacketed hollow points, in a ten-round magazine.

Neil gave a nod, then turned and started walking in the opposite direction.

"Hey," one of them called.

Neil cursed under his breath but turned back, pushing Kiana behind him. With a wave, he answered, "Hi."

"Where are you two headed?" the man asked.

Both Neil and Kiana recognized the mask. He was the one who shot the couple.

"I'm trying to get my daughter to…" He paused, quickly glancing backward, not wanting to give them any information as to where they were headed. "…to her mother's house. My car broke down."

"Need a ride?" the man questioned, slowly stepping forward. The other two men stepped behind him.

"No, thank you. We aren't far."

"We're just trying to help," he replied. There was something in his voice that felt insincere.

"Thank you," Neil answered. "We better be on our way."

Neil took hold of Kiana's hand and tugged her down another alleyway, heading away from their destination. He quickly went a few more blocks, and then stopped for a moment in a small alcove on the side of one of the buildings.

Kiana bent over, resting her palms on her knees, trying to catch her breath. "Those guys scare the hell out of me."

"Yeah, they're trouble. We have to be more cautious."

Neil pulled his phone from his pocket and checked their location. In another few blocks, they could be back on track. But before they moved, he faced his daughter.

"You have your gun right?"

"Yeah."

"If you need to…if we're put in a position of trouble—"

"I know, Dad. If I have to, I'll use it," she assured him.

"Good. I just need to make sure you aren't afraid to defend yourself."

"What about you?" she asked with a raised brow.

"Don't worry about me. I can manage," he affirmed. "Let's get out of here."

"The sooner, the better," she agreed.

They quickly weaved their way through more side streets, passing a few pedestrians wearing medical masks. But they didn't give them the time of day.

Then, out of nowhere, gunfire began to explode somewhere in their vicinity, along with agonizing screams and shortly followed by screeching tires.

Neil grabbed his daughter and dragged her into another small alleyway.

"Dammit," he cursed, realizing there was no way out.

"Those men!" Kiana exclaimed. Her heart hammered against her chest.

Engines roared down the streets.

"Keep moving!" Neil grabbed her arm and pulled her with him.

As they ran, two familiar vehicles sped right by them. The driver of the white lowrider glanced back and slammed on his breaks. After a brief pause, he threw it in reverse.

"Run!"

He and Kiana sprinted down the street, but the lowrider was too fast. As it swerved toward them, Neil shoved Kiana out of the way.

"Nooo—" she screamed.

In an instant, Kiana's world came to a crashing halt. The horrific event played in slow motion. Terror-stricken, she watched the lowrider collide with her dad. His body flew through the air and tumbled across the pavement like a rag doll until he lay still. His gas mask was a few yards away, cracked in half.

"Dad. Dad!" she wailed, rushing toward him. She dropped at his side. "Dad, please!" Terror and despair encompassed her, making her unaware of the driver who had stepped out of his car, heading toward them.

A firm hand suddenly clasped tightly around Kiana's arm. She screamed, struggling to release the grip, but the long fingers squeezed even tighter. She kicked and punched, but he wouldn't budge. He was much too strong. Then, he paused, his tinted mask faced hers.

Frantic, she reached into her pocket and wrapped her hand around the grip of her revolver. As the man jerked her toward him, she panicked. Raising the gun, she pulled the trigger.

Bam! Bam! Bam!

Three shots fired directly into the middle of his chest. He glanced down at his wounds.

"Oma," he exhaled.

His grip released as he dropped to his knees, then fell backward to the ground.

Kiana froze. Her mind and body went numb; the mask felt asphyxiating. The gun fell from her trembling fingers.

Through her blood spattered mask, she stared at the man lying on the ground. But before she could process what had happened, another set of tires screeched to a halt behind her. The two men in the red car jumped out. One pulled a shotgun and lifted it at her.

As she turned to run, gunfire erupted. Screaming, she dropped to the ground, covering her head and ears.

Shortly after, everything went silent.

When Kiana raised her head, she saw her dad sitting up with his gun aimed behind her. As she twisted back, two bodies lay motionless on the ground with blood seeping from fatal wounds.

"Dad!" Kiana bellowed. She ran over and fell at his side, wrapping him in a hug. "I thought you were dead."

"I did too," he moaned. Blood trickled from a wound on his forehead.

Trying to pull himself up, he immediately fell back down, gasping for air.

"What's the matter?"

"I think I cracked a rib and I can't move my leg." His right leg was bent at an abnormal angle.

"I think it's broken," she noted, trying not to faint.

"Yeah." He cringed in pain.

"You're unprotected," Kiana gasped.

She shot up and ran over to the man she shot and lifted his mask. Underneath was a white man. His head was shaven and he had a tattoo of a skull and crossbones directly in the middle of his forehead. His wide-open eyes were blood red.

"Oh my God. He's infected," she gasped, releasing the mask and quickly scooting away.

Not risking a chance with the other two, she pulled a medical mask from her pack and handed it to her dad. "It's better than nothing."

"Thank you," he breathed. "I'm so proud of you."

"I thought I'd never see you again," she wept. Tears pooled in her big brown eyes. "How are we going to make it to the bunker now?"

"We've acquired transportation," he noted, nodding toward the cars. "You've gotta drive us."

"That, I can do," she willingly responded.

Kiana pulled the red car closer and helped lift her dad into the back seat. It was hard and painful, but they managed. Neil suppressed the pain as best he could, but it was nearly unbearable and he found himself blacking out.

"Which way, navigator?" she asked, turning back to him.

Neil had become pale and was fading in and out of consciousness. He raised his phone. "Sorry, sweetheart. You're in charge now."

"Don't worry, dad. I'll get us there," she said confidently, but inside she was terrified.

As she checked the map, another message popped up.

PFD 117: Where are you?

Kiana texted back, her fingers were trembling.

10 minutes away. Ran into trouble. Need medical assistance.

PFD 117: I'll have a team waiting. Have you been exposed?

No. But not sure about my dad.

PFD 117: Kiana?

Yes.

PFD 117: Just get here. We'll take care of you.

On our way.

Kiana studied the route and knew exactly where to go. Glancing back, she noticed her dad's eyes getting heavier. "Hold on," she begged.

Instead of swerving past the man she shot, she ran directly over him.

"Bastard," she said, gritting her teeth.

He hit her dad. Plus, the infected asshole was senselessly murdering others like him. Hypocrite. He deserved to get run over.

As she turned onto the highway a police car passed by, heading in the opposite direction. Her stomach twisted in knots as she watched him turn around, flash his lights and blare his siren.

"Dammit," she exclaimed, slamming her hand on the steering wheel. She wondered if the car was tagged. "Dad. Dad?" she called, but he was unresponsive.

Kiana pulled to the curb and stopped, but the cop flew right past them.

Exhaling in relief, she put the car back into drive. As she glanced into the rearview mirror, fear overcame her. Her dad looked on the brink of death.

"We're almost there," she said out loud, hoping he could hear.

When they finally arrived at their destination, a man in a white moon suit with a clipboard greeted her. He waved her over and then held his hand up for her to stop.

"Name?" he asked.

"Kiana and Neil Reed," she answered. "My dad is injured. He needs help."

"Pull ahead and take a left around the building."

Kiana did what he said, and as she pulled around the corner, three more men in moon suits were standing with a gurney. She stopped the car directly in front of them.

One of the men approached her. "Kiana?"

"Yes. My dad. He's hurt," she pointed to the back seat.

The man motioned and the others went to retrieve him.

"Was he exposed?"

"I don't know. He didn't have a mask on for a few minutes. He was hit by a car. I…I don't know," her voice wavered and tears began to spill down her cheeks.

Once Neil was on the gurney, they lifted a plastic covering around him.

"Is he going to be okay?" Kiana asked, standing beside him. His skin was nearly colorless, and his breathing was labored.

"Let's hope so. He will remain under close observation for the next twenty-four hours. If he's clear of the virus, we will be able to concentrate on his injuries."

"What happens if he's *not* clear?" she cried. "What if I'm not able to say goodbye?" Speaking those words made her heart feel as if it would shatter into a million pieces.

"If he *is* infected, he will have the best care until the end."

"He's the only person I have. He can't die," she sobbed.

"Most of the residents inside have lost loved ones. Your father risked his life so you could live. Bringing you here was his top priority," he said. "But let's not put a death sentence on him yet."

"Do *you* think he'll live?"

"I have hope. There are people who have formed natural immunities to the virus. There's a small chance he's one of them or that he hasn't been infected."

As they began to wheel Neil away, Kiana yelled, "Wait!"

She ran over to the gurney where her dad lay unresponsive and leaned close to his ear. "Be strong. I need you," she pleaded.

Everything inside of her ached. They were supposed to be safe, together. He was supposed to take care of her.

A gentle hand lay on her shoulder. "You just have to believe you'll see him again. For now, you need to go through decontamination, and will be placed in a holding room for twenty-four hours, just so we know you aren't infected. Then, we'll introduce you to the rest of the residents."

Kiana glanced up at the man, blinking her tears away so she could see his face through the transparent mask. Sincere green eyes met hers.

"Are you PFD 117?" she questioned.

"Yes, but I prefer Andrew," he grinned.

"Thanks, Andrew. For helping us."

"Of course. We're part of your new family," he replied. "You're safe now. Come." He held out his hand to her.

Kiana paused for a moment, then placed her hand in his, letting Andrew lead her through a large steel door where she would finally be safe from the outside world and the virus. Existing only because of her father.

"I love you, Dad," she whispered under her breath. "Thank you."

She needed to hold on to hope. It was all she had left, and she would tuck it in her heart until she saw him again.

SIX: *Trust*
by John Gregory Hancock

Dangerella used the flat of her hand to shade the screen of her tablet computer. The hot sun picked up so many greasy fingerprints and half-arcs from swiping the touchscreen it created a glare.

She used to be such a clean freak about her electronic devices. Those days were in the past. Nothing to be done about it now. The future she could change. Would change.

Her plan found her here, at the southern end of Manhattan, threading her way around cars abandoned on the sidewalk, the small mountains of rotting bags split open from overflowing garbage, and things she'd rather not think about. A large city like New York seemed odd without traffic or the bustle of people going to and fro. She grew up on the Upper East Side, near 77th and Lex, where the only obstacles to dodge were the occasional wino or crack dealer setting up shop on the corner. But the police always came and then they'd magically melt away into alleys, stores, and unlocked apartments. They came with the city. A package deal.

She was slight of build, a freckle-cheeked redheaded girl. Ripe for the picking from nearly everyone, including the creeps that hit on little girls from their long black cars. Her parents couldn't be with her everywhere. And even if they were, it offered no guarantee of safety. Her dad was easily distracted while he read his stock reports and prattled into the mechanical cockroach-looking thing that was always in his ear. He called it his "tooth." Facing the perils of the city on her own was why she came up with "Dangerella," a persona she jacketed herself in to enable her to walk the streets without fear.

Her dad had pet names for lots of things, but never a pet name for her. She wasn't a thing. She was his little princess. He treasured her more than his things and his money. Almost. She was born half him. He recognized himself in the set of her eyes and the shape of her jaw. He loved himself completely and therefore loved her half as much as that.

None of that prevented him from using her as a bargaining chip against her mother. He established his dominance, controlling the days of visitation, of who presided over holiday celebrations and birthdays. He even coerced easy sex from her mother post-divorce.

Oh, she knew. They tried to use discretion, but Dangerella knew everything that happened in her house. Dangerella was an accomplished spy. It wasn't even a challenge. Her mother's weaknesses were writ large for all to see. Her father exploited them as pressure points to get what he wanted.

For one thing, her mother was openly addicted to his money. She married him for it, and eventually divorced him to get more.

Dangerella vowed never to be that stupid. Her mother deluded herself into thinking she held the upper hand in the relationship, but there was no contest. She was a rank amateur. Her dad brokered million dollar transactions every day. He could easily attract or arrange to rent younger and better looking women than her mother, a fact her mother never seemed to figure out. She was oblivious enough to the world around her to let him manipulate her. The contempt she held for her mother was the whetstone that she sharpened herself against.

But all that family angst was ancient history, her former dismal existence. Before the *Prep for Doom* website. When she signed up, she was afraid the screen name 'Dangerella' would already be taken. She was grateful to find it available.

Her whole life was survival of one kind or another. A website that connected followers to prepare to survive any impending apocalypse was a social group she could get behind.

* * *

The rotten smells from the street assaulted her nose, breaking through the menthol cream barrier she wore on her upper lip. It was a hot summer, and the authorities had stopped gathering up dead bodies long ago. Eventually, even the androgynous people in HAZMAT suits started dropping, and there was no one left to come and collect bodies. People often just fell where they were. Sometimes they crawled a foot or two before their grisly deaths. The roads and sidewalks became their final resting place. Carcasses littered the streets or rotted in cars like overripe melons in the heat. No burial, no markers. No dignity.

The dwindling number of survivors piled the bodies on the sidewalk until they resembled forgotten mounds of brightly colored trash. A trash collector's strike organized by the grim reaper. The common color among them being the streamers of bright red, dingy brick red, and brown. The fatal colors of spent blood and fluids.

Clouds of flies rose up if she stepped too close. The insects seeded the cadavers, laid their eggs. There would be an unholy plague of flies soon.

Sweat dripped down the back of her neck as she swiped a finger across the tablet.

Dangerella: I'm somewhere around 8th street now. Can you see my blip on the GPS?

Bull3tBoy: nope. But no surprise there. Tall buildings and whatnot.

Dangerella: Where are you?

Bull3tBoy: Jersey still. In a sporting goods store.

Dangerella: oooh! Can you pick me up some more throwing knives? I only got 5

Bull3tBoy: *sigh* What are we? Married or something? Aren't there any places there in the big rotten apple?

Dangerella: C'mon, dude, you're already in a place. I'd have to find one. Puhleeze?

Bull3tBoy: It's gonna

She lost the end of his message. For the first nanosecond she thought she'd maybe tripped over something. But she kept falling, down into darkness. A powerful jerk yanked on her backpack straps and they dug painfully into her underarms. Her tablet jostled from her hands and hit something hard below, with the gut-wrenching sound of breaking glass. So lost was she in the throes of mourning for her tablet, for a minute she didn't register her own pain. Her tablet was the only link to the other preppers. To Bull3tBoy.

Then the pain rose up and demanded her full attention. Her right leg was burning. She felt hot blood dripping into her shoe. She looked around, but there was no light, except for the angled shaft from the surface above, and it only pushed so far. The rest was nothing but darkness to her unadjusted eyes.

Her movement was sharply restricted from her own weight pulling against straps. She was awkwardly suspended, her feet dangling in nothingness. Every move she made increased the pressure under her arms and added to the wave of pain radiating up her leg. She forced herself to remain calm.

Dangerella tilted her head up toward the opening in the sidewalk, to the open square of light. Shiny metal hung down behind her head from the hole and she realized that she was hung up on the grate, still attached to one edge. She had no idea how securely the grate was connected. She didn't want to end up like her tablet, broken somewhere below.

How far it was to solid ground, she had no idea. She was getting light-headed.

Dangerella closed her eyes; the only clear thought in her head was to first get free.

While she was trying to come up with a step two, the humid heat and thickened air made her drowsy.

* * *

"Well, what do we got here?" A voice sounded, waking her up. "Somebody throw a broken doll into my house? Ha!" It was hard to tell if that was a friendly laugh.

Dangerella squinted and made out a silhouette directly below her.

"Please, can you get me down?" she said through gritted teeth. Her leg felt soaked. The pain had moved from sharp edge to dull ache. It almost seemed worse to be on the verge of rescue, but have it delayed.

"Why you asking me? I don't know. Maybe. You're up kinda high, little girl."

She made a mental inventory of exactly where her throwing knives were hidden. She played out different scenarios, figuring out which knife afforded the quickest access.

She could sense him moving around below. Metal screeched painfully against concrete as the man scooted a large trunk underneath her.

"Hmm. Not quite high enough, no sir," he muttered to himself. He shuffled away and was gone for a long time.

"Okay, this oughta do it." He came back into view and kicked over a small number of sturdy plastic milk crates. From these and the trunk he fashioned a homemade staircase, two block steps up to the large trunk, and one step on top of it. His actions were deliberate and maddeningly slow.

He climbed the steps up, standing on the last crate. Still, the top of his head only reached the level of her stomach. She saw an older African-American man, with unkempt dreads and the tracks of hard-lived years written on his face. He wore a heavy grey overcoat, even though it was the middle of summer.

He examined her predicament with the straps and let out a low whistle, rubbing his bristly chin hairs.

"Name?" he asked, out of nowhere.

"Oh God. Does it matter? Just please get me down."

"Oh, I'm getting to that. But first I gotta have a name. Not going to even try anything until I get that."

"Why?" her voice was edged, the pain and discomfort evident.

"Well, see here, this is how it go. If you don't make it, I want to know what to call the redheaded baby doll that fell through my roof and died on my floor. I've cleaned up too many dead folk already with no names. Or no names that I knew, anyhow."

"Oh," she bit her lip. "Dangerella."

He laughed.

"That's no proper name. Is that the name your parents gave you? I don't think so. Say your real name, or I don't get you down."

"GET ME DOWN!" she hollered.

"You in no position to bargain, child. I can just walk away, or call you a museum piece of hanging art, or throw darts at you. But whether I get you down is up to me. This here's my castle, and I'm the king of it. Your name."

She dropped her head down and sighed.

"Angelica."

His face broke into a broad grin, his teeth amazingly clean and intact.

"Okay then, Ms. Dangerella, let's get you down."

He stretched up suddenly and deftly grabbed the knife she'd hidden in her belt. The one she was sure no one could detect.

"Hey!" she cried.

"What? Didn't think I knowed you had that?" He winked. "Old Earl is nobody's fool."

For a scary moment, she wondered if this was how it would end, with her trapped and hanging like a side of beef, stabbed to death by a stranger using her own knife. Didn't seem fair, after surviving the outbreak.

He flipped her knife from hand to hand in a way of someone well-versed in bladed weapons.

"Now, I can't unbuckle both your straps, with all your weight on 'em, that'd be impossible. The only way I can see it is to unbuckle one, get that arm free, then hold you up and cut the other one. It'll ruin your backpack, but I can scrounge you another, maybe a pretty kitty cat backpack, all pink and stuff." He laughed at the horrified look on her face. "Maybe not, then."

He grunted with the effort of trying to unlatch a backpack strap that was cinched as tight as it could be. Soon, he gave up and sawed back and forth on it instead.

"Change of plans, little girl. Get ready. I think gravity's going to be a beeyatch."

The knife cut through enough of the strap that the remaining fibers suddenly frayed and broke. They awkwardly tumbled to the ground in a heap, plunging their way through the blocks.

Dangerella shrieked when her injured leg hit the hard floor. The pain made her see red winking lights around her field of vision.

She heard the man yelp in the darkness.

"Jesus, girl, how sharp did you go and make this knife?"

* * *

Dangerella watched as Earl pulled the needle and thread through her leg again. She was biting down on a rolled up piece of cloth, her saliva running down her chin. She was grateful that the worst of it was over. She had almost popped her jaw out of joint when he poured the alcohol directly into her wound.

"This is the germ kind of alcohol, not the kind you drink," he'd said, right before a hot river of pain lanced through her leg. He told her he didn't have anything for her pain, besides aspirin. And the other kind of alcohol. He had lots of that. He'd been pouring whiskey down her throat to try to keep her mind off the pain, but at first that just made her throat burn.

Working on her wound was aggravating his own. When they fell, he fell on her knife and sliced up his palm. Earl winced as he pulled the thread. His right hand was wrapped in gauze, and blood was beginning to stain the dressing.

As she lay there, being stitched like a quilt, and more than a little drunk from the whiskey, her mind bounced all over the place. She started crying. She spit out the cloth.

"I'm not going to catch up with Bull3tBoy now." Her lower lip made a quivering furrow. Tears dripped off her chin. "And I don't know how to message him."

Earl stopped, and looked at her.

"Who's bullethead?"

"Just some guy I'm in love…met online."

"Ah. 'Love.' Good for you this is just an online deal. There's no such thing as love."

"What?" Dangerella tried to sit up.

The room spun around her.

She laid back down in a hurry.

"People always think they're in love. Really they're in love with the *idea* of love. Anyhow," he said as he used his teeth to end the knot of the sutures on her leg. "Young love is the worst kind. He's probably dead by now with the bleeding thing. Most people are."

His words hit her like punches. "What the hell do you know? You're just a bum living under the street."

Earl pulled back then. His face was unreadable. He got up and walked away to sit on a milk crate. His eyes looked far off, unfocused.

"I'm sorry. I didn't…I mean you just fixed up my leg and all and here I dump on you. I didn't mean it."

"Oh hell, don't do that. Don't act like you didn't tell the truth. I guess I am a bum. I gave up on the world long before the latest trouble, but you have no call to know about that."

"I should have said thanks for—she started softly.

"But let me give you some free advice," he interrupted. "Speaking the truth will only get you in big trouble someday. I know it did me."

He bowed down and shook his head. "I know it did me."

They didn't talk for a while, both of them feeling their own flavor of prickly and neither sure how to shift into something else.

After a time, Earl came over and quietly finished up dressing her leg. He elevated it on a rolled up quilt and threw a thin blanket on top of her. She stuck out her good leg and both arms to try to keep cool. The whiskey didn't help. It made her warm from the inside out. Still, when he offered her another drink of it, she didn't turn it down.

She spent a fitful night trying like hell to go to sleep. As far as she could tell, Earl sat in the same place on the crate all night. She watched him in the dark. He was a big man, or was once. His dreads came down to the middle of his back.

He muttered things under his breath.

She wondered where Bull3tBoy was, and if he was okay. She thought about his online picture, the one that wasn't an avatar and showed what he really looked like. He said he was clumsy and tall, that's as far as he went describing himself. She wanted him to be a hero and come tearing into the city to find her. But she knew that would be nearly impossible without her tablet's GPS.

It hurt her to think she would rather have him safe and at the compound than wasting his time looking for her. It made the inside of her chest tingle. Because she also wanted to be with him more than anything else she could think of.

* * *

Dangerella's leg swelled, sporting angry red skin around the wound. She tentatively tried to get up and put some weight on it, but ended up falling back down.

She tried to talk to Earl, but he was still angry, or absent. He frequently seemed to get lost in his own mind. Her voice turned small.

He continued to take care of her. He didn't have anything to drink that wasn't liquor, so she only took enough to wet the insides of her mouth, and stretched out the time between sips. She felt light-headed and feverish enough from infection; she didn't want to be drunk all the time too.

Finally he came over to check on her leg, lifting up the bandages. His eyes grew wide and he cursed under his breath.

“Did you bring any meds in your backpack? Penicillin? Antibiotics?”

“No. I only brought stuff, well, you know, for girls.”

He ran a hand over his face.

“Well, here's the thing. The pharmacies were looted and picked over right off. Necessary drugs and things that got you high disappeared first. Antibiotics are necessary drugs. I need to go topside and see if I can find you something.”

“Okay,” she answered weakly.

“I don't like leaving you here like this, but I can't take you with me either.”

She shrugged, not knowing how to answer that.

“But I got no choice. You sure messed up my life, you know that?”

“I didn't…”

Earl's face screwed up in rage, and he shouted, “I didn't ask to be born on your planet!” He picked up random things and started smashing them against the walls.

She felt around, looking for something. Something that should have been there. In spite of the sickness and the haze in her mind, she snapped awake.

"My knives! Where are my knives?"

"See, now, I can't trust you to have weapons in my own house, little girl. Your knife about split my hand in half." He waved his arms, describing an invisible box, like a mime.

"This is a weapon-free zone, is Earl's house."

"I'm going to need those when I leave, Earl."

He jumped as if bitten by a snake.

"You can't leave right now. Not with your leg infected. You ain't leaving." His eyes were burning brightly.

Dangerella's face became grim, but she remained silent.

Earl grabbed a wireframe grocery cart with damaged wheels. "I got maybe another place I can look for meds. I'll be back."

"Wait," Dangerella requested. Earl looked at her impatiently.

"If you can find a laptop or a tablet, could you grab that for me?"

Earl frowned, his dreads swaying. "What do you need that for?"

"I can use it," she assured him. Then, her stomach cramped up and she curled into herself on the makeshift cot.

Angrily, Earl looked at her. "So you can leave."

She pretended to not hear him, and groaned. Eventually, he left, dragging the cart behind him, making as much noise as he possibly could.

* * *

Earl stood in front of the Grand Arthurian Plaza: home of luxury condos with excellent security. However, he knew where the extra emergency key was kept. He removed the third brick down on the right side of the door.

He entered the marble-clad lobby and carefully looked around. Every little noise contrasted with the complete silence.

The first floor condos had doors flung open. Earl saw signs of a struggle or hurried exit, belongings strewn everywhere. There were stiff brown stains on the expensive carpeting. No one had gotten around to cleaning up the blood.

The first floor didn't matter. Earl's objective was the elevator. He stepped into the open car and double-pressed the basement and lobby keys simultaneously. He was heading toward the basement. In the Super's office was the skeleton key. At least it always had been. He smiled when he was rewarded by finding the dull brass key and ring hanging off the metal key box.

He pressed the lobby and penthouse keys together to go up.

The penthouse was where Mr. Diamond lived. That's what his entourage and the staff called him. He had the whole floor to himself. Earl felt himself half-bowing as he entered, though he doubted anyone was there to bow back or dismiss him. Old habits die hard.

He ignored the immaculate living area with the huge picture windows. There was another more important room here. When he reached it, he slowly opened the door and felt a puff of trapped air escape. Air rich in oxygen. It really perked Earl up and brightened his eyes. For a moment, he thought the hermetically sealed room might have miraculously saved Mr. Diamond throughout the blood virus trouble. But he saw in the expensive hospital bed a different story.

The bed was covered in dark spent blood, and after observing his dying position, Earl felt a little sorry for Mr. Diamond, unable to move, and already old and unhealthy. He must have let in someone he completely trusted. Someone who entered and carried the virus within them.

The bed was curtained with plastic barriers, and as he walked through them, he saw the culprit, already punished, dead on the floor. Mr. Diamond's nephew, in front of the opened wall safe. He died hugging bricks of cash and platinum bars to his chest as he bled out of his orifices. Earl didn't like Mr. Diamond's nephew, but nobody deserved to die like that.

He stepped over the body, and opened a large standing cabinet that filled one wall.

Pay dirt.

He stepped into a massive medicine cabinet, larger than a walk-in pantry. Mr. Diamond had his physicians stock every medicine one could think of, in the mad struggle to keep him mostly alive. Some bottles had names on them Earl had never heard of, but there were several antibiotic prescriptions, different versions of penicillin, ciprofloxacin, and broad spectrum infection eradicators. There was also a refrigerated section with bags of drawn blood, probably Mr. Diamond's own. Earl quickly shut that. He held his jute bag under the shelves and shoveled all the meds in.

He stopped at the foot of Mr. Diamond's bed.

"What good did it do you, huh? Now you're dead, and I'm still walking around. Where are your boys now? Carmine probably took the coward's way out and kissed his own gun barrel goodbye. What it's worth to own everything, when everything goes to crap? Nothing. That's what."

As he was leaving the place he found something lying on a glass table. He started to pick it up, and then set it back down gently. He stared at it for a long time. He lifted it again in his rough hands. Things warred in his head that paralyzed him. He wondered whether it was the proper thing to take it with him.

* * *

Pills were placed in her mouth, and washed down with whiskey. She wasn't aware of it. Her mind was filled with nightmares, intricate maps and unbelievable birds. Dangerella dreamed of losing her leg and walking with a prosthetic limb, the interior of which cached several knives. She was a killer robot and Bull3tBoy rode alongside her on his mechanized horse.

* * *

Earl sat patiently next to Dangerella on his milk crate. He was drinking very expensive 25 year old scotch taken from Mr. Diamond's penthouse.

"Beats the hell out of cheap wine," he told himself.

He sipped slowly, savoring each blended flavor.

The last time he'd had liquor this good was in Da Nang, Vietnam. He'd been assisting an interrogation.

"Don't let him die," they told him. They wanted Earl to patch the prisoner up so they could start again. Sometimes there was nothing he could do, the body was a machine and sometimes it could be damaged beyond repair. But the eyes of the prisoners would plead with him.

That duty whittled away little bits of his soul, leaving gaping holes that he now filled with alcohol. The Vietnamese general had very nice liquor, and primo cigars. Not as good as Mr. Diamond's, but still good.

He dozed a few minutes at a time. His head would start to drop, and he'd jerk himself back awake. The girl slept on, the antibiotics working their way through her system. He'd popped a few himself, as a precaution for his own knife wound.

* * *

When Dangerella's fever broke, Earl stood over her, staring.

"Where you going to go after you leave?" he asked her, devoid of emotion.

"Just nowhere, anywhere."

"Staten Island, right? You're going there." Less of a question, more of a declaration.

"Yes." She tried to pull herself up. "It's safe."

He laughed bitterly.

"Safe? Who told you it was safe?" He crossed his arms, looking very intimidating.

"They did. On the site." She stuck her chin up defiantly.

"And 'they' are?"

"Well..."

"You don't even know, do you? All you know is they are asking people to come. Now why would they do that?" He shook his dreads at her. "Why wouldn't they just keep their own selves safe?"

"Because they're trying to save mankind. We're all that's left."

Earl grunted to himself, and then said, "Okay, let me tell you something, baby doll. Mankind has always been crazy selfish as hell. Just because there's less of them don't make them less crazy." His eyes connected with hers and she felt them bore through her.

"Good advice, and you best take it. Don't go. Stay here. You don't know if you can trust them."

"And I should trust you? The guy who stole my knives?"

"Safe keeping, is all." He said, though he did look around the space to see if anything had been disturbed.

She sat up all the way, and glared up at him.

"I *am* going to leave. You can't stop me. I appreciate the help, but I can't stay in a hovel under a sidewalk. Besides, Bull3tBoy..."

"Bullethead."

"Bull3tBoy is waiting for me. If I don't show up, he could do something stupid, like come looking for me."

Earl was rigid. He continued to stare for a minute. He reached for a bundle behind a shelf and almost threw it at her. Then he stalked away and left.

Dangerella unwrapped the cloth and found her knives in the first layer. But there was something hard underneath them, wrapped in more cloth. She set it in her lap and pulled the material away. She gasped.

It was a tablet. Much better than the one she broke.

"Thank..." she started to say, and realized he wasn't there anymore to hear it.

Before she turned it on, she looked at the back and saw the engraving.

'G. Bandorelli' it said.

"The gangster?" she whispered to herself.

"Huh." She shook her head, amazed.

Dangerella: Hey! Are you there?

Bull3tBoy: OMG. Where have you been?

Dangerella: Guess what? I am on Gianni Bandorelli's tablet!

Bull3tBoy: The mobster?

Dangerella: Alleged.

Bull3tBoy: yeah, ok, whatevs, like the rule of law still applies. So how did that happen?

Dangerella: Long story. I'll tell you when I see you. Right now I'm a little slowed up.

Bull3tBoy: We still going to meet at the bridge?

Dangerella: I'm going to try to make it as soon as I can.

Bull3tBoy: Are you still walking?

Dangerella: Not really. Sort of. Going to find a different way, though.

Bull3tBoy: I'll wait for you. I kinda like you, and stuff.

Dangerella: lol. Giggle.

Did she really just type 'giggle' at the end of her chat? Is that something Dangerella would do? Is it even something Angelica would do?

* * *

By the time she got done chatting, Earl had come back to his house, dragging his shopping cart, full of expensive looking liquor bottles. He was smoking a cigar.

"Gag. That cigar smoke!" she objected.

He pulled it out of his mouth, looked at it, pulled another draw and blew a smoke ring.

"These are the best cigars money can buy, if money could still buy things."

She motioned for him to sit down on the milk crate. Warily he lowered himself, watching her closely.

"We need to settle some things, you and I," she began.

"You're looking better. You're welcome." Another puff of smoke drifted up. Earl smiled to himself.

“Okay, yes, thank you. Thank you for everything. I really can't repay you, not with anything that means anything.”

“Nope.” He grinned. He was really enjoying his cigar.

“So, here's my thought. I need to get to Staten Island, and I can't hoof it at the moment.”

“Nope.”

“But if I could be driven, it would be much, much faster.”

He stared down his cigar at her.

“And you can't drive, I guess.”

“Never needed to. I don't know the first thing, honestly.” She spread her hands wide, like someone showing they had nothing in their pockets.

He leaned back and looked at the ceiling, thinking. Smoking.

“Well, I could drive you. But then, like you said, what's in it for me?”

“I've been thinking, and I think I came up with something in trade.”

Earl nearly choked and shook his finger at her.

“Hey now, you're too young for that sort—”

“No! Jeez. Ewww.”

Earl mouthed the word 'ewww' and raised his eyebrow.

“No, I mean right now, you're living under the sidewalk.”

“It's not bad.” He looked around, appraisingly.

“But what if, in exchange for driving me there, I put in a good word, and get you into the haven?”

The old man got a serious look on his face. He leaned forward and cleared his throat.

“Okay, I'm gonna tell you a story. A story about Earl. A true story. I did something once. It was supposed to be a good thing. All the lawyers and the DA and the feds, they all acted like I was some kind of hero. Up until then, I was no hero. For some reason, I wanted to be one.”

“So, they came to me. 'Oh, we'll protect you until the trial,' they said. 'We're going to put the guy behind bars so he can't hurt you,' they promised. Then they said, 'We'll protect your family.'“

He brushed his fingers across his eyes.

“I buried my wife and my two sons. Laid them in the earth like they were someone else's family. Like I wasn't me. It was a message from a former employer.”

“Bandorelli,” she guessed. His face recoiled in horror, or guilt. Earl got up and started pacing.

“I used to do…enforcing. For Mr. Diamond. I knew everything about his operation. My wife suspected. She was the one who persuaded me to tell the truth, to work with the feds."

He stopped, facing away from her in the dark.

"That's not the point. The point is they promised me safety, the DA, the police, the task force. They had no idea how powerful Mr. Diamond was, how many fingers he had in all the pies. When they took my family, it was proof I couldn't trust anyone. I became Earl, the homeless guy. No one thinks twice about a bum you see on the street. And now, it's happening again. Staten Island is promising you safety."

"But I have to try. I have to get there, there are people waiting on me," she said. "The world has changed. Maybe for the better."

"I doubt it, Angelica."

He got up and rummaged around in a corner. Finally, he pulled out a long device like it was Excalibur.

"Here we go. I got this while scrounging. While you was deciding to wake up or not." Earl handed her a metal rod with a round cuff at the top and a short bar just under the cuff. It was a hi-tech crutch.

She got up and put the crutch under one arm, took a few wobbly steps around the place. Her leg still hurt, but she could use the brace to get around.

"Okay, enough practice. You need to come with me," Earl said, while packing things in his cart.

"Where?"

"Hopefully to a place that'll knock some sense into you."

* * *

The view from Mr. Diamond's penthouse was beautiful, encompassing large sections of the city. Earl motioned her over to a telescope mounted on a platform before the large bulletproof windows.

"Look through this thing. You got to squint one eye and bend down to see anything."

Dangerella started to bend, letting her crutch drop to the floor.

"Make sure it's the eye not looking that you squint."

"Really, you think?" she shot back.

"Hell, I don't know if you used a telescope before. Okay, what do you see? I had it aimed before."

"Is that…is that Staten Island?" she asked, almost to herself.

"Yep, but what else do you see?"

In the distance she could make out the huge concrete barrier at the end of the bridge leading onto the island.

Dangerella stared at him. He was waiting for her to put things together. He motioned at her to look again.

She focused on the streets. She had to take a breath quickly. What she saw shocked her. There was a knot of armed men, patrolling the streets in what looked like a very organized routine. That's what she saw. But what she *didn't* see worried her more. No children. No families. Nobody out enjoying the day. And it was a really nice day.

"You know, baby doll, concrete is such a faceless thing. It's grey, a neutral color. It can be used to make a daycare, or a prison," Earl said.

"That's true," she agreed.

"And this here concrete is not telling us which one it is." He pointed out the window. "Is it the concrete of a sanctuary, or..."

"Only one entrance..." she said, holding her hand to her mouth.

"You gotta ask yourself: Are they keeping people out, or keeping people in? If they were so all-fired, bent on saving mankind, why would they need to do either one?" he added, watching her carefully as she sat down in a large over-padded chair.

Earl saw her break down, from the inside out. He knew what a shattered dream looked like on someone's face.

Dangerella's face became animated, "O.M.G. We've got to stop Bull3tBoy!"

* * *

The dingy yellow cab bounced along Highway 278, which would become Goethals Bridge, the only entrance to Staten Island. The cab's suspension was shot, so they felt every little bump.

The sides of the cab were scratched with the paint of various cars, from when they had been forced to squeeze through some tight spaces. The roadways to the island were clogged with unmoving vehicles. Some were abandoned, but most were manned by the dead.

"This is it, coming up," Earl said to Dangerella. She had her head buried in her tablet, frustrated by the lack of a Wi-Fi signal.

"Bull3tBoy is supposed to meet us at the bridge. He said the beginning has concrete posts to stop the cars, and you have to walk on foot from there."

"How you gonna know who is Bullethead?"

"I've seen his picture online."

"That could be fake, anyhow."

She didn't answer. She'd been thinking of that as a possibility and didn't want to go there.

"Got your crutch?"

"Aye aye, cap'n," she answered.

They came upon the bridge. Newly restored, it was designed with what looked like delicate cords that pulled at the towers to keep it structurally sound. It seemed like a graceful futuristic creature lounging across the water.

Earl dropped any chatter they'd been having. He stopped the cab, hung his hands on the top of the steering wheel and peered out at the bridge.

Dangerella got out and walked over to the driver's side window as she pulled on the straps of her new backpack, leaning on her walking crutch.

"Thank you," she said, and appeared as though she meant it.

"Just go find your boy," he said quietly, turning the key to stop the cab from idling. He leaned back in the hot seat and watched her as she hobbled away from him toward the bridge.

Earl pulled out another fine cigar and chewed on the end a bit. He hoped this wasn't going to take long.

* * *

People came to the bridge on foot. They flowed around Earl like a rock in a stream. Every once in a while, he'd nod if someone noticed him sitting in the cab. One or two people eyed him suspiciously.

"Hurry up, baby doll. Things could get a little tense out here," he muttered to himself. His cigar was about halfway smoked. He reached down and swigged another drink from his liquor bottle.

Earl sat up straighter in the cab, keeping an eye out for Dangerella. He'd lost sight of her when she bumped her way into the crowd waiting at the bridge. Some people must have been waiting for others to join them, and Earl figured some were scoping out the situation.

On his right he saw some bushes move. There crouched a young girl peering at the bridge between the leaves. She wasn't making any moves to head out there herself so Earl kept watching her, intrigued.

She turned her head in his direction. She didn't see him in the glare off the windshield, but it gave him a chance to recognize her.

"Well, I'll be…" he said, as he grabbed his cigar and stepped out of the cab. He walked slowly and carefully, because he didn't want to spook the girl. He'd almost gotten within fifteen feet of her before she caught sight of him.

She looked like a worried rabbit, making ready to jump. Then, she narrowed her eyes and took a good look at him.

"You," she said.

"You back."

"You're still alive?"

Earl patted himself down. "Looks that way."

The girl darted her eyes over the scene, making sure no one else approached.

"You're a long way from the bakery," Earl finally said.

"I know. You remem—"

"Yeah, yeah, I remember you making me take your day-old bread. I felt sorry for you, so I went ahead and ate it." Earl smiled.

"What? That's not how I remember it." She smiled back. "I seem to recall you didn't want to accept charity."

His expression turned hard-edged. "No, you're right, little girl, I don't accept charity. Earl can look out for himself. I told you those rolls and biscuits were going to be just a loan. And Earl always pays back his debts. I'd have gotten around to paying."

"Well, you don't owe me anything now, the world has gone crazy. Nothing means anything anymore."

Earl drew slowly on his cigar and looked past the bushes to the general area of the bridge. He noticed she couldn't help but flinch when he did.

"Something bothers you about that wall, ain't that right?"

She nodded slightly.

"You *should* be bothered. Hell, we should *all* be bothered. Something ain't right about all of this."

The girl ran to him and collapsed into his massive chest, tears flowing.

"Hold on now," Earl said to the top of her head.

"And who the heck is this?" said a voice behind them. Earl turned his head, still holding up the distraught girl, to answer Dangerella.

"Her name's Linnie, or Alex or something like that."

A muffled word came through the lapel of Earl's coat, "Lexia. My name is Lexia."

Dangerella hobbled over to them and put her hand on Lexia's shoulder. She patted it a couple of times. It seemed like she wanted to comfort someone besides herself, for once.

"So, where's Bullethead?" Earl asked.

A pained expression crossed her face. "Either he never showed…" she said, before taking a breath deep into her chest. She let it out heavily and scratched her freckled forehead. "Or he's already in, and it's just too late. Either way, I guess we should head on back."

Earl nodded, like he fully expected that to be the situation. He pushed himself apart from Lexia, holding her gently by the shoulders.

"You. You got a place to crash?" he asked her as he bent down and looked into her eyes.

"I…don't want to go in there. Not on the island. Something smells wrong about it."

"Well," said Dangerella as she readjusted the straps on her backpack with a bit of struggle, "You ever thought about living in a luxury penthouse apartment in Manhattan? It's safe."

Lexia flinched at the word 'safe.' For a moment her shoulders hunched and she looked about to cry. Then she wiped the back of her hand across her face, smearing the tears and what little makeup she wore.

She nodded, making a firm decision, "I do know how to bake."

SEVEN: *Roland*
by Kelsey D. Garmendia

Roland looked in the mirror at the black skull and crossbones tattoo burned into his skin. Even with everything happening on the streets, that tattoo was still the worst decision in his life. His music career and choice in friends were questionable, but it was the tattoo that still made him cringe. The music, the booze, and the dumb decisions were things of the past though. The news was the only music in Roland's run-down bungalow now.

"Why can't we watch something else?" his mother yelled over the fizzling sound from the television.

"Oma," Roland said over his shoulder through his medical mask. "This is important stuff here. We gotta listen—"

"I'm going to be late for class," she screamed, knocking her oatmeal to the ground. "Class is starting in fifteen minutes!"

Roland sighed and picked up the bowl, scooping the oatmeal off the carpet. Without her medication, his mother's Alzheimer's worsened with each day. Most of the time, she had no clue where she was. School seemed to be the most important thing to her these days. He emptied the bowl of oatmeal into the garbage and tied up the bag.

A sigh escaped his mother's lips followed by a chuckle. He looked back over his shoulder at her, wishing that she would come back to him. The old her, the one who would constantly watch MTV just to make sure she was keeping up with the times. The one who would come to all of Roland's shows regardless of the venue. The one he saved from going to a nursing home after her house burned down; he still kicked himself for not noticing the symptoms of Alzheimer's then.

"What are you doing in there, Rolo?" Oma called from her chair in the living room.

The nickname made a smile flash across his face. Sometimes the old her would appear out of nowhere. He lived for those moments. But he knew better than to get his hopes up. "I'm taking out the trash Ma," he said. "I'll be back. Stay here."

"Don't take too long," she responded. "I've got to be at the school in an—"

"Yeah, I know," he responded, pulling the gas mask his brother gave him over his head. He opened the closet door to his right and pulled a pistol from the top shelf.

The metal object felt foreign in his palm. It was another *gift* from his brother Paton before he disappeared. It was the kindest gesture his brother had made since getting sober. He hated carrying it when he did mundane things like taking the trash out, but after seeing the looting and mass hysteria on the news, it was the only thing he had to protect what was left of his family.

"Keep your mask on, Ma. I'll be right back."

"Rolo," she said. "Don't forget about the school assignment—"

He shut the door before she could finish. He'd heard enough of her for today.

The street had been quiet since the Fever spread like wildfire. At first, Roland thought it was great compared to the pre-virus hum of his neighborhood. By pre-virus hum, he meant gunshots and shouting from midnight to five in the morning.

But the silence eventually grew past its nice stage. Now, the silence meant that death was waiting to knock on each door until there was no one left. A roaring purr of an engine bounced off the siding of the houses around him. He gazed around the corner of his house at a red car with dark windows; skulls floated in bright flames painted down the sides. Without warning, the car took off in a loud roar down the street and squealed around a corner.

That car had been doing laps around the neighborhood for the past few days. Each time Roland saw it, another stream of smoke would pop up somewhere in the neighborhood. He went to the source of a smoke cloud one day and found the charred remains of an elderly man that lived three houses down. Sometimes he found himself thinking that the person in that car was Death himself.

Laughter billowed out from inside Roland's house. He marched across the yard toward the backdoor while the rest of the trash burned. The news on the television filled his ears again along with his mother's soft laugh. He closed the door behind him and slid the bolt action closed.

"Rolo, your brother is here," she responded. "I let him in the front door."

My brother? Roland hadn't spoken to his brother since he gave him the gun and gas masks about a week ago. They fought about their mother. Paton wanted him to move her to his house with his family so that they could all stay safe together until help came, but Roland knew that moving her would only make her more confused. He disappeared back to his wife and kids when they couldn't come to an agreement. It was hard being his brother at times, but he knew what Oma needed and Paton didn't.

Roland flipped around to spot a man with a gas mask and a sweat-filled hairline tearing their kitchen apart. The front door was wide open, letting a cool breeze pass through the house. He looked to Oma's face and felt his heart stop. His mother's gas mask sat on the table next to her, along with her backup medical mask. She smiled wide when she saw her son—her lips pulled back over her teeth like they would if this were any other time.

Pain flared up somewhere between his stomach and his heart. The years he had cared for her meant nothing now. The years of fighting over taking her medication were washed away with the breeze that rolled through his house. She could be infected now all because she opened the door for someone.

"Hey!" Roland screamed.

The man in the kitchen jumped, sending dishes shattering to the ground. He pulled down his mask, turned around, and leaned back against the counter. Roland noticed the front of his jacket was covered with a spray of blood. The looter grabbed a knife from the dish rack behind him. "I'm not infected—"

"Whose blood is that!"

The stranger inched toward the front door with the butcher knife held out in front of him. "I—I was just looking for meds and food," he said. "I'm not infected—"

"Why do you keep saying that?" Roland asked.

"Just let me go," he responded. "I'll go. And I won't come back."

Roland looked closer at the looter. Something about his gas mask looked off. He peered into the reflective eye holes. "Your mask is cracked," Roland said pointing at the clear line through the eye. "That won't protect you." Roland stepped toward him. The intruder swung the knife at him. "Jesus! Will you chill out man—"

"Get away from me!" The stranger sprinted from the kitchen out the front door. Roland threw himself out the door and into the street after the dark figure. He lunged toward the stranger and latched onto the straps of his gas mask. The masked man swung with the knife again and stumbled out of Roland's grasp. The knife clattered about two feet away until it went silent. His gas mask fell to the ground, the Plexiglas cracking as it hit the pavement.

Without his gas mask on, he pushed himself to his knees and vomited blood onto the road. *No.* He cried out in pain and gripped his stomach with his arm. *Please, no.* The stranger turned his head over his shoulder and two blood-red eyes stared back at Roland.

"You killed her," Roland growled. He looked into the fear-filled eyes of the man and felt his blood boil. "You killed her!"

Roland reached for his pistol. The man tried to run but stumbled over his feet in his attempt and collided with the pavement once more. Roland pulled back the slide and pressed the muzzle into the infected's forehead.

"Please, sir," he begged. "I'm sorry—"

Hearing his plea stung, but his anger won. "You lied to me!" Roland yelled. "You lied to me and now my mother is dead because of it!" The gun fired once, and the looter's head snapped back. His body fell backward while Roland emptied the rest of the clip into the man's chest. Then, the silence returned. Death had taken another soul from the streets.

"Rolo?" his mother called from inside the house.

Roland walked through the open door in complete nausea. *I'm a murderer. Just like that person with the flamed car. Just like all the people on the news.*

"Rolo, honey," she said. "Did you call the school? Do they know that I'm going to be late?"

Roland began to take his mask off, but then stopped himself. *She's probably infected now.* He reached out and rubbed his finger across her cheek. "I'm so sorry Ma," he whispered. "I'm sorry I couldn't keep you safe."

"Oh honey," she said smiling. "Don't worry about that now. We're still together right? That's all that matters."

Roland nodded. He was grateful for the mask now; it hid the tears. Twenty-four hours. Twenty-four hours was all he had left with her.

* * *

A knock at the door woke Roland from his sleep. The Spanish soap opera Oma requested to watch blared on the television. He turned to her and saw the sheen of sweat on her forehead. "Stay here Oma," he said through his mask.

"Okay dear," she said. "Don't be gone too long now. You're going to miss something."

Another knock, louder this time, boomed throughout the house. Roland gripped his pistol and pulled it from behind him. "What?" he asked through the door.

"Roland?" a voice called from the other side. "Please tell me that's you."

Roland frowned at the voice. He unlatched the chain to the door and pulled it open. A loud purring from an engine filled the house in an instant. He saw the vibrant red and orange flames first, followed by large shiny rims and then the tattooed hands of his brother.

"Paton?" Roland peered closer into the reflective eyes of the person's gas mask, and then behind him at the red car with skulls and flames painted along its sides; a stream of smoke floated up from behind the car.

Roland felt sick. He thought the man who had been slaughtering and burning people in the streets was Death, but he was wrong. The man burning people in his neighborhood was his own flesh and blood. He backed into the house and aimed at Paton's chest.

"Stop," Paton said. "Let me explain—"

"You killed off more than half the neighborhood and now you want to explain!"

"I know this looks bad, Roland. Please just give me a chance," he responded, inching his way into the house with his hands raised.

"Shhh!" Oma said from behind them both. "I can't hear my show."

Paton looked past Roland at their mother with wide eyes. "Ma?"

"Oh, you must be mistaken," she responded. "Rolo, who's this you invited?" Her eyes reflected red in the television's light. She coughed several times into a white handkerchief. When she pulled it away from her mouth, it too was stained a dark red.

"You've been keeping her here like this?" he said pulling a long-barrel rifle over his back. "Tell me you didn't take off your mask."

"What are you doing Paton!"

"Answer me!" Roland's brother yelled.

"No, okay! I didn't!" Roland answered, stepping in front of their mother. "What the hell's gotten into you?"

"My life was *destroyed* because of the Fever, Roland!"

"She's our *mother*!"

"She's suffering," Paton growled.

They stood with weapons drawn at each other for a few moments. Roland released a strained breath from his lungs. "Okay." He lowered his pistol. "I don't feel up to shooting anyone else tonight—"

"Who else did you shoot?"

"The one that's burning on the other side of that car you came out of, Paton. He's the reason Ma's sick."

The horn honked from the flamed lowrider outside as if on command. Paton looked over his shoulder and let out a long sigh. "Listen," he said. "I've been doing circles around the house for a couple days now. I didn't feel right leaving things the way I did. I've been trying to keep this place safe for you two until I was able to move the both of you elsewhere."

"By murdering people?"

"If you mean infected people, then yes. And it's not murder, Roland. Not exactly. I don't expect you to understand—"

"Help me understand." Roland reached a hand out to his brother.

"My wife and kids are gone," he responded. "A police officer stopped by our house while I was out scrounging for groceries. It was after I tried to get you and Ma to leave. He was informing my family of the new curfew. My wife wasn't wearing her mask."

"They're—*dead*?" They both stood in silence looking away from each other. Roland loved his brother's family. As much hell as Paton put Oma and him through while they all lived under the same roof, turning his life around was his saving grace. Roland disengaged the pistol and slipped it back into his belt.

"Yes," Paton said turning his head back to his brother. "I didn't know she was infected until she started throwing up. She didn't separate herself from our kids, Roland. The news says it takes hours for this disease to kill its host, but it felt like years watching my family die."

"Paton, I'm sorry—"

"You're doing the same thing to Ma," his brother responded.

"No, I'm not—"

"She's dying in front of you right now. The amount of pain she's in—even if she has a bit of sanity left in her, it'll disintegrate. And then, she'll die a shell of the woman who raised us."

Roland glanced over at Oma feeling his temper burn again. "Yeah, well, where were you when that guy came in here?" Roland yelled. "You left us both so many times just so you could get drunk with your low-life friends. Ma doesn't even know you anymore—"

"I'm here now." Paton shifted uncomfortably on the balls of his feet. His sobriety was not something spoken about out loud. "I know it may not mean much, but I can't just leave both of you here without trying to help. Whether you like it or not, I'm the only family you're going to have left."

Roland turned his gaze over his shoulder at Oma. She laughed at something on the television and coughed into her handkerchief multiple times; more blood soaked into the white cloth. A groan escaped her lips as she attempted to push herself up in her chair.

"I listened to my wife beg me to kill her; her screams still haunt me," Paton whispered. "I couldn't do it. I was so stuck on not losing her. I kept telling her help was coming. Just hold on. When the kids started getting sick, she made me promise not to let our children suffer like she did." Paton's voice cracked. He turned away from Roland and cleared his throat. "I had to kill my kids, Roland."

Roland listened to Oma's hacking cough fill the room. Her laughter was replaced by wheezing now.

"I hunted down the police officer who came by our house," Paton continued. "But I was too late. And all that anger I had towards him. It just lingered there."

Roland looked away from Oma back to his brother feeling his throat tighten with tears.

"You've got to give Ma that peace. Don't watch her suffer anymore, Roland. I can't lose you both because of this. I can't."

A knot grew in Roland's chest. Their mother turned to both of them and smiled—blood staining the front of her teeth.

"My friend, the one in the car—his name is Sanderson. He found me at my apartment. He's been keeping the infection at bay in this area," Paton continued. "He's intense, but his plan is working."

"How?"

The horn honked again. Paton turned and held out his hand toward the car, motioning him to wait. "He has a story similar to mine, but we don't talk about it. He's been cleaning out neighborhoods to honor what he lost. He was heading this way. I knew you would still be here, so when he made the offer to join him, I said yes. I was a mess, Roland. I needed something to make this anger go away and prevent me from putting a bullet in my brain or drowning myself in liquor, you know?" he continued.

"Yeah, I guess."

"Listen, I know we've had our differences. I know I screwed up more than once. I've brought holy hell into this family so many times that I've lost count all because our dad left. I thought I was doing the right thing when I left you guys here back before the virus spread. I knew you were capable of taking care of Ma. If there was a nurse that said she'd stay with her twenty-four-seven, I'd still choose you to be her guardian. I thought that someone eventually would come for us after the outbreak. Then I lost my wife and kids, and all I feel is hatred and resentment for anyone who's infected. Sanderson helped me from falling apart by showing me how to channel those feelings into something useful."

"The news said to—"

"Oh screw the news, Roland! I'm your brother. *I* care about you," he said poking a finger into his chest. "No one else cares that we're suffering out here. If they did, they'd be helping us. Not ignoring us. Not sending infected police officers to people's houses. Not coming into our homes and spreading the Fever *knowingly*, and especially not making us play God with a rifle."

For once in Roland's life, his brother was right. He knew that Paton was the only other person who would look out for him. And the anger over losing his mother to this virus boiled just under the surface. He looked into the eye holes of his brother's gas mask and felt his humanity teetering dangerously on a ledge. Paton reached out and gripped his brother's arm and squeezed.

"How do I do this?" Roland said shaking his head. "I took care of her for so long. And now what? It just—ends?"

"No," Paton said lifting the rifle off of his shoulder. "This is where we start making a difference. We need to take matters into our own hands. *That* is something Oma would be proud of."

Paton held out the rifle to his brother. Roland gripped it with a shaky hand. He walked behind his mother and ran his hand through her thinning hair. "Is it time to go, my Rolo?" she asked through wheezing.

"Yes," he responded, aiming the rifle at the back of her head. "Close your eyes Ma."

"Okay," she said, leaning her head back against the muzzle of the rifle. "You know I love you, Rolo. No matter what happens."

His palms sweat against the grip. Oma hacked another bloodied cough up, then, as clear as day, a soft laugh escaped her lips. Before the disease took her memories, she was always laughing like that—a soft reminder that she was happy. Roland stifled a sob.

"Roland—"

"Tell me I'm doing the right thing here. Please."

Paton's hand gripped onto his shoulder. "It's what she needs, Roland," he said into his brother's ear. "Don't let her suffer anymore." Roland tightened his grip. His brother backed away toward the front door, but he didn't leave.

Before the infection, Roland, Paton, and Oma would go to the town's drive-in movie theatre every Friday night. Roland wasn't sure why the memory popped into his head while his brother was offering up her death sentence, but it calmed the knot in his gut.

She would always get her popcorn with so much butter that Roland was sure her doctor's ears were ringing. That was before Paton was married. Back when he was still the black sheep with an alcohol problem. Even with him like that back then, the memory was good enough to make Roland smile. Their family was never about perfection—and Oma never pointed that out.

I love you, Ma.

The gunshot exploded, leaving nothing behind but the smell of burning flesh and the silent swoop of Death's grasp.

Roland fell back against the wall letting the rifle clatter to the floor. Sweat covered his skin as he forced vomit back down his throat. He never really knew how much he depended on her. It sounded ridiculous to him to even think that now. She had Alzheimer's so bad that she needed directions on how to open a jar of peanut butter, but she was his rock. Oma was the one good thing left in his life.

His sobs filled his gas mask and the living room until his head pounded. It wasn't just the pain of losing her that made him snap. It was blood—the blood on his hands made the old Roland die with Oma. Paton sat next to him with his head in his palms. "Her suffering's over, Roland," he said just above a whisper.

"What do we do now?" Roland straightened his aching muscles out.

"We get back what this virus has taken from us." Paton gripped his brother around his shoulders. "We get back our reason to live."

Things were almost normal in his life. That's all Roland wanted. He wanted Oma to have her memories. He wanted to play music again. He wanted no more fear of the Fever.

But the anger he had for the man that infected her was what he *needed*. He needed vengeance. Something that gave him purpose. "Let's go."

* * *

"You know I love you Rolo. No matter what happens."

"Roland," Paton said nudging his brother's shoulder. "You still with me?"

"Yeah, I'm here," he responded. It had been one week with Paton and Sanderson. Roland was beginning to feel the aftereffects of ending people's miseries. What started out as something that felt like murder now felt like the noble thing to do.

Paton's description of Sanderson as a savior was far from the truth. Roland recognized that during their first run through a building. But if he had to choose between curling up in a ball of depression or staying with his brother, he'd always choose blood over his feelings. Paton was the only person left that mattered to him—and he clung to that with a strangling grip.

The shooting got easier. His feelings, aside from anger, were like ghosts. Sanderson said he was giving people mercy from their pain, but there was something in the way he killed that seemed manic. He saw glimpses of that in Paton's eyes, in the way he carried himself into a building filled with the dead. If he was honest with himself, he'd say that he was most definitely following in his footsteps. *I'm doing this to honor Oma—right?*

"You're still okay with this right?" Paton said, checking his rifle. "Our whole mission?"

"Taking back what was taken from us?" Roland laughed. He let out a long sigh as memories flooded him again. "Yeah, I'm good."

"You know I'd put a bullet in anyone that tried anything with you, right?"

"Yeah, it's why I came with you." The truth was that he felt hopeless without his brother and Sanderson. He'd have nothing to fight for if they weren't there. "You're the only blood I've got left. You're really the only one I can trust."

"I'm glad you didn't leave us," Paton leaned against Roland's car with his rifle pointed at the ground. The silence swooped over them as they stood outside of the last apartment building. "It's not your fault that Ma's dead—"

"I get that, Paton. It was that damn looter's fault."

"Just making sure you keep that in your head," Paton said gripping his brother's shoulder. "That fire? That's what drives me. Screw all those people who made this happen to us. Just focus on the people we're helping one at a time. Things'll be back to normal before we know it."

Roland nodded and looked down at the cracks in the concrete.

"All right," Paton said. "There are several people inside. They haven't been there long, but I heard a lot of muffled cries on the first floor. We go in, clear the floors out one by one and burn the building to prevent anyone else from getting infected. Then you, Sanderson, and I go to the next town."

"This is the last building here?"

"Yup. Sanderson went to fill up on gas so it's just you and me this time," Paton said loading his rifle. "Thank God we're almost done here. I'm sick of this town."

"I'm sick of everything." Roland cocked his shotgun. "I'm hearing screams in my damn nightmares, Paton. It's all I hear anymore." Roland leaned heavily on the hood of his white car.

Paton's hand clamped down on his shoulder and squeezed.

"For our family?"

"For our family."

The gunshots stopped sending chills up Roland's spine by the time they reached the third floor. By the looks of the people in this building, the pain had already kicked in from the Fever. Roland hadn't run into anyone who didn't want to be killed, since the looter that infected Oma back in Scotchtown. Most people looked at him as an angel and begged him to end it. At first, it felt redeeming. He thought taking people's pain away was the one good thing coming out of this virus.

But nothing was changing. The death toll from the virus continued to rise. Roland hadn't seen a police officer since the early days of the outbreak. Putting people out of their misery wasn't making a difference and now, his anger and resentment over that fact was winning.

He chose another door to his left, and Paton took the apartment across the hall, kicking in the door.

Roland landed the ball of his foot on the door by the knob. A girl screamed from the other side and muffled shuffling followed. He kicked again, and the door exploded into the room. He raised his shotgun and shined his flashlight around the apartment. A crashing sound from the right drew him in further.

"Don't kill me," a small voice said from his right. He turned to find a woman with blood seeping down from her eyes. "Please."

She was young—early twenties, late teens maybe, but the Fever made her look much older in the dim moonlight in the apartment. Something in the sound of her voice made Roland stop from shooting her. He let his shotgun lower.

"You're sick." He tried to find better words to say, but nothing came. The silence hung over them both. In that moment, he realized neither of them would back down. Roland watched the girl's face change from afraid to animalistic in seconds.

She leaped from the corner of the kitchen tackling him into the wall. He kicked her off of him, sending her crashing into the counter. Roland sprung to his feet while the girl came slashing at him with a knife. He felt the first swing of the blade make contact before he was able to fire a shotgun round at her chest. The shot hit her with a muffled thud, and she fell in a heap.

His breathing echoed inside his mask. He didn't feel any pain where the knife had made contact with him, but to be safe, he illuminated the front of his body with his flashlight to check himself out. It lit up the front of his jacket and stopped just at the beginning of his gas mask's filter tube. A small slash through the ridged material glared at him.

Oh shit. He looked down at his body to see if there were any wounds.

"Roland!" his brother yelled from the other room. "You good?"

Oh God. It's only a small gap. There's a backup in these masks, isn't there? "Yeah," he said, zipping his jacket over the slash mark in his hose. *She was infected. Why didn't I just shoot her? Why did I hesitate?*

He drenched the girl in gasoline and dripped it out into the hallway.

"That last apartment down there is empty," Paton said making his way back toward his brother. "It was covered in plastic on the inside. But no one was in there. I doused it all."

"Let's get the hell out of here then."

They both drained the rest of their gasoline down the staircase. Paton got the matches while Roland jogged out to his white lowrider. Sanderson pulled in behind his car.

"Everything go okay in there?" he called out the cracked window.

"Yeah—"

"Help us, please!" a voice shouted from the alleyway.

"Paton," Roland called out. "Someone's out in the alley."

"I'll take care of them," he answered. "Take off and meet us in Highland."

The phrase made Roland's skin crawl. *Will he take care of me when the time comes?* Roland climbed into his car and turned over the engine. He peeled out from the parking lot and sped down the alleyway. A woman and man with white medical masks were on the ground in between the buildings. The woman lay in the arms of the man—she was covered in a deep crimson.

That's going to be me, and no one will be there to help it end.

The infected reached out toward Roland's car, but he sped past without a second look.

* * *

Roland rubbed the tips of his fingers together. The back of his shirt stuck to his skin with sweat. He knew the Fever got him hours ago, but he kept it to himself. All he felt was regret and resentment for anyone who wasn't infected. He killed because the Fever took everything that mattered from him. It kept the anger at bay. But now he was dying because of bad luck with an infected girl. *This isn't fair.*

Paton leaned on his car next to him and slapped him on the back. Pain shot down Roland's body—*good thing these masks cover my face.*

"One more town in the books," Sanderson said squeezing his shoulder. "You were really sucking wind back there man."

"It gets hot in these masks," Roland responded, leaning back against the car. "Sue me."

"At least the Fever won't take anyone else coming through here," Paton said.

"You got that right." Sanderson leaned back on the car between Paton and Roland.

Shuffling echoed in the alleyway and all three of the men turned toward its source. Roland squinted at two people dressed in full protective suits and masks. They hesitated before the taller one nodded once and turned away from them.

"Hey!" Sanderson called out.

The two figures flinched at the sound of his voice. The one closest turned and pushed himself in front of the smaller person. "Hi," he responded with a wave.

"Where are you two headed?" Sanderson asked.

"I'm trying to get my daughter to…" the man started. He turned a slight glance over his shoulder at the girl. "To her mother's house," he continued. "My car broke down."

"Need a ride?" Sanderson pushed himself from the car and stepped forward.

"No, thank you. We aren't far."

"Well, we were just trying to help." Sanderson looked over his shoulder at Roland and shook his head slightly.

"Thank you," the man responded, pushing his daughter away from them. "We better be on our way." And then, they were gone.

"That's was weird," Sanderson said once they were in silence again. Roland took a step toward where they ran off to, but Sanderson stopped him. "Where are you going, Roland?"

"I'm going after them," he responded.

"Dude, we'll get them when we get them. No need to go chasing." Sanderson nudged his shoulder.

"They might know where more people are," Paton said pointing his pistol in the direction of the man and his daughter. "They could be hiding something—"

"Roland, we don't go hunting people," Sanderson commented, nodding his head where the two once stood. "They'll end up crossing paths with us again."

"So we're just gonna let them go? They might know something!"

"Roland, what are you talking about?" Paton said gripping both of his shoulders. "You sound crazy—"

"You know how much blood we have on our hands? And all of it for what? Making a difference?" He shoved his brother away knocking him to the ground. His voice echoed off the walls of the surrounding buildings.

"Roland, what the hell's the matter with you?"

His breathing pained his lungs while he braced himself against Sanderson's car. The Fever was like a ticking time bomb. Each agonizing second reminded him he was one step closer to dying. It toyed with emotions he thought were too fractured to still be there—emotions that were pushing him over the edge into a consuming spiral of anger.

Paton pulled himself from the ground and brushed off his blue jeans. "Paton—"

"Forget it," he responded. "It's fine."

Sanderson took a step toward Roland getting within inches of his gas mask. "You good, man?"

He nodded while swallowing down vomit. "Yeah," he responded. "I'm just...this doesn't feel right."

"Sure, I get it. You're feeling guilty for what we've been doing. You feel like a murderer, right?" Sanderson took a step into his car, leaning casually on the driver's side door. "Unfortunately Roland, that's the only way to help these people. And if no one else will, that's where we come in." He slammed the door leaving Paton and Roland outside.

"What the hell man? Something's been up with you since that last apartment building." Paton shook his head and folded his arms across his chest. "What happened?"

"Nothing," Roland responded stalking away to his car.

"I've been your brother for a long time, Roland." Paton cut in front of him before he could reach the handle to his car. "You're either gonna tell me what's going on in that head of yours or I'm beating it out of you—"

"I'm infected." The silence that followed was like a heavy footstep crashing down on him. There was no relief to be given from the secret he kept when death was the only ending. Roland couldn't tell if Paton was making eye contact with him through his gas mask, but he could feel the tension in an instant. Roland swallowed another mouthful of vomit—it tasted like blood.

"How?"

"I hesitated in that apartment building," he responded. "My filtration tube was slashed."

Paton let out a panicked laugh. "Please tell me you're joking."

"I'm not."

Paton shook his head. "Why would you tell me this?"

"Because you're my brother. Because I don't know what to do, Paton. And I feel like I'm going to die being a murderer." Roland reached out to him.

"Get away from me," he said holding his hands up.

"Paton, please—"

"Why would you keep this a damn secret, Roland? You realize that's how that policeman infected my family. He kept a secret that was toxic. It's how Ma got infected." Paton shook his head and turned his gaze away. "Get in your car and go. Don't follow us."

Paton marched past him without looking up. "We're supposed to look out for each other," he called out. "I need my brother."

Paton opened the back door to Sanderson's car and looked over at Roland. He shook his head once and then climbed in. The door slammed leaving Roland with a hole in his chest. He climbed into his car and turned over the engine.

A memory that Roland thought was long gone flashed before him. He was in the hospital—Paton lay on a bed after getting his stomach pumped for the third time that month. He had lied to Oma and Roland about where he was going. Somehow, he ended up at the wrong side of a bottle. A psychologist that Oma had hired for the family sat next to him. "It's okay to feel angry at him," she said.

"Why would he do this to himself? Why won't he talk to me about any of this?"

The psychiatrist sighed and laid a hand onto his shoulder. "Some people build a wall in their head when something tragic happens, Roland," she said. "It's fragile, but we keep it there to ensure that the things we don't want getting out, stay put. Your brother uses alcohol to keep his demons at bay. That's his wall. He doesn't need to talk about things because the drinking keeps it hidden."

"Well what happens to a person when he can't build that wall anymore?" Roland looked over his shoulder at the psychiatrist. "What happens if he loses everything and it's just too much?"

"He breaks."

The memory faded with the sound of Sanderson's tires squealing.

He laughed as everything came crashing down on him all at once. *I've got nothing. There's nothing else to lose anymore.* He peeled out behind Sanderson's car and out of the alley.

The nausea made his head burn. He shifted the car into the next gear and turned his head out toward the driver-side window. For just a split second, he caught a glimpse of the father and daughter from earlier running toward him.

Roland slammed on his breaks and threw the car in reverse. With Sanderson and his brother out of his life, the only thing to cling to was the anger. He didn't want to feel the hole festering in his chest, and the anger was the only thing that hadn't left him. A fire filled his lungs until he felt like he was drowning in it. *I've got nothing. No one is watching my back. Nothing is keeping my demons at bay. What's one more death on my hands before this virus kills me too?* He turned the car down the alley.

A coughing fit splattered blood onto his mask, blurring his vision. The figures both stopped short. One made impact with the car and flew several feet away. Once he came to a complete stop, Roland watched the remaining person sprint toward the one he hit. Roland grunted and lifted himself from the car. He stumbled in her direction and gripped the girl by her arm.

The girl struggled against his throbbing fingers, but his anger empowered him. He squeezed tighter. He tried to tell her he was sorry. Tried to tell her that she would probably be the last person that he took from this horrible world. *That's what this is, right?* The blood in his throat tangled with his vocal cords.

Three crisp gunshots boomed in the air. Roland released the girl and stumbled, glancing down at his chest. "Oma," he sputtered and fell backward.

He thought he knew death. He'd caused it more times than he could count; all the apartments cleared, people left in the wake of destruction—his mother. But it wasn't until he was dying that he truly realized what it was.

It wasn't salvation. It wasn't filling the missing piece.

It was relief. A relief that was only realized at your final breath.

EIGHT: *Second Chances* by Amy Bartelloni

Some mistakes you can't take back, and Sierra had made a slew of them lately. One right after the other, like a snowball rolling down a hill that she was helpless to stop. It had resulted in her wallowing in self-pity on her couch, watching a four-day marathon of *Pretty Little Liars* and *The Vampire Diaries*. Sometime during the second day, she'd turned off the home phone so she wouldn't have to hear the recording from school saying that she was absent again and in danger of failing her senior year. She thought about her father's warning to stay out of trouble and decided if he really cared, he'd just come home from his business trip. With the trial still pending, the court could go after her for truancy, but after everything that had happened she couldn't bring herself to care.

Her cell phone buzzed from under the pile of empty containers that littered the coffee table. She was just about out of food, and with her parents still away, she knew she'd have to face the world eventually. Even if it was only to fill up on Chunky Monkey with the cash they'd left behind, though the prospect of facing anyone was too daunting to think about.

Quite accidentally, the news turned on after she switched off the DVR. She hadn't seen the outside world in days, and she was avoiding her parents' voicemails, which were few and far between. Not like they cared, anyway. She flipped through the channels, and every station was reporting some stupid epidemic. Her heart skipped a beat as she thought of Jake. If she were a conspirist, like her ex-boyfriend's family, the news of the epidemic would have freaked her out.

She'd been avoiding Jake for months, though, even before the accident. He'd called a couple times to check on her, but she didn't answer. She told herself she didn't know what to say, but the truth was she was embarrassed. She'd been awful to him. The final straw between them had been when he took her to that preppers meeting with his folks, and she said some awful things that she couldn't take back. She cringed at the memory of calling his family a bunch of crazy freaks. That was her first mistake, the moment the snowball dislodged and started rolling down the hill, taking her life with it. She'd convinced herself that if she wanted to be popular she couldn't have Jake at parties sporting his stupid theories about contrails and GMOs. That was when she started hanging out with Mason anyway, and Mason was much safer, socially anyway. Captain of the football team, and every girl's dream—he'd already accepted a full scholarship to Boston College. She didn't have to worry about nuclear war or safety bunkers when she was around him. She didn't find out until after the accident that safe didn't mean anything. It didn't mean loyal, or kind, or loving. The news of widespread outbreaks brought to mind all of Jake's warnings. She wouldn't be surprised if he was right after all. He was a genius, in his own way, and he had a smile that could make her melt.

At the moment, though, she had other problems.

When she got up to grab the last tub of Ben & Jerry's from the freezer, the light on the machine blinked an ominous red, flashing off and on in warning. It illuminated the trash and empty cartons that littered the counter, bringing up a momentary pang of guilt. She'd heard the lawyer's calls earlier in the week, each message increasing in severity. Her arraignment was next week, and though her dad's lawyer was confident they'd go easy on her, she'd never forgive herself. It was only a few weeks ago when she'd taken her eyes off the road for a second, but that was long enough for Kelsey to dart out from between two cars in the school parking lot. Now Kelsey might never walk again, and Sierra's life as she knew it was over.

Mason was supportive in the beginning, but he was friends with Kelsey too. He couldn't take the pressure at school, he said, especially since Sierra wasn't there anymore to defend herself. And he probably felt guilty too; he was the one she was texting. To tell the truth, it was a relief when he bailed. Every time she looked at him she thought of the thump when she hit Kelsey, the blood that matted her blond hair, and her legs stuck out at unnatural angles.

Though it was only mid-morning, she took the carton and a spoon back to the couch. She glanced at the coffee table, strewn with trash. Her dad's *Wall Street Journals* were piling up. She'd finally stopped taking them in, and there was another pile outside the door, along with the remains of the eggs someone had thrown the previous week. At least they hadn't graduated to graffiti, not yet anyway. After people started to talk, all bets were off as far as vandalism went. The lawyer went ballistic about that, but there was nothing her parents could do. *Especially since they were on another business trip*, she thought with an inward roll of the eyes. The company her parents both worked for, Peter Franklin Donalds, was always more important than things at home. At least they asked if she would be okay this time. They even offered to get a *babysitter*. *As if.*

Her cell phone buzzed under all the newspapers and Pop-Tart wrappers, vibrating the table. Sierra switched on the TV to *The View* and tried to ignore it, but there was another news flash on. She swore and pushed all the garbage to the floor, grabbing the phone at the last minute to save it.

She looked at the number and froze.

Part of her wanted to give in and talk to Jake. At least he probably knew what was going on, but she couldn't bring herself to answer. He might have had some crazy theories, but he was sexy as all hell, and right now he was her only friend. He'd always been that weird, goofball kid that could make her laugh, ever since they were kids. But those last few months, his obsession with conspiracies became intense and she had to break it off. She didn't deserve his friendship, anyway.

As the phone stopped vibrating, she wondered where her life would be if she'd stayed with him. A lump formed in her throat as she looked up to the TV, where a reporter was standing outside a hospital, ambulances flying back and forth while she interviewed some military official who was trying to remain calm. The same kind of bullshit Jake could see from a mile away. She could almost hear him saying that when the government says things are all right, it's time to get out of town.

Before the reporter could finish her question, there was a loud bang at the door.

"Sierra, I know you're in there! Open the door."

Sierra glanced down at the phone still in her hand, as if the noise were coming from there. Jake must have called from the front step. She smiled. That was just like him. He knocked again, louder.

"I'm not leaving!" he said. She got up and shook her head. The reporter was saying something about casualties and death rate. Jake would have a field day about it. She swung the door open just as his hand was in mid-knock.

"Quiet down!" She looked past him to the family across the street who was frantically packing their belongings in their minivan. Not just suitcases, but crates of food and boxes of supplies. She froze in the door, watching the toddler crying on the front step as his parents stepped around him. The same toddler she used to babysit before the accident. Before she became untrustworthy. What was happening?

"We need to talk," Jake said. He dropped a backpack inside the door, pushed past her, and closed the door. Instinctively, she tucked a stray lock of her brown curls behind her ear in an attempt to look decent. How he could still affect her like that, she didn't know.

"Sierra." He grabbed her arm, but he didn't seem to know what to say after that. Maybe too much time had gone by, after all. Maybe there was nothing left to say. After all, 'you and your friends are a bunch of crazy freaks' speaks volumes.

"What are you doing here?" She pulled her arm out of his hand and took a breath when she walked into the living room, kicking trash aside on the way by. She cleared off a place to sit on the couch, brushing all the crap to the floor, but he didn't sit down.

"I've been trying to call you," he said, his tone somewhere between accusatory and sad.

"Yeah. Well." She picked up the ice cream carton and twirled the spoon in her fingers. "My parents have been out of town on some emergency business trip. And Mason broke up with me after the accident, so I've kind of been wallowing. I guess you were right about him after all."

"He's an idiot." Jake shook his head, and took a step toward her. He gently pulled the carton out of her hand and placed it on the table. "I'm not sorry to hear about the breakup, though."

"Jake—" she began.

"It's happening, Sierra."

"Your apocalypse?" she said, a hint of the old incredulity in her voice. Jake frowned.

"Have you been watching the news?" He gestured to the TV and Sierra was startled to see a line of gurneys on the street in front of the hospital. The bodies were covered in sheets.

"Not...really," she admitted.

"My parents got a tip," he continued. "There's a safe zone. They left already, but I snuck back for you."

Sierra's head swam. Reality crashed into skepticism. That was the thing about Jake. There was always a certain amount of sense to his madness, until it pulled you under.

"No." She sat back on the couch, paper crinkling under her. There were so many reasons she couldn't go with Jake, but her disbelief turned to fear. If there were some kind of emergency, surely she would have heard from her parents? Why hadn't she heard from them?

"You don't have a choice. It's getting bad out there. Look." He took the remote and cycled through the channels. All showed the same thing. How long had it been like this? She flipped through her text messages, but she hadn't heard from her parents in days. She tried to call her dad but it went straight to voicemail.

This is Richard Brook, Vice President of Marketing at Peter Franklin Donalds. I can't take your call right now, but please leave a message after the tone.

She didn't realize she was crying until she left the message.

"Daddy, I'm scared. What's happening? Please call me back."

She tried to count the days since the accident, since Mason broke up with her, and her parents left. They all melded into one, and some days she hadn't even bothered to get out of bed. She was only just coming around, and that was because she had to eat.

"How long has it been like this?" she asked.

"Not long," he said. "It's fast moving, and it's airborne. We should be in masks, but I don't know if we need them." He looked away. *Airborne*, she thought. She knew what that meant. They were dead.

A laugh escaped her mouth, hysterics, she supposed, as Jake retrieved his backpack from the hall. He unzipped it and pulled out a facemask, the kind they ask you to wear at the doctor's office when it's flu season.

"It's not the best, but it could help," he said. She took it from him and held it up: a tangible, concrete item to show that she had gone crazy.

"I'm not supposed to leave the state, Jake." She tried to hand it back to him. "I can't do this right now."

"That doesn't matter anymore, Sierra. If you don't come with me, you won't even make it to next week."

She'd heard him talk about the end of the world before, and she'd always brushed it off and laughed at him. He knew what it sounded like, and he'd laugh right along with her, even while attempting to convince her to buy a bunker with him when they graduated and go off the grid. This time, there was no laughing. Even with the end of the world pending, the accident weighed heavily on her mind.

"It was my fault," she said. He sat next to her on the couch and put an arm around her. "I was texting Mason. I didn't even see her." The words came out as muffled sobs, the last ones almost unintelligible. She cried into his shoulder as he smoothed her hair back.

He didn't attempt to make her feel better by changing the subject or telling a stupid joke, which Mason used to do. Jake just held her. She didn't know how long she cried. Time was something that had lost meaning after the accident. She finally lifted her head to see the destruction on the television. The reporter her parents always watched, Amy Savino, was almost frantic.

"It's really happening?" Sierra sat back and wiped her eyes. "You were right about everything."

"I don't know about that," he answered. He pulled his arm back and met her eyes. "There were some things I screwed up on." The last statement hung in the air, and Sierra's thoughts turned to her parents again. She pulled out her phone and dialed both of them, but she couldn't get a signal and the phone's charge ebbed down below twenty percent.

"I should pack, I guess." She stood up and looked around the living room. The mess was everywhere, and she couldn't begin to think about what she needed. The biggest baggage she had was coming with her whether she wanted it or not: guilt, sadness, regret.

"Just a backpack. A few changes of clothes," Jake slipped into his planning mode and Sierra couldn't help but think how quickly her world had turned upside down. She thought back to all his disaster talk, and seemed to remember him talking about taking weapons. If that's what he was expecting, he'd be disappointed. The only weapon she had was a nail file.

"Okay." She followed his orders, and went upstairs. She dumped her schoolbag and filled it with clothes, slipping in a photo of her and Kelsey from drama club the year before. Sierra ran her hand over their faces with their innocent smiles, and swore she wouldn't forget her. She'd spend the rest of her life paying, one way or another.

"Let's go." She came down the stairs and handed the backpack to Jake in the kitchen. He took a couple jars of peanut butter—the only thing left—threw them in the pack, and zipped it closed. Before they reached the front door, he pulled a mask over his face, then adjusted hers. He let his hand linger by her ear for just a minute before he turned and opened the door.

The neighbors had packed their van so full that their kid looked pressed against the window in the back. Sierra gave them a sad wave as the dad swerved out of the driveway and took off down the street. Around them a couple of other families looked in the throes of packing and leaving, but other than that, the street was mostly silent. It was late afternoon, but there were no kids outside playing.

"Where are they going?" Sierra asked.

"Out of the city," he said. The minivan stopped at the end of the street and honked, but whatever was in the road didn't move. The van drove up and over the sidewalk, but still hit part of the object with a loud thump. The familiar noise made Sierra want to gag.

"Is that—"

"A body. Let's go."

The SUV had always been cluttered, but now it was filled to the brim; there was just enough room in the passenger's seat. Jake let them take the masks off in the car. She let hers hang on her neck, like a piece of costume jewelry.

"Is that where we're going? Out of the city?" She placed the backpack with her meager possessions by her feet. Once, she would have prized so much more than what was in the bag. Stylish clothes and jewelry were left behind, even the diamond earrings her dad had given her for her sweet sixteen. A consolation prize, as he'd been away on a business trip that week. She picked up her phone and tried to call them again, then sent a text, which remained undelivered. She sighed as Jake pulled away from the curb, keeping her eyes away from the body as they turned the other way. They reached the top of the hill, and smoke rose like a plume from the direction of downtown Greenwich, Connecticut.

"We can follow my parents into the safe zone. I copied their map of Staten Island." He leaned forward and concentrated on the road. She opened her mouth to ask another question when he stopped short, holding her back from the dashboard even though she was wearing a seatbelt.

A police car swerved around them, zigzagging up the street. Jake held his breath as it careened straight into a telephone pole. Sierra screamed at the sound of the crash, as the hood crinkled and smoke rose from the cruiser.

"We have to help!" She reached for the handle, but Jake stopped her.

"We can't," he said, sadly. The officer shouldered the door open, and stumbled out. He was covered in blood and yelled something incoherent. The noisy siren had shut off, but blue lights flashed and made him look like a nightmare come to life. Sierra sobbed and looked away as Jake inched the car forward.

"We're going as far as we can by car, then we'll head out on foot." he said. "It's not far. The safe zone is on Staten Island."

"How are we going to get there?" she asked. Already the streets didn't seem safe. A gun went off in the distance.

"Leave it to me," he said.

New Haven wasn't far from Staten Island, and the car ride was filled with things that they didn't say. Sierra wondered where Mason was, and fiddled with her phone as she thought about warning him. Then she thought about the snide comment he'd made about Kelsey the last time she'd seen him. It was the lowest point in her life. She called him anyway, thinking she could use the karma points, but her phone wouldn't connect. She managed to get through to her mom's phone, which went right to voicemail, and this time she left a message. She tried to control the panic in her voice when she told her mom where she was going, and asked her to please call back. As she disconnected, she realized she didn't even know where they had gone this time. Peter Franklin Donalds sent them everywhere, so they might not even be in the country. They weren't close, but she had an ache in her chest at the fact she might not ever see them again.

Jake crept slowly through trashed suburban areas. They tried to keep the radio on, but it was all depressing newscasts. Sierra switched it off.

"Back at my house, you said something about the masks," she said. The closer they got to Staten Island, the more people they saw headed the same way, in cars and on foot, a slow shuffle of refugees.

"I don't think we need them," he said. He drove past a suburban convenience store. The front glass had been broken and people were taking armloads of stuff out. Jake slowed down as someone ran across the street carrying cases of soda balanced one on top of the other. Sierra trembled and slid down in her seat as one kid pointed to their car and started shouting, but Jake sped past them.

"Why don't we need the masks?" she asked, once they'd passed all the commotion.

He risked a sideways look at her, and the corner of his lip pulled up into that familiar half smile.

"You're going to think it's crazy," he teased.

"I think we've gone past that," she said, a mixture of humor and guilt in her voice.

"I think we're immune."

"Why would you think that?" He looked at her with that sideways smile again, so she knew what he was about to say would be out there.

"Spit it out," she said with mock anger.

"Some people just are," he shrugged. "I took care of my uncle Nick, in the beginning. He was one of the first ones to come down with this thing. I stayed with him the whole time, even went to the hospital with him. They were overflowing by then."

"Did he make it?"

"No." Jake paused for a minute. "They made me leave the hospital, eventually, but he was out of it by then. That's when my parents got serious about leaving for Staten Island."

"I'm so sorry," Sierra said. She liked his uncle, and remembered that Jake was really close to him. Jake cleared his throat.

"Anyway, I never came down with it. I got some mild cold for a couple days, which is why we didn't leave right away. My parents kept an eye on me but none of us got it."

Sierra let his story sink in. Nick was dead, and how many others?

"Do you remember when your dad started working at PFD?" Jake changed the subject.

"Yeah, what about it?"

"All those tests they put your family through? I think that was some kind of experiment, for a cure or something." Sierra had to fight an urge to roll her eyes. Old habits die hard.

"They were for a physical," she argued. Her parent's employer had been a huge source of tension between them. Jake was convinced that PFD was up to no good, then his family joined the preppers which fueled his paranoia. Sierra had to admit, the company took up all her parent's time the last few years, but that didn't make them evil.

"I think it was more than that," Jake said, becoming animated. "What if PFD knew this outbreak was going to happen? What if they were already testing people for it before? Like to find natural immunity or something. Or maybe they tested something on you? There are rumors of an inoculation—"

"Jake—" she began. It was an old argument between them.

"They have the contract for the vaccine!"

"What?" That threw her off kilter. She was used to his arguments, but he rarely had facts to back it up.

"They announced it a couple days ago," he said. "They say it's not finished—but…" He trailed off.

"Oh, my God," she said. "My parents were part of this. They could be involved." She rolled the phone back and forth in her hand, but even if the charge weren't dead she couldn't get a hold of them.

"It's not your fault."

The words were a trigger. Maybe that wasn't her fault, but there were plenty of things that were. She tried to focus. They'd driven off the main road on to an abandoned side street in a residential neighborhood.

"You think we're immune, then?" she asked. Jake put the SUV in park and let the engine idle while he took a CB radio out to fiddle with the dials.

"It's possible," he said.

That didn't sit well with her. As he worked with the CB, she laced the mask over her face and got out to get some fresh air. He reached someone on the CB, one of his parent's friends. She strained to hear the conversation, but only heard something about a bridge. She'd only gone off a couple of paces when he swung the door open behind her.

"They're screening people," he said spoke through the mask. "At the bridge. As long as you're healthy, you're in."

"In where? Is anywhere really safe?"

Sierra looked up and down the street. They were in a neighborhood of single-family homes. All were empty and quiet except for the wail of a distant siren. She fought the urge to climb into one and just fall asleep until the nightmare passed.

"Everyone in the group is headed to Staten Island," Jake said. "It's safe there."

"I don't know," she said.

"You'd rather take your chances out here?" he asked.

"No, I guess not," she said. She started toward the car but froze when a curtain moved inside the house.

"What is it?" Jake asked. Sierra shielded the sun from her eyes.

"I think it's a kid," she said. She pointed to the window, where a head was barely visible over the windowsill, two wide eyes imploring her to help.

"So?" Jake said, but he cut the engine.

"We have to help her," she said. She thought of the accident and Kelsey. It wouldn't make up for it, nothing would, but maybe it was a start. She took a step toward the house, still not sure what to do. Sure, she used to babysit, but that only involved some Disney DVD's and an early bedtime. And Jake was an only child himself. They couldn't leave her there alone, though.

"I'll go," he said. He got out of the car and joined her in the yard. The kid had disappeared from the window and the house was quiet again. She reached for Jake's hand and gave it a squeeze. He was risking a lot taking her with him, and now the kid. She'd forgotten how much she missed his kindness.

"Can I, like, cover you or something?" she asked. He laughed.

"If you'd actually taken those shooting lessons I suggested, then maybe. As it is, I'd fear for my own life if I left you armed." He handed her the keys to the SUV, and let his hand linger in hers.

"I never stopped loving you, Sierra. Even when you changed."

"I didn't change." She shook her head. "Not really. I just forgot what was important."

He smiled, like he was going to say more, then let go of her hand. She had to look away when her chest tightened from the emotion of it all. She heard him climb the steps and knock. The kid looked through the glass to the side of the door, but didn't open it.

"Is your mom or dad home?" Jake asked. The kid shook her head and Sierra got her first view of the little girl. She was six or seven, maybe. Sierra was never very good at ages. Her oversized shirt was a ripped mess, even from this distance, and her brown hair was matted. But her tears were what struck Sierra the most. No kid that age should have that haunted look in her eyes. It was a look Sierra understood.

"I can help you." Jake knelt down to the kid's level, and the door opened a crack. "There's a place that's safe, I can bring you there." He turned to give Sierra a thumbs up as the door opened, and he disappeared into the house. Sierra hovered by the car for several tense minutes before he came out holding the girl's hand. He opened Sierra's door and Sierra squeezed in with the girl on her lap, the only open space in the SUV.

"She's six, and her name is Kylie," Jake said.

"Um, hi," Sierra said. She shifted uncomfortably on the seat. "I'm Sierra." She took stock of the kid, who was in rough shape. Tear-stained face and brown hair that was matted and tangled at her shoulders. She'd changed into a pink shirt and sweatpants that were a size too small. Sierra softened, and put her arms around the girl's waist.

"You're safe, now," she whispered as Jake got in and pulled away.

"Her parents?" Sierra asked quietly. Jake shook his head.

"The virus," he said. "They've been gone for a few days. Kylie was surviving on her own." Sierra felt a rush of sympathy for the girl.

"What about her?" she asked.

"All this time, she's probably immune."

They didn't speak for a while, but Kylie cried softly on Sierra's lap. She held a small bag that Jake had hastily packed, along with a stuffed elephant. Sierra shifted so she could hold Jake's hand over the console. She thought about apologizing to him, but she had no idea where to even begin. The list of crappy things she'd done was at least a mile long. Besides, her daddy used to say that a real apology was in actions, not words; but it didn't hurt to try.

"I'm sorry, Jake," she began. It wasn't just because she had no choice. She'd realized it before the accident, before she made a mess of things and before Mason dumped her. Before the world proved that Jake was right. She just didn't know how to make it right.

"Not now," he said. He'd tensed when she took his hand, but he softened and ran his thumb over the back of her hand. "I heard from one of my parent's friends over the CB. He said Goethals Bridge is the only one that's open. There's some kind of checkpoint; he was about to go in. My parents are already in there."

"Okay," she said. "But have you heard from anyone who's actually inside?" He pulled the car into a parking lot and cut the engine.

"Well, no, but what choice do we have?"

She couldn't argue with that. It wasn't like she had made any apocalyptic plans, and the Four Seasons was out of the question. He got out and stuffed as much as they could carry in the backpacks. He pocketed the keys to the SUV and handed her a folded map to hang on to. She shoved it in her pocket.

"We can walk from here," he said, putting on his mask and taking out an extra for Kylie. She didn't fight him when he laced it on her. Sierra knelt and adjusted it for her.

"This is going to keep us safe, until we can get into the safe zone. Can you keep it on for me?" Kylie nodded, and the level of trust in her look humbled Sierra. She hugged the girl and swallowed her tears so Kylie wouldn't see. She needed to be strong.

They made their way to the highway, and the crowd got heavier. The groups around them were a ragtag mix that ranged from full HAZMAT suits to stragglers who were obviously sick. Jake kept them away from the infected as much as he could, and when fights broke out, he helped them avoid those as well. By the time they got to the bridge, it wasn't just the virus Sierra was scared of, but the other survivors too.

Sierra's fear kicked up a notch as they joined the queue at the entrance to the bridge and people approached in various types of protective gear. It all looked so alien to her, especially the masks with the big bug eyes, but the ones not wearing anything, and the ones with flimsy masks like Jake and Kylie, looked so vulnerable. Behind her, someone sneezed, and the person next to her wiped blood off his nose. There was the smell of death in the air, of desperation and humanity, as they were jostled along in the line toward the concrete barriers. The guards holding guns over the crowd did nothing to ease her fears. Her shoulder ached with the weight of the backpack, and Kylie was so close, she was almost hugging her leg.

"I heard there's a vaccine in there," someone said. The guy next to her snorted a laugh, which broke into a coughing fit.

"They'll probably just shoot us all," he said, wiping blood on his sleeve. "Decrease the surplus population."

A scuffle broke out between the two men, and a punch flew close to Sierra's head. Jake moved them away, and worked his way through the swell of people trying to stay away from anyone obviously diseased. Sniffles and cries echoed through the crowd, and the feeling of loss hung over everyone. It was more than Sierra could take. She stopped to make sure Kylie's mask was secure.

"Almost there," she told the girl, but she couldn't stop wondering what they were walking into. She was no scientist; in fact she was close to failing anatomy before the accident, but she was pretty sure an airborne virus couldn't be contained on an island. There was no going back, though. The force of the crowd propelled them forward and she felt protective of Jake and Kylie.

They reached the entrance to the bridge, where guards leered at the crowd from behind their masks. Once in a while gunshots echoed from the other side of the bridge, past where the tents were set up. She couldn't see beyond them, but it didn't give her a good feeling. They passed a set of concrete barriers with the next wave of refugees, then they were separated into lines where they waited to go into the tents. Ahead of her, people shuffled nervously as they entered the tent a few at a time.

"This is it, then?" Sierra asked. She tightened her hold on Kylie's hand. Many of the refugees were in pairs of two or three, but some were alone. There were mostly adults, with a few kids mixed in. Sierra shuddered to think what would have become of Kylie if they hadn't found her. Already she'd become attached to the little girl.

"No going back now," Jake said. His voice didn't inspire confidence.

They kept to the back of the line that had formed on the bridge and waited their turn to enter the tented-off section. The refugees were pulled aside one by one and screened by men in black tactical suits with facemasks. She had a bad feeling when an older man and woman wearing olive green rubber suits were pulled out of line ahead of them and fought with the guards.

"What's happening?" Kylie asked softly. Sierra just had time to turn the girl's head away when two gunshots rang out. They were so close that Sierra's ears rang. She couldn't even hear the sound of her own screaming for several seconds. The group started to break out in hysterics. People shoved and Jake grabbed Kylie just before Sierra was pushed down to her knees. She was close to being trampled when someone yanked her up by the arm. She turned her head to see the diamond shaped logo for PFD on her savior's arm. The crowd quieted as he shot his gun in the air to get control.

She met Jake's eyes through the sea of people. He had Kylie by the arm, but he couldn't get to Sierra. She turned to the soldier to plead her case, but she couldn't get past the PFD patch. Was Jake right about the company after all? As the chaos of the shooting subsided, Sierra tried to jerk out of the man's hold.

"I don't think so, sweetheart," he said. She couldn't see through the mask, but she didn't know many of her dad's coworkers anyway. While Jake fought to get back to her, she took a chance.

"I'm looking for my father," she said in a voice full of false optimism. Jake had gotten them this far, but she'd have to get them the rest of the way. It wasn't just her and Jake any more, but Kylie's life depended on it. The guard's hold never wavered. If anything, it got stronger.

"Nice try," he said, and he pulled her away from the line. She got a view of another guard pushing Jake and Kylie back in line before she was dragged to the other side of the tent. They were dangerously close to the side of the bridge. The wind whipped her hair up and around her face, and she had the feeling she was going over.

"Richard Brook!" she yelled, and held her other hand up. "Richard Brook is my father! He works for PFD!" Her hand trembled as she pointed to the patch on the man's arm. His hold wavered for just a minute.

"Marketing!" she said, miserably. "He works in marketing, or at least I thought he did." She had a feeling that many things about her parents, and Peter Franklin Donalds, weren't what she thought they were.

The guard took out a radio and mumbled something about her father's name. She thought he kept his eyes on her, but it was hard to tell with his mask. Her arm was starting to throb from the pressure of his fingers. It would leave a bruise for sure, which was the least of her problems.

"Lucky girl," he loosened his hold. "You're in." He shoved her toward the tent, and before she knew what was happening, he grabbed her hand and she felt a prick on her finger.

"OW!" she cried. She scanned the tent for Jake or Kylie but couldn't find them.

"She's clear," a voice echoed. She was pushed along to the other side of the tent, and fell back into another crowd as she emerged and was shuffled into another line.

Staten Island wasn't yet visible through the crowd. She stood on tiptoe, but no one was familiar. Far ahead, someone who looked like Jake carried a young, brown haired little girl that could have been Kylie. They were approaching another checkpoint. Sierra yelled as loud as she could, but either they couldn't hear her over the noise or it wasn't Jake. They disappeared in the sea of people and Sierra started to panic.

She tried to get to them any way she could, pushing and elbowing her way to the front. Someone swung at her, and when she ducked, he connected with the man beside her instead and a fight broke out. She used it to her advantage, and shoved her way through the next checkpoint. It made her a target and the guards started to come at her from every direction. Every instinct told her to flee. She dropped her backpack as she ran, pushing people aside here and there. Gunshots fired behind her and people screamed, but she tucked her head in and kept running. She lost the guards soon after she made it off the bridge, but she kept running as far and fast as she could.

When she finally stopped, she'd lost not only the guards but Jake and Kylie as well, and she had no supplies. She'd ended up on a street full of stores, or one that used to be full of stores. For a safe zone, it was eerily empty. She ducked in an alley and leaned against a building to catch her breath. She could have let the guards take her, but she couldn't drag Jake and Kylie into this mess with PFD before she knew exactly what her parents' role in the company was. And to do that, she'd have to find Jake and Kylie too. Not just because she needed his help, but because she needed him. He'd been right all along, but she had been too stubborn to see it. This time, when she found him, she wasn't letting go. And she would find him. If she had to comb Staten Island, even if she had to resort to her father's help.

She felt her pocket and realized she still had the map Jake had given her. Staying in the building's shadow, she pulled it out and unfolded it. There was an address circled three times in red. A warehouse, it looked like. It was just like Jake to think of everything. She looked up to the horizon where the sun was just setting. If she had any luck, she'd make it by nightfall. Luck hadn't been on her side much lately, but it was about time for that to change. It was about time for her to have a second chance, and she'd fight for it. Somewhere, Jake and Kylie were waiting for her, and she'd do anything to get back to them.

NINE: *Nan Tapper*
by Laura Albins

Owen watched the yellow lines in the centre of the tarmac reel past, listened to the gentle hum of the wheels as his bike sped down the deserted street. The air was hot and heavy but so long as he was moving he could keep alive the illusion of a breeze.

The incline steepened as it took him toward the western edge of town and the bike's whirring intensified as it sped up. Owen racked his brain, trying to recall the layout of the suburb. He'd never been there before the outbreak, but the side of town where he'd grown up was getting trickier. Survivors coming in from the villages, stealing, causing trouble. There were still a few people around but those left alive were dealing with the sick, or were sick themselves. The Fever had struck fast. Within days everything had been turned on its head and Owen had found himself stuck in a strange other world where he could no longer guess how people would behave or who he could trust.

The stores in town had been cleared before the sickness even arrived. Twenty-four-hour news reports had whipped panicked shoppers into a frenzy, stocking up for the worst, when it was already too late. Probably eighty percent of all the food, water, medical supplies…everything deemed necessary to survive the end of the world…lay untouched, surrounded by the recent dead.

Turned out survival wasn't a choice, a reward you could earn, a product you could buy. It was luck, pure and simple. Random selection: those the virus took…and those it left behind. For some reason Owen had yet to fathom, he belonged to the latter.

He steered left and freewheeled down the crescent to the gated community at the bottom. Straddling the entrance was a gaudy sign emblazoned with '*Sunnydale Retirement Village.*' The gates were open, just like the day before, only this time he'd come prepared. He adjusted his empty backpack and removed the panniers from the bike.

Sunnydale was deserted, the elderly residents long gone. A few of his nana's friends had lived there, though Owen didn't know exactly which ones. What did it matter? Whoever they were, they were long gone. One way or another.

Owen wheeled the bike round the side of an outbuilding and eased it behind a bush to hide it from view. The place might look deserted but he'd learned the hard way that things had a nasty habit of disappearing, even—or especially—when you least expected it.

He'd already picked where to go, and marked where to avoid. He passed the doors with the four, bold letters spray painted in black from the day before: DEAD. The markings were hardly necessary—in the midsummer heat, most times you knew which places housed the dead without even having to open the door—but he liked to make sure he didn't stumble across dead bodies any more times than he had to. He kept going until he reached the ones without the spray paint, the ones he wanted.

After just two apartments his backpack was full. Packets of pasta, rice, and beans. Batteries and matches, band aids, dressings, bottles of pills. He had no idea what the pills were but had a feeling his nana would.

Owen returned to the bushes, his heart thudding—suddenly filled with a sense that he wasn't alone, that his bike would be gone… He breathed out. There it was, exactly as he'd left it. But on the first count he was right. He was no longer alone.

She was just a girl. Around his sister's age, fourteen or so. Average height, dark brown bangs that hid half her face. On her back she carried a weird looking sling full of supplies while in her hand she held a tatty, lumpy string bag. It didn't look like she'd washed in a while.

"I saw you here yesterday," she said, stepping forward as he dragged his bike out of its hiding place. "Where are you staying?" Owen attached the bulky panniers to the bike, determined to ignore her. "Do you have somewhere? Somewhere safe?"

"I can't help you," he said.

"Please," she added, turning her head at a faint sound from behind her. The sound turned into a high pitched hiccupping and then a full blown cry. Owen stared as the sling on her back wiggled and twisted before a chubby, angry arm flailed out from the top. "We're all alone. My parents…" The girl stopped, the word lodged in her throat.

Owen took a carton of milk from one of the panniers and held it out. "There's plenty more inside."

She accepted the milk, but it was clear she wanted more than food.

"Can't I come with you?"

"No. I'm sorry." He nodded his head back up toward the hill. "Town's that way. You'll find help there." His gut twisted. Guilt.

He turned, cursing under his breath at the sight of the hill up ahead. No chance of a quick getaway, not with the heavy backpack and the panniers. He set off anyway, sensing without looking that she would follow.

"Please," she called. "Wait."

Owen pushed on and her voice faded as his mind zoned out, retreated into nothingness. A place where he was numb, where nothing or no one could reach him.

Finally he reached the brow of the hill. Without looking back he threw his leg over the saddle and pedalled like the very devil was behind him.

He arrived back at the farm just before sundown. The gate into the long driveway was kept locked against strangers but on impulse he tugged at the faded sign, turning it round until the neat stencilled letters spelling 'Hollow Tree Farm' faced backward. On the blank side he scrawled with his spray can 'FEVER HERE.' Nan Tapper wouldn't make it down the drive in her wheelchair, at least not without his help, in which case he'd be able to sneak the sign back around before she saw it.

"You're late," said Nan as he arrived at the porch steps. Her beady eyes took in the backpack and the panniers. "Did you see your mum today?" she added when Owen didn't answer.

He shook his head. "She's too sick for visitors right now. I told you that."

"Hm." She didn't look satisfied, but with Nan Tapper that wasn't unusual.

Owen dumped his pack on the bottom step and unstrapped the panniers. "Nana, you're meant to stay inside when I'm not here. Remember?"

The old lady huffed. "You'd have me roasted like a chicken…"

"Nana…"

"Oh, I know," she grumbled, releasing the brake on her chair and wheeling herself indoors.

"Just give us a sec and I'll make dinner," he called, wheeling his bike round the back and up the rickety wheelchair ramp.

"I can make dinner. I'm not totally incapable," she replied, amidst a loud clattering from the kitchen.

Owen wiped sweat from his eyes and walked back to the front, scanning the yard, the driveway, the woods, looking for any sign of strangers. The farm was secluded, surrounded by thick forest at the front and the river out back, but Owen felt sure that someone would remember the old farm at the end of the lane. One day, probably soon, someone would come.

What he would do then, he didn't know.

"You coming in then, or you just gonna stand out there all evenin'?"

With one last glance, Owen turned and headed inside.

Hollow Tree wasn't really a farm anymore. As his grandparents got older they'd been able to do less and less and when Grandpa Tapper passed, Nan stopped the working side completely. But the farmhouse was still home and she would never leave without a fight.

"Something happen today?" she asked, ladling pasta onto his plate.

Owen fingered the knife on the table. He knew he should be hungry but the sudden knot in his stomach wouldn't let him enjoy the food. "I went to Sunnydale."

"And?"

"There's a lot of stuff there." He forked up some food and put it in his mouth, made himself chew and swallow.

"See anybody?"

He shook his head and concentrated on his plate—chew and swallow, chew and swallow—but he could feel her eyes on him. As though she knew what he'd done, leaving that girl and the baby... Was it the right thing? The wrong thing? He still hadn't decided.

After a few moments of silence she finished her last mouthful and wiped her lips with a napkin. "You'll go and see your mum tomorrow?"

Owen stopped, the fork an inch from his mouth. "I'll try."

Unbidden, unwanted, a memory sneaked through the wall he'd built in his mind.

Sunlight and sweat, white fingertips pressed against glass...

"She needs you more than I do. And there's your sister to think of..."

"I know."

"You can take them some of my applesauce," she added, putting the plates and the cutlery together. "See how they're getting along. Then you can come back here and tell me all about it."

* * *

The next day he went to Sunnydale again. Owen didn't need more food right away but the more they could stockpile, the better.

That's what he told himself.

He found himself heading for the same place behind the bushes, waiting there awhile before heading into another apartment. Then when he was done collecting supplies he waited again, longer this time. But there was no sign of the girl.

Perhaps she'd headed into town like he'd told her, found help after all. Or perhaps…

He stopped himself, determined not to think about it anymore, but before he left he took Nan's jars of applesauce from his backpack and set them on the ground. Then he set off up the hill back toward the woods.

The man came out of nowhere.

One moment Owen was pedalling along the path, the next something big and heavy crashed into him, knocking him into the dirt. He grunted in pain as gravel scraped down his whole left side and before he could even recover his bike was ripped away. "What the hell?" Looking up he saw a skinny man in overalls hovering over him, Owen's bike in his grasp.

"Stay down, kid." The man talked tough but his eyes were nervous, darting around like he didn't know what to do next—or maybe, Owen thought with a stab of fear, he was waiting for back-up. Back when he'd still dared to head into the centre, when there had still been a chance of finding his dad there, he'd seen a lot of survivors. At first they'd been disoriented, stunned into a state of co-operation. But soon enough they'd started forming groups, some good, some bad… Owen had quickly decided to avoid them all.

"Give me back my bike," he said, getting to his feet.

The skinny guy shook his head and gestured to Owen's backpack. "What else you got?"

"Give it back!"

"Or what?"

The man didn't look that strong, but that didn't stop Owen feeling scared. He wasn't used to fighting. He didn't want to get hurt. But he really, really needed his bike. Before he could think about it he lunged.

They struggled over the bike in a surreal tug of war, as intense as it was brief. The man was taller but Owen's backpack lent him momentum and he managed to wrench the bike away, swinging it round like a weapon until it smashed into his opponent, knocking him to the ground. Both of them were panting hard, the man's disbelief turning to anger as he fingered the blood pouring from a deep gash on his head. "You little shit," he said.

His anger shook Owen into action. He mounted the battered bike and took off.

The man started yelling, his voice following Owen all the way down the street. "I know you—Owen Tapper!" he said. "I know you!"

When Owen reached the woods, he dismounted, almost falling down in his haste to get under cover of the trees. He stumbled over the uneven ground, pushing his bike like a battering ram. His nerves were singing from the fight, stomach churning at the thought of all that blood. He hadn't meant to hurt the guy, but it had been instinctual. A visceral reaction to protect what was his. To escape.

The woods were quiet but he kept looking back, scared that the man had followed him. But that was impossible; he'd left him way behind. Still, Owen couldn't forget the man's words:

I know you! Owen Tapper!

He knew Owen's name. Did he know where he lived? Where his nana lived?

Owen tried to calm down, but it was no use—and when a figure stepped out from behind a bush he jumped a foot in the air. "Jesus! Dammit!"

"You," he said. "What are you doing here?" The girl looked guilty. "You followed me?"

She looked even dirtier than before. And scared. "I didn't know what else to do. I went into town like you said but...it's bad there. They're stealing, fighting...and worse." She swallowed. "I couldn't..."

"Quiet!" His head whipped round, listening. For a second there was silence, then he heard it again. The unmistakable sound of bodies moving through the forest...and men's voices. "You followed me. And they followed you," he added. "You led them right here!"

Her eyes widened. "I'm sorry..."

"Shh." The men were close. Owen knew that running was hopeless. He scanned the trees for a hiding place. "Over there."

They crammed themselves into the half decayed trunk. A few paces away, Owen's bike lay hidden underneath a heap of ferns. The girl pressed closer and his nose stung with the smell of dirt and sweat, while in its sling the baby whimpered. "Can't you keep it quiet?" he whispered.

"*It* is a she. And no, I can't. She's five months old." Still, she adjusted the sling to angle the child into her chest and the whimpering subsided.

Finally they were quiet. For a precious few moments the sounds subsided and Owen began to hope…but within seconds the rustling and snapping started up again. Closer. The men had ceased their chatter, concentrating on finding their prey, but Owen could hear them all the same. Heavy, laden with weapons and supplies, swaggering through the new world like they owned it.

When they reached the area by the tree, Owen held his breath, hoping they wouldn't look too closely. The trees were full and lush, heavy with midsummer, but if any of the men poked around too much they'd find the hollow trunk. He sensed them moving outside, pacing like sniffer dogs.

"She's not here," said one, sounding bored.

"Oh and where'd she go then, smart ass?"

"I'm beat," said another, younger voice. Owen gave a start as he recognised the lazy drawl. Cam Starling. Beloved quarterback and supposed all-round nice guy. Maybe not anymore. "Let's just go back." Cam came closer, until he was only yards from their hideout.

"Kid's right," said the first speaker. "There's other girls back at Pete's." At that moment Cam came into view and Owen's heart leapt into his mouth. Another step and he'd be right on top of the bike. Seconds slowed, dripping like treacle as Owen fixed his eyes on the boy's feet, praying he wouldn't come any closer.

"Yeah but she was real pretty…" said the second man. He cursed. "Fine. Let's go."

Owen let out a shuddering breath as their footsteps receded, though it was a few minutes before he dared set foot out of hiding. Even after they were sure the men had gone, the girl clung onto his arm, as though fear had frozen her to him. Angry, Owen shook her off and strode over to snatch his bike from underneath the ferns.

"Don't follow me again," he said.

* * *

Back at the farm Owen let Nan help clean up his cuts and grazes from the fall, too exhausted to protest. It was only when they'd finished, sitting on the back porch with comforting tea, that she asked him what happened.

"I fell off my bike."

Nan didn't ask any more questions. She just stared at the river until darkness slid over the sky. When the light was gone, Owen wheeled her inside and helped her get ready for bed. All the time he was distracted, thinking about the girl with the baby, the men in the forest…the man who tried to take his bike.

I know you!

There was still a world out there and he couldn't avoid it forever.

It was a long time before he could sleep. He thought about Nan, about how he could protect her if the men came to the farm. The short answer was, he didn't know. He didn't know what he would do.

His father would have known. His mother would have smoothed Owen's brow and told him it was going to be all right. But the Fever had come and nothing was ever going to be all right again.

The next morning when he came down for breakfast, Nan was already up. On the table lay a glass of tea, a bowl of oatmeal…and a 9mm brushed steel Luger pistol.

* * *

Owen knew how to use a gun. As a cop, his dad had wanted Owen to know how to handle one should the need arise, but Owen's mother had drawn the line at keeping a gun in the house. Grandpa Tapper kept a shotgun, rifles for hunting…and apparently a 9mm Luger, which now sat snug in the front pocket of Owen's backpack.

Even with the pistol for protection, he decided to take a day off from foraging. There was plenty to do around the farm, sections of fence to mend, ground to be cleared.

In the woods it was peaceful. He could forget the day before—the weeks before—and remember how life used to be. Him and his sister playing hide and seek, sent off for the day with a picnic and their swimsuits. Long summer evenings lying in bed, his parents downstairs—the soft tones of their conversation lulling them to sleep. Before he knew it, the day was almost gone.

When he got back to the house, it was quiet, the front porch empty. He headed round the back, pleased that his nana had finally listened and stayed indoors. Until he saw the blood on the ramp.

Owen scrabbled in his pack for the pistol, thanking the Lord he'd loaded it already, as a man's voice sounded inside the house. His heart pounded as he crept up to the back door, ears straining to make out the words. The voice sounded strange and the words ran on in a constant stream, without pause. Owen took a deep breath and swung the door open wide.

There was a crash as the pot Nan was holding slipped from her hands. "Owen! What the heck? You scared the bejeesus out of me!"

He stopped and stared, taking in the empty room. "There's blood outside," he said. "On the ramp."

"I know." Nan reached up to lower the volume on the radio perched atop the sideboard. "Been waiting for you to get back and clean it up for me. We got a visitor, well two…" She considered. "Maybe one and a half."

Owen stood in the doorway, speechless. Visitors… the radio… He didn't know where to start. "How long have you been listening to that?" he asked finally.

Nan hoisted a pan of water onto the stove and lit the gas. "Every day since 1978." She wheeled the chair around to face him. "I know what you've been doing, babe. And I appreciate your trying to protect me, but I'm eighty three. There's not much gets past me anymore. Now why don't you go and clean up outside while I make us a nice cup of tea." A cry came from upstairs. "Looks like we woke baby," she said, looking up as the girl appeared at the top of the stairs, feet sporting one purple spotted sock and one tight, white bandage. "How's your foot, love?"

"It's better. Thank you."

"Ester, this is Owen." The girl stared at him. "Owen, this is Ester." Owen stared back. "And Jojo," said Nana, smiling at the baby who stared at everyone and everything.

Dinner was tense, Nana acting like they entertained visitors every day, Owen avoiding the girl's gaze while she eyed him as though she thought he'd chase her out of the house given half a chance. Which right now he had to admit he felt like doing. Only the baby seemed to be enjoying herself, kicking her legs in the air.

"Why didn't you tell me you knew?" Owen asked Nana later, once the girl had gone to bed. "About the Fever?"

"I figured you'd tell me, when you were ready."

"Mom…and Hope…" Owen tried to swallow the lump in his throat, but it wouldn't go down. "I don't know where Dad is…"

They were silent, the ticking of the clock the only sound. Owen felt like he was holding his breath, but the truth was he'd been holding in a whole lot more, for the longest time. He couldn't do it anymore.

Nan didn't say anything. She just took his hands between hers, like she had when he was a child, and let him cry it out.

In the morning when he woke the world felt different—like a page had been turned or a line crossed over.

The baby had been up most of the night and by the time he got down for breakfast Ester was upstairs asleep again. Nana watched him eat, like a dog waiting for the leftovers, and the second he'd finished she gestured to the back door. "We need to talk," she said.

They settled themselves on the back porch. In front of them the water drifted by, calm, meandering. Hard to believe that their gentle river wound along into the Hudson, the current taking it all the way down to New York City, to the Atlantic...gateway to the world. Owen had often dreamed he might go there someday. But like a schooner in a storm, the world had been sunk, taking his dreams down with it.

"That girl's been telling me about the gangs in town," said Nan. "How they're stealing stuff, hurting people. Not enough police left to stop them taking what they want." She paused. "They're going to want what we've got, Owen—and we're not going to be able to stop them from taking it. You know that, don't you? It's time to think about getting out, before they come."

Owen was silent. He thought she was right, but leaving was a scary prospect. He'd felt safe at the farm. No bodies, no looting or fighting, no emergency broadcasts on the TV. At Hollow Tree Farm he'd almost been able to pretend that none of it was real.

"But where would we go? The Fever's everywhere. Even if I could drive we don't have a car—and most of the roads are blocked."

Nan folded her hands in her lap. "Back when we were younger, before I got sick, your grandpa built us a boat. Took him all his spare time for most of the nineties, beautiful little thing she is—big enough to live on for a while, until things get better. It's down in the boathouse. You take it; take yourself and Ester and the baby."

"And you," Owen added.

Nan smiled and gestured to her useless legs. "Reckon my cruising days are over don't you?"

"I won't go without you."

Her smile faded. She looked out at the river drifting by. "I'm dying, Owen. Not like that," she added, seeing panic in his eyes. "Seems maybe I'm immune to this Fever thing—don't that just take the biscuit?" With that she shook her head. "What I got's slower, but just as deadly. And it's going to get worse—a lot worse—before the end. I don't want that. Not for me. Not for you."

"But that's even more reason for me to stay and take care of you!"

"I'm not planning on getting that far. I've lived on a farm nigh on thirty years. I know how to put an animal out of its misery." She put her hand on his. "Everything passes," she said. "That's what age shows you, for better or worse. You know, I grew up in England, didn't come over here 'til I was twenty?"

"Yeah, I know."

"When I was at school we visited a records office, where they keep the births and deaths, parish registers, that kind of thing. As a girl I found it dead boring but I remember seeing something that stuck with me. They had this book from a village long ago, 'bout this big." She held her hands wide apart. "Thick it was, old yellow pages that crackled when you touched them. It had the names of burials, month by month. Most months there was just a half page, sometimes a little more. Then I turned another page and the names...they just went on and on. Page after page after page...in just one month...until almost the whole village must have gone. It was the plague. The plague had come." Nan's hands settled, her gaze far away. "So you see, it's not the first time this has happened. It's just the first time it's happened to us."

* * *

They spent the next day loading the boat with supplies, Nana supervising from the porch. Getting the boat onto the trailer and into the water was the hardest part, though between them, Owen and Ester managed it. Lucky for him, the girl was stronger than she looked. But for Owen the toughest task still lay ahead, because he knew for sure that he wasn't going to prise Nan Tapper out of that house without one heck of a fight, but was just as sure that he was no way going without her. He'd left enough people behind already. If he had to leave, they would leave together.

But there was something else he had to do first.

Owen sneaked out early, before Nana was awake, creeping past Ester crooning to her sister in the kitchen. With any luck he'd be back before they even realised he was gone.

The wheels of his bike spun along the dark grey tarmac of his home town for what he knew would be the last time. He passed his old high school with its boarded up windows, the hospital car park overflowing with stretchers full of putrid bodies like a war zone, stores with broken windows...until finally he turned into the street that was as familiar as his own reflection.

He rode past the first few houses: Mr. Emerson's, Mrs. Clark's, the Booths' with their faded stars and stripes hanging forlorn out front, Kendra James's place where he'd had his first kiss not three months ago... Back when things like that seemed important.

At the last house but one, Owen stopped. He waited a moment, studying the outlines of what he now saw had been a perfect world. The polished, wooden door with its brass knocker, the neat square windows with the carefully chosen ornaments and photo frames on the inside ledges. The dove grey porch that he and his mother had painted together after giving up waiting for his dad to do it. Remnants of a life that was gone forever.

Skirting the house he headed round back, heart thumping, throat thickening with every step. He let the bike fall onto the brittle grass, took one step after another until he was back there, in front of the french windows. Scene of his longing dreams and fevered nightmares.

Sweat and sunlight, white fingertips pressed against glass.

But the fingertips were gone, a dark rust-like stripe the only evidence that she had ever stood there.

He peered through into the darkened room, saw the slumped body on the floor beside the couch. It was positioned exactly as it had been the last time he'd come. "Mom," he whispered.

Last time he'd said her name out loud he'd been yelling through the glass, rattling the door handle, scared out of his wits at what they'd seen on the news at school.

She was inside, leaning over the couch, but spun round at the sound of his voice. "Mom! I can't get in. The bolt's on."

"Honey, I know." She came right up to the glass door, her face a riot of emotions. He watched her tamp them down, trying to put on a brave face that, even through the confusion, he understood was for him. "You can't come in, baby..." Her voice had cracked. "It's Hope..."

His eyes flicked behind her back to the couch where his sister lay stretched out—her thin, white arm dangling from the cushions. She wasn't moving. "Mom, let me in," he'd pleaded. "Please."

"Owen, no! You can't come in. You have to go. Go to your nana's. I'll leave a note on the front door for Dad; he'll come find you there. Okay?" She wiped her face with a trembling hand and when she was done she pressed it up against the glass, fingertips white with the pressure, like they would break through to reach him if they could. "I can't let you in, baby. You know that."

So, helpless and sick with rage and grief, he'd left them. And now he was leaving them again, for good this time.

"Owen!" she'd called as he'd turned to pick up his bike. "I love you!"

"I love you," he whispered, wiping at the hot tears scalding his face. He crouched and sobbed then, wild like an animal, chest heaving like his heart wanted to escape.

He'd meant to come back and bury them, but he couldn't even do that. There was no time. The past had slipped through his fingers while he wasn't looking and all he had left was the future, whether he wanted it or not.

* * *

No blood on the steps this time, but as soon as he pulled up to the farmhouse he knew something was wrong. Tire tracks in the dust, and a stillness that felt unnatural. He followed the driveway round to the back and stopped. There, right by the back porch. Ugly and alien. A truck.

For a moment he was paralysed, his brain refusing to accept the fact that strangers had come. They were finally here. Then with trembling fingers he took out his pistol and crept inside.

The house appeared to be deserted, but as he made his way into the kitchen, he realised that it wasn't. His brain slowed again, taking several seconds to process the puddle of red that edged its way across the floor, curling round the wheels of Nana's chair. He let out an animal shout of shock and pain as he saw her body stretched out on the floor beside it.

"Nana!"

" 'wen?" It came out like a sigh and he dropped to her side. The head wound was deep and her face was pale as death, but by some force of will, she was awake. On the floor beside her lay his grandpa's shotgun.

"No, no, no, no…"

"Men here. Ester…" she croaked, her breath bubbling between the words. She grasped his arm, already trying to pull herself back into her chair. "The woods…" She bumped him with her weakened fist. "Go!"

Owen ran outside. Which way had they gone? All of a sudden he heard a noise—a baby crying. He pelted toward the sound, head filled with the sounds of his breathing, feet crunching over dried branches as he sprinted into the trees.

He came across the baby first, set down in a blanket among the mossy stones. Then he heard a shout and saw Ester a short distance away, locked in a desperate struggle with a man in blue overalls.

"Hey!" shouted Owen. "You!" He held the pistol out in front, trying to keep his hand from trembling. It was the man who'd tried to steal his bike. *I know you.*

The man froze but didn't release his hold on the girl. "Guess I was right," he said, a sickly smile crawling over his face. "Owen Tapper. Told 'em we'd find you here."

"Leave her alone," said Owen, trying to sound brave.

The man looked unimpressed, though his eyes flickered to the gun in Owen's hand. "Relax, kid. There's no need to be shooting anyone. That thing with the bike, it was nothin' personal. It didn't mean nothing. We don't want trouble with you...but you don't know her, she's nothing to you. Just leave her and we'll let you go—okay?" He held up one hand, placatory, but his eyes told a different story. Owen hesitated and for a split second he wondered what his father would have done in his place. But his father wasn't here. It was just Owen and a gun...and a man trying to take what didn't belong to him.

He pulled the trigger.

They were running, him clinging onto Ester's hand as she dragged him through the trees, while on her back, the baby squalled. Behind them the man's shrieks were fading, but other shouts rang out in the distance. "Hurry!" said Ester, hauling him along until finally they staggered into the driveway. "There are more of them," she said, nodding to the woods as she adjusted the sling to make Jojo more comfortable. "Where's your nana?"

Owen looked around, dazed. "She's...right there," he said, confused.

Nan Tapper was sitting on the front porch in her chair, just like always. The only difference was the drying patch of red on one side of her face. On her lap lay the old tartan blanket that Grandpa said came from way back. "What are you doing?" he said, snapping out of his stupor and running to the front steps.

"They're coming!" said Ester, as the sound of another vehicle reached them from the farm gate.

Owen turned, frantic. "Nana, we have to go!"

"Yes, you do," she said, her voice sure and steady. "But I'm staying right here." She twitched back the blanket to reveal the tip of the shotgun barrel. "Got to give a proper welcome to our guests first, see?"

"Nana…"

"Owen, don't be arguing with me. You may be the last of this family but I'm the eldest and what I say goes—and I say you go. Right now."

The engine noise grew louder. Ester grabbed his arm. "Owen…"

He looked up the drive and then back to Nana, the battered remains of his heart tearing itself in half. "Owen Tapper," Nan snapped. "Get going or I'll shoot you my damn self!"

He pelted up the steps and threw his arms around her, breathing in her scent: lavender and cookie dough—the scents of his childhood—but even that was tainted now, infected with the rusty tang of blood. "I'll come back," he said.

Nan didn't reply. She just pushed him away. "Enough now."

Owen and Ester cleared the side of the building just as the first car screeched to a stop in front of the house. They ran full tilt to the boat and threw themselves on board, Owen fumbling with the mooring rope before starting up the engine. The revving burst through the air, like a gunshot. Then, like echoes, real shots rang out from the farmhouse. One, two, then a crackling exchange that didn't stop until they were almost to the middle of the river.

"Get down!" called Ester as first one man, then another, arrived at the river bank. More shots sounded as the men fired at the boat, but the bullets fell short, peppering the water instead. When they saw that the boat was out of range the men gave up.

Owen and Ester stared at one another, shell shocked into silence. Against all odds, they'd got away.

After a while Owen cut the engine and let the current carry them downstream. For a long time he was numb, unable to talk. He was aware of Ester moving around, straightening out the supplies, taking care of Jojo, but he felt detached, like he'd left the core of who he was back there, at the farmhouse.

"What do we do?" asked Ester eventually. "Carry on downstream or head to the shore?"

She stood in the prow, waiting for an answer. A fourteen-year-old girl with a baby to care for. Owen realised that Ester and her sister hadn't asked for this any more than any of them had, and all he'd done was push them away, keep them out. Not anymore. This was his world now and they were in it.

He'd spent so long doubting and wondering what was right and what was wrong. But he knew exactly what Nan Tapper would have said.

"We go on."

TEN: *CDC*
by Jon Messenger

A rock struck the window, startling Cassandra Morin. She slid across the back seat, further away from the angry mob huddling around the car, but it was useless. More protesters were crowded around the passenger's side as well. Looking into the crowd, she could see people with red streaks marring their faces, a telltale sign that they were infected.

She wanted to scream at them, to warn everyone that gathering in a tightly packed crowd would only speed up the rate of infection, but she knew no one would listen. They were scared. Their loved ones were dead or dying and they wanted answers. The Centers for Disease Control office in New York seemed like the right place to find them.

Cassie adjusted the respirator covering her nose and mouth and tapped on the driver's shoulder.

"How long have they been out here?" she asked, though the mask muffled her voice.

The driver glanced over his shoulder as the car slowly pushed its way through the crowd and approached the makeshift chain-link gates blocking the way into the CDC offices. He mumbled something, but it was unintelligible through his mask.

"Say that again," she said. He seemed to repeat himself, but she still couldn't understand him. Frustrated, she pulled down her mask, letting it dangle from her neck by its rubber straps.

"I asked how long they've been out here."

The driver turned toward her, startled. His eyebrows arched in surprise and he started to reply, but she held up her hand.

"Take off the stupid mask, John," Cassie said. "We've both already tested immune. All the masks are doing are scaring the people."

Begrudgingly, John pulled down his mask. "They started gathering ever since the first reported outbreaks. They think we have some miracle cure hidden inside."

"That's ludicrous," she said, tucking some flyaway hairs back into the severe bun at the back of her head. "Why the hell would we have a cure and not share it with the world? What possible gain is there for us? I think people have a very different view of what the CDC actually does."

John gestured toward the angry protesters, waving signs that read "The Government's Killing Us" and "Our Pain, Their Gain."

"Try telling that to them," John said.

The car rolled forward once again, blocked on either side by National Guard soldiers in full protective equipment. She frowned as she saw their loaded weapons. No one, it seemed, knew how to avoid panicking the population. They rolled through the gates, which swung closed behind them.

The CDC building was a wall of glass windows facing the busy street. A few cars were parked near the front of the building but the lot was mostly deserted. John parked and climbed out, opening the door for Cassie as he walked around toward the trunk.

Cassie climbed out, smoothing her pants suit as she stood. Before John could unload her suitcase from the trunk, the front doors opened. An older black man emerged, blinking against the harsh summer glare. His hair was white at the temples and there were deep wrinkles around his eyes, but he smiled broadly as Cassie waved.

"Chuck," she said, stepping forward and hugging the older man.

Charles Westmore hugged her tightly back. They quickly separated, though, and she tried her best to replace her serious demeanor.

"Welcome to New York," he said. "I hope your flight wasn't too bad."

"It was a private chartered plane," she explained as he led her into the building. "Those are pretty much the only planes still in the air. All things considered, it wasn't half bad. How are things here?"

Chuck shrugged. "Probably just as bad as they are in Atlanta. The hospitals are overflowing and medical supplies are running dangerously short. We're trying to disseminate information about how to stay healthy—pretty much the same advice we give for the seasonal flu: wash your hands, don't have too much direct contact, wear a mask if you're feeling sick. There aren't that many papers or television stations still operating, so getting the word out has been tough."

They walked past an empty reception desk and stepped onto an elevator. Chuck selected one of the top floors and the doors slid closed.

"I was glad to hear you were immune in your email," Chuck said as soft music filled the elevator.

"You, too," Cassie replied.

"I was kind of surprised to hear from you, to be honest. I didn't figure even the Atlanta office would have an investigator left to send up our way."

Cassie glanced over at her counterpart and arched a brow. "You're ground zero for this disease. Of course they would send someone."

The elevator door opened onto a floor with a wide bank of cubicles. They were immaculately kept: pictures still sat on desks, potted plants looked a little dry but otherwise healthy, and some jackets even still hung on the backs of chairs. The cubicles, however, were practically abandoned.

A blond haired woman approached, holding out a folder for Chuck. "Thanks, Joanne," he said as he took the binder from her. "Joanne, this is Cassandra Morin, an investigator out of Atlanta. Cassie, this is my administrative assistant."

Cassie barely acknowledged the other woman. Her eyes were drifting over the sea of empty chairs. "Where is everyone?"

Chuck gestured toward Joanne, who quickly walked away. "They're not here. I sent them home."

"You did what?" she asked incredulously. "We're in the middle of the biggest epidemic the world has ever seen. This is a hundred times worse than the 1918 Spanish Flu, and you sent everyone home?"

Chuck started walking away and Cassie was forced to hurry to keep up. "These people had families, Cassie. They had parents, spouses, even kids dying of this disease. They needed to be with their families."

"They needed to be in the office, trying to find a way to stop it! That's what we do; we're the CDC!"

He stopped and turned toward her, his jovial expression replaced with a stern glower. "There is no way to stop it. It's way beyond us now. Yeah, we're the CDC. We train for disease outbreaks, but not like this. We talk about superbugs in brain trusts but it's all theoretical exercises. No one's really prepared when something like this happens."

He sighed and sat down in the closest chair. "Some people did come to work, until the first one of them tested positive. They were symptomatic and getting the rest of the office sick. I couldn't risk it anymore; the CDC is ineffective if we're carrying the disease. Joanne, John, and I stuck around. We're all three immune, so I wasn't worried about us getting sick. So like it or leave it, we're all you've got here in New York." He waved his hand dismissively. "Write me up in your report if you want to, but I know I did the right thing."

Cassie didn't have much of a response. Sensing that the discussion was over, Chuck climbed back to his feet and led her down a side hallway. There were individual offices lining the hall, most with their doors propped open. John stepped out of one, running a hand through his shaggy brown hair.

"This is you," Chuck explained, pointing toward the office. Cassie looked inside and saw her suitcase already sitting at the foot of a foldout cot. The rest of the furniture had been removed, except for a small office desk and chair pushed up against the wall. "It's not much, but it's safer than any hotel right now. There's a bathroom and shower down the hall."

She glanced inside once more and shrugged. "It'll do."

"I'll let you get situated. We'll start first thing in the morning."

Cassie nodded as the two men left. She closed the door behind her and drew the blinds over the window. Sparse as it was, it would work for the next couple of days.

She meticulously unpacked her bag. There weren't any dressers to speak of, so it mostly consisted of retrieving her previous reports on the virus and its virility. She laid them atop the small desk and sorted through them, rereading her own handwritten notes from Atlanta's outbreak response. After a couple of hours of absently perusing her work, she gently closed the folders and walked out of her room.

In the main room, there was only a single office with light filtering through its blinds. She walked to the door and knocked softly. She heard Chuck scooting his chair back and walking to the door. He didn't bother looking through the slats to see who was there; there were only three other people in the building.

He opened the door and smiled as though he knew she'd be visiting. "Come in and have a seat."

Cassie entered before sitting opposite Chuck. She crossed her legs and drummed her fingers on her knee. "I'm sorry about earlier," she said abruptly.

He shook his head. "There's no need. We're all under an incredible amount of stress."

"No, Chuck, you don't have to be the good guy. I was out of line. I came barging in like a bull in a china shop, throwing my CDC credentials around like they meant something here. I'm sorry. You clearly have this situation under control."

He laughed heartily. "Under control? Are you out of your damn mind? I'm holding on by a thread, while a crowd of the—pardon the expression—*walking dead* try to break down my gates every day. I'm a lot of things but 'under control' probably isn't one of them."

Cassie sat back in her chair and ran her hand across her forehead, as though staving off the start of a migraine. "You're doing a better job than I'd be, is all I'm saying. I don't know how you do it. We have our own problems in Atlanta, but at least we've been on lockdown since all this started. I've got a full staff working around the clock to figure out how to stop this disease and you're doing it here with three."

"Including me," he emphasized.

Despite her best judgment, the corners of her mouth curled into a smile.

Chuck stood and walked around his desk, finally sitting on the corner next to her chair. "I know our situation here hits home for you. There's a reason only the four of us are here. We have no living parents. No kids. We were either never married or long since divorced. The only thing we're married to is the job. So, in the face of the apocalypse, we keep on doing what we do best."

"She's a harsh mistress, this job," Cassie joked.

"Don't I know it. Listen, don't stress about it. You and I are fine. Go get some sleep because bright and early tomorrow morning, we're going to try to solve this mystery."

Cassie smiled and nodded. She climbed back out of the chair, glad for even the brief conversation, and walked back to her room.

* * *

She showered quickly the next morning, tying her hair into a long braid rather than the bun on the back of her head. It soaked the back of her shirt as she finished getting dressed, but she ignored it. It was an austere environment to begin with; she wasn't going to manage perfect.

Dressed, she made her way back to the main offices. Most of the lights were turned off, but a bank of lights burned brightly at the far end of the room. She could see Chuck and John hovering around a massive dry erase board, talking in low tones between them.

"Morning, gentlemen," she said as she approached.

They turned abruptly and smiled. "Good morning. Want something for breakfast?"

She glanced around curiously. Chuck held up a protein bar. "The very finest the CDC's vending machines can provide."

When she looked disapprovingly at his offering, he smirked. "Don't worry, we get real food for lunch and dinner."

She ignored the meager snack and stepped between the men, examining the expansive white board. Multicolored lines spread like a spider's web, expanding in ever widening concentric circles from the center. Hospitals and business names were printed in small letters around the outside, obviously Chuck's meticulous handwriting. Closer to the center, however, the writing gave way to actual photographs.

"Disease spread?" she asked.

"As best we can tell." He tapped a photo of an olive skinned man near just outside the center of the web. "The first confirmed death was Bradley Scaglione, a paramedic."

"But he's not our patient zero," she surmised.

"No. The day he died, he responded to..."

"Six," John offered.

"Six runs. Three car accidents, two home accidents, and one suicide. It had been a light day so far for a paramedic in New York. We think it's one of the car accidents that actually started the spread."

Cassie's gaze fell to the uniformed man in the center of the complicated epidemiological web. "I don't get it. If you've got all this figured out, why did you request an investigator from Atlanta? It looks like you've got this all handled pretty well on your own."

Chuck set down the dry erase marker he'd been holding and turned toward her solemnly. "Because this," he said as he tapped the board, "doesn't make a bit of sense. One of the last runs of the day was for a truck accident—an armored car, actually."

"Armored car?"

"An armored car owned by, and this is where it gets good, Peter Franklin Donalds."

Cassie furrowed her brow as she glanced back at the picture at the center of the whiteboard. "The pharmaceutical company?"

"One and the same. Best we can guess, our truck driver," he tapped the picture in the center of the complicated web, "Kevin Mahoney, seems to be our patient zero. We called PFD and they admit he was supposedly carrying an untested Ebola vaccine."

She frowned deeply and walked away from the whiteboard, pacing the carpeted floor. "That doesn't make sense. PFD was recently approved as one of the companies authorized to pursue a viable vaccine against the disease. What the hell were they carrying in that truck?" She stormed away and approached the window overlooking the front of the building. She pulled open the blinds and pointed at the gathered crowd. "Take a look out there, Chuck, and tell me they were carrying a *vaccine*."

He put up his hands defensively. "You're preaching to the choir, lady. At least now you understand why I called you. If PFD was involved in creating this virus, I'm going to need a lot more clout than I can manage as a regional CDC manager."

She glanced out the window at the throng of protesters. The hastily erected chain-link fence around the New York office strained to keep them at bay. She felt for the National Guardsmen manning the gate. She was sure they'd rather be anywhere right now than facing an angry mob of infected people, even if they were wearing their MOPP gear.

"You said that your paramedic…"

"Bradley Scaglione," John offered, staring at his notes.

"Right, this paramedic responded to a vehicle accident involving a PFD transport moving what was supposed to be a vaccine and next thing you know he's infected? What do we have for the timeline?"

Chuck turned to John, who clearly had all the pertinent details in front of him. John cleared his throat as he read. "Scaglione presented at Mount Sinai approximately nine hours after responding to the accident. His medical report claims he was complaining of flu-like symptoms."

"That's consistent with what we've seen."

"He was brought into the Emergency Room for observation. Within an hour, vomiting and diarrhea had begun. They gave him Zofran, which controlled the vomiting, but symptoms progressed to nose bleeds." John looked up from his notes. "From there it's everything we already know. Abdominal pain, migraines, and eventually bleeding from damn near every orifice he had. He died fourteen hours after being admitted, which is twenty-three hours after his encounter with the truck."

Cassie walked back over to the whiteboard and stared at Mahoney's picture. It was a company photo and he was wearing a polo shirt with the PFD diamond stitched on his chest. "Who examined the contents of the truck? If it was transporting medical supplies, we should have been called."

"We were," Chuck admitted morosely. "We sent out a team in full PPE and collected samples. There wasn't much left; the truck caught fire during the accident. Almost everything was destroyed. We were starting to go through what samples we could salvage when Scaglione died, followed by the nursing staff that had been tending to him. It snowballed from there. We only got back to examining the samples days later and...well, you can guess what we found."

"The virus," Cassie concluded.

She traced the path of the disease with her finger, from Mahoney to Scaglione to a slew of nurses and a doctor. It was after the nurses that she sighed. There was a direct line from a nurse to the John F. Kennedy Airport. "We could have contained this," she muttered. "One crappy break, one nurse who wanted to go on vacation, and this thing spread across the country. Just like that," she said, snapping her fingers. "It needed a perfect storm to get out of New York City before we could lock it down and it got it."

"I think our crappy break came when the PFD transport happened to slam into the barrier on the interstate on-ramp," Chuck corrected.

Cassie paused, her finger hovering over the airport. It quickly traced backward to Mahoney. She furrowed her brow. "The truck crashed into a barrier?"

"Yeah," John replied. "It drove through a couple of the orange barrels and hit the concrete wall head on. The police said the fire started almost immediately afterward, probably from a crack in the engine and leaking fuel line."

She turned toward the two men, biting the inside of her lip as she thought. Eventually, she shook her head. "These trucks are made to withstand a direct hit from a rocket. Anything they'd be carrying in the back would be strapped down and insulated from an accident. There's no way a crash with a wall, even if Mahoney here was driving a hundred and twenty, would have broken the vials in the back."

She glanced back at the whiteboard as the two men shrugged. "I'd kill to get a look at that truck."

"Then I've got good news," Chuck said. "When we identified Mahoney as our potential patient zero, I contacted the NYPD and had the truck shipped over from their impound. I've got it in quarantine in the basement."

Cassie shook her head as she laughed softly to herself. "Chuck, we really need to work on what information you should lead with."

* * *

John waved as the elevator doors closed and Chuck pushed one of the buttons marked for the garage. The elevator music drummed overhead as Cassie leaned back against the cool metal wall.

She tilted her head to the side as she looked at the older black man. "Where is Joanne? I haven't seen her since I got here yesterday."

"She's our social media monitor," Chuck said with a soft laugh. "She watches the couple remaining TV stations and monitors the few websites here in New York that are still updating regularly. Without a field staff on site, we're kind of relying on the media, for as long as it lasts."

The elevator dinged as it came to a stop. The doors slid open to a well-lit garage. Cassie's attention was drawn to a corner where long plastic sheets had been hung. Behind the semi-transparent plastic, she could see the outlines of a large armored truck.

Chuck led them to a table just outside the quarantine, where he handed her static-free coveralls, booties, and gloves. She slipped them over her clothes before picking up a surgical mask. Finally, she pulled up the jumper's hood, covering her long hair. When they were both dressed, Chuck unsealed the plastic partition and they walked through.

The truck was in terrible condition. The front end had been smashed inward, warping the frame and twisting the body all the way up to the cab's doors. Most of the damage, however, had come from the ensuing fire. Flames had gutted the cab. The sides of the truck were likewise blackened, starting about halfway up. Cassie walked around to the back of the truck, where the back door was hanging slightly ajar. With her gloved hands, she pulled the heavy door open. The rear of the armored truck was just as destroyed, blackened almost to the point of being unrecognizable.

"Did the police forensic team go over the truck?" she asked.

Chuck shook his head. "They never had a chance. They were swamped with 911 calls. You're the first to really inspect it."

Cassie nodded. She knew the truck should have come straight to the CDC first, rather than to a police impound lot, but she wasn't about to start that argument with the New York regional manager right now. "Would you mind being my recorder?"

"Not at all," he said, pulling a tape recorder from the pocket of his white coveralls.

"Damage to the hood of the truck is consistent with a vehicular accident," she began, as she walked around the front of the truck and examined the vehicle. "There's extensive damage to the right front bumper, where it must have struck the concrete barrier."

She climbed up on the step outside the driver's side door and peered into the cab. "There's extensive damage to the dash and front of the seats. Fire damage seems worst in those areas, also consistent with the police report of a fire starting in the engine block."

Her eyes drifted toward the back of the truck, which was completely separated from the cab. She furrowed her brow as she climbed down and walked slowly toward the back of the truck. Glancing into the back once more, she shook her head at the extensive burn damage throughout the inside of the rear compartment.

"What are you thinking?" Chuck asked, as he followed her with the recorder.

"We're assuming the accident caused the virus to be released, right?"

Chuck nodded but didn't figure she needed a response.

"But we've already covered that this compartment was self-contained. The padding alone should have been enough to keep the vials from breaking."

"Yes, but the fire could have damaged the casings around the virus."

Cassie shook her head. "If it was hot enough to destroy the clamshell casings, it would've destroyed the virus, too. I think our timeline is wrong. The virus had to have been released *before* the fire broke out."

Chuck stopped the recording and lowered his arm. "That sounds great in theory, but even if the vials had broken first, the virus would have been contained in the back of the truck. The doors weren't opened until the fire built inside and blew them open."

"At which time the virus would have already been destroyed by the heat."

She grabbed the door to close it but withdrew her hand sharply as something stabbed her in the finger. She looked down and noticed a tear in her glove and blood welling from a small cut.

"Damn it," she muttered as she stripped off the glove. "Can you grab me another glove and a Band-Aid?"

"Are you okay?"

She nodded. "Yeah, just cut myself on the door."

Chuck turned and walked away as Cassie sucked on the blood pooling. It wasn't very sanitary, she knew, but she wasn't concerned about getting the virus. Her natural immunity would keep her safe. She looked up at the door, trying to find the metal edge that had cut her. As she peered closer, her eyes narrowed. There wasn't a single edge, but a long row of sharp metal slivers, all pointing inward. The metal around the slivers was slightly bent.

As the older man returned with the medical kit, Cassie quickly waved him over. "Did the police have to use a crowbar or Jaws of Life on this door?"

Chuck sighed as he handed her the medical bag and walked back over to the table, retrieving the police report. "Nope. Says here the door was already opened by the blast. Why?"

"Because someone opened this door from the outside…without a key."

He lowered the report and stepped closer. She pointed to the bent metal and he frowned. "Let's just lay our cards on the table. What are we saying here?"

"The fire's been bothering me since you mentioned it upstairs. The back of the truck is completely separate from the front. There's no reason why a fire in the cab should have affected the back of the truck at all. We know the virus had to be released before the fire broke out, or there wouldn't have been an epidemic in the first place. Now someone pried this door open, probably before the fire."

"Say it, Cassie," Chuck said sternly, raising the recorder and pushing the record button once more. "We need it for the report."

"I think the virus's release was intentional. Someone set the virus free after the accident."

"Kevin Mahoney?" Chuck asked.

She shrugged. "It doesn't really fit, does it? He survived the crash but died before the paramedics could get him to the hospital. By that point he was already infected. If he was going to release it, wouldn't it make sense that he survived?"

"So he had an accomplice?"

"Or an enemy," she replied. She walked around the side of the truck, stooping as she did so. "If Mahoney wasn't involved, then I doubt it was a coincidence that he happened to get into an accident."

Most of the vehicle was marred by smoke and fire, leaving the damage indistinguishable from any signs of the accident. Only the hood shows evidence of the crash. Cassie ran her hands along the separation between the burnt and bubbled paint near the top of the truck and the still relatively pristine white paint below. On the side of the truck, she traced the bottom of the gray diamond and what remained of the letters, spelling out "PFD."

As she walked toward the cab, her gaze drifted lower and she furrowed her brow. She paused near the front wheel well and gingerly touched scrapes on the paint. Her fingers traced backward, as she followed one scrape as it stretched past the driver's door.

"What do you have?" Chuck asked.

She withdrew her hand and noticed a metallic blue clinging to her glove. "Paint transfer." She glanced up at him. "Definitely not from the armored truck."

"Could it have been from the barrels he hit?" he offered.

Cassie held up her fingers so he could see the blue paint. "Someone rammed him into that wall."

Chuck whistled softly. "I know a lot of people who aren't going to like this report."

* * *

The elevator opened onto the fifth floor once more and Cassie followed Chuck to his office. She collapsed into one of his chairs, this time without being invited.

"This thing is giving me a headache," she complained, pinching the bridge of her nose. "We have a pharmaceutical company that's supposed to be working on a vaccine, but instead they actually created the virus in the first place. We have a truck carrying the virus run off the road. We have someone prying open the back door and releasing the virus intentionally, then setting fire to the truck to cover their tracks." She covered her face with her hands and tilted her head backward. "This is normally the part of the day where I'd head to a bar and drink cosmos until this all made sense."

"I can't help with cosmos, but…" Chuck pulled open a bottom drawer and withdrew a bottle of clear liquor and a couple glasses. He rattled the glasses, offering one to her.

She read the label on the bottle and frowned. "Vodka?"

"Cheap vodka," he corrected.

"That's the best you've got?"

Chuck shrugged. "Apparently when everyone starts dying, hard liquor becomes a commodity. Push comes to shove, beggars can't be choosers."

With a sigh, she held out her glass. He filled it most of the way. Despite it being a short cup, he easily poured six or seven shots worth of vodka into the tumbler. He poured his own and raised it in a toast.

"To the end of the world."

She raised her glass before bringing it to her lips. She paused as the smell hit her, a combination of rubbing alcohol and paint thinner. Wrinkling her nose, she took a swig, feeling the sensation of fire rolling down her throat. She coughed involuntarily and her eyes watered, but Chuck merely laughed.

"Good?" he chided.

"Toxic," she replied. "Good enough it should be shared with John and Joanne."

Chuck looked longingly at his bottle and she quickly realized it was all he had left. With a sigh, he leaned around his desk and yelled into the cubicle farm beyond his door.

"Come in here, John!"

John appeared at the door, brushing his shaggy hair out of his face. Cassie raised her glass, offering him a drink. He looked surprised for a second before taking his own drink. His face immediately went scarlet and he exhaled slowly.

"Go grab Joanne, too," Chuck said.

John tried to respond but it came out in a wheezing gasp. Nodding instead, he handed Cassie back her glass before vanishing back into the room beyond.

Cassie lowered her glass, unsure if she wanted to take another drink. It felt like a celebration, but her mind was a million miles away. The smile on Chuck's face faded and he lowered his glass.

"Who would make a virus like this?" Cassie asked. "They had to know it would get out of hand. You don't weaponize one of the deadliest viruses in the world and then act surprised when it does exactly what you want it to."

"Did you get a look at the virus?" Chuck asked.

She nodded. "We had some samples down in Atlanta. Ebola mixed with Influenza H5N1, plus a little something extra for added virility. Whoever designed this is a real bastard."

"Yeah, but the real bastard is whoever let it out."

Cassie absently ran her finger around the lip of her glass. "Do you honestly think it could have been PFD?"

Chuck shrugged. "Do I think a pharmaceutical company is capable of being, basically, a stereotypical Bond villain? Just thinking about it makes me imagine that Peter Franklin Donalds is run by a guy in a high-backed chair, petting a cat."

She chuckled as she shook her head. "I just want to give them a call, to find out what the hell they were thinking."

"PFD? Wish we could. All the phone lines have been tied up for the past few days. Nothing goes through."

"You don't have a satellite phone?"

"We do," Chuck said, "but it won't do us any good. The only numbers I have for PFD are commercial lines."

Cassie swirled the vile liquid around her glass. She opened her mouth to speak, but a crash from the main room startled her. John slid to a stop in front of the door, out of breath. He pointed over his shoulder. "You two are going to want to see this."

Without a word, they set down their glasses and hurried from the office. John led them to the far end of the room, where a break room sat open. Joanne stood against one wall, watching a blaring television. On the screen, a dark-haired female reporter was talking frantically. The label at the bottom of the screen said, "Amy Savino, WNMN News." She was near the end of a report, but it didn't take Cassie long for her breath to catch in her throat.

"The virus continued to spread relentlessly from there. As you probably know, Peter Franklin Donalds is a well-known pharmaceutical company that was manufacturing a vaccine for the AVHF virus at the time of the outbreak here in New York.

"New York, this may be my last broadcast, but it may also be my most important. This reporter believes that the virus here in New York has too many coincidences. I will not rest until I find out the truth. My heart is with you, New York. God bless you all."

Cassie turned sharply toward Chuck. "I need to talk to her."

Chuck was a step ahead of her, turning toward John. "Get one of the vans and bring her here. Now."

John ran from the room as they turned their attention back to the television.

* * *

Cassie glanced through the narrow window on the door. Amy Savino shifted nervously in her chair, glancing around at the narrow room. The CDC offices didn't exactly have an interrogation room like a police station, but the makeshift office would do. A table had been placed in the center with a couple chairs. Light streamed through the closed blinds.

"She looks nervous," Chuck whispered, trying not to be heard by their guest inside the room.

Cassie glanced toward him briefly. "We grabbed her off the street and stuffed her in a van. You'd be nervous, too. What do we know about her?"

"Joanne pulled her bio off the WNMN website and Facebook-stalked her for a bit. Honestly, there's not a lot on her. She was born here in Brooklyn and has worked at WNMN for the past few years." He handed her a folder, which just told her the same thing he'd already said. "You want me to come in with you?"

"And freak her out more? No, I should be good."

Cassie softly touched the tight bun at the back of her head and smoothed out her pants suit. She had changed to look more professional, rather than wearing her button up shirt and having her hair in a braid. She turned the handle and Amy jumped slightly at the sound.

Cassie offered a smile as she entered the room but it did little to put the reporter at ease. As she sat, she opened the folder in front of her. Amy eyed the folder's contents curiously; she looked as though she expected half the paperwork to be redacted, with broad black lines marking out entire sentences. When Cassie caught her eye, the reporter quickly looked away and glanced around nervously, looking everywhere except into Cassandra's gaze. Cassie wasn't surprised. She looked down at the folder splayed out in front of her. Pinned to the left side of the folder was a picture of the reporter. On the right, a description.

"Miss Amy Savino, of the World News of Manhattan," Cassie said matter-of-factly. "Originally from New York City, aren't you?"

"This is about my story, isn't it?" Amy said hastily. "I won't retract it, if that's what you're expecting."

Cassandra looked up, surprised. "That's not what I want at all. Quite the opposite, I'm interested to find out what you know."

Amy glanced over her shoulder, to the plain mirror hanging on the wall. "Is that how this works? You find out what I know and then make me disappear?"

Cassie closed the folder and shook her head as she looked at the reporter. "Miss Savino, I don't know what you've heard about us, but we're the CDC, not the mafia. We don't make people disappear."

"Who are you?" Amy asked.

"I'm Cassandra Morin, a CDC field investigator out of Atlanta." She extended her hand, but Amy refused to take it. Cassie leaned back in her chair and crossed her arms over her chest. "This impromptu meeting is, however, about your news report. We caught the tail end of it. You seemed to be implicating Peter Franklin Donalds in this outbreak."

Amy crossed her arms as well, glaring defiantly at Cassie. "Am I being accused of something? I'm guessing the CDC doesn't really have the authority to detain someone anyway, even with the world going to crap, so unless I'm being charged with something, I'm leaving."

The reporter began to stand when Cassie sighed.

"I believe you."

Amy seemed startled. Her posture relaxed visibly, but her expression still seemed skeptical. She placed her hands on the table and leaned forward toward Cassie. "You know something, don't you?"

Cassie bit the inside of her lip and frowned. "I…I can't tell you. I'm sorry."

Amy shook her head and stood upright. "Then we're done here. Thanks for the kidnapping."

She took a step toward the door before Cassie held up her hand. "Wait."

Amy paused but didn't turn toward her. After a second of silence, the reporter started toward the door again.

"Okay," Cassie said, standing. "Please, come back and sit. I'll tell you what I can, but this can't go into your next report."

"Off the record, then?" Amy said. She smiled slightly.

Cassie smirked and pointed at the chair. "Sit."

Amy sat and the two women talked for nearly an hour. Cassie felt her stomach drop as they compared notes about PFD potentially conducting preliminary experiments in Africa and about Cassie's findings here in New York. As they talked, the sun began to drift lower in the sky. Cassie caught herself looking out the window, dreading the next day when she had to fly back to Atlanta. Everything about her report was inflammatory and it was only getting worse the longer they discussed.

"So you really don't know about the safe zone?" Amy asked as the conversation was winding down.

"I haven't heard a thing," Cassie replied. "On Staten Island?"

"Yeah, supposedly they've blocked off the whole island except for the Goethals Bridge. It wasn't widely publicized—just a handful of online forums and one news station—but they were advertising a virus-free zone, with food and shelter. All the amenities."

Cassie shook her head. "How do they expect it to stay virus-free? This is one of the most virulent diseases I've ever come across. All it'll take is one infected person getting in to devastate the island."

"I don't know," the dark-haired reporter admitted, "but I intend to find out."

Cassie frowned. "Are you crazy? If someone took over the island and was able to block all the bridges, that indicates some sort of armed guard. It's not the type of place you want to go wandering into."

"Aren't you a regular Sherlock Holmes," Amy teased.

"I am an investigator, after all. But I'm being serious. Staten Island isn't a place you want to go."

Amy shrugged. "I'm a reporter, and probably one of the last ones in New York. I go where the story is."

"Be careful," Cassie pleaded.

"I don't think 'careful' is a word we use during the apocalypse."

The door to the room opened and Chuck stuck his head in. "Sorry to interrupt, ladies, but it's getting dark. If Miss Savino is leaving, it'll have to be soon. We'd hate to be caught outside, violating curfew."

The two women exchanged glances before they stood. John joined them as soon as they walked out of the room and the small gaggle moved together to the elevator.

"Is there somewhere we can drop you off?" Cassie said, before quickly adding, "Somewhere that isn't Staten Island?"

"My apartment in Manhattan would be fine," she replied.

"Give John directions and he'll get you there." Cassie hesitated for a second before leaning forward and embracing Amy. "I'm serious. Be careful."

Amy hugged her back before they separated, then Amy and John got onto the waiting elevator while Chuck and Cassie stood by as the doors slid closed. For a second, they just watched the numbers decrease as the elevator rolled toward the garage levels. Eventually, Chuck tapped her on the shoulder.

"We still have drinks to finish before you fly out tomorrow."

Smiling but shaking her head, Cassie followed him back to his office.

* * *

John pulled Cassie's suitcase behind him as they walked toward the elevators. Joanne and Chuck followed closely behind, talking genially between them.

"I wish I could say this was a fun trip," Cassie said before patting the folder in her hands. "They are going to hate me once I get back to Atlanta with this report."

Chuck laughed. "I don't envy you."

"Thank you all," she said, more seriously. "For everything. I may not have liked what we found, but at least we might be able to find a cure because of it."

"The plane is waiting for you at the airport?" the older man asked.

She nodded. "I sent an email to the office with my preliminary report and got confirmation that the plane would be waiting when I got there. Speaking of which," she said, looking at her watch, "we'd better get on the road."

She hugged them each in turn before walking to the elevator. "The fact that you three are still here is pretty amazing. I just wanted you to know that before I left."

Joanne blushed but Chuck merely smiled. "Don't be a stranger. It shouldn't have to take a pandemic to get you to come visit us."

Cassie smiled as she stepped onto the elevator. John pushed the garage button and she waved as the doors closed.

They left in the same sedan in which she'd arrived. The crowds were still protesting at the gate as they left, the National Guardsmen working diligently to keep them away from the car. Even so, she could hear the fists and feet banging off the car's exterior.

Once clear of the crowd, she sunk back in the seat and opened the folder in her lap. She had printed off her report before leaving and the folder that had once only contained Amy Savino's basic demographic information was now swollen with typed pages.

Her heart thudded in her chest as she glossed through the pages, one after another, each doing everything but blatantly accuse PFD of manufacturing and releasing a deadly virus. She would have loved to have been more direct in her report, but the CDC was a government organization and, as a result, a slave to political vagaries.

The car rolled through the mostly abandoned streets, dodging past parked or abandoned cars, some of which blocked most of the roadway. She had grown accustomed to the relative quiet and loneliness of the drive, the city feeling like a ghost town. Looking down at her report, Cassie was startled when headlights fell over the passenger's side of the car. She looked up as tires squealed and a van rushed out of a nearby alleyway. The van crashed into the side of their sedan, sending it spinning.

Cassie felt the window next to her shatter and the bite of glass cutting her cheek. She flinched and covered her face as the car slid to a rest. She slowly glanced up and saw John slumped over the steering wheel.

"John?" she asked as she reached forward, shaking his shoulder.

Beside her, the back door was wretched open. She screamed as firm hands closed over her arms and neck and she was dragged from the car. She looked up at the men, all of whom wore balaclavas, concealing their features. She started to wriggle free before a hood was pulled over her head and she was lifted unceremoniously.

The men threw her in the back of the van as another retrieved her report from the back of the sedan. With Cassie bound and trapped, the men closed the van's doors and sped away through the city.

ELEVEN: *Lucky*
by Hilary Thompson

Arie woke to a crash followed by nothing. She blinked around her, taking stock. A strip of starry night was visible at the top of her window, above the cardboard she'd taped there last week. Her bedroom door was closed, but the walls were thin enough that she should have been able to hear Uncle Bas snoring.

There was still nothing.

Before the virus wiped out most of her neighborhood, it was never this quiet unless something was going down. The same instinct that had her locking doors had her pushing out of bed now. She slid her feet automatically into worn black boots, yanking the scuffed leather above her kneecaps and stretching a lightweight t-shirt down over her black leggings. Always prepared. Family motto and all.

The boots were really too hot for mid-summer in the city, but they looked tough, and they covered her hack job of a prosthetic leg. Plus they were awesome for collecting and concealing—extra space everywhere.

She slid her Beretta from the pocket of her pillowcase and tried to be quiet as she eased open her door. Still nothing from Bas, but no sounds of anything else either. That was a relief, at least. Looters had been through the neighborhood several days ago, but Bas had emptied a few clips into the street, scaring them off. Now that someone knew they were here, though, she had been expecting a second attempt.

Her steps thudded along the bare plywood floor as she peeked into the bedroom across from hers. Uncle Bas wasn't in there. The bathroom was empty. Kitchen too.

Finally, she found him in the living room—slumped across the armrest of his recliner. He probably needed the sleep, but he'd be stiff and grouchy if she let him stay that way all night.

"Bas," she whispered, shaking his shoulder. "Wake up. You dropped your computer again." No response, so Arie bent down to pick up the laptop before shoving him harder. She bit down a scream as he slumped forward and toppled to the floor. His face rolled up and she could see the blood leaking from his nostrils.

Arie cursed softly as she backed away, the laptop clutched in her cramping fingers. Specks of dried blood stippled the screen. How long had he been in here, dying? Alone…

"Not this… God, Bas. I thought you were safe. *We…*"

Then he blinked at her and she dropped the laptop, kneeling beside him.

"Bas? What can I do?" She cradled his head as his eyes tried to focus. Oddly, the familiar panic was gone from his eyes. The PTSD had retreated, and he seemed to be lucid.

"Key," he whispered, the sound barely discernible from his raspy breathing. A trickle of blood was gathering at the corner of his lips. Arie tried to push down her own panic—how could she function without Bas? Everybody was losing everything, but she had stupidly thought maybe she would be allowed to keep just one person in her life. Maybe she'd lost enough already.

But apocalypse or not, the world wasn't interested in changing her luck.

"Key…crossroads," Bas tried again, then shook with weak coughing that did nothing but bring up more blood.

"Shh," Arie said, smoothing the creases in his forehead. She blinked away tears—she hadn't cried since her father died three years ago, in the car crash that took her leg.

Bas's hand clutched at her fingers, pulling them from his face. His eyes remained closed, but he brought her palm to his neck, where his old military tags hung. "Key!" he tried again.

"Okay, Bas. Okay—I'll take your key," Arie said, trying desperately to keep her voice reassuring. She had no idea what the hell he was talking about, but obviously the necklace meant something to him. He was dying—she'd say anything he wanted.

"Go…crossroads," Bas whispered, then fell silent. She continued brushing his cheek with her hand, skirting around the blood. She had thought they were both immune—it had been weeks and everyone around them was dying, but not Bas. Not her.

What did it mean that he had caught the virus now? Would she catch it too?

Her stomach lurched as she looked down. He was gone. Her fingers still clutched the tags and blood smeared one palm where it had held Bas's cheek.

Her stomach rolled with a new knife-twist—guilt. Did she bring the virus home with her, hidden in the folds of her clothing? Did she collect the germs that killed him? Stumbling to the bathroom, she hunched over the toilet. At the sink, she scrubbed fiercely at her face and hands. As though it would help. If she had the virus too, it was only a matter of hours and she'd be choking on blood.

She stared at her reflection in the mirror. Pale face. Reddish hair that needed to be washed. Sunken brown eyes. She could be sick already and not even know it. Arie tried to remember what Bas had been like yesterday, but she'd gotten home late, tired from picking carefully through the dying neighborhood. And he had been in the shower.

She hadn't even said goodnight. Her only living family member, and she hadn't even said goodnight.

Emotions are just chemicals, she reminded herself, pressing her shaking hands flat against the bathroom counter. Eventually they would run out.

After her dad died, she'd learned this sit-still-and-wait strategy from her therapist. Bas used a similar method, but neither of them was good at being still. So she collected for the pawn shop, and he collected for the end of the world. She trolled the neighborhood, and he trolled the internet.

Bas had always been paranoid about conspiracies and all that. But he'd barely left the apartment since that news story broke about the crazy death counts in Africa. Then that truck accident and the driver and paramedics dying from the same symptoms—Bas had gone nuts, spending all his time online in his prepper forums, trading advice and outlining possible "hunker-down" plans. Being a realist, Bas had never expected to escape the city. Just survive it, like he'd survived Afghanistan and PTSD.

Her pawn shop and the apartment above it were crammed with the kind of stuff people wanted in an apocalypse. They'd been so prepared.

Fat lot of good that did Bas now. Not to mention that dumb prepper website.

She blinked at herself in the mirror as her chemicals shifted from shock and grief to an adrenaline-infused need to stay alive.

The website.

There had to be something useful somewhere on there—surely some of those overachievers had made it through this alive. She stumbled into the living room and lunged for the laptop, turning her back on Bas. The browser loaded slowly, but sure enough, there was his obsession: *Prep for Doom*.

Arie scrolled through the main website, which was full of generic articles even she could have written. Then she noticed a second open tab: *Members Only*. Luckily, Bas's password completion was turned on, and she skimmed as the emotions she saw rewound from panic and grief to outright glee that *they* had been right. After all these years and dollars and sealed buckets of rice and bricks of water.

They were right.

She flicked the page back up, where the newest threads were. She clicked on one, barely registering its news that a bunker had been secured in Kingston, New York. Good for them, but who the hell was in Kingston? Everyone here was dead. Another message warned people away from the Staten Island safe area. Staten Island was close, but Bas had just laughed when she told him about it a couple of weeks ago.

"Conspiracy!" he had said, automatically dismissing any plan that wasn't his own. But she'd heard something similar on the streets a couple of weeks ago, when people were still moving in the daylight, looking for shelter.

A shattering noise sounded from downstairs, and fear surged in her gut. The sound was muffled, but undeniably coming from within the shop below their apartment. Almost like the looters somehow knew that Bas was dead, and she was alone. Arie palmed the gun and stepped over Bas to the door.

She moved down the back stairs as quietly as the clunk of her leg would allow, stopping before the thick wooden door that separated her home from the storeroom. She looked into the peephole, gripping her gun more tightly.

Nothing but dark shadows and darker shapes. She flipped the deadbolt and opened the door, feeling her way through cabinets and furniture to the showroom door. For at least two days, she had been the only one coming and going in this neighborhood. She paused and took a deep breath before pressing her eye to the next peephole.

A flashlight beam nearly blinded her, and she instinctively ducked, pressing herself against the lower half of the door. She heard heavy footsteps, and the doorknob rattled. She breathed through her mouth, forcing her chest not to shake.

Before the virus, nobody would have dared touch her pawn shop. When she inherited her dad's business at fourteen, Arie had quickly become known as a ruthless collector of others' treasures. Bas and his two Marine buddies they had hired for security were always around to back her up when a customer didn't take her seriously—which happened less and less as she grew into the role of shop owner.

But as skilled as she was at making money out of misfortune, Arie protected people's treasures as well as she collected them. Four years later, the whole area had known Silver Lining was the best place to deal and the last place to steal.

But that was before the virus, and before both her security men succumbed to it. *Before the looters*, she thought with another burst of anxiety. People who would kill to get what they wanted—not collectors like herself.

The doorknob twisted again and Arie thought she heard a muffled curse. Then the wood behind her head shook, and her grip on the gun slipped. Someone was trying to kick down the door.

Why were they trying to get inside the back room? There was plenty to steal in the showroom. How many were there? She had sixteen bullets in the clip, one in the chamber. She'd been practicing with Bas's Marine buddies for a few years now, but she didn't exactly have experience with live targets.

Then she realized: if they had a gun, they would have shot the lock.

The door shook again, and Arie grimaced. Time to talk.

"Hey!" she yelled, and the kicking stopped. She stood on shaky legs and pointed the gun toward the door. "I've got a loaded Beretta aimed at your heart, and my kill shot ratio is better than your average cop."

Silence, then, "Arie?"

She froze. Who was out there? Everyone she knew was dead. Was it a trick?

"Arie? Is that you? It's Enrique!"

Her heart pounded as she looked through the peephole one more time. Enrique. She hadn't thought of him in weeks. Okay, that was a lie. She'd thought of his teasing smile way more than she'd ever admit.

The flashlight beam swung up to illuminate a form and face she hadn't ever expected to see again. She bit down hard on her bottom lip, more than a little ashamed of the flush of warmth that flooded her cheeks and filled her lower belly. It was the freaking apocalypse, and she was blushing.

She fumbled with the lock and pushed the door open. "Aw, crap, Enrique. I could've really hurt you."

He gathered her immediately into a hug, his tall frame wrapping around her. The gesture undid her completely, and she sank into him, hating herself the whole time for her weakness.

"I can't believe you're still alive," he whispered.

"Takes more than the end of the world to kill me," she answered, slipping automatically into the tough-girl role he would expect. Then her fingers brushed the barrel of a gun at his waist. She leaned back and narrowed her eyes. "Why didn't you just shoot the lock?"

He shrugged and an embarrassed half-smile tugged at his lips. "I don't have any bullets."

She blinked at him and finally managed to push him away. "You're such a damsel," she murmured, a smile twisting her lips. He grinned back, not denying their standing joke.

"So you've been out on the streets without a functioning weapon?" she asked, sliding her own gun back in its holster.

He ran a hand through his wavy brown hair. "I didn't know where to go. Thought if you were…if Silver Lining was still here I could, you know, stock up or something. Make this my compound."

"Compound? Like with red Kool-Aid and everything?" she found herself teasing him. It felt good to smile a little—forget what was really happening. Beautiful boys were historically bad news for her, but if it came down to it, Enrique wouldn't exactly be a bad choice for the last man on earth scenario.

"What? I could so defend us! You're not the only one who can shoot a gun, yeah?"

She grinned wider, thinking of their target practice together, only a few short weeks ago. It could have been a first date, although she never would have admitted that to him. Dinner in the city at a tiny, authentic Italian place, then an adrenaline-filled shooting session where he left more holes in her resolve than in the paper target.

Those butterfly feelings had intensified on the drive home. Waiting at a stoplight, Enrique had turned his bedroom eyes and insane dimples on her, trying to smirk his way into a first kiss.

But that was the night the PFD truck was hit—emergency vehicles had streamed by them, breaking apart the moment. She'd watched the news footage over and over—less than a mile from their stopped car, the truck had smashed into the concrete barrier before catching fire. The virus had been released, and the world had been smashing and burning ever since.

Arie sank to the floor, leaning against a case holding handguns and knives. The room was gradually growing lighter as the sun began its slow climb. Enrique joined her, his legs stretching more than a foot past hers.

"Bas is dead. Virus."

Enrique's brown eyes widened, and he muttered something under his breath.

After a few minutes, he said, "My mom, too. I found her phone in the clinic." Arie leaned her head on his shoulder. He reached in his jeans pocket and pulled something out. He opened his fingers as if it was physically painful, and she saw the shattered screen of a cell phone. His thumb flipped it over to reveal the photo on the case—Enrique grinning as he hugged a woman with caramel skin and the same floppy, dark hair that was now hiding his eyes again.

The picture was smeared with dried, brownish blood.

"I'm sorry, En." She remembered his mother had been a nurse—all the local medical personnel had gone down quickly. Killed either by the virus itself or by desperate people looking for medicine and supplies.

"We gotta get out of this city, Arie. Like now."

"I know. There's this place… Bas had some contacts in New York."

A few seconds passed in silence. Then, "Okay. I came here to find you, so I'm in. Tell me what to do."

Her heart pounded double-time at the idea that he actually came for her. Nobody did that kind of thing for her. "Do you have a car?" she managed to ask.

He nodded. "My mom's old Blazer. It's got most of a tank, though."

"Okay. I'll get my stuff from upstairs," she said. "You take some weapons and gold from the cases. Not more than we can carry, though."

She punched the code into the safe behind the counter and retrieved the display case keys, tossing them at Enrique. He glanced around, looking a little lost.

Upstairs, Arie kept her eyes averted from her uncle, willing herself to shut down. There wasn't time for grief, despair, or fear.

Her basics bag was already packed—Bas had taught her about those bags years ago. A change of clothes, select personal items, med kit, a canteen with a water-filtration straw, and a few dozen of Bas's homemade MREs. Everything you needed to survive, pre-packed in case you had to run immediately. She also grabbed Bas's bag from his room—Enrique wouldn't own anything like that.

There were a few more options to consider. She rifled quickly through her stash, opening each drawer and cupboard methodically. She chose carefully. Packed light. Certain items went into the hidden pockets inside her left boot, where the metal below her knee left plenty of room: gold coins, a second handgun, and spare ammo.

She braided her long red hair and shoved it under a ball cap. After zipping up the ballistics vest she'd collected from an abandoned police cruiser last week, she cinched the basics bag across her chest and added one of Bas's loose shirts to hide it all.

The last item she chose was a single picture from her narrow dresser. Arie removed the paper from the frame—her parents, before she had even been born, backlit by the best sunrise God had ever pulled together.

Taking a deep breath, she knelt next to Bas one last time, driving the tailspin of emotion in the other direction. Bas would tell her to keep moving: the chemicals would run out soon. She'd lost people before. She'd make it through this. Find new people.

Humanity was just one big lost and found now.

Saluting Bas's slumped form, she muttered his favorite prayer—his only prayer, really. "We pray for our sisters and brothers who fell. They lived the good life, and we'll see them in hell… See ya, Bas. Hopefully not too soon."

God, she hoped not too soon. Forcing herself to turn and leave, she shut the door on the only home she'd ever had.

Enrique had chosen several different weapons and piled jewelry on the counter. Arie checked to make sure he had the right ammo for each gun. She popped open the register and dug out the short stacks of cash, then did the same with the safe. She had no idea if cash would even be used anymore, but it seemed silly to leave it here.

She turned to Enrique. "We make one trip. Only what you can carry. Got it? I don't want anyone seeing us and getting stupid."

Enrique nodded, his eyes shifting away from her. He emptied his duffle bag onto the counter, replacing clothing with the guns and gold.

Arie eyed the stacks of designer jeans and pressed shirts. "Wow, En. I never realized the apocalypse would be so fashionable."

He offered her half a smile, and lifted a shoulder. "Didn't know what to bring," he said softly.

She handed him the basics bag. "Put it on." He buckled the strap across his chest obediently.

"So how were the roads up north?" she asked, changing the subject. She knew he lived near the medical clinic where his mother had worked.

Enrique shrugged. "Pretty open, I guess. But I came through a while back…"

Arie narrowed her eyes. "How long ago?"

"Um…four days? Five, maybe?"

"You've been on the streets for *five days*? Looking for me?" Her voice was too sharp so she tried to soften it with a smile. In her gut, though, she wasn't sure she trusted his story.

Enrique scowled. "Look, Arie, I know you're better at this stuff than me. That's why I'm here. My mom is gone. My aunt and uncle never came home from the medical center either. I can't find any of my friends. Everyone I know is dead or missing! So yeah, I came here. And yeah, I wandered around too long, but I'm here now, right?"

His tirade over, Enrique hunched over a glass case. He massaged his temples with both hands. A new thought set her brain spinning—what if he'd been seen by one of the street gangs? What if he'd led them right to her? She tried to ignore the feeling, but Enrique just wasn't the survival type.

"Hey…" Arie started, her hand tentative on his back. "I'm sorry, En. I didn't mean anything. Let's get going, okay?"

He sighed, but straightened and shouldered his duffle bag. He slipped out the door and she followed close behind.

There was nobody in the streets. Not a single movement in the shadows between the buildings. Despite Enrique's tall form next to her in the alley, her brain had begun to buzz with the word *alone.* Did she even know him well enough to trust him with everything that was about to happen? The old feeling of panic from losing her father was beginning to unravel her edges again, now that Bas was gone too. Her movements were clumsy with anxiety as she tossed her duffle bag in the back seat of the black SUV.

She had just opened the passenger door when she remembered Bas's necklace. His key.

"Hang on, I forgot something!" She bolted before Enrique could ask. She couldn't believe she'd almost forgotten Bas's dying wish. It took less than two minutes—she yanked the military tags from his neck and hid them beneath her shirt, then rushed down the stairs, not even trying to be quiet. But when she swung open the door between the storeroom and the shop, she came face-to-face with a scruffy, grinning man. She stumbled backward, hitting the wall too soon.

"Hey man, we got a cute little girl here all alone!" he called, glancing over his shoulder. Arie flinched. Ever since freshman year when a particular beautiful boy had shattered her, the word *little* had always been a trigger. And where the crap was Enrique? She shouldn't have left him alone.

The man advanced on her, and she noticed a hunting knife at his belt. A bell jingled as the shop door opened. A second man entered, holding a gun loosely. Scruffy looked back at his partner just long enough for Arie to yank her own gun up and flick off the safety.

Scruffy saw it and laughed, a low and menacing sound. "It's okay—come with us and I'll show you how to use that. Feisty little thing."

It was the wrong choice of words. Black memories flooded Arie's mind and she pulled the trigger on instinct. The recoil slammed the gun back into her face and she cursed her nerves, her cheekbone throbbing. The man staggered as red blossomed across his shirt, and he fell against a case.

The second man shoved past his fallen partner, aiming his gun at her chest.

"You little—"

Arie panicked and fired again. Turns out her kill shot ratio was even better under stress. A strained giggle escaped her shaking lungs as hysteria started to take hold. She had just killed two men. Bas was dead on the floor upstairs. She *still* didn't know where En was.

The door jingled again, and Arie swung her gun wildly toward the sound. "Wait! Arie, stop!" Enrique yelled, his hands high in the air. A third stranger ducked out from behind En, a glint of metal in the man's hand.

"Out of the way, En!" she screamed, trying to aim around him.

Enrique didn't move. "It's okay, Arie. They're not…" His voice faltered as he took in the two bodies on the floor in front of her and the smear of blood down the glass case.

"A little trigger-happy, aren't ya?" the third man said, stepping into range. "That's okay. I didn't like those guys anyways. Now be a good girl, and we'll let you and your boyfriend come with us." He stroked his goatee and grinned at her.

Arie's eyes flicked back and forth between the man and Enrique, who was staring at her with saucer eyes. He nodded slightly, and she cursed. Her freaking gut. Why did it always have to be right?

Arie took a deep breath, steadying her grip on the gun. "Sorry, but I work alone."

"Well, now that's a shame," Goatee said. "Sweet little thing like you'd be most welcome back at camp."

Arie's arms shook, but her adrenaline was evening out. She could hear that word without killing someone else. Probably. "Look. I'm leaving. You can have whatever's left. Store's yours." She began to edge toward him, angling around so she could see the door. No other movement outside.

"I'm planning on that. But I had my heart set on that Blazer too. And a fresh face back home would make everyone feel a little better," the man grinned.

The metal in his hand shifted, and she saw it was a hunting knife, not a gun.

"No," she said, her voice more firm. "I'm leaving in that car. En too, if he wants." She wasn't sure about that last part, but she figured he'd been pretty desperate the last few days.

Anyone might have done the same.

She was only a few feet from them now, and the path to the door was clear. She darted for it, seeing the shine of metal hurtling for her just as she dove for the door, shooting blindly toward Goatee.

A scream and a thud and a crack. It took her a few seconds to sort everything out. She'd cracked her shoulder on the door, and she was lying halfway out of it. The man was on the floor, blood seeping through his jeans near the knee. And Enrique was slumped face-down.

Arie stumbled to her feet, keeping her gun trained on the man. He scrabbled around for his knife, cursing her continuously.

She shoved at En and found the knife—she released a breath. Just a shoulder wound. A scratch, really. His eyes fluttered open, and he groaned. She slid the knife into her belt.

"Suck it up, buttercup," she said, glaring at him. She grabbed his hand and pressed it onto the wound, causing En to suck his air.

"Get in the car. I'm driving."

En nodded and rose awkwardly, holding his hand over his shoulder.

"Now," Arie said, looking down at Goatee. "I can kill you. Or you can sit here like a good boy and watch us drive away."

Goatee just sneered at her, the hatred in his eyes showing that he knew she had the advantage.

She walked backward out the door, her gun trained on him. Ducking into the alley, she jumped in the idling Blazer. En watched her warily as she threw the vehicle in reverse. The engine was loud in the empty neighborhood, and she was grateful for its speed as they careened toward the highway.

"I'm sorry, Arie," Enrique whispered, touching his hand to her shoulder briefly. She resisted the urge to shrug him away, but she also couldn't bring herself to answer yet.

So they drove in silence. The roads were surprisingly clear, as though nobody in this part of town had tried to leave. Of course, there hadn't exactly been a chartered bus for virus evacuees.

Once they hit 87 North toward Kingston, it was a different story. She had to reduce her speed and drive around accidents and clumps of abandoned cars. Some still had passengers, and Arie was glad the Blazer had air conditioning. She squirmed to think of the stench of bodies melting in the July sun.

Maybe thirty minutes into the drive, Arie relaxed enough to talk to Enrique again. She still kind of wanted to hit him, but she let it go. He had made a crap decision, but she was okay. They were okay.

"There's medicine and gauze in your basics. You should treat that cut."

He opened his eyes. "Probably needs stitches," he grumbled.

"Probably. Or you could just leave it. Chicks dig scars."

He cracked a smile, and she allowed herself the same luxury. She took a deep breath. "I don't blame you for falling in with those guys, you know."

Enrique snapped his face toward her. "How did you know?"

She shrugged. "I could just tell. Anyways, all I'm saying is that anyone might have done the same thing."

"Would you?" he asked softly.

"Probably," she lied. Maybe it wasn't a lie—she'd done plenty of things today that she never thought she'd do.

En sighed and dug through the basics bag, finding a tube of antibiotic cream. Arie watched him out of the corner of her eye as he cleaned and dressed the wound. His movements were efficient and assured.

"My mom taught me some things," he said, sliding her a glance that said he'd seen her watching. Arie felt her cheeks heat in embarrassment and she stared straight ahead. "Arie…I never would have suggested Silver

Lining to those clowns if I'd known you were still alive."

"I know," she said. And she believed him.

"But I'm really glad we're doing this together, yeah?" His voice was sincere and almost hesitant.

She glanced at him and smiled. "I know. Besides, a knight doesn't just leave the damsel."

"Hey, I can't help it if I like tough chicks," he grinned. A fluttery feeling began in her chest, so she turned back to the road.

They passed a mileage sign listing the next few towns—Kingston was less than an hour away. *This just might work*, she thought.

A few miles later, Arie found herself squinting at the road ahead—cars were everywhere, blocking her path. There was an exit sign for Route 299 just before the blockade.

"Does 299 go to Kingston?" she asked En. He pulled a map from the glove box. "Can't believe you still have one of those," she teased.

"299 crosses over to 9W, which goes up to Kingston."

"Good enough." She didn't see a way around the pileup.

She slowed her speed as she neared the jumble of cars. Then her stomach dropped as she realized they weren't jumbled. They were parked neatly in a grid. Someone had planned this detour. Her gut screamed *trap*, but she didn't know what else to do.

I-87 didn't have many cross roads—299 East would *have* to be good enough.

The exit ramp loomed ahead and she pushed the gas pedal as she left the curve, giving the Blazer a burst of speed. But even as the road straightened, she saw they were closing in on toll booths.

"Gates are smashed! Go on through," En laughed. So she did, half-expecting sirens or tire spikes at any moment. But all was still and calm.

Then she saw how more empty cars were gridlocked at the junction of the ramp and 299, forcing her east. Her entire body pulsed with nerves, but she had no other alternatives.

Just as she swerved onto 299, a single car peeled out from the formation.

Chasing them.

She gripped the wheel tighter to keep her hands from shaking and pressed the gas even harder, but the Blazer just whined. It was no match for the Mustang in her rearview mirror.

"What are they doing?" Enrique asked, fear finally evident in his voice.

"I think you know what they're doing. Get a gun and be ready to shoot!"

She wished their positions were reversed—her leg made it harder to regulate speed, and En's aim was questionable.

"Find me a place to hide—we'll never outrun them!" Arie demanded, her voice high with panic.

"It's too open!" He was right—this section of 299 was a mess of suburban sprawl—box stores and gas stations and too few trees.

"There!" he yelled, pointing to the right. "Turn there! A park!"

She jerked the car, nearly rolling it onto the side road. At least there was more cover here. Then she cursed as she realized they were only following the *signs* for a park—still not enough woods to shelter them. The Blazer bounced hard over a pothole. The road was too curvy to see how close the Mustang was to them, but Arie glimpsed it a few times.

"Left!" En yelled, and she saw the park ahead.

The Blazer skidded to a stop at the parking lot entrance, and Arie threw open her door. They scrambled out of the car just as another engine revved behind them.

"Go," she hissed at En, who was struggling to pull the duffle bag from the back seat. He glanced up and dropped the heavy bag. They sprinted toward a wooded area.

She heard a car door slam, and the sound dropped her to her hands and knees like a gunshot. She ducked and rolled under a large bush. Enrique kept running, crashing through the trees. Arie knew she couldn't outrun anyone—she'd just have to rely on her shooting skills. She grabbed her Beretta and was about to unzip her boot to get a full clip when she froze: voices—two men.

"Couple of kids! Took off into those trees."

"Eh, don't bother. We got the car. Looks like some sweet guns in these duffels, too."

"What if they come back?"

"Then we'll get 'em then. They'll probably double back anyways. Nothing out here."

"Where do you want me to take this SUV?"

"Drive slow and watch for the kids, but head toward the bunker."

Two doors slammed and two engines started up. Arie pushed aside some leaves and watched as the Mustang and the black Blazer drove away.

So much for transpo, she thought. *Now, where was En?*

Arie clomped through the woods, cursing her special brand of luck. Those men were probably on their way to Kingston, too. Maybe she should have just shown herself and hitched a ride with them. Maybe they wouldn't have been bad news.

She huffed. *Right. Maybe had never gotten her anywhere but disappointed.*

The trees bordered a large baseball complex, and beyond them she could see another parking lot. Her knee throbbed from the jar of the prosthetic against her skin. She wasn't used to this sort of thing. Plus it was really hot now. She could feel her t-shirt stuck to her body under all her layers. She unbuttoned Bas's shirt and looped it around the strap of her basics bag, leaving the ballistics vest on.

"Enrique?" she called quietly.

His head popped out from behind an abandoned van.

"Thank God," he said, rushing to her. "Are you hurt?"

She shook her head, but he reached out and pulled her close anyways, wrapping his arms around her. Her face smashed against his broad chest and she could barely breathe.

He still smelled pretty good, too, she noticed as she managed a deep breath. Arie rolled her eyes at herself for noticing something like that at a time like this.

But disassociation was how she had always coped with the crap in her life. Don't focus on the bad. Focus on something else.

En pulled back and held her cheeks between his hands. The look in his eyes made her nervous in a whole new way.

So she disassociated again. "They took the Blazer and our bags. Said something about heading toward a bunker."

"Kingston?" he asked, zeroing in on her suspicions.

She shrugged. His thumb stroked down her cheek and she shivered, despite how thick and heavy the summer air was. She lowered her eyes, but he lifted her chin with a finger.

"I can't believe we got away again. I think you're lucky, Arie," he said, his voice low.

She started to laugh at the absurdity. Bas had taught her to never rely on luck—better to just be prepared. But the laugh stuck in her throat as she glanced up. En gazed down at her, his hair falling into his wide brown eyes. Arie had always sneered at movies where people pause to kiss in the middle of battle or tragedy—unrealistic. No time for that. But suddenly she got it.

There was nothing crazy about wanting a connection to life and love when you were walled-in by death and hate.

He bent toward her and his lips brushed hers, soft and warm. Her fingers slipped to his waist, gripping at the fabric of his shirt, at desire and dreams, and all the things she had tucked away a lifetime ago. Her eyes slid closed and a whisper of his breath found her collarbone as he gathered her closer. His fingers trailed up her bare arm and she allowed herself to brush the hair from his face.

He made her feel *maybe*.

Then he leaned back, just a little too soon. He smirked, all dimples and bedroom eyes again. His fingers still caressed her neck, tangling in the rope of Bas's necklace.

The tags slipped outside of her shirt and distracted her. She looked down.

"Your uncle's?" En asked, keeping his arm around her waist as he pulled the necklace up. Arie nodded, staring at the tags as they twisted in the sunlight.

Then she grabbed the tags and twisted away from En, holding them closer to her face.

"Sorry, Arie, I—"

"Look!" she said, waving off his apology. One of the tags was different—not military issue. The metal was thicker and engraved on both sides. She examined the lines, an idea skipping just beyond the reach of her exhausted brain.

En bent his head over the tag. He ran a finger along its edge. "There's something in here. Like a pocket knife or something."

Arie dug a fingernail into the slit on the edge and it caught on a ridge. She pulled and something rotated out.

"A key!" she said, laughing. En looked at her, his eyes narrowed in confusion. "A key to the crossroads…" Arie repeated Bas's words.

"What crossroads? What does it open?"

"I don't know. Just something Bas said."

En flipped the tag, examining it. "What are these lines?"

She shrugged, but the pattern already seemed more familiar. There were two vertical lines, intersecting at the bottom and top, like a teardrop. Another line crossed them, about halfway up. A crossroads?

"Key to the crossroads," she repeated, as if it might help solve the puzzle. She started walking absently, following a paved trail that circled the park. Pacing had always helped her think, and they needed to move anyways.

"So if those guys were heading to Kingston, should we still go?" En asked as he fell in step beside her along the shaded trail.

"Do you still want to go?" she asked. Their eyes met for a long second before she blinked away.

"If you do," Enrique answered.

"Okay. Yeah. The food in these basics bags might last a week. So we can head that way and scope it out carefully."

He nodded, his hand gripping the small bag strapped across his chest. *Lucky*, she thought, still flipping the tag over and over in her fingers.

"I don't have a gun, though," En said.

Arie grinned. "Now, don't freak out, but I've got you covered." She stopped walking and knelt down. He squatted next to her, his head tilted in question. She unzipped her boot and peeled back the leather to reveal her homemade prosthetic and the boot's inner compartments, fitted like a puzzle around the leg.

"Nice, huh?" she said, but her eyes stayed on the ground. Not many people knew about her leg. Fewer had ever seen it.

En leaned forward and brushed his fingers along the slim metal of her leg and foot. He grinned and she felt less self-conscious.

"I pieced it together myself after insurance gave me one of those crap plastic ones. Looked like a department store mannequin."

"How did you lose it?" he asked. "Sorry. I mean, I never knew, yeah?"

"It's fine. I don't really talk about it. My dad and I were in a car accident when I was fourteen. He died and my leg was crushed."

"I'm so sorry."

"It's okay," she said again, ignoring the pang that always came when mentioning her dad. "Anyways, old news. But here's a gun for you." She zipped the leather back over her knee.

Enrique stood and held his hand out. She let him help her up.

"Don't worry. You can still be my knight," he said with a smile.

"If you're lucky," she answered.

They followed the path right out of the park and into a more heavily wooded area. Now and then the trees were replaced by rock on both sides—as though the path had been blasted through.

"Where *are* we?" she finally asked, giving way to her curiosity. She'd never seen a park trail like this.

Enrique dug in his basics and pulled out the crumpled map.

"You had that this whole time?" Arie asked, snatching it from him. "Nice," she smiled, and spread the map flat on a tree trunk. "So we got off on 299, then turned somewhere…"

En reached around her, and she couldn't help but notice how close he was again. She watched his finger trail across the line and stop at a side street. "Here's the park. We're on the Rail Trail," he read. "Like an old railroad?"

"That would explain the rock. Here's another old railroad," she pointed. She squinted at the map, feeling like she was forgetting something.

Suddenly she dropped the map and grabbed the tag again. "Look!" She traced the lines on the map. "Two vertical highways, joined here and here by cities. Crossed in the middle by 299!"

The map matched the lines on the tag perfectly.

"But what about this side?" En flipped the tag over. A network of lines crossed each other, forming several crossed roads.

Arie compared them to the map. "I think that's Black Creek, and this is the trail we're on. That line could be this old rail bed. Somehow we're exactly where we need to be."

"See? Lucky," En grinned.

Arie shook her head. She'd never been lucky—not really. Just prepared. Family motto, right? They approached a bridge over the Black Creek and Arie paused to look around. "Maybe we should take a break and eat something."

En dangled his legs over the edge of the bridge as they ate Bas's reconstituted cheesy pasta. "Not bad," he shrugged.

"Not good, either," Arie said, but she grinned anyways.

"Wish we had some spray paint. I'd love to tag this bridge. Right over there—by the one that says 'BE PREPARED.'" En laughed. "How about 'the end is near'?"

Arie leaned over to see where he was pointing. The dull green paint was blocky and small on the mossy stone of the bridge—not the sort of splashy tag she was used to seeing.

"Who tags crap way out here in the suburbs, anyways?" she asked.

En hopped down and skidded down the bank, knocking rocks into the shallow creek below. "Check this out, yeah?" he called up to her. She leaned even farther over, grabbing the railing to keep herself steady. The stone supports of the bridge were massive—they reminded her of an old castle drawbridge.

"Arie! Get down here!" En yelled, and she shoved to her feet, climbing down as fast as she could with her awkward leg.

"What? Are you okay?"

He just pointed, his eyes round with wonder.

There was a door in the bridge support, right beneath the words they'd seen. And a lock.

"I feel like we're in a movie," she giggled nervously. But she pulled the key off her neck. It slid into the lock and clicked over with only a very small push. The metal door screeched as they both pushed, but it opened.

As soon as they stepped inside, Arie knew.

This was Bas—everywhere she looked, this was Bas.

A double set of bunked cots on one wall. Canisters, labeled in small block print, were shelved on another wall. Bricks of water stacked ceiling high. A generator. Blankets. A drum of gasoline. Board games.

Her eyes could barely take it all in.

Enrique cursed under his breath, and all she could do was nod.

"Lucky, yeah?" he laughed, whooping. He squeezed her from behind, his arms strong and shaky all at once.

"Prepared," she whispered, and tugged the necklace back over her head.

TWELVE: *Proof Falls Down*
by Brea Behn

Amy was stuck in a New York City traffic jam on her way to work when her cell phone chirped.

Amy pushed a button on her dashboard to answer. "Amy Savino, WNMN news, can I help you?"

"Miss Savino," a male voice said. "I have a story that you might like to look into."

Amy frowned. She got calls like this all the time, but usually from people she knew. She did not recognize this man's voice. She looked down at the caller ID. It said, 'unknown.'

"May I ask who's calling?"

Ignoring her question the man said, "A woman by the name of Rosa Manuel resigned without any warning from a pharmaceutical company called Peter Franklin Donalds after working there for decades."

Amy rolled her eyes. It was another waste of her time. She was about to politely brush him off when he continued.

"Shortly after her resignation, she was admitted to the hospital in an unexplained coma."

Amy waited a moment to see if there was anything else. "I'm sorry to hear that. Was she a relative of yours? Or a co-worker maybe?"

Once again, he ignored her questions. "Peter Franklin Donalds is responsible. I don't know how yet, but they are."

Amy heard the distinct click of the man hanging up.

That was creepy, she thought. Ordinarily, she would brush a phone call like this off, but something about the vehemence in the man's voice made the hairs on Amy's arms stand up. She decided she would look into it when she got to the office.

Amy breezed into the WNMN news building a short time later. Her cameraman, Vince, was leaning against the young blonde receptionist's desk when Amy walked past.

"Hey Amy!" he said when he saw her.

"Morning Vince," she said distractedly, pulling her hand through her dark brown hair.

"I hear we are heading out for an interview later, yeah?"

"Aren't we always?" Amy said looking at him for the first time.

He smiled and stared for a moment before turning to go back to his own work area.

"Amy!" Amy's boss yelled her name across the room.

"Morning Mick!" She waved in his direction but kept moving.

"Got anything good for me today?" Mick followed her with a cup of coffee near his lips.

"Got a tip on the way in. I'm going to follow up on it."

"That's what I like to hear. Keep me posted."

Amy went straight to her office, before anyone else could intervene.

She fired up the computer and typed in Rosa Manuel. A local newspaper story popped up immediately.

Rosa Manuel had faithfully worked for Peter Franklin Donalds for decades before suddenly resigning with no explanation. Shortly after her resignation, she was admitted to the hospital in an unexplained coma.

Exactly like the man had said.

"Rosa, you ticked off the wrong people," Amy whispered to herself.

She typed in Peter Franklin Donalds on her keyboard and waited. Once she found their website, she clicked on it. For some reason their logo immediately caught her eye. It was very simple. Just a grey diamond with the blue letters, PFD, in front of it. Somehow she felt like she had seen it before, but she couldn't remember where. She brushed it off and quickly ran through the page, clicking relevant links and copying information into her notes. It didn't take long. No matter how much she searched, there was not much to find.

She tapped her pen on her desk for a moment thinking. She pressed a button on the screen and a mechanical voice said, "Calling Peter Franklin Donalds".

It rang only once before someone answered. "Hello, thank you for calling Peter Franklin Donalds, how may I direct your call?"

"Good afternoon, I would like to speak with Mr. Donalds please?" Amy asked hoping they did not trace her to WMNM right away.

"I'm sorry he does not receive unscheduled calls. Would you like to schedule a time to speak with him?"

Amy was swearing in her head. "Yes, please. As soon as possible."

She had really hoped to get an interview for this evening's news report.

"May I have your name?"

"Amy Savino," she told the operator. She figured it was better to tell the truth than have them trace her call and catch her lying.

"I'll look at his schedule. Hold, please."

Amy tapped her foot while she waited impatiently. Her boss was not going to be pleased if she didn't get this interview.

Amy heard a click in the receiver, "Ma'am? I'm sorry Miss Savino, our company does not speak with members of the press by phone or in person. They only speak at press conferences. If you would like our press schedule or any other information, it is available on our website."

Amy heard the click of the connection breaking. She stared at the screen stunned.

"Oh no you didn't just..." Amy began. She immediately called back. This time it went straight to voicemail. Amy left a message knowing that she would not be hearing from them again.

Fuming, she decided then and there that she would get to the bottom of Rosa's story. That hers was going to be the one story Peter Franklin Donalds would take notice of. *Never tick off a reporter,* she thought, smiling.

Amy spent the rest of that morning attempting to reach members of Rosa Manuel's family, her friends, former co-workers, all to no avail. As much as she wanted to run the story, she just couldn't get any solid proof. Which in itself was suspicious.

By noon, she decided proof or no proof she was running with the story. She typed up her report and emailed it to Mick. Then she moved on to some other stories that she was supposed to be working on.

Before long, Mick appeared in her doorway.

He didn't need to say anything. Amy could tell he was not happy.

"Before you jump me Mick, hear me out," Amy said with her hands in the air. "Something about the Rosa Manuel story just got to me. I have a feeling about it."

"Amy..." Mick began.

Then suddenly Amy remembered something. The Peter Franklin Donalds logo. She remembered where she had seen it.

"I'm sorry Mick," she interrupted his scolding, "I've got to look something up."

"You better be right about this Savino," her boss said leaving the room.

She brought up the Peter Franklin Donalds page again. She stared at the logo. She remembered where she had seen it before. It was in Africa! Months ago she had done an interview with a deputy health minister in Sierra Leone. There had been a bad outbreak of a particularly dangerous hemorrhagic virus. Amy remembered it was called AVHF for short. It was a big story for a while, thousands had died, but they had contained it and, like anything, with time the AVHF virus became something people talked about less. More out of denial and fear than anything else. As if not talking about it meant it didn't exist at all.

Amy pressed the button for her camera man's personal phone. He picked up almost immediately.

"Hey gorgeous, what's up?"

"Hey Vince. I need you to look through our past recordings for the Africa interview and send it to me."

"Ugh. Why would you want to be reminded of that? All those people bleeding out of their—"

"Just do it. As fast as you can," Amy interrupted him.

"Already on it. You okay?" Vince asked more seriously.

"Of course. I just thought of something I need to check out."

"Okay it should be there any second."

Amy watched the file pop up on her screen. "Thanks Vince."

"No problem."

She hung up without even saying goodbye.

Amy pressed play on the recording. She fast forwarded through much of the interview. When she thought the interview was mostly over she pressed play. She watched herself saying to the doctor beside her:

"Doctor, the virus has been confirmed as airborne, correct? Has there ever been a hemorrhagic virus that was airborne before?"

"No, there has not."

"Some conspiracy theorists believe that means that this particular virus was engineered—can you confirm that to be true?"

"I have no comment on that."

Amy had seen enough. She didn't need to be reminded of how terrifying that virus was. She fast forwarded to the footage that was tagged onto the end. The footage she and Vince had both had nightmares from seeing. Men in containment suits were carrying children on gurneys. They had blood dripping from their eyes.

Amy paused it. On the arms of the containment suits was a gray diamond with the letters PFD. Just like the Peter Franklin Donalds logo.

Amy printed the image on the screen. She stared at it, her mouth going dry.

She had never gotten over the virus in Africa. She'd gone there and seen what this virus did in person, making it personal for her. In between her assigned work, she had been digging into this previously unknown strain of a virus. Something about the whole thing felt off. The fact that it came out of nowhere and then was somehow miraculously stopped with no vaccine or cure had her naturally suspicious side tingling.

Amy's phone buzzed, breaking her out of her thoughts.

"Amy Savino, WMNM news," she said automatically.

"Hello, Ms. Savino, my name is Gloria. I am calling on behalf of a patient here at New York Hospital here in Queens. A Mr. George Pascelli."

"How can I help you?" Amy asked when she paused.

"I know you are a very busy woman, but Mr. Pascelli would like for you to come see him. He is sure he has something newsworthy to share with you Ms. Savino. He is quite adamant."

Amy smiled at the exasperation in the woman's voice. "What is this regarding?"

"You will have to ask him. Something about one of those prepper groups."

"Do you know which group, Gloria?" Amy asked more interested.

"That Prep for Doom one I think."

Amy was instantly excited.

One of the results of the AVHF virus in Africa was that a whole new seriousness about prepping for disasters sprang up throughout the country. So much so that Amy and several other stations did stories on the various hardcore prepper groups. Prep for Doom, in particular had the New York area buzzing. Mostly because of the wide variety of people that were supposedly involved. Including church officials, medical professionals, and even members of government.

"Okay, I can stop by and see him. I am on in a bit, but can swing by after."

"I'm sorry dear, visiting hours will be over then."

Amy was disappointed, but decided it would just have to wait.

"First thing in the morning then?"

"Oh you will make him very happy. Not much makes him happy these days," she said whispering the last.

"I'm sorry to hear that. I will be over in the morning."

"Wonderful. Oh and one more thing. He asks that there be no cameras. He doesn't look too well these days."

"Of course. I will come alone."

"Wonderful," Gloria said again. "Goodbye dear."

"Goodbye."

No one had landed an interview with a Prep for Doom member before and Amy was buzzing by the end of the call. She hung up and instantly typed the name George Pascelli into her computer. It turned out he was a former government official. She spent the next hour researching George Pascelli and the Prep for Doom group. When she was convinced she knew enough for an adequate interview, she printed it all and put it into a folder. By that time she had to get ready to be on camera. Despite what Mick thought, she was going to deliver a story on Rosa Manuel and Peter Franklin Donalds. One New York would pay attention to.

* * *

"Could you tell me which room Mr. George Pascelli is in?" Amy asked the hospital receptionist the next morning.

"Oh," the young woman in scrubs said, looking up in surprise. "Of course Miss Savino."

Amy smiled. She was used to being recognized.

"He is in room 342. I just love you by the way. I watch your station every night."

"Thank you," Amy said.

She made her way to the appropriate elevator and stepped in with a large group. When she was on the third floor, she found her way to Mr. Pascelli's room easily. She knocked on the open door before stepping into the room and approaching the man in the hospital bed. He looked terrible. His skin was a grayish color and he had several tubes attached to him.

"Good morning, Mr. Pascelli. I'm Amy Savino from WMNM news. Is this an okay time?"

He attempted to speak, but had to cough instead. He swept his arm in a 'come here' gesture and pointed to the chair beside his bed.

Amy politely took a seat. When he finished coughing, he tried again.

"Yes, Miss Savino. I know who you are." He sucked in air. "Even if you weren't beautiful, you are also a damn fine reporter," he finished, breathless.

Amy smiled and tucked her hair behind her ear. "Thank you, Mr. Pascelli. I appreciate your request for me to come see you. Before we get started, can I have your permission to record our conversation?"

He waved his permission dismissively, obviously anxious to get on with the interview.

Amy tapped a button on her watch and a red light indicated it was recording.

"I am Amy Savino with WMNM news with Mr. George Pascelli. Former Federal Judge. As you know, Mr. Pascelli, I have reported on several stories about the group known as Prep for Doom. Can you confirm that you are a contributing member to this organization?"

Mr. Pascelli smiled. "Straight to the point. That is why I asked for you specifically." He coughed a few times before clearing his throat to continue. "I don't have much time. Yes, I am a member of the group Prep for Doom. Although I did not choose that name for it," he laughed which led him to more coughing.

Amy reached for the water in front of him and helped him get a drink.

"Thank you," he said when he had control again.

"I assume your role in Prep for Doom is investment?"

"I see you have done your investigative work well Miss Savino. Yes, I have contributed large amounts of funds to the organization."

"For what exactly?"

He widened his eyes. "To prepare of course."

Amy didn't think her line of questions was going to lead anywhere, but had to ask anyway.

"And what does Prep for Doom have that makes them more prepared than any other prepper group?"

He smiled. "Safety, Miss Savino. A promise of safety, of food, of maintaining life."

He looked sad then and Amy realized why he was willing to talk to her now. His life was ending anyway. What did he have to lose?

"Can you tell me, Mr. Pascelli, who is the original creator of Prep for Doom, and why has this group, above all the others, gained the interest of such influential people, such as yourself?" Amy asked.

Mr. Pascelli ignored her first question. "Prep for Doom is not a game. Although some of those online kids treat it as such. Viruses like the one in Africa are very real threats."

Amy's pulse quickened.

"Of course, but it was contained, Mr. Pascelli."

"Ah yes, but for how long?" He let the question hang in the air for a moment.

"Are you implying that AVHF is still a threat?"

Clearing his throat again he said, "Well, no but I do know there is a company working on a vaccine for it as we speak."

Amy nodded. "That would be Peter Franklin Donalds. Everyone knows they won a contract to begin preliminary testing. What does a vaccine have to do with the virus?"

"Hopefully to prevent future outbreaks, Miss Savino."

Amy smiled. He was a sly old man, she would give him that.

"So what does Prep for Doom have to do with Peter Franklin Donalds? Are they related?"

"No," he said again quickly. "Although, at the moment, they both seem a bit focused on the AVHF virus."

Amy nodded, her eyes widening at the thought. All kinds of theories were taking bloom in her mind. "What do you know of the original outbreak in Africa?" she asked.

He shrugged. "Only what I have seen in your reports on it. It is the first time in history a virus like this has been airborne. It kills faster than anything we have ever seen. It has a seventy to eighty percent mortality rate. Some are immune and some can survive it. That is about it." He trailed off at the end, succumbing to a coughing fit.

Amy's attention piqued. "I never reported that some are immune because I could never confirm it. How would you know that?"

He shrugged again. "Maybe it is just wishful thinking."

Amy wasn't so sure.

"Mr. Pascelli, is Prep for Doom promising its members safety here in New York if something were to happen?"

"That would make sense wouldn't it?" he paused then to cough violently again.

When he was done she placed her hand on his arm. "Where? Where would it be?"

"How would I know? I am just a rambling old man wishing to help those who are still alive."

Amy smiled then and believed him. "Thank you for your time Mr. Pascelli. I will let you get some rest now."

"No, thank you Miss Savino. Don't ever stop, you hear? You keep telling it like it is."

She smiled and squeezed his hand. "Now, that, I can promise."

Amy left feeling sad for the man, and with her head swimming with theories of conspiracy. She was heading out of the hospital when her phone buzzed in her pocket. She stuck her ear bud in without even looking.

"Amy Savino, how may I help you?"

"Amy! This is Miguel."

"Miguel! How are you?" Amy asked, smiling. He was a many-time informant who often had the uncanny luck of being in the right place at the right time. She had known him for years and they had grown to become friends.

"No time for small talk, Amy. Something is happening at the hospital. Something major. They are locking it down."

"Which one?"

"Mount Sinai."

"Okay, I am on it. Thanks Miguel! I owe you boxed seats for this one."

"Sweet girl! I'll take them."

Amy smiled. She liked Miguel.

She cursed that she just happened to be in Queens. She called her boss and Vince on the way. Vince was going to meet her there.

Amy was not expecting the chaos that was already erupting around the hospital when she arrived. Guards in full containment suits were standing outside the hospital doors. People were gathering in front of the hospital getting louder about getting in to see loved ones or because they themselves were sick or hurt and being turned away. Determined, she double parked, not caring about a ticket.

Amy scowled to see two other news stations already rolling cameras.

Amy looked around. She saw a building scaffold adjacent to the hospital and climbed it quickly. She turned to see into the hospital windows. It was too far to see too many details, but what Amy did see made chills sweep down her back. Men in containment suits were everywhere.

People were vomiting in the hallways, screaming and crying. She watched as a patient was wheeled by the windows. Even at this distance she could see blood staining the white bed around his head. She had seen enough. She climbed down and went back to her car and paced, fighting the fear building inside of her. AVHF was back.

The second Vince arrived, Amy pulled him around to the back of the hospital.

"Why are we back here?" Vince asked her.

"You'll see," Amy said.

They waited a long time until the back doors opened and a man in a doctor's coat came out.

"Sir!" Amy yelled. "Can you tell us what is happening in there?"

"No!" he yelled, waving her away.

"Is it the AVHF virus? Is it here in America?"

"No! I don't know! No comment!"

Armed men in containment suits burst out of the back door, heading straight for Amy, Vince, and the doctor. Amy took off running and luckily Vince paused to keep filming as they surrounded the doctor and corralled him back into the hospital. When one of them noticed Vince, the men in suits started running toward them. By the time Vince caught up with Amy, they still had a head start. They got around to the front of the hospital and lost themselves in the crowd still gathered there. Eventually they made it back to his van.

"Whew!" Vince said bending over, breathing hard. "I need to start working out to keep up with you girl."

Amy laughed, breathing hard herself. "Did you get all that?"

"Yeah, that was freaky."

Once they had recovered, Amy recorded a piece with the crowd and suited guards in the background. She spoke as if the virus AVHF had found its way to America.

Hours later while she was just finishing editing the recording back at the studio, her worst fears were confirmed. It was AVHF. It did not take long for the virus to escape the hospital and pop up all over the city. The phones around her were soon ringing nonstop as New Yorkers called in to report cases. With the virus being airborne and fast acting, it was impossible to contain and obvious where it had traveled. It was hard not to notice someone bleeding from their eyeballs.

Amy worked tirelessly for hours that soon stretched into days. She reported almost constantly, throwing herself into her work to keep the fear at bay. Since she was an orphan with no family, her work was her life.

People were dying by the thousands. She and Vince were driving to various places throughout the city to get coverage on every aspect they could. Both trying to keep the news flowing but also trying to avoid getting infected themselves. It was getting harder to avoid as the virus continued to spread and Amy saw things she knew she would never be able to forget. Children clinging to their dead parents. Babies bleeding from their eyes. Amy's sleep was filled with nightmares of the horror that was now known as the Fever.

Story after story began trickling in of a safe zone that had opened up on Staten Island. Hundreds were supposedly going there. New Yorkers were scared and so was Amy. Supposedly Staten Island was safe because only those who did not have the virus were allowed in. They were keeping people out by cutting off all entry onto the island except by the Goethals Bridge.

Amy was researching Staten Island very early one morning when her ear bud started buzzing on her desk. She shoved her ear bud in and pressed it quickly.

"This is Amy Savino of WNMN news," she said, rubbing her eyes.

"Hey girl," Miguel said. He sounded strange.

"Miguel, is that you?" Amy asked worried.

"Yeah, it's me. I'm sorry, I'm just a bit…drained."

Amy was instantly scared that he had the virus. "Miguel, are you okay?"

"I don't have it. At least not yet, if that's what you're asking. But a lot of people I know do…or did. But that's not why I'm calling. You need to know who started this. Who to rip apart in one of your best stories yet, girl."

"I'm listening."

"It started at Mount Sinai, Amy. They think the first was an ambulance driver. He was coming back from a Peter Franklin Donalds truck that crashed."

Amy stood up out of her chair so fast she knocked it over. "Did you say a Peter Franklin Donalds truck?"

"Yeah. The driver died on the scene. My ma is a nurse. Was a nurse. She worked at Mount Sinai. She never got out. She died before they gave up keeping the staff locked in, but she called me. Told me everything. Told me she was never coming home."

Amy could hear him break into tears.

"I'm so sorry, Miguel. Is there anything I can do?"

"Yes. Make them pay, girl. Make whoever did this sorry they ever messed with New York. Can you do that for me?"

"I will Miguel. I promise."

"Bye, babe. Keep it real."

Amy held her breath for a moment, fighting the tears burning in the back of her throat. She had no way of knowing if she would ever speak to him again. Either one of them could get the virus and be dead in a day.

"Bye, Miguel."

She hung up not knowing if she would ever talk to her friend again. Anger soon replaced her fear. She had work to do. She worked for hours researching Staten Island, following up on leads and pinning confirmed cases on the New York City map on her wall. Anything to keep her busy. Waiting for it to be morning and what was left of the staff to come in. She called the ambulance company that worked for Mount Sinai and was able to use her pull as a well-known reporter to find out the location of the actual crash of the Peter Franklin Donalds truck.

She became impatient and decided to call Vince at home. She rarely did so, but she was growing worried. He was late and it wasn't like him to just not show up without calling.

"Hey, I'm sorry I didn't call," Vince said as a weak hello.

"Are you okay? Where are you? I got a hot lead I have to follow."

"I'm sorry, Amy," Vince said pausing. "There won't be any more news from this kid."

"Vince?" Amy said, tears springing to her eyes. "No, Vince, no!"

"I'm sorry babe. I got it. I got the virus." Amy let the tears slide down her cheek as she heard him sob for a moment on the other end.

"I should have called," he said finally, his voice still hoarse with tears, "but I was busy puking my guts out. I thought maybe it was something else at first, you know…"

Amy covered her mouth with her hand, tears streaming down her face.

"I'm so sorry, Vince. This is my fault. I shouldn't have dragged you into all those places for a stupid story!"

"Not your fault Amy. You know the camera is what we live for." He paused for a long time again. So long Amy was not sure he was still on the line. Then finally he said: "You keep bringing the news to New York though, okay?"

Amy nodded, taking a shaky breath. "I will, Vince."

"You know," he laughed then coughed. "I always had a crush on you. I don't know why I never told you that."

Amy laughed irrationally. "You should have. Who knows? Maybe you and I could have actually gone on a real date. That would've been real nice, Vince."

"Yeah, it would have." Vince's voice was so quiet, Amy could barely hear him now.

"Well I'm going to go now," he said eventually. "See you."

"Oh, Vince," Amy broke into sobs. She couldn't hold them back.

"Goodbye, Amy."

"Goodbye, Vince," Amy heard the click in her ear and let her grief overcome her. Not just for Vince, but for the horror of it all. For all those dead and dying. For a virus that killed without thought or remorse. She'd never let it sink in before. Not even with Africa being ravaged by it. Now it was real. It was home.

Eventually her grief hardened once again. Suddenly she was furious.

She washed her face and re-did her makeup. She had a story to shoot.

"Mick," she said, walking into his office without knocking. He looked horrible. Haggard really.

"Amy?" he asked.

"I need a cameraman. Vince won't be...he can't make it in," she struggled to keep her resolve. "I found the source Mick. I found out where it started."

Mick nodded, suddenly more alert. "Alright. Marcus can run a camera and he is still here, but I have to warn you Amy. This may be our last shoot."

"I know," Amy said sadly. "That's why I need to do this now. The people responsible for all of this need to be held accountable, Mick."

He nodded again. "Then let's make this good, huh?"

"Best of my career, Mick. I promise."

He reached for her hand and held it for a moment before reaching over and pushing a button. A young man answered and Mick explained the situation.

"He will meet you at the van. Stay safe out there."

"Safe as I can."

* * *

"Hello, New York. I am Amy Savino reporting to you live. WNMN news has found the likely source of where the Airborne Viral Hemorrhagic Fever outbreak in NYC originated."

The camera zoomed out to show the blackened pavement and dented rail beside Amy.

"A transportation truck owned by Peter Franklin Donalds crashed at this very spot. The driver was killed. However, not before transferring the AVHF virus to an ambulance driver. The virus quickly spread throughout the hospital."

Amy knew she did not know that as fact, but at this point she figured she had nothing left to lose. She was angry and so was New York. They needed someone to be responsible for the virus that was killing their city and so did Amy.

"The virus continued to spread relentlessly from there. As you probably know, Peter Franklin Donalds is a well-known pharmaceutical company that was manufacturing a vaccine for the AVHF virus at the time of the outbreak here in New York."

She left that hanging for a moment, letting New York put their own pieces together.

"New York, this may be my last broadcast, but it may also be my most important. This reporter believes that the virus here in New York has too many coincidences. I will not rest until I find out the truth. My heart is with you, New York. God bless you all."

Amy let her eyes fill with tears when Marcus indicated the feed was done. She had never allowed a report to be so personal before. Time was running out though. She knew it, and she was going to keep doing what she did best until she could no longer.

"That was great, Amy," Marcus said, putting a hand on her shoulder.

"We are not done yet, Marcus. I just wish I had more proof."

Amy watched Marcus pack up the equipment. She was reluctant to leave. She felt like she was right on the edge of something, but wasn't able to see any further.

"You okay Amy?" Marcus asked, stepping up beside her.

"Yes, it's just that this whole thing," she said waving her hand around her indicating the city. "I can't believe it's real."

"I know what you mean."

They both leaned up against the van talking quietly for a long time. Amy learned that Marcus had already lost family to the virus. His parents and his younger sister, who was in college, were already gone. Amy told him about Vince.

"Well enough of that," Marcus broke into Amy's dark thoughts suddenly. "Where to next?"

The truth was Amy wasn't sure.

Suddenly a van came screeching toward them. It stopped right by them and a young man got out.

"Amy Savino, you need to come with me."

Amy froze. "No way, I'm not going anywhere."

Marcus had already started backing away when the young man drew a gun.

"We don't have time for this. I'm not asking."

Amy put her chin up high. She would not show him fear.

"Fine." She turned back to Marcus. "Tell Mick it was worth it." While she was talking, she indicated her watch, widening her eyes. Marcus looked to the watch and back to her eyes, nodding.

She got in the van. After they were speeding down the interstate, she looked over to the man driving. He looked perfectly normal. A bit nerdish even.

"Are you going to tell me where we are going?"

He said nothing.

They drove through a small crowd into a gated area in front of a huge building.

"The CDC?" Amy asked curiously.

"Please, just go inside and listen."

"Okay," she said and followed him inside.

He led her to what was obviously not an interrogation room, but rather an office cleared out to be one. He locked her inside. She looked through the blinds over one of the windows and could see nothing but an empty hallway. She sat down in one of the chairs.

While she waited, she thought about what her next move would be if she was given the opportunity. She decided that Staten Island was the answer. She felt dumb for not thinking of it sooner. She needed to get there and record what was happening. Maybe even catch someone with a PFD uniform. She laughed at the thought. Just then the door opened, making Amy jump.

A woman came in and opened a folder on the desk between them. It had Amy's picture on it and what she assumed were her credentials. She looked away quickly. It made her nervous.

"Miss Amy Savino, of the World News of Manhattan," the woman said. "Originally from New York City, aren't you?"

"This is about my story, isn't it?" Amy said. Her mind was whirring with possibilities of what the CDC could want with her. She answered the woman's questions cautiously and vaguely, not ready to give in until she knew the woman's motives. In the moments that passed, Amy learned the woman's name and little else. If Cassandra wasn't willing to show her hand, neither would Amy. She stood and made her way to the door.

"I believe you," Cassandra said.

Amy leaned forward on the table between them. "You know something, don't you?"

"I…I can't tell you. I'm sorry."

"Then we're done here. Thanks for the kidnapping."

Amy moved to leave again before Cassandra said, "Wait."

Amy paused, but the woman didn't speak, so she reached for the door.

"Okay," Cassandra said, standing. Amy grinned, knowing she had won.

"Please, come back and sit. I'll tell you what I can, but this can't go into your next report."

Happy to finally have Cassandra talking, Amy gave in and shared everything she knew. As did Cassandra. It turned out the CDC had no more definitive answers than Amy had, but the overwhelming sense that PFD was responsible was becoming more and more likely. And Amy wasn't done with this case. Not by a long shot.

The door to the room opened and a man stuck in his head. "Sorry to interrupt, ladies, but it's getting dark. If Miss Savino is leaving, it'll have to be soon."

Cassandra had firmly insisted Amy not go to Staten Island before sending her on her way, with the driver she'd arrived with, a man she now knew as John.

They got in the van and she gave him directions to the studio. They rode in silence.

Amy had told Cassandra she was going to her apartment because she didn't want her to worry, but the truth was she hadn't been there, except to pack a suitcase, in days. She had no intention of letting more time pass before finding out the truth.

"Thanks for the ride," she said when he had parked the van in front of the studio.

He didn't seem all that surprised she wasn't really going to her apartment.

"Listen, I'm sorry about earlier…" he began.

"Hey, no hard feelings," she said smiling. "Your boss helped me actually."

He smiled too. "Goodbye, Miss Savino."

"You take care of yourself."

"You as well," he said before she closed the door and made her way up the many flights of stairs to her office.

She intended on taking some notes, regrouping, and going out again, but as soon as she sat down on her makeshift bed, also known as the couch, she felt fatigue hit her like a brick. She decided to give in and let herself get some rest before what really would be her final report.

* * *

Next thing Amy knew, sunlight was seeping into her window. She chastised herself for sleeping for so long. She had things to do! She quickly pulled some clothes together and went down to the bathroom, which luckily for her had a shower. She showered quickly, got dressed, and spent extra time on her hair and makeup. If today was her last report, she wanted it to be perfect.

Amy made her way to Mick's office. He was slumped over his desk sleeping. Amy smiled and went to the office kitchen. She got her and Mick coffee and stale doughnuts. The breakfast of the media world.

When she came back he was awake. He must have smelled the coffee.

"Morning, sunshine."

"Glad to see you're alive, Amy. Marcus came running in here beside himself. Of course we were both relieved when your watch radioed us your whole conversation, so we knew you were not only alright but on a gold mine."

"I'm assuming you got it recorded."

"Every word. Even the part about you going to Staten Island. Is that still your next move?"

Amy didn't answer right away. She knew how dangerous it would be. She had made some very powerful people look bad, and worse than that, had deterred New York away from them.

"Yes, I'm going now. Alone. I won't risk Marcus's life just because I think it is necessary to risk my own."

"I don't think so," Marcus said from the doorway. "It's my life to risk. We're all dead anyway, right?"

"Gotta die someday," Mick said, shrugging. "Alright, you two better get out there. By the way, Amy—we are officially the last news station still operational. I just thought you should know. This is it."

Amy nodded. Now even more determined. If this was the end, she was going to end it doing what she loved. With no family and her friends dropping like flies it was all she had left anyway. She didn't dare think about what was next.

* * *

They drove in silence to Staten Island. Each lost in their own thoughts.

They reached a blockade of cars several blocks away from the Goethals Bridge.

"Now what?" Marcus asked nervously.

"Now we walk, I guess," Amy said, squeezing his arm reassuringly.

They both got out and Amy waited as Marcus unloaded his gear from the back. They started walking, weaving their way around hundreds of cars.

They started walking into the crowd of people. Amy had warned Marcus to keep the camera hidden until there was something to record. She didn't want to cause a panic. It didn't take long before people recognized her. She heard people saying her name around her. Soon it became a sea and people began to part, letting her go to the front.

At the front of the line, she looked down a row of armed men in black military-grade armored containment suits. A woman at a table told her to come forward.

"Give me your hand please," she said to Amy.

More out of curiosity than anything she did so. The woman stuck her finger in a device that briefly pricked her finger, making Amy jump. The woman watched the device for a moment and looked up at Amy.

"Go to the right. Next!"

Amy did so and waited for Marcus who was told the same. They walked together into yet another line.

"What was that?" Marcus whispered.

"They were testing our blood for the virus."

"So were we infected or not?" he asked nervously.

"We're about to find out."

After shuffling with the line for a while Amy looked behind them. She noticed that her view of the previous line, those waiting to be tested, was now cut off. There was no going back now.

Suddenly, a group of men in black containment suits came marching from somewhere up ahead. They weaved around the smaller group of people, and before Amy knew what was happening, they were all around her and Marcus.

"Amy Savino. You are to come with us."

One of the men stepped forward, grabbing Marcus's camera out of his hands before he could record them. Then they threw him like a ragdoll to the ground.

Terror suddenly slipped down her spine. On their arms was a patch with the letters PFD. Flashes came to her then. The dying children in Africa being carried by men with the same symbol, the PFD transport truck, and now armed men with the same symbol. It had been a mistake coming here.

She watched in horror as they unceremoniously shot Marcus in the forehead. The people around them screamed and backed away from the group of men.

Amy was in shock as the men grabbed her. She watched as they stepped over Marcus's body like he was no more than garbage.

They half dragged, half carried her in the direction of Staten Island. Fighting was pointless. They were too strong. Suddenly her world went black.

Hours later Amy woke up with a gasp. She was in the most claustrophobic room anyone could imagine. The floor she was laying on was concrete. The walls were black and concrete as well. It was cold and she instantly was freezing. She tried to get up, but realized her ankles and wrists were bound behind her. There was not much to see. There was a solid black door in front of her with a small slat at the bottom. Above her was a grate of lighting in a concrete ceiling. That was it. Thinking quickly, she felt her wrist. She was relieved to find her watch still there. She pressed a button on it quickly.

"Mick. I know you can hear me. They killed Marcus. I am in a concrete holding cell. They are going to kill me too. I know that now. So you are going to have to make the last report, Mick. Use my voice."

She took a moment to think about the last thing that she wanted to tell the world.

"New York, this is Amy Savino. You cannot see me because I was kidnapped and I am now in a holding cell on Staten Island. They killed my camera man and my guess is they are going to kill me as well. Please listen to my final report. Whoever is responsible for this virus—they will do whatever it takes to keep it a secret. I don't have much time New York. So I will leave you with this. Staten Island is a trap. Please stay away from Staten Island. If you are not infected hide or leave, but do not come here. Peter Franklin Donalds is involved somehow. I don't have any proof, but you have my word. I have loved you my whole life. You are my family. May God bless you all and keep you safe. This is Amy Savino with WMNM news signing off. Goodbye, New York."

Amy paused again before speaking, choking back tears. "And goodbye to you Mick. I always thought of you as a kind of father. I'm sorry I didn't tell you that in person. I will leave my transmitter on so you can record everything they do to me for proof. I'm sorry you have to hear it, Mick. I am."

She went quiet then and waited, crying. Even her tears dried up after a while and her anger settled in once again. The longer she waited the angrier she got. Eventually she heard her watch begin to beep indicating the battery was dying. Finally it beeped for the last time and went silent. She was now completely alone. No one would hear her final story.

THIRTEEN: *Escape to Orange Blossom*
by Yvonne Ventresca

The deadly outbreak, nicknamed the Fever, had killed nearly everyone Bailey knew. Her teachers. Her neighbors. Her former best friend, Hannah. Mom and Dad.

Like a cockroach, her cheating ex-boyfriend Derek had managed to survive. It figured. He sat across the kitchen table from her, drumming his fingers in that annoying way, studying a map online. Her Golden Retriever, Scout, sat close enough for Derek to scratch his head. It irritated her that Scout didn't sense Derek's unfaithfulness, his betrayal. Weren't dogs supposed to detect untrustworthy people?

"The sooner we leave, the better," Derek said. His parents were dead, too. They didn't talk about it. The bleeding, the screams of pain, the horror. The only good thing—if there was anything good about a fatal, contagious illness—was that it was quick. Victims only suffered a single day before dying. "Four guys from school are heading to Staten Island. One of them has prepper relatives in New York and his cousin, Jake, told him about a safe haven."

She nodded, trying to absorb how few people from school were left. Six weeks ago, they had danced at the junior prom. Derek bought her a coral-colored rose to match her dress. Pictures on her phone showed happy, smiling friends. Those friends were gone, along with Mom and Dad. But she couldn't think about that now. She needed to focus on survival.

"I think we should go to Staten Island, too," he said.

"I don't know. My dad wanted to take us to Kingston," she said. "There's supposed to be a bunker, some type of shelter. It's more rural than Staten Island so it should be less crowded. Nate will do better."

"If it actually exists," Derek said.

"My dad said so."

"Staten Island is closer, Bails."

"Don't call me that," she said. "Only people I love can call me that. Besides, half a million people live in Staten Island. Nate can't function there."

"Half a million people *used* to live there. Most of them are dead. But the infrastructure still exists."

"Exactly. It will draw the masses. That's what we need to avoid."

Her brother wandered into the kitchen. He opened the fridge even though it was almost empty.

"Orange juice?" he asked.

"Sorry, Nate. How about peaches?"

"Want peaches." He sat at the table next to Derek and waited.

Nate was nearly thirteen, but autism severely limited his vocabulary. He knew his snacks, though, and he was in an orange phase, so Mom had stocked up on canned peaches, macaroni and cheese, and carrots. Bailey opened a can and gave him a fork.

Nate devoured it and then drank the syrup. "More peaches?"

"More peaches later. Right now we have to get ready for a trip. Maybe you should decide where we're going, Nate." She took a quarter from the family change jar and handed it to him. "Heads is Staten Island. Tails is Kingston. You flip it."

Nate loved his version of flipping coins. He wiggled his fist, then plopped the coin on the table.

"Tails! Tails Bails!" He left the room giggling.

Bailey smiled. "Kingston it is."

"Flipping a coin is no way to decide," Derek said.

"We don't have hours to debate it. I'll drive."

"No way." He frowned. "You've never driven outside of Pennsylvania."

"Like the highway in New York is much different?"

"How much gas do you have?" he asked.

Dad's Jeep Cherokee was nearly empty. "Fine," she said. "But I get to pick the radio station."

"Bailey." He took her hand in his. For the first time since their breakup, she didn't pull away. "You know there's no music on the radio anymore."

She nodded. "Listen, if Kingston doesn't work out, it's two hours to the Goethals Bridge. Staten Island can be the backup plan."

In theory, she could go without him. But it made her nervous to travel to an unknown place with Nate alone. Who knew what craziness existed out there. Nate was comfortable with Derek, so it made sense to stick together even if she was still angry.

"Nate wins," he said. "We should pack. Let's leave after dinner."

She walked him to the door. There was an awkward pause during the moment when he would have kissed her goodbye if they were still in love.

"I'm sorry," he said, "about what I did. Are we ever going to talk about it?"

She hesitated. Now with her parents gone, with everything so screwed up…somehow his betrayal almost didn't matter. Almost. "I'll see you later."

After Derek left, she walked with Nate to visit their surviving neighbor. Mrs. Alvarez had already been exposed to the disease, too, caring for her grandchildren. They didn't make it.

Nate bounded up the porch steps and sat next to her in the small rocking chair she kept for him. He barely fit now, but he loved to rock and watch her knit. Even though winter was months away, she'd nearly finished a scarf in shades of orange. It reminded Bailey of a sunset.

"Nate and I are leaving today. We're going to a place where other survivors live together. It might not stay safe here. In other towns, looting started and…I can't take any chances. Why don't you come with us?"

Mrs. Alvarez shook her head. Like Nate, she was a person of few words—another reason he probably liked her.

Bailey sat on the step, listening to the squeak of the rocker, watching the rhythmic motion of the needles. Exhaustion seeped through her. There was so much to do, so much to worry about. She absentmindedly braided and unbraided her hair.

They sat without speaking on the deserted street. From blocks away, so faint she almost thought she imagined it, a woman screamed. Someone was sick.

Unless it was something worse.

"Are you sure you don't want to come with us?"

Mrs. Alvarez nodded.

On a normal day, Bailey would let Nate stay and rock in his chair. Not today.

"Time to go, Nate."

He ignored her.

"Come on. Time for peaches. Peaches, then car."

"Get in the car." Nate loved to go for rides.

Mrs. Alvarez held up her hand: wait. She tied off the loop at the end of the scarf and handed it to Bailey. "For you."

"Oh," she said, surprised. "Thank you. It's beautiful." Not wanting to cry at the unexpected kindness, she gave Mrs. Alvarez a quick hug. When they waved goodbye, Bailey had the sinking feeling that they wouldn't see each other again.

"Want to play red light, green light?" she asked Nate as they walked. She needed to feel normal, to do something ordinary, even for a few minutes. He rewarded her with a grin.

"Red light!" she said.

He stopped.

"Green light!"

He began walking.

"Super green light!"

Nate laughed as he ran and then skipped with joy. It lightened her heart a little.

Back at home, while Nate ate his snack and watched an old Sesame Street DVD, Bailey searched through Dad's neatly stacked folders until she found it: the one labeled Kingston, containing an address and directions.

She dragged herself upstairs to pack. It should be organized—clothes in one suitcase, food in another, the most important items in their backpacks. But it was too overwhelming to think logically. She sat with her head in her hands. How long would they be gone? Forever? Bailey didn't know how to pack for forever. There was no one left to help her.

Rushing to get it done, she grabbed a mish-mosh of canned goods, first aid, books, clothes, Nate's softest blanket. Her favorite family picture would fit, too. In the photo, she already stood taller than Mom, but they all shared the same dark hair, brown eyes. She wrapped it in her new scarf, then packed Nate's iPad, squishy toys, Matchbox cars.

And dog food. She couldn't forget dog food. Bailey thought about leaving Scout with Mrs. Alvarez, but it was too painful. They'd already lost too much to leave him behind.

Before her last trip downstairs, she hovered outside her parents' bedroom. She'd called the town but no one came for their bodies. Behind the closed door, they rested side by side in bed, covered with extra sheets from the linen closet. She wanted to say goodbye, but she couldn't stand the thought of looking at their bloody faces again.

After Mom and Dad became sick, Bailey had tried to care for them, but in the end her mother had made her leave them to die alone. "Promise me…" Mom was too weak to finish, but she didn't have to. Bailey knew that she needed to take care of her brother.

She'd given Nate a bath because he loved splashing in the tub. Then she'd dressed him in his orange-striped PJs, put in his favorite DVD, and held him while they waited for the Fever.

Only it never came. Somehow they were immune.

"I promise," she whispered to the closed door. "I promise to keep him safe."

* * *

"Get in the car?" Nate put on his coat despite the July warmth.

Derek arrived in his little Honda Civic with a bag of cheese crackers for Nate. He wore the pale blue shirt Bailey had given him, the one that matched his eyes. She pretended not to notice.

She pretended, too, that this was an ordinary road trip and that they weren't leaving home for an unknown future. Nate ate his snack quietly in the back with Scout's head resting on his knee like any other day.

They'd hoped to arrive in Kingston before dark, but it was slow going. There were no other moving cars on the road, so traffic wasn't an issue. The problem was the stopped cars. People had fallen ill and died as they tried to escape. Vehicles littered the sides of the road, often blocking a lane, with the driver still behind the wheel. Some cars had entire families in them, dead. She didn't want to see the bloody eyes, the bloody everything.

"Ouchy," Nate said, pulling the hood of his coat over his head. Sometimes he processed more than she realized.

She wiped her face frantically, relieved to see tears instead of redness. If Derek noticed her crying, he didn't say anything.

Bailey was almost grateful for nightfall, the darkness that helped hide the horror. As they traveled farther north, the abandoned cars lessened and Derek picked up speed.

"We're going to spend a lot of time with each other," he said. "Don't you think we should clear the air?"

Bailey gazed out the window into the blur of trees that lined the highway.

"About Hannah," he said. "I screwed up. It didn't mean anything."

"It doesn't matter anymore." Their fourteen months together happened in another lifetime. Weariness settled over her.

"I'm sorry. I—" A loud clunking from the front of the car interrupted him. "That's not good."

"Do you think it's a tire?" she asked.

"It sounds more like the engine."

She checked the GPS. "We're miles from the exit."

The noise grew more insistent. Scout whined in the back seat.

"We should stop. I need to walk the dog anyway," Bailey said.

"Go potty," Nate chimed in.

"Okay, I'm pulling over," Derek said. "Maybe I can figure out what's wrong."

He found a spot away from any abandoned cars. They clunk-clunked to a halt.

"Can you take Nate?" Bailey turned her phone light on. "I'll take Scout. I have to go too."

"Backpack," Nate said when they got out.

"We're not going to school."

"Backpack," he insisted.

It was easier to give in than to argue. She popped open the trunk and handed the backpack to Nate.

"You should lock the car," she told Derek. "Everything we own is in there."

"Like there are so many thieves around." He gestured with outstretched arms. "We're probably the only living people for miles. But if it makes you feel better." He clicked the remote before pocketing the key. The beep sounded obscenely loud.

"Come on, big guy," Derek said to Nate.

They went right; Bailey headed to the left. She didn't want to venture too far from the road. Scout wagged his tail, sniffing the ground. "Let's be quick," she told him. It was eerily quiet except for wind rustling the leaves and an empty plastic bag trapped on a branch.

On the way back to the car, Scout stopped in his tracks. He growled, a low, menacing sound from the back of his throat, staring through the trees. Bailey could only see shadows. What was taking them so long?

Then Derek yelled like he was in pain. She ran toward the edge of the woods with Scout by her side. "Derek?" she called into the darkness. "Nate? Where are you?"

"Go!" Derek screamed. "Run!"

No. Bailey couldn't go anywhere without Nate. Scout pulled hard on the leash, barking toward the woods. "Nate!" Moving in the direction of Derek's voice, she glanced around frantically. She spotted a flash of orange—her brother's coat. He walked toward her as she rushed to meet him.

"Hurry, Nate!" She wasn't sure what the danger was, exactly, but if Derek told them to run, it must be bad. What made him scream?

"Super green light," she encouraged, trying to sound calm as she finally clutched his hand. She couldn't panic him or else he would cry and shut down. "Let's go to the car."

"Bang," Nate said.

"Bang? Like a hammer?" She didn't have time to analyze Nate's reaction. They kept moving until they reached the yellow Honda. Maybe she could drive it closer to the woods and shine the headlights to find Derek.

Bailey grabbed the door handle. Locked. She'd insisted that Derek lock it and he had the key. They were stranded without it.

Somewhere nearby, firecrackers exploded. Then she realized: not firecrackers. Gunshots.

"Bang bang," Nate said.

Someone in the woods had a gun.

"We need to find another car. Fast." In the distance, a white sports coupe rested on the highway's shoulder. She pulled Nate along. Scout growled but kept pace. She checked around them, but didn't see anyone. "White car, Nate." She gripped his hand. "Run to the white car."

They raced ahead. She needed the car to have keys in it. But that meant there would be a dead person inside. It was a morbid thing to wish for—a car with a dead person and keys.

They were in luck. A girl about Bailey's age slumped over the wheel. Another victim of the virus, but at least she didn't seem like she'd been dead for too long. Keys dangled from the ignition. "Get in, Nate." Scout hopped on the seat beside him.

Summoning her nerve, she leaned over the dead girl and unclicked the seatbelt. Scout started barking as she reached under the legs and around the back of the corpse. Nausea threatened but there was no time to be ill.

She'd pulled the girl halfway off the driver's seat when Nate yelled. "Bang bang!"

He faced the woods. Bailey turned to follow his line of sight. Then she spotted him: a tall man in camouflage clothes had emerged from among the shadows. He held a small gun.

Terror froze her in place. Then Scout tried to leap from the car. She stopped him with her hip. "Stay!"

Grunting, she jerked the body from the car. "Sorry," she apologized, dumping it on the ground. She slid into the bloody seat as the man charged toward them.

Bailey slammed the door closed. Locks. She searched for the lock button, jabbed it with a trembling finger. The man approached, gun drawn. Her hand fumbled as she turned the key. She tried again.

As the engine revved, she looked back one last time. No sign of Derek. She hesitated, but the shooter came closer. Time to go.

She floored it, swerving left off the shoulder and onto the highway, but turned too hard. Cursing, she corrected toward the right. When they straightened out, she pushed harder on the gas. The speedometer climbed: 55, 65, 75. She'd never driven that fast and it scared her. "Seatbelt on," she told Nate through gritted teeth.

Scout stopped barking. A good sign. She glanced back. The door to the Honda was open.

Their supplies. Everything they needed was in that car. All they had left was her phone and Nate's backpack. She could only hope the man was more interested in their food than in following her. Still, she kept her foot steady on the gas. The car didn't smell, but she opened the windows anyway, needing the fresh air.

She continued north, but with a jolt she remembered that the exact address was still in her backpack. They'd also programmed it into the Honda. Maybe if she saw the street on a map, the name would come back to her.

Another thought had been rattling below the surface of her mind. The man had opened Derek's car. That meant he had taken the key from him.

Bailey couldn't lose hope. Derek knew where they were headed. He would figure out a way to meet them, maybe find another car the way she did.

They had half a tank of gas, Nate's backpack, and the car's navigation system. It could be worse, she reminded herself as she gripped the steering wheel. Still, she checked the rearview mirror every few minutes, fearing the man would appear behind them in the Honda. She accelerated with her heart pounding as she realized: *he could find them.* He could follow the directions in the GPS.

"Peaches, please."

She jumped at the sound.

"You're hungry?"

"Hungry," he said.

"Okay. A few more minutes, then we'll stop."

As much as she wanted to reach the bunker tonight, her nerves were at the breaking point. She would feel safer once they were off the highway, off the GPS route, in case the man in camouflage came after them.

Maybe they should have stayed home, down the block from dear Mrs. Alvarez. Her stomach twisted at the thought of her own bed, of the couch Nate loved to snuggle on, of Derek at her kitchen table.

She could turn back. She could go home, get help, look for Derek.

But even as she considered it, she knew it wouldn't happen. Going home wasn't necessarily safer, not for long. They needed to find a community of other survivors.

Finally, they reached the sign for their exit. She checked the mirror for the hundredth time. Still clear. They crossed an overpass. To the right, lights twinkled in the distance. Lights meant life, people, and safety. For the first time in hours, she relaxed her shoulders.

She followed the exit ramp off the highway. Miles later, they still hadn't reached the twinkling lights, but the area seemed quiet and Scout had relaxed.

None of the road names sounded familiar, but Nate fidgeted in the back, so she turned onto the nearest side street. Darkened houses lined the block, but the streetlights offered a comforting glow. She stopped the car and listened. Crickets chirped. No one screamed. She took that as a good sign. "Hand me your backpack. Let's hope we have something left to eat."

She surveyed their remaining supplies. One family photo. Her sunset scarf. Five cans of peaches. A box of granola bars. A large baggie of dried dog food. Toy cars. A box of crayons she didn't remember packing.

It would have to do.

They ate in the car: Nate slurped his peaches, Scout gobbled kibble from her hand, but she couldn't bring herself to take more than a bite of a granola bar. During a short walk with the dog, she stayed alert for signs of danger but the street seemed calm.

"We're going to sleep in the car, Nate. A special sleepover."

"Blanket?"

She sighed. "We don't have a blanket."

"Blanket!"

Uh oh. Nate had held it together the entire day. He couldn't last much longer.

"You need a blanket?"

"Mommy?" he said. "I want Mommy."

Bailey could barely breathe. She bent over with her hands on her knees. She wanted Mommy, too. She forced herself to inhale deeply, to exhale, again and again, until she could finally function. "Okay. We'll find a blanket."

The third house she tried was unlocked. A single lamp lit the family room. "Hello?" she called. When no one answered, she took two blankets from the couch and a chair.

She spotted a bathroom next to the kitchen. "Use the potty," she told Nate. After he went, she scrubbed off the dead girl's blood. Then they used the blankets to carry some food and bottled water. She tried not to think about possible bodies upstairs.

They holed up in the locked car, as comfortable as she could make it. She stayed in the front seat in case they needed to leave quickly; Scout nestled against her brother in the back.

He rubbed Scout. When Nate finally looked at her, she had to ask.

"When you were with Derek, did he go to sleep?"

"Sleep."

Bailey closed her eyes a moment, tried to compose herself. She couldn't tell if Nate was repeating words like he often did or confirming her worst fears. "Derek was sleeping in the woods? He was lying down?"

"Derek sleep."

"Okay. Night night, Nate."

"Night night." Without prompting, he added, "Love you."

"I love you, too."

When he slept, she used her phone to call Derek. He didn't answer. Listening to the recorded sound of his voice made her ache. "Hi Derek. It's Bails.... I know you're sorry. I'm sorry, too." Hanging up, she sobbed quietly.

Weariness settled inside her. Inside her bones. Inside her heart. Bailey stared into the night for a long time.

In the morning, a rhythmic zipping noise jolted her awake. She jerked her neck to check on her brother. He rolled an orange Matchbox car back and forth, back and forth, along the edge of the seat. Two cans of peaches littered the space next to Scout's sleeping head. Nate had been up early and he'd been busy.

Sunlight streamed through the car. "Go potty," Nate said when he noticed she was awake.

Bailey forced herself to eat the rest of the granola bar while they walked Scout, then summoned her courage to return to the house from last night. It seemed worse in the daylight, somehow, but they used the bathroom and washed as best they could.

Back in the car, she started the engine, opened the windows, and checked the GPS. Finding the shelter could be tricky. The more she studied the map, the more each street name sounded vaguely right.

She wondered what it would be like there. Dad had said that some people were better prepared for an outbreak than others and that if they were lucky, those in the bunker would help them. Would they let just anyone enter? As an EMT, Dad's skills would've been in demand. But not everyone would welcome a girl, her autistic brother, and their dog. Turning off the car to save gas, she considered their options. Bailey wished she could find the source of the lights from last night.

Nate put his toy car away. "School bus?"

"Not today."

Closing her eyes, she tried to remember school, the hum in the hallways on Friday at dismissal. She could almost hear kids laughing.

Her eyes flew open. She *did* hear kids laughing.

"School," Nate said.

He must have heard it, too. Somewhere, nearby, a community existed. A joyful community.

Bailey drove with the windows down, trying one street, then another, until she turned onto a road which ended in overgrown shrubs. Behind them stood an old chain link fence, the same kind that surrounded the playgrounds at home. It would be better to investigate alone, to make sure it was safe before bringing Nate along, but leaving him wasn't a possibility.

She knew they were running out of choices. The gas in the car wouldn't last much longer and driving aimlessly wasn't exactly a plan. Turning off the engine, she strained to listen. For a moment, she heard loud clunking, exactly like Derek's yellow Honda. Was the killer looking for the bunker, too?

Someone shrieked. Bailey gripped the steering wheel, but the shriek was immediately followed by giggles.

"My turn!" a little girl's cheerful voice yelled in the distance.

"School?" Nate unbuckled his seatbelt.

"Wait." She undid her own seatbelt, then hurried to his door, grabbing Scout's leash before he jumped out. As they walked through the gate beyond the thick shrubs, Bailey grasped Nate's hand while keeping Scout close on her other side.

Ahead on the left, a group of kids played on the swings. Some of the parents sat on benches, smiling as they watched. It looked like a normal morning except for the adults with guns who guarded the playground.

Nate pulled her along. Scout wagged his tail at the excitement. The guards wouldn't shoot two innocent people and a dog, right?

"Orange!" Nate said.

"I don't have any oranges."

He pointed. Someone had propped up a large piece of plywood facing the gate. "Orange Blossom Community" was painted in block letters, with a big orange peace sign underneath.

Relief washed over her. For the first time since leaving home, hope fluttered in her chest. Anything with orange in the name couldn't possibly be bad.

Bailey heard the Honda again, clunking even closer now. "Come on, Nate. Let's meet some new friends."

FOURTEEN: *As The Pieces Fell*
by DelSheree Gladden

It was all a lie. Sidney wasn't sure why that surprised her, but it did. Distracted from her musings by the rhythmic stomp of the PFD soldiers marching by the front of the house, she cringed. Why exactly did a company that made medicine and vaccines have a private army already on staff, ready to go when the local government turned to them for help shortly after the outbreak happened?

A better question was, why hadn't she seen the signs before she let her mom drag her and Vivi here?

It all seemed so obvious to her now, but when her mother was shoving clothes in suitcases and screeching at them to get in the car, they were too terrified to think of anything but escaping. Staten Island. Safety. She had promised. It wasn't the only promise she had broken.

The cracks started to show before they ever made it out of their apartment building that day. Sidney shivered at the memory of slipping on the first floor landing. She had stopped herself from falling completely, but her sister hadn't been so lucky. Vivi's hysterical screaming at finding her backside and left hand covered in blood when she tried to stand back up was a sound Sidney would never forget.

She stunk of bleach for days afterward.

Of course, her mother knew the bleach was useless against the virus. She just had to get rid of the blood from Vivi's hands and clothes so no one would suspect the truth. Sidney knew she should have seen it then, should have asked questions, demanded answers. Instead, she followed blindly. She trusted her mother and got in the car. It seemed like such a relief to sit down on the soft seats that day. She should have savored the feeling, because she suspected she would never feel it again.

"Sidney," Vivi whispered from the back door. She peered out timidly.

"Is she gone?" Sidney whispered back. Vivi's eleven-year-old head bobbed quickly, her fear making her movements sharp. Sidney dropped the broom and abandoned the chores Mrs. Otis had assigned her. It wasn't like sweeping the back stoop was going to help this place look any better or feel less like a prison. It was simply a task to keep her busy, to keep her from asking too many questions or coming up with an escape plan.

Like so many other plans Peter Franklin Donalds had laid since the outbreak, attempting to distract her failed just as surely. The endless, mindless chores only gave her time to think. Scrambling up the steps, Sidney slipped into the house and shut the back door to keep the nosy neighbors from investigating.

Sidney gently pushed her sister to the side and yanked open the broom closet. A ratty old mop and dust pan was all it contained…on the surface.

Shoving aside the mop, Sidney pushed and prodded at a board. The old wooden floorboard had to be pried up from under the house the first time, which meant venturing into the rat and spider infested crawlspace. Blood oozed from scraped knuckles before Sidney was successful. Two more came easily after that. The basket she had hung beneath the opening contained the two backpacks they had arrived with, both of which were now packed with food, matches, and a couple of screwdrivers.

The screwdrivers weren't much in the way of weapons, but they were the best Sidney had been able to ferret away. She yanked both bags out and slung them onto her shoulders. Vivi reached for one, wanting to help, but the purple bruises and needle tracks caused Sidney to grip the straps even tighter.

"I've got them," she said.

"I can help," Vivi protested. Her accusing finger pointed at the marks on Sidney's arms.

At seventeen, Sidney had stood up to the relentless blood draws and invasive tests better than her sister. Vivi had always been tiny and frail. If anyone should have succumbed to the virus, it should have been her. She usually caught every bug and virus around, spending most of her early years taking medications and staying home from school. Somehow, she seemed to have more natural immunity now than any of the other survivors, including Sidney.

Of all the things Sidney had figured out since coming here, that one unanswered question still bothered her. How had her mother known that PFD would want Vivi so badly? She knew the truth about this place because she helped set it up—Sidney learned much too late—but still she brought them here, expecting them to accept her daughters as payment for saving her life.

Part of Sidney felt like her mother deserved what had happened to her after attempting to trade in her own children as science experiments. She clearly hadn't cared about them as much as she had cared about herself, but no matter how angry Sidney was at her mother for what she'd done, she was her mother, her only parent. She was furious, but still missed her so badly she almost couldn't stand it some days.

"Did Mrs. Otis say where she was going?" Sidney asked her sister.

Vivi shook her head. "I was pretending to be asleep, like you told me. She peeked into my room to check on me, then I heard the front door close a few minutes later. She probably won't be gone long."

The fact that Mrs. Otis hadn't told Sidney she was leaving didn't offer any clues. She had been keeping the sisters away from each other as much as possible. Sidney was supposed to be locked out of the house while she cleaned. Mrs. Otis didn't know Vivi usually snuck down and unlocked the door as soon as they were alone.

Even still, she hadn't called a replacement to watch them. They were always guarded, because of Vivi's value. If she'd left Vivi alone, she probably just went to the neighbor's. Rations, even on the island, were becoming scarce, and Mrs. Otis couldn't survive without coffee. They only had a few minutes.

"I'm going out first," Sidney said.

"I wish we could do this at night," Vivi said. Her eyes were wide, darting around anxiously at every creak and groan the old house made.

Sidney echoed the wish silently, but only said, "This is our only option. We can't get out of the restraints at night. Be brave, Vivi, and trust me. I'll keep you safe."

Vivi bit her lip as her hands twisted. Sidney knew she was thinking about their mom's promise of safety. It hadn't been true then, but Vivi nodded, putting her trust and her life in the hands of someone she loved one more time, hoping for a different result.

With a quick nod, Sidney slipped out the back door. She walked as casually as she could to the middle of the yard. Anyone who saw her with the bags would be instantly suspicious, but this was the time of day when the morning coffee had worn off and the stress of living on an island prison caught up to everyone.

There was an unnatural halt to the noise and motion of this compound, watched over every second by a deadly militia. For the first few days, it made Sidney's skin crawl. After three weeks, the silence was beautiful.

Closing her fingers into a fist, she put her right hand behind her back where Vivi could see it and motioned for Vivi to follow. The muted creak of the door opening was followed by the soft patter of Vivi's worn sneakers as she scurried down the back steps.

As soon as Viv was near enough, Sidney gripped her hand and they walked with deceptive calm to the back fence. Weeding the garden had shown Sidney the way out. She had no idea who might have lived here before the outbreak, before PFD had done just as much killing as the virus to secure this area. She tried not to think about it. She did discover that the previous occupants had a dog.

The soft earth where the unknown dog had dug its escape route had been lazily pushed back into the hole. The bottom portion of the partially chewed fence slat had been left as it was. It hadn't taken much time for Sidney to pry off the broken piece and turn it into a makeshift shovel. She'd carefully scooped all the dirt back into the hole each day, but loosely.

Dropping to their knees, both girls pushed and scooped the soft earth furiously. They were careful to shove it out of the yard, into the alleyway, so it could be replaced after they left. Getting out from under Mrs. Otis's harsh eye was only the first hurdle. They still had an entire city to navigate before they could reach the outer edges of the island. They couldn't leave any clues behind.

Vivi was the first to squeeze under the fence. Her waif-thin body made it through easily. Sidney struggled a bit more, but wrenched herself through with only a few more scrapes and cuts than she had started with. The pain was nothing compared to what she had already been through.

The desire to run gripped both girls once they were upright. Sidney, especially, wanted to sprint through what was practically a ghost town. There were thousands of refugees living in the buildings. None walked about freely, though. PFD soldiers made sure of that.

They also made sure no one escaped.

Grabbing Vivi's hand, Sidney led her sister forward. They reached the end of the alley too quickly. Sidney's heart was racing, and she could feel her sister's terror through her death grip. Sidney had tried so many times to get out of the nightly restraints. The monitor's wires and electrodes were frightening all by themselves, but even more terrifying was being strapped to a bed all night so various needles could be inserted into her arms to collect and analyze samples.

The worst, though, was the amber liquid that hung above her every night. It slowly dripped down the tube and into her arm, burning its way through her body all night long. Not screaming the first few nights was torturous. Listening to Vivi beg for them to stop was even worse.

It would never happened again, Sidney promised herself as she scanned the empty street. The other residents were all safely tucked inside their apartments with the curtains drawn and the blinds down to shield them from whatever gruesome activities might be going on. There was no one there to stop them, but Sidney's stomach twisted at some unknown fear.

"Walk slow, normal. No running. Pretend it's perfectly natural to be out on the street for a walk."

"That used to be true," Viv said quietly.

Sidney's heart ached at all the horrible things her little sister had been forced to endure over the past few weeks. "It will be again someday."

The dead silence that answered her said everything that was running through Vivi's mind. Deep down, Sidney wondered if Vivi felt the same clutching hopelessness she did. Even if they did somehow get off the island, the scars were too deep to ever heal.

"Let's go," Sidney said before her fears could steal away her courage.

Nodding, Vivi didn't resist Sidney's pull. Her hand tightened around her sister's, but she didn't say a word. They moved as quickly as they dared from one sheltered location to another. Once, taking a walk would have meant Vivi chattering endlessly, her arm swinging Sidney's back and forth like a pendulum that never slowed or ran out of momentum. That was gone.

Sidney shoved thoughts of *before* out of her mind and concentrated on the present. She eyed curtains and blinds for movement, checked alleys before walking in front of them, inspected abandoned vehicles as they passed them, and strained to catch even the smallest sound. They had gone almost six blocks before she saw the fabric of a pale blue curtain flick back into place. It stopped her in her tracks.

"What's wrong?" Vivi whispered.

"A curtain, it moved. Someone saw us."

Vivi's gasp was weak and fearful. "Will they report us?"

There was no way for Sidney to know. She shrugged her shoulders and nudged her sister forward. "Just keep moving."

Speaking to others was rare. Especially after the PFD soldiers had found their mother infected and shot her in the head in front of everyone. Sidney doubted that knowing she had been on one of the many research and development teams at PFD would have spared her life anyway. Infected meant dead.

Sidney and Vivi had cleared as non-infected and been shoved into a containment room for further testing. Neither of them had a clue what was going on. When the doctor who had examined them gave them the news that they were naturally immune to the virus, it had sounded like a good thing. It wasn't.

Since then, they had seen or spoken to very few. The glimpses Sidney caught of others through the windows revealed they were all terrified, but she wasn't sure if they were more scared of PFD or getting sick. All she could do was keep leading Vivi further and further away from the labs and hospitals where they were tortured.

The further they walked, the safer they should have felt, but that didn't happen. Darting behind a broken fence at the sound of heavy boots, Sidney yanked Vivi down next to her and clamped a hand over her mouth. They huddled against the grimy slats in the dirt and the weeds, Vivi squeezing her eyes shut as Sidney watched the street. Her sister was too terrified to make a sound. Thud after thud pounded against her mind until her fears came spilling out to mix with Vivi's silent crying.

The wait to start moving again was interminable. Sidney's heart felt like it was on its last leg before the clomping boots finally faded away and the girls slipped back onto the street. This time, it was impossible not to speed up. Even in their weakened and battered state, their legs were humming with unspent energy, desperate to move faster. Another twitch of blinds on the second floor of an apartment building held them back.

By the fourth time, when she saw movement in a window from the corner of her eye, Sidney knew something was wrong. They dodged PFD patrols twice more, but none of the people peeking out at them did anything to alert the soldiers. Maybe they were all hoping they'd get away, that they would succeed in escaping this nightmare.

Sidney couldn't pinpoint why that seemed so off, but the creepy-crawly feeling continued to worsen with every block. Something was very, very wrong, but she had no idea what it was. The similarity to those last few moments before reaching Goethals Bridge set her on edge.

Something had seemed off then as well. The diamond shaped logo was all too familiar. She saw it every day on the folders and notebooks that her mother brought home at night. Including the last time. Except, she hadn't taken her paperwork to her office that night. Sidney remembered hearing the popping sounds of a fire, but had passed it off as nothing. Who would start a fire in June?

Standing near the middle of the Goethals Bridge that day, she'd noticed the soot stains on her mother's jeans, but hadn't said anything. There hadn't been any time. They'd left their SUV with the others in the graveyard of abandoned cars that clogged the street to be pushed around with the mob of people all trying to get into the supposed safe haven. As soon as they neared one of the soldiers, Sidney's mother had tried to explain who she was and why they needed her, but he didn't even hear her.

He'd ignored her words while keeping a rifle trained on her head. Vivi was bawling next to Sidney, but she just held her hand and stared as some guy in a yellow plastic suit jabbed a needle into their mom's finger. She kept talking, ranting about being able to help. The guy in the suit stepped back without hearing and shook his head.

Even without understanding what was going on, Sidney knew enough to grab her sister and bury her head against her chest to block her from seeing. It spared Vivi from witnessing their mother's murder, but not from anything else. Sidney felt the need to shelter her sister again, but from what?

"How much farther?" Vivi whispered when they crouched down behind an abandoned car to avoid another PFD patrol. It was the fifth patrol they had seen in the last hour, which wasn't normal.

Sidney had no idea how much further they needed to travel in order to find safety, but she said, "We're about halfway there."

Nodding slowly, Vivi gave no hint of whether or not she believed her. She didn't ask again, even when the hours stretched on longer than they should have and the sun disappeared behind the towering buildings and left them with only half-light with which to navigate the streets, which had been made clear by too many deaths.

Sidney had no idea how long they'd been walking when she finally heard the soft lapping of water against rocks. At first, she thought she was just imagining it. Nearly convinced they were walking in circles, her tired limbs and starving body had just about given up hope of ever reaching the docks.

In the darkest corners of her mind, she felt certain Mrs. Otis and the others were just playing with them, sending out patrols to watch them fumble around, just waiting for the right moment to swoop in and capture them. Perhaps they were simply waiting for the two girls to give up and realize there was no escape. That wouldn't have surprised Sidney in the least.

The sweet sound of water freely washing up against the docks made her giddy. Her breathing picked up and she yanked on her sister's arm. Vivi stumbled behind her, half-asleep as she walked, but her eyes snapped open in fear a second later.

"Where?" she demanded, thinking they had been found.

"Water," Sidney gasped as she dragged Vivi along behind her.

Hope replaced fear, and her pale limbs came alive. She broke free of Sidney's strangling grip and sprinted into the open to find the source of the sound. Sidney was running as well, too high on the idea of being free to watch for danger. She just ran and hoped and begged for this to be a way out.

She didn't see the dark shape running toward Vivi until he was nearly on top of her. Her scream came too late. Vivi was tackled to the asphalt of the dock, her breath whooshing out of her on impact. Terrified that the force of the impact had crushed all the bones in Vivi's fragile little body, she launched herself at the attacker.

The fear coursing through her was solely for her sister. Somewhere in the back of her mind she suspected she was about to die, but the hint of rationality she managed to hold onto said it would be worth it. She dove for the black-clad head, intent on ripping the figure apart. Weak and hungry as she was, she knew her chances of success were just a shade above zero. The chance to find out how much desperation accounted for in a fight never came.

The impact of a body much larger than hers smashing into her from the side reminded her of the first time one of Mrs. Otis's gigantic needles was shoved into her spine, only about a dozen times more painful. She wanted to scream at Vivi to run, to bite or kick or fight. Her burning lungs were incapable of breathing after the impact. Screaming was a fantasy. Convulsing as the heavy weight pinned her to the ground, tears poured down her face. She had failed.

"Focus. Breathe," a rough voice commanded.

Confusion bounced around in her head like a gunshot inside a metal room. Her entire chest burned like the amber liquid seeping into her veins at night. She was trying to breathe, desperately!

Why was he trying to help her, anyway?

"I know it hurts," he said more calmly. "You have to try, though. Breathe in slowly. Don't gasp."

Her wild eyes scanned his uniform—what little she could see while he was lying on top of her. The PFD diamond wasn't there, which only confused her even more. Despite that, she did her best to take his advice, and slowly was able to suck in the fishy, oily air of the dockside. Only once she didn't feel like she was suffocating, did her mind clear enough to think about Vivi.

Darting a panicked glance over at her sister, she had no idea what to think when she saw another guy, covered head to toe in black, gingerly picking her up. Sidney snapped her eyes back to the guy pinning her to the ground and demanded, "Who are you?"

"Not a PFD soldier, if that's what you're worried about." He let his hands fall from her shoulders to the ground and shoved himself up to a crouch. Reaching a hand out to Sidney, he clearly expected her to take it, but she pressed herself into the asphalt instead. "I'll explain everything," the guy said, "but not here. It's not safe."

"And going with you is?" Sidney demanded.

Hissing at her to be quiet, the guy's face contorted in irritation. "We just saved your life. Could you be quiet and just trust us for a few minutes until we can get you back to the safe house?"

"Saved my life?" Sidney was dumbfounded. They had stopped them from escaping. Why would she trust them?

Clearly out of patience, the guy yanked Sidney up from the ground and dragged her over to the edge of the dock. For a moment, she thought he was going to toss her over, but instead, he pointed to a rounded beacon that flashed a soft light every few seconds. It wasn't the only one. They were lining the dock, like a barrier. Like…

"It's a fence," the guy grumbled "Like the kind used to keep dogs from running away. Except this one isn't electric. It's biologic. It doesn't need a collar. All it needs is the biological deterrents that PFD has been pumping into you since you got here."

"What?" Sidney gasped. She wasn't exactly surprised by the idea that PFD was somehow monitoring her and Vivi. In fact, she'd suspected it after the first hour when no alarms announced their escape. She'd suspected something more traditional, though, like cameras.

"The amber liquid in the IV," he said. "It's loaded with deterrents. It won't let you leave."

Sidney sagged against him. "No."

It wasn't a refusal to believe. It was her last, empty protest. His words were enough to convince her that escape would never come, but he must have felt she needed proof. Sidney didn't bother to struggle when he put his hand over her mouth to smother the inevitable screams and shoved her arm toward the beacon, where it immediately began to burn her skin. The pain was horrible, but nothing compared to the way she broke in that moment.

There was no way out.

"We have to go," he said.

She nodded, but she had no strength left to move on her own. The last of her effort went into looking behind her for Vivi. Relief flooded her when she spotted the second guy in black cradling Vivi against his chest. She couldn't tell if her sister was asleep, unconscious, or just too exhausted to lift her head—but she was safe. Maybe.

"My name is Harley," the guy holding up Sidney said. "Ellis is the one carrying your sister. We're going to take you somewhere safe, but we need to leave now before PFD finds out we've made contact. They were happy to let you two wander around when they thought you couldn't escape, but if they find out we have you, all hell will break loose."

His words inspired a thousand questions, but Sidney was too numb to ask any of them. She knew she should be more curious, or wary, or careful. Why? What was the point? She was trapped here. Forever. Did it really matter if they were in the hands of PFD or whoever these guys were?

Harley pushed her to run, and she did. The fear that had pushed her all day was strangely absent…until Ellis and Harley came to a stop in front of an old metal door hidden behind a false wall that looked like something off of *Lost*. Sidney balked, but sirens began to wail through the night air a moment later, and Sidney was shoved forward into the darkness.

Stumbling, she struggled to get her feet under her before she face planted into the damp earth beneath her. A hand reaching out to grab her was the only thing that saved her. "Sorry," Harley mumbled. "I didn't mean to shove you that hard."

He helped Sidney steady herself, and someone else flicked on a light. Blinking in surprise, Sidney gripped Harley's arm, even though hiding behind him was the last thing she wanted to do. From the corner of her eye, she saw Ellis setting Vivi gently down on a cot to her left. Sidney reluctantly let her concern shift to the group of anxious faces staring at her in amazement.

"Where am I?" she demanded.

Sidney doubted Harley was the leader of this group, given that he looked like he was barely older than she was, but he was the one to answer her question. "This is our safe house. PFD has no idea it's here. It used to be an old bomb shelter, built completely under the table, so it's not on any city schematics."

"How do you know that?" Sidney demanded.

"Because this is where I grew up," Harley said. "My great grandfather built this."

That was the first piece of news to really shock her. "You lived here, before the outbreak?"

The few answers she'd been able to get out of the other residents had convinced her that Staten Island had been completely sterilized before being turned into a promised safe haven. On the outside, everyone had been told that the majority of Staten Island's original inhabitants had been taken down by the virus and those that remained were being kept safe from further contamination.

The survivors willing to talk when they first arrived told a different story. Even those who had outlasted the virus were now gone, either put down as punishment for rebellion or escape attempts, or victims of the same experiments Vivi and Sidney had been subjected to.

"I thought everyone who lived here was dead," Sidney said quietly.

"Most are," an older man said, "but a few of us survived and went into hiding."

"What's the point?" Sidney asked. "There's no way out."

Harley and the older man shared a look. A whole conversation seemed to pass between them in a matter of seconds. Sidney had no clue what the details were, but she saw enough to understand that they were trying to decide whether or not to trust her. A few minutes earlier, she had been the one fearing them. She wasn't exactly sure when that fear had turned into acceptance, if not outright trust, but whoever these people were, they were at least better than PFD.

That thought heartened her, but the memory of rantings from her mother put her on edge only a second later. "Are you part of that Prep for Doom movement?" Her eyes darted around the room, pausing only a split second on each face.

"Why does it matter who we're aligned with?" Ellis asked. "We saved you and your sister's lives. Isn't that enough to earn your trust?"

His expression was indignant, but Harley put a restraining hand on his arm. "Of course it matters to her," he said to his friend. Turning to Sidney, he continued. "No, we're not preppers. We're just survivors. Somehow, we didn't fall to the virus or the experiments PFD put us through. We want the truth, Sidney, and we think you and Vivian have it."

"What?" Sidney backed up against the concrete wall behind her, pressing herself against its cool surface as fear bubbled up inside her chest. A million questions sprang to her lips, tumbling over themselves until one tipped the balance and stumbled out. "How do you know our names?"

Sidney had assumed—well, as much as she'd actually had the presence of mind to think about it—that these guys had been watching the docks when she and Vivi ran up, and that they had tackled them to keep them from getting burned up by the beacons in their foolish escape attempt. Could they have actually been searching for them? Why would they think either of them knew anything? They didn't.

"Everyone here knows your names," the older guy said. "You're the only two girls here who are guarded around the clock. Even when Mrs. Otis steps out, there are always a dozen cameras on you, guards put in place around the city to watch for you, patrols that know your faces better than their own mothers."

Shaking her head, Sidney stared at him. She knew they were being watched carefully, but she thought everyone was. "Why?" her mouse-like voice asked.

The older guy and Harley shared another look. When Harley received a nod, he turned back to Sidney. "Your mother brought you to Staten Island, right? Edith Jaynes?"

"Yes, so?" Sidney shrugged in confusion. He asked the question like the answer was important, but who cared if her mother had lied to them, tricked them into following her as a trade for her own life. It didn't even work.

"Do you know who your mother was?"

Now Sidney was really confused. "Of course I do. She was my mom. She worked on vaccines for PFD. Chicken pox. That's it. She wasn't anything special."

Ellis's eyes narrowed, as if he were trying to discern whether or not she was lying just by looking at the freckles sprinkled across her cheekbones. “Your mother didn’t work on a chicken pox vaccine. That’s been around for a while now.”

“But she…she was you know, adjusting it. Viruses, they change. She had to keep working on it.”

The older guy shook his head slowly. “If she were working on minor adjustments to the chicken pox vaccine, why did she run from PFD?”

The soot stains. The fire in June. Every night she brought home her folders and binders, all with that horrible gray diamond on the front. She didn’t always bring home the little box with the matching logo, but they were never allowed to touch any of it.

“She burned it all,” Sidney whispered before thinking better of it.

Ellis, Harley, the older guy, and the others in the room all leaned forward. Their interest and eagerness was palpable. “She burned what?” the older guy demanded.

Glancing up at the sound of his voice, Sidney immediately pressed herself back against the wall. The older guy was less than a foot away from her, his eyes burning for answers. “I don’t know,” Sidney gasped. “She never showed me what was in the binders or the box. She came home that night, went to her bedroom, started a fire, and I never saw any of it again. She didn’t bring it with us when we left our apartment for Staten Island. I swear, I don’t know what it was.”

Harley put a hand on her shoulder, making her jump, but he didn’t remove it. Instead, he squeezed lightly and said, “Sidney, your mother wasn’t just another virologist at PFD. She studied viruses, sometimes to find a vaccine or cure, sometimes to make them worse, more deadly. To weaponize them.”

“No,” Sidney argued, “she wouldn’t do that.”

The older guy stepped back, letting Sidney breathe, but reached for a plain manila folder on a table behind him and held it out to her. Sidney didn’t need to be any closer to see her mother’s name on the index tab. Her head started shaking back and forth.

“We’d heard rumors from the others, gossip that they’d overheard from some of the chattier soldiers, about a woman scientist on the AVHF virus team who was supposed to have answers about the virus because she’d been studying it longer than anyone else,” the older man said.

“Why? Why was she studying something so terrible?” Sidney asked.

Harley’s expression tightened. “Because of Vivian.”

“What?” Sidney shoved his hand away and scurried back, along the wall, to gain some distance and room to think. "What does Vivi have to do with the virus? She's immune, just like me."

Everyone else in the room stood stock still, not willing to risk frightening her. Only Harley took a step toward her. "You are immune, but Vivian isn't. She never has been."

"But, if she wasn't immune, she'd be dead already," Sidney argued.

"No," Harley said slowly, "if your mother hadn't been treating her with a mutated form of the virus since birth, she would have died as an infant from the blood disorder she was born with."

"What blood disorder?" Sidney demanded.

"She nearly died after birth from blood clots that kept forming," Harley said slowly. "A mutated form of AVHF saved her by attacking the platelets in her blood instead of the blood vessels. Your mother helped develop it."

Sidney's head was spinning. He had to be lying. It just wasn't possible that her mother had done something like that. But she remembered how sick Vivi had been when she was born. The doctors told her parents to prepare for the worst, and then, two nights after Vivi was born, there was the fight that changed everything. The words were lost between layers of walls and doors, but the screaming was terrible.

She remembered how angry her dad had been, how her mom had pleaded with him. There was another voice, a man from her mom's work named Luca. He sided with her mom, telling her dad it was the only way. It wasn't just the fact that her dad mistrusted Luca that had put Sidney on edge, but something about his insistence that they do what he was suggesting. At six years old, Sidney didn't understand what he meant or why they were fighting when Vivi was so sick, but when she heard the front door of the apartment slam shut, leaving only her mom and Luca's voices, she knew in that moment that her dad would never come back.

The file was still there for her to read, but as the pieces fell into place, her knees buckled and she sank to the floor. That was why he left. He had always been leery of her mom's work, fearing it. Sidney could imagine the words behind their fight then…her mother suggesting the virus, using it to save their daughter…her father being terrified and angry that she would even think about infecting their child with something so deadly and unpredictable. It was a rift they couldn't cross.

Conflicting emotions raged through Sidney as she tried to process the idea that Vivi had been saved by a virus that had killed so many. Was it her mother's fault the virus became so deadly? Had she twisted and manipulated it too much in her search for a permanent cure for her frail little daughter? Was it her fault so many people had died? Sidney knew her mother wouldn't have done something like that on purpose, and her blame began to fall on the man who had pushed her to use the virus on Vivi in the first place. Saving a child had never been his end goal, Sidney was sure of that now.

That stuff her mother had burned, it must have been about Vivi, but that realization brought up a new question. "How did you know about Vivi?"

A girl who looked vaguely familiar stepped out from behind Harley. "My parents," she said quietly. "They knew about Vivi. They used her case to market the potential of the virus to investors and buyers."

On top of everything else, that revelation was crushing. The company her mother worked for was using Vivi to sell weapons to terrorists? "But, the virus they used on Vivi, it wasn't a weapon."

"It is very much a weapon," Harley said. "Used on Vivi, it saved her life. Used on a healthy person, it would be devastating and very hard to trace."

This was all too much to take in. Sidney could barely process everything. Oddly, the only thing she could really focus on was the girl. She had seen her somewhere before. Narrowing her eyes, she demanded, "What's your name?"

"Sierra," she said quietly. "I had no idea about any of this until Harley found Kylie and me and brought us here." She gestured behind her, at a little girl and the teenage boy holding her. "Jake's the one who actually found out about it. We were separated, and well, it's a long story, but he made it to a prepper compound, hoping someone would help him come get us, but he accidentally overhead this foreign sounding guy talking about my parents…and Vivi. He came back to find me, and…" She shrugged.

And they ended up sitting in this strange room, dismantling what was left of Sidney's life.

As more questions than she could count poured down on her in a deluge, her lips formed a single question. "What do you want from us?"

Harley kneeled down next to her, not risking another attempt at a comforting touch, but near enough that his body heat crossed the space between them and hummed against her skin. "We want the virus in Vivian's blood. It's the only one that's stayed stable without killing the host."

"So?" Sidney asked, her voice empty. "PFD has been taking her blood for weeks and they haven't saved anyone."

"PFD isn't trying to save anyone," Harley said. "They're just trying to cover up their mistakes. Maybe they'll find a cure using Vivi's blood and swoop in as the world's savior before the virus runs its course; but if they don't, they'll need to hide any evidence of what happened to Vivi in order to protect themselves."

"So PFD did this on purpose? Released this virus in New York?" Sidney asked.

"We know they created it," Harley said. "The outbreak was supposedly an accident, but what we've been able to learn suggests there's more to the story, and Luca is somehow involved."

Sidney finally looked up and met Harley's eyes. "What do you want the virus for?"

"To show people the truth." His voice and eyes were earnest. Everything about him begged her to trust him. He was a stranger. Sure, he had saved them from being charred by the beacons, but how could she bring herself to trust him? Trust any of them? She hadn't even been able to trust her own mother.

"How?" Sidney asked.

"Vivi carries the virus. It's a different form, but it can be linked to AVHF and they can both be traced back to Peter Franklin Donalds," Harley explained. "We still don't understand how or why the virus was released, but we do know PFD created it. Exposing their role in this is the only way to take away their power. People keep coming here, becoming prisoners and lab rats. It's only going to get worse until we stop them.

Stepping forward, Ellis squared up in front of Sidney. "You only have two choices. You can let PFD find you and keep draining your sister until they finally get what they want, or you can help us put an end to the war that's brewing."

"War?" Sidney asked.

"A few weeks back, we caught someone trying to escape."

At the mention of leaving, Sidney honed in on what he was saying. "Escape? But I thought…"

The older man shook his head. "What we told you about the beacons is true. This person, he somehow managed to pose as a survivor to get in, but then disappeared before they could give him any injections."

"Why did he sneak in just to leave again?" Sidney asked.

"His goal wasn't to find safety. It was to gain information," the man said. "He was trying to find out about PFD's defenses, and how to get around them."

Maybe Sidney was just too tired to follow the logic of that. "Why?"

"Those preppers you mentioned, they're hardly the biggest threat to us right now." The older man pressed his hand to his chin as he studied Sidney. "We *questioned* the man we caught, extensively. He never told us the name of the group he worked for, but we were able to discover that whoever this group is, they know the truth about PFD."

"Isn't that a good thing?" Sidney asked hopefully.

"Not if they believe PFD has no hope of coming up with a cure and blames them for destroying the world," the older man said. "Add in the fact that they're hell-bent on revenge and will stop at nothing to keep PFD from gaining control of what's left of the world. So no…this group is not a good thing."

Sidney's last straggling hope of getting her sister to safety died a short death. More concerned with the impending war, the older man seemed unaffected by her dashed dreams. He squatted down next to her and met her eyes. "You and your sister will either die at the hands of the monsters who helped create this hell, or the lunatics intent on destroying what's left. Those are your options if you choose not to help us."

Sidney swallowed hard, glancing over at her sleeping sister before turning back to the man. "And if I agree to help you?"

"We'll do everything we can to protect you both," he said. "We can't promise this will end the way we want it to, but we can promise that you'll be doing something right, something good, with whatever time we all have left."

She and Vivi had escaped experimentation and prison only to find themselves stuck in the same situation all over again. They wanted Vivi's blood. They would be locked up more tightly than they had been with PFD. They could die in this bunker without ever seeing the light of day again.

Or they may save the world. What was left of it.

Vivi had never been given a choice in any of this, but now it was up to Sidney to decide. Pushing up from the ground, she looked at the man. "If we're going to be working together, maybe you should tell me your name."

"Abraham," he said as he extended his hand.

The relief on his face was echoed throughout the room. Even Sidney felt the tension release from her shoulders as they shook hands. She had no guarantee that she was making the right decision, but at least it had been her choice this time. She wasn't being pushed blindly along a path set by someone else who had their own interests at heart. Fear and anger had driven her father away. Desperation caused her mother to do terrible things, and eventually led to her own death.

The need to protect her sister had been the fuel behind everything Sidney had done lately. That certainly hadn't changed, but Sidney was done being driven by circumstance and terror. Hiding and running away would accomplish nothing. She was ready to take a stand and protect her sister, and just maybe do something that would matter, that would help others and not tear apart what little was left of humanity. Sidney was taking control.

FIFTEEN: *Edge of a Promise*
by Casey Hays

The shovel point cracked against the hard dirt and a thin layer of topsoil spun into the air. Wendy paused, rubbed her blistering hands together rapidly, and tried again. The impact vibrated up her arms, but the shovel bit no deeper. It was pointless; the dirt was like rock. With a choking sob, she crumpled to her knees and buried her face in her hands.

The breeze kicked up slightly and rattled the chamisa bushes lining the back fence. It's where Wendy had hoped to bury her mother. In her mind, the empty spot in the middle was the perfect choice. But she'd never buried anything in her life, and contemplating it any further was a waste of time.

Yesterday, her world had been a different place. Yesterday—even though her mother's eyes were bloodshot from lack of sleep due to a terrible headache—she'd made pancakes for breakfast. Yesterday, as usual, the wind had blown hot over the valley. And despite the horrific stories of death that poured from the television hourly, yesterday had been a relatively good day.

Then, late afternoon, her mother had vomited up a lunch laced with traces of blood. Wendy, and her younger sister Julie, had stared in shock as she'd bent over the sink—blood smatter spotting her chin. She'd collapsed with aching fatigue, and she could hide the cause of the headache no longer. The virus had arrived at their doorstep.

Wendy fiercely wiped her tears, stood, and gripped the shovel. She stabbed it at the ground again and again, a rage bubbling up inside. The shovel never hit the same mark twice. Another jab, and she flung it as hard as she could across the yard and into the barbed wire fence that divided the two properties.

It wasn't fair. She shouldn't be the one disposing of her mother's body. But there was no one else. No neighbors, no emergency responders, no one. Everyone had fled the city…or died.

Her sweat-drenched hair clung to her forehead, and she pushed it away in frustration. She eyed the navy-blue sleeping bag at her feet.

Three weeks ago, they'd gone camping at Ute Lake. Rain had been scarce all season, and that night had been extremely hot and dry. Her mom had smiled from across the campfire, her short, dark curls still wet from her swim. Wendy hadn't told her how beautiful she'd looked. It was not cool for a sixteen year old to tell her mom she was beautiful, so she'd kept the thought to herself. They'd climbed into their sleeping bags without another word.

She wished she'd said something. But on that night, she'd never dreamed her mother's sleeping bag would one day be a coffin.

Yesterday, her mom had climbed into it for the last time.

"When, I'm gone," she'd wheezed, her lungs caving under the last, gruesome symptoms, "you zip me up in here, and take me out of this house. Do you understand?"

Wendy had simply nodded, tears threatening, and pressed a cool cloth to her mother's forehead.

Now, the sun beat heavy in the windy, dry heat; the sleeping bag beckoned to her, and she cursed the hard ground. She had no choice but to concede to option two. She loathed option two, but she had to lay her mother's body to rest somehow. The necessity ate at her.

Hesitantly, she took a fistful of the sleeping bag in each hand and lugged her precious load across the yard and through the side gate to the garage. This wasn't her mom any more. No. Her mom was singing in the heavenly choir.

Her mom had sung like an angel—another unspoken compliment that Wendy regretted. Every week, her mom was the first member of the choir to arrive at the large church in the Heights—an hour early. It was a drive for them, and every week, Wendy complained.

"Why do we have to go so early, Mom? I mean, we could sleep another forty-five minutes if you weren't so anal."

"Hush," her mom would say. "You need to get your priorities straight, Wendy. It's one day out of the week. Can you not devote one day to God without complaint?"

Wendy didn't remember the scolding now. Only the sweet sound of the voice she would never hear again.

She pulled the sleeping bag to a stop and straightened. She didn't mind church. But many times, she would have rather been somewhere else. Sleeping, listening to music, making out with her boyfriend. Her chest tightened.

She hadn't heard from Chad. Three days since the virus struck Albuquerque, and no call. No text. She was beginning to worry. He lived north, in Rio Rancho, but they talked every day. *Every* day. She sighed. There had to be a logical explanation for why he hadn't called. The alternative was not acceptable.

Her life had changed dramatically since she'd met Chad two years earlier. He made her feel safe and loved. He was her prince. Her singing, guitar-strumming knight in shining armor. Even in her grief, this made her smile.

They'd grown closer this year—close enough that he'd finally let her meet his father. A pilot with the National Guard, he cared about two things: flying and "prepping" for the end of the world. One consisted of a search and rescue helicopter; the other involved much more, including a very popular apocalyptic website that even her friend, Billy, had been sucked into. Wendy didn't understand the obsession, but Charles Montgomery was always nice to her. Chad didn't talk about it, and they spent very little time at his house. Wendy knew he was embarrassed, so she didn't pry. In truth, Mr. Montgomery was kind of a fanatic.

But now, she wondered if he'd had the right idea. Not that it could have stopped the storm that had swept in so quickly to take them out one by one.

She squeezed back the tears. Chad would survive. She needed him to with every bit of her heart. Everyone else had slipped out of her grip. Her dad had died of cancer five years ago, even though Wendy had prayed every day that he'd beat it. And now her mom…

Wendy bit her trembling lip. Julie waited inside. She was all Wendy had left. Sweet Julie, who never complained about anything. Never argued. Always did what she was told. So accepting. And she was brave. Wendy wasn't. She didn't feel one ounce of bravery, and she wrangled with their mother as the garage door ascended. *Get up! I can't do this without you!* She wanted to scream it. The answer was silence.

She sighed, and the hollow sound magnified her grief.

Inside the garage, the deep freezer chest squatted against the wall. Wendy left the sleeping bag, moved to the freezer, and lifted the lid. It was half-filled with sirloins, ground beef, chicken breasts. Still, there was plenty of room. She cringed. Her mother's body would be laid to rest alongside the frozen remains of potential dinner foods that would never be eaten. The image was ugly, but it had to be done.

She tugged the sleeping bag across the smooth floor, sliding past her mother's black Ford Escort. She didn't think, she simply scooped her hands beneath her mother's body and lifted. It bent in the crook of her arms and Wendy shuddered in revulsion, straining against the weight. Her mom had been gone two hours; she still felt so lifelike. But she was dead, and this sent Wendy into a nervous panic until she managed to jostle her mother's small frame into place.

She didn't know how long it would take for her mom to decompose, but she hoped this would hold it off. She pressed the fabric down and slammed the lid with a resounding thud. With the sound, her heart cracked. She spread her palm flat atop the freezer for a brief moment, sniffled once, and turned on her heels. She entered the house through the screened door. It fell shut with an angry smack.

* * *

"Here Julie. Try to eat something."

Julie lay on the couch under a heavy multi-patterned quilt, her legs draped across Wendy's lap. She'd refused to stay in her bed. The sunroom—her favorite place in the house—this is where she wanted to die. Wendy hadn't argued with her. Instead, she'd helped her to the room full of sunlight.

She raised her little sister's head, tipped the cup of soup toward her lips, and Julie truly did try to comply. Her lips worked weakly against the edge of the cup. She slurped, swallowed, slurped again. Still, the soup was barely disturbed. Julie fell back against the pillows with a tiny, aching sigh.

"It hurts to breathe," she whispered.

She pried her lids open and Wendy fought the urge to turn away. The whites of Julie's eyes were gone. Every blood vessel had exploded; it was painful to see. Wendy set the soup aside and tightly clamped Julie's hand.

"Just take shallow breaths, okay?"

Julie nodded, her eyes drooping, and Wendy brushed a strand of sandy-colored hair away from her sister's eyes. Her fingertips grazed Julie's forehead, and she was astonished by the heat. Julie grimaced, coughed once, and a trickle of blood oozed from of the corner of her mouth. Wendy dabbed at the blood with a wadded napkin.

Julie was severely dehydrated. After spending hours rotating between diarrhea and vomiting, she had nothing left. No energy, no strength, nothing but purple bruises and hemorrhaging lungs. The virus proved its ruthless determination to kill her with every cough.

"Did you bury Mom?" Julie whispered, and Wendy froze. She could not tell Julie about the deep freezer. It was too morbid.

"Mmm-hmm," Wendy nodded.

"Did you pray? And say her favorite scripture?"

Wendy bit her lip. Of course, Julie would have remembered to do those two simple things. And so why hadn't she? *Say a prayer; recite a verse.* It was that easy. She took a breath, ready to lie again, but Julie saved her from it.

In a coughing fit she bolted upright. Her eyes widened in a panic, and before Wendy could react, blood spewed in a river of crimson. It splattered over the quilt, sprayed Wendy's face, her chest. Julie raised her hands to her own face in horrified shock.

"I'm sorry," she wheezed. She dragged the back of one hand across her mouth. "Wendy…"

Wendy didn't move, stunned. Their eyes locked. Julie's fingers grappled for Wendy's hand as her lungs rattled.

"Pray with me," she whispered, tears in her voice. Her fingers tightened weakly. Wendy simply stared. She had no clue what to pray at a time like this. And so Julie began.

"Dear God," her voice was a mere whisper. "Thank you for the life you gave me. For my parents. For my sister." She dragged in a choking breath and forced out the words. "I'm ready to come home to you, but it means I'll leave her to face this all alone. Please be with her, God. And please, please don't let her get sick. She won't have anyone to take care of her. That's all I ask, in Jesus' name."

Tears edged the corners of Wendy's eyes. "In Jesus' name," she whispered.

Julie blinked, and Wendy saw the end in the motion. Another fit of coughing. Blood gurgled from Julie's mouth; she fell back, her body stiffening as she gasped for air.

"Julie?" Wendy leaned in. "Julie? Julie! No, no, no…"

She leapt to her feet. Her hands hovered frantically, but she could do nothing.

Julie, her face smeared with blood, released one final wheezing breath—and she was gone.

Like a statue, Wendy stood over the lifeless form. She forgot about the blood; she forgot about the fear of infection. She fell to her knees, gathered up her baby sister, and wept.

* * *

She wept as the shower washed away the last evidence of her sister's life. Pink-tinged and mocking, the water swirled around her feet and fled down the drain. She scrubbed her skin with a pedicure brush until it was raw and aching—like her heart.

She would be next; she would die alone. The thought wrenched her gut. She pressed her back against the cold tile and slid down its surface to the shower floor. She hugged her knees to her chest and rocked as the water, mingled with her tears, pummeled her.

She couldn't stay here. She couldn't just wait to die. As far as she knew, everyone in her small town of Tijeras Canyon was dead. By all rights, she should be dead, too. Both her mother and her sister had succumbed to the infection virtually overnight.

So why had it overlooked her?

She rested her chin on her knee. Dwelling on that question would send her to the edge of insanity. And she didn't need that right now. She needed a human touch.

She wanted Chad.

The shower began to cool, and she shivered. She didn't know what she might find out there on the streets of the city. The thought of leaving the house terrified her as much as staying put, but she had no choice. So she settled her mind; she would go to Rio Rancho.

She stood and shut off the water. It was overwhelmingly possible that Chad was dead. And if not, he still may not be home. It was probable that his dad had taken him and his sister Annee out of the city. And if he had, what then?

She shook her head and reached for a towel. She'd go to Chad's anyway. What would it hurt? And if he was gone, then she'd find Billy.

Billy Young was undoubtedly one of her more eccentric friends. She'd known him since middle school. He had an overly-active imagination due to far too much online gaming, and his membership on Montgomery's website only strengthened his eccentricity. But mostly, Billy was a computer wizard. He knew the infrastructure of this city because he'd climbed inside the system more than once while sitting at his own desk. Last summer, he'd hacked into the city's power grid and turned every single stoplight red. Mass confusion had erupted, along with not a few angry commuters, until he'd switched it back after an hour. A month later, he'd managed to weasel into the online security system at the Metropolitan Detention Center and unlock all the inside prison cells in the female ward.

He never did get caught, but he did share his high-tech escapades with Wendy and Chad, who told his father. Charles Montgomery was impressed, and Billy's feat earned him high clearance status on the website—and a nickname. The Ghost. He was beyond proud of his new title.

Yes, if she couldn't find Chad, Billy would know what to do.

Wendy scrambled into her clothes, and rummaged through a drawer for a comb. Lately, Billy had become as obsessed with prepping as Montgomery, talking about it every time Wendy saw him at church. Once, when Chad had been with them, he'd mentioned a stocked bunker in New York. Chad had had very little to say in response, so Wendy had only half-listened. And Chad's fingers, tangled with her own, had tightened.

Wendy scooped up her cell phone from the bathroom counter and checked her messages. Still nothing. The tears came again, and the screen blurred out of her vision. She blinked the tears away and punched her outgoing calls tab. Chad's number was at the top of the list. She pressed his name and waited. It rang…and rang.

"Please pick up." She hated how desperate she felt. "Please pick up."

After the twelfth ring, the line clicked.

"This is Chad. Leave a message."

Wendy bit her lip at the sound of his voice.

"It's me again. Listen. If you get this message, I'm heading for Rio Rancho. I'm okay, but—" Her voice cut short. She couldn't bring herself to tell him about her family. She exhaled deeply. "I'll be there in an hour." A pause. "Chad…please be home."

Afterward, she stared at the phone for a full minute. The screen went black, and a teardrop splattered the dark surface. She furiously wiped her eyes.

She felt the anger creep in. Jaw tense, she clenched her fists against her thighs, fighting the urge to throw something. The world was all wrong. Backward. Her mom was dead; Julie was dead; Billy might be dead. Why not? And Chad?

With a harsh intake of breath, she stifled her thoughts, and his brown eyes flooded her memory. Living eyes, full of laughter.

She closed her eyes and prayed for strength. And for peace.

In her room, she tugged a duffel bag from her closet and packed four changes of clothes, a toothbrush, soap, all the essentials. She yanked every picture off the mirror where she'd taped them through the years. Her mom in Hawaii, sipping a piña colada. Julie dressed for her first school dance. Prom night. Chad's arm draped around her while he kissed her cheek. She ran a thumb across his face before quickly tucking the pictures into her bag.

Downstairs, she grabbed a basket from the laundry room and loaded it with every non-perishable thing it could hold. Canned foods, water, items from the medicine cupboard—just in case. She loaded the car and returned to the sunroom.

She had nowhere to put Julie, so she simply took the quilt, and with a final look at her sister, pulled it over her face. It was covered in blood, and as an afterthought, Wendy lugged the pink-striped comforter down from Julie's bed and flung it over the entire couch. It was the prettiest coffin she'd ever seen.

She closed her eyes, and quoted Julie's favorite Bible verse from *Hebrews*.

"Now faith is being sure of what we hope for and certain of what we do not see."

The verse stung, spilling from her lips. Silently she prayed for something left to hope for. Her fingertips brushed the striped fabric.

"I love you, Julie."

They were the last words she ever said to her sister.

* * *

She parked her mother's Ford in Chad's driveway and cut the engine. The large, adobe-styled villa stretched out before her, intimidating as usual. But today, it felt more ominous than ever as she took the walkway up to the front door.

She rang the doorbell and cupped her face to peer through the thick, foggy glass panel in the door. Nothing. She knocked, four quick raps.

"Chad? Annee?"

She rang the bell again, and then tried the knob. Surprisingly, it turned. She pushed the door open.

She stood in the doorway, uneasy. It wasn't like the Montgomerys to leave a door unlocked.

"Chad?"

She stepped into the foyer, and she felt it immediately—emptiness. No one was here.

No one alive, anyway.

Droplets of blood splattered in a ragged line across the foyer tiles.

"No," she whispered. Her hands flew to her mouth.

Wendy followed the trail, which ended in a messy pool of blood and bile in the kitchen doorway. Gagging, she stepped around the crimson puddle, her eyes searching the kitchen. Smudges of blood smeared the countertop and the floor near the dining room. The blood ended there. She peered into the empty room, bent to see under the table. Nothing. She turned away as desperation flooded her.

Back in the foyer, she paused at the foot of the stairs, her hand on the railing. The white-carpeted steps were clean, not one stain. She raised her eyes.

"Chad!"

She expected no answer, but she called anyway. She rested a foot on the bottom step just as her phone buzzed against her hip, startling her. She quickly tugged it from her back pocket.

It was Billy.

"Hello?"

"Wendy?" Static accompanied his voice.

"Oh, Billy," An involuntary sigh escaped her. She spun, plugging her free ear and straining to hear. "I'm so glad to hear your voice."

"Where are you?" His voice cut out. "—at home? I've been trying to reach—"

"No. I'm—"

She stopped as Billy's hacking cough filled her ears. Her heartbeat thudded inside her head.

"Billy, are you sick? Please tell me you aren't sick." The phone blanked out, and Wendy panicked. "Hello?"

She moved into the den, and the connection strengthened. His raspy breathing crackled in her ear.

"Are you sick?" he asked.

"No." Her answer was filled with a stark shame. She should be sick. "Julie and Mom are gone."

"I'm sorry," he answered quietly. "You must be immune."

She straightened. "What?"

"It's what they're saying." He coughed again. "Not everyone is sick, and some people get well."

She digested his words in disbelief.

"Wendy, where are you?"

"Chad's."

"Good. He'll know where to go."

"No, Billy." She shook her head and slumped against the sofa. "He's not here."

"What?"

"I don't know where they are." Her eyes scanned the den. "No one is here."

Billy began to choke, and Wendy held her breath. She couldn't take this. She couldn't witness another death of someone she cared about.

"Billy?" His name was shaky on her tongue.

"Listen to me," he rasped. "Prep for Doom has a safe house in Moriarty. The Sunset Motel. If Chad's alive, he'll go there."

Wendy's hope soared. "Okay."

"But if he's not there, those guys won't just let anybody in, so you need to take something."

"Like what?" Her nerves bounced across her skin.

"You have your I.D?"

"Yes."

"Okay. Find something to prove you know Montgomery. Something they would want or need."

"Okay." Her eyes darted around the den. She spotted the large gun case against the far wall full of rifles. It was open. Three guns were laid side by side on the floor in front of it.

"There are a lot of guns here."

"Guns? How many?"

"Fifteen or Twenty."

"That's weird."

"Why?"

"Montgomery wouldn't leave behind that much weaponry."

Wendy swallowed hard as her hope of finding Chad alive lessened a degree. She dreaded going upstairs, but she couldn't leave before she checked.

"Take the guns. Anything else? Something to prove they came from Montgomery's?"

She reached into the case and pulled out a small wooden box with the initials CJM carved into its lid. It was filled with bullets.

"His initials on an ammo box?"

"That's a start."

She scouted the room. The desk in the corner was cluttered with documents, bills, and a pile of notebooks stacked neatly on the edge. She flipped one open. Slanted handwriting scrawled across the pages. She skimmed them until she began to see a clear pattern of survival tips and "how to" advice. These were Montgomery's notes.

"Okay, I found something that should work."

Billy wheezed in her ear.

"Good. Wendy?"

"Yeah?" She held her breath. *Was this goodbye?*

"You're going to be okay. Just get there." His words trembled and Wendy heard his tears. "I'll leave a post on the site about you. So tell them to check it."

"Billy…" A sob accompanied his name.

"Don't, Wendy." He tried to sound firm. "I'm going to be okay, too. Live or die, God is with us. No fear, right? You know it just like I do. Hold onto it."

She nodded with another sob. "You—you watch out for Julie up there, okay?"

"You bet." She heard his smile in the wheezy response. "See you on the other side."

"See you," she choked out.

The phone clicked. Wendy sank to her knees.

* * *

The sun was setting when Wendy pulled into the motel parking lot off Route 66. It was empty, and the lobby was dark. For a moment, she feared it was the wrong place. Then a light flickered at the entrance, and a shadow exited the building. A boy.

Wendy gripped the steering wheel as he neared. He wore an oversized short-sleeved white tee, untucked. A bandana graced his forehead, but his most prominent feature almost made her put the car in reverse. An automatic rifle was slung against his shoulder, his finger on the trigger.

Cautiously, he moved closer. His face was covered with a medical mask. She gawked at him until he tapped the glass with his knuckle, and she jumped.

"Hey," he hollered. The sound was muffled. Hesitantly, she cracked the window an inch.

"Name?" he asked. He peered at a clipboard he carried.

"Wendy Mitchell." Her voice sounded small.

He studied the board, looked up. "You're not on the list." His Hispanic accent was thick.

"I know." She swallowed. "My friend, Billy Young, left my name on the website."

The boy's eyes narrowed. "Who?"

Wendy thought a moment. "The Ghost."

His brows lifted.

"Asa and Juan will have to clear you. You can't park here." He tipped his head. "Take your car to that gas station."

"I have something for you." She thumbed toward the back.

He peered through the back window at her basket, then stepped away and motioned for her to get out. She popped the trunk first. At the sound, the boy's gun swung toward her. She froze.

"In the trunk," she said quickly.

Cautiously, he stepped to the back of the car and peered in. His eyes widened and he shifted his rifle defensively. Wendy held still in her seat.

"Where'd you get the guns?" His voice was wary.

"Charles Montgomery." She used her bargaining chip. "Is he here?"

She waited for his reaction. He slammed the trunk closed.

"Come with me."

She grabbed her duffel bag and left the car, a silent prayer in her heart. She had no idea what came next, but this boy was the first uninfected person she'd seen in a while.

The boy stopped at the room closest to the lobby entrance and inserted a key in the door. Wendy studied him uncertainly.

"This is the holding room. Everybody comes here first."

He pushed the door open. The room was sparsely furnished with a double bed, a table, and two chairs. Mask still intact, the boy picked up a walkie-talkie from the table and called someone. A voice crackled in return. He gave Wendy's full name and mentioned Montgomery's weapons. She shifted, hugging her duffel bag close to her as he closed the door.

"You can sit down," he waved a hand toward the bed. She didn't move.

Soon, voices rang out in the parking lot. The boy parted the curtains. A group of armed shadows surrounded Wendy's car. Someone popped the trunk. Wendy held her breath. The boy let the curtains fall to.

Fifteen minutes later, another masked figure entered the room. Young, Hispanic, with dark suspicious eyes. He made no introduction.

"Do you have an I.D. on you?"

He took a threatening step toward her. Quickly, she produced her license. He took it in a plastic-gloved hand and examined it. He looked at her.

Behind him, another boy entered. He was tall and broad with muscles bulging under his green t-shirt. His dark, brown hair fell loosely against his collar, and a thin, fuzzy beard crawled along his jawline beneath the mask he wore. He studied her, cast his eyes to the first boy and back to her.

"Wendy Mitchell," he said.

She nodded and clutched the strap of her duffel bag. A large hunting knife hung from his belt.

"I'm Asa Brown." He nodded toward the other boy. "This is Juan Montoya. And you've met Carlos."

He exchanged a glance with Juan, who held up her license with a nod to verify that she was indeed Wendy Mitchell.

"We checked out your story," he continued. "The Ghost left a message about you."

Juan huffed and gave her the license. "Are you sure about that, Asa? She could be a hacker. Why didn't The Ghost come with her?"

"We don't know who The Ghost is. Maybe it's her."

Her heart thudded. "It's not," she confessed. "But I know who he is."

That got their attention. Asa dropped his hands to his sides. Carlos slowly lowered his arms until the butt of his rifle thumped against the worn carpet.

"Ay Dios mio," he whispered.

"You know him? Personally?" Asa asked, his brows rising at the question.

"Yes. He's one of my best friends."

"Where is he?"

Her heart sank. "He's…dying."

Juan frowned. "She's lying."

Asa crossed his arms over his chest, and tilted his head. "I don't know, Juan. Did you see the stash in her trunk?"

"I'm not lying," she said, a hard edge to her voice.

All three studied her.

"How do we know those weapons came from Montgomery?" Juan's voice was just as hard. "You could have gotten them from anywhere."

"But I didn't." She unzipped her bag and pulled a notebook from it. Asa took it when she offered. "This is his. He's signed several pages."

Asa studied it, looked up in astonishment. "Where did you get this?"

"At his house. His son is my boyfriend." Wendy's voice cracked. "I'm assuming they aren't here."

"No," Asa replied.

Wendy's shoulders slumped.

"All right." Asa tucked the notebook under his arm. "Next order of business: making sure you aren't infected. When was the last time you were near someone with the virus?"

Wendy raised her eyes, and her heartbeat quickened.

She could lie—say she hadn't seen anyone in days. But she had a suspicious feeling they would know, and she needed their trust. She had nowhere else to turn.

"I left my sister on our couch a few hours ago."

Asa straightened, his eyes narrowing. "She's infected?"

Wendy shook her head. "Was," she said quietly.

The boys stiffened simultaneously. Carlos visibly swallowed and readjusted his mask. Juan edged toward the door, but Asa merely tilted his head.

"Yet you aren't sick." His tone was even. "You were with her the whole time?"

"Yes. And my mom before that."

Asa rubbed at his chin. "I guess you're immune." His eyes roamed up and down her arms. He squatted and peered at her bare legs. "No bruising. Eyes aren't bloodshot. Have you had any nosebleeds?"

He stood.

"No," Wendy answered. She fidgeted. Her duffel bag grew heavier by the minute.

"Come on, hombre," Juan interjected. His hand rested over a pistol on his hip. "She's been with the infected. We need to cut her lose."

Cut her loose? They were going to make her leave?

"We've all been with the infected," Asa replied quietly, crossing his arms over his chest. His eyes softened. "She's not sick. Plus, she's kind of cute."

At this, Wendy's face turned every shade of red.

"Asa." The sharpness in Juan's voice cut through her. "We don't need another mouth to feed."

Asa characteristically tilted his head. "That's not who we are, Juan. We're here to help survivors."

"But—"

Asa held up his hand.

"They're saying it takes eight hours for symptoms to show." He addressed Wendy. "We're going to hold you here 'til midnight—just as a precaution. If you don't get sick, we'll get you settled in with a roommate. But understand. If you're cleared, we each pull our own weight around here. Nobody's a babysitter."

"Okay." Wings fluttered in her belly with sudden relief.

"We're waiting for Montgomery." Asa paused, weighing whether to say more before he continued. "He's supposed to airlift us to New York, if he can get to his chopper. Either way, we're moving out July 31 as planned. Okay?"

Wendy nodded rapidly as the wings in her belly lifted. They were going to wait for Charles Montgomery. Which meant, by default, they were waiting for Chad. Wendy's shoulders relaxed.

Juan left in a huff. Carlos nodded at Wendy as he moved to the door.

"I hope you don't get sick," he said. "I'll bring in your basket."

Asa faced her. "See you at midnight."

He extended a plastic-gloved hand, and Wendy took it. It swallowed hers up in size and warmth. Up close, she saw the color of his eyes. They resembled honey.

* * *

Wendy ate a can of cold pork and beans for dinner, and the hours inched by like crawling snails. She tried to sleep, but her nerves were on edge. Every time she closed her eyes, she saw the puddle of blood in Chad's kitchen. She'd checked the rest of the house before she'd left. She'd found nothing. So whose blood had it been?

She sighed and settled back onto the bed. She didn't want to think. But the waiting was nerve-racking. She pressed a sweaty palm to her forehead. No fever.

Asa and Juan returned just past midnight. Asa turned on the lamp and

Wendy sat up, squinting in the sudden light. He straddled a chair and leaned in scrutinizing her closely. She leaned away.

"No symptoms," he said with satisfaction. "How do you feel?"

"I'm fine," Wendy retorted irritably.

"Okay," Asa leaned back and tugged the mask down to his chin. His mouth tipped slightly into a half smile. "You've passed inspection."

He eyed Juan.

"Get Brooke."

Juan removed his mask, scowled, and left.

"What's his problem?" Wendy asked.

Asa shrugged. "He's afraid. Cautious—as he should be. Worried about the infection. Running out of supplies if we keep taking people in."

"But…this is a safe zone."

"Yes," Asa nodded. His honey eyes danced. "And I balance him out with my reason once we see there's no threat." He smiled again. "It's a good system."

Asa reached into his pocket and retrieved a folded piece of paper.

"The rules for this zone." He held it out, and she took it. "Read them. Let me know if you have any questions."

The door swung open. A girl wearing a silky, pink robe glared at them.

"A roommate?" she exclaimed. "Really, Asa?"

Her eyes found Wendy. She squinted.

"Wendy? Wendy Mitchell? No friggin' way!"

A hint of disdain laced her voice, and she settled her pink-tipped fingers against her hips. Wendy blinked.

It was Brooke Applegate, one of the most self-absorbed girls she'd ever known. Self-absorbed…and mean. Her blue eyes were riddled with irritation at the inconvenience. Because virus or not, Brooke only cared about Brooke. A wave of nausea flooded Wendy at the thought of spending the apocalypse in Brooke's company. But Wendy wasn't surprised. Mean girls always survived. Like cockroaches.

"I take it you two know each other?" Asa inquired. Wendy glanced at him. He rubbed at his whiskery chin with an amused expression.

Brooke, leaning against the door jamb, rolled her eyes at him before settling her gaze on Wendy. "Well, come on then, roomie."

She spun and traipsed off, pink slippers slapping against concrete. Wendy gave Asa one last annoyed look before she lifted her duffle bag.

"Wendy."

She faced him.

"You're going to be fine now."

"Yeah," she whispered.

Outside, two boys were guarding the perimeter, automatic rifles in hand. Wendy shuddered and hurried past them. This "preppers" life was going to take some getting used to.

* * *

"How are you here?"

Wendy sat on one of two double beds and waited for Brooke to answer. It was a valid question. Clearly, Brooke was not the "prepper" type.

"My brother," she answered indifferently. "He and Asa were tight."

Brooke was sprawled across the other bed on her stomach flipping through a fashion magazine, which was humorous considering the world was coming to an end. "He was a nerd." She rolled her eyes. "All he ever did was play video games. It was completely out of control."

She paused, flipped a page. Wendy pursed her lips.

"He didn't make it, did he?"

Brooke didn't look up. Her voice went hard. "Nope. I'm it. The last of the family line."

Wendy nodded. She knew that feeling. Brooke tossed the magazine onto the nightstand, pulled a sleep mask over her eyes, and turned off the lamp.

"I don't want to talk to you about this," she proclaimed. She rolled over to face the opposite wall.

Wendy sat unmoving in the dark. Clearly, she and Brooke were never going to be friends, even under the worst of circumstances.

She slipped beneath the sheets. The room was stuffy. She would have stripped down to her panties, but that wasn't an option. She'd read Asa's rules. They were as follows:

1. Food packs served in the lobby at 8:00 a.m., 12:00 p.m., and 6:00 p.m. only.
2. All doors locked by 8:00 p.m.
3. Keep your bags packed.
4. Sleep fully clothed, including shoes.
5. Keep curtains drawn.
6. Use lights sparingly to avoid outside attention.

7. Weapons are to be fully loaded and ready for use. Safety first.

8. Members found to be infected will be put out. No exceptions.

9. If you don't like the rules, leave.

Brooke had broken several already. Her bare feet dangling off the end of the bed were proof. But Wendy refused to tread on thin ice. This place could be her only chance to reunite with Chad. She kept her tennis shoes on.

She stared at the ceiling, willing sleep, but it didn't come. Too much had taken place today with no time to compartmentalize. She'd rather forget. To remember meant blood-tinged vomit and her mother's last wheezing breaths. It meant staring into Julie's painfully bloodshot eyes.

She would give anything to look into them now.

With a sigh, she dug into her pocket and drew out a *Fender* guitar pick. She held it above her in the dark. She didn't need to see it. She'd memorized it. A neon green vintage with black script across the front. Chad had given it to her at church camp two years ago. A promise. She always kept it with her.

She clutched it and pressed her closed fist to her lips.

"Dear God," she whispered. "Please keep Chad safe. Please let him be alive. And Annee and Mr. Montgomery, too. Please."

A tear raced backward down her temple. Chad was the only one left in this world that she truly cared about. She would cling to her faith that he was alive. She refused to let herself believe anything else.

* * *

Wendy collected her breakfast pack from the lobby in the morning: a cup of instant oatmeal, a bottle of water, a fruit roll-up, and a granola bar. She ate seated on a bench just outside the lobby doors.

During the day, Asa allowed a bit more freedom. But he always had two guys on duty, walking the perimeter, checking the surrounding lots, looking out for infecteds. Members could sit outside, take walks—as long as they were armed. He'd given Wendy a small army knife; she'd left it in her bag. She was naïve about potential danger, and in her mind, everyone was hiding, dying, or already dead anyway.

She munched on her granola bar and thought of Julie. She'd only been thirteen. Her death—it didn't seem fair, and for the first time, Wendy wished it had been her instead. Sweet Julie…

Her breakfast stuck in her throat. She squeezed her eyes closed. She would not cry. Today, she would stay strong.

"Where'd you come from, Wendy?"

She jumped at the voice. Asa had taken a seat at the opposite end of the bench without her noticing, his arm draped across the back. She shook her head to steady herself.

"I hope you aren't planning to do that every time we meet."

Asa laughed. "Sorry."

Wendy glanced at him, then looked away.

"I'm from Tijeras Canyon," she answered.

"How do you know Brooke?"

"I don't, really. She was just in my pre-calc class last year."

"Oh." Asa leaned forward on his knees and clasped his hands. He hesitated a moment before he continued, his voice full of sympathy. "You lost your mom and your sister? Who else?"

Wendy bit her lip. There went her plan not to cry. She blinked several times.

"I think—" She cut herself short, staring at the ground. She couldn't voice her fears. "What about you?"

He sighed deeply. "I lost everybody. And I'm the oldest of eight." He laughed softly, a sad, bitter laugh. "It was a real slaughterhouse at my place."

His lower lip trembled, and Wendy felt his aching inside her. She hesitated, and then reached over and placed her hand on his forearm. His eyes, moist and full of sadness, met hers. He smiled.

"Asa!"

Carlos raced up the sidewalk, his rifle hugged to his chest. Asa leapt to his feet.

"What is it?"

Carlos, bent at the waist, breathlessly forced out the words.

"It's Devon, man. He just threw up all over the bathroom sink."

Asa straightened, and his role as leader slid into place.

"I thought he was cleared," Carlos insisted.

"Get everyone to their rooms," Asa ordered. "Find Juan. And Carlos…" He paused until Carlos met his gaze. "We'll do what has to be done to protect the rest of us."

Carlos nodded and sped off. Asa faced Wendy.

"Go," he said. He pulled a mask from his pocket. "And stay inside."

Wendy gathered up the remainder of her breakfast as Asa thundered off to "do what had to be done."

She didn't like the reference one bit.

* * *

Brooke paced back and forth in front of the curtains while Wendy sat cross-legged on the end of the bed and chewed on her thumbnail. They listened to Devon's screams.

"Please! Please don't do this! I don't have anywhere to go!"

His pleas came from the parking lot. His voice was hoarse, and every once in a while a ragged coughing fit attacked him. It had been thirty minutes since Asa had sent them to their rooms. It felt like hours.

"Why are they letting him yell like that?" Brooke stopped pacing and peered out a tiny crack in the curtain. She had a clear view of him. "He's going to bring a lot of attention on us. We're supposed to be safe here. This isn't helping."

Wendy didn't answer. She was thinking that today was the Fourth of July. She and Julie had an armory of fireworks stashed in the laundry room, and if this had been any other Fourth of July, they would be at their grandparents' ranch eating barbeque. Her grandfather had called on July 1 to tell them not to come. He was sick. Wendy knew he and grandma were both dead by now.

Through the thin motel walls, Wendy heard Devon choke on a sob and bellow again.

"You can't do this! Oh, God. God it hurts…"

His misery penetrated her conscience, and she couldn't take any more. She scrambled off the bed.

"They shouldn't be doing this," she said. "They should have allowed him to die in his room."

Brooke whirled. "That's not the rule, Wendy. If you get sick, you leave."

"And this is better? To let him die in a motel parking lot?"

"He's supposed to go," she insisted. "He's not following the rules."

"There are no more rules!" Wendy screamed, and Brooke's eyes widened. "Don't you get it? The only rules now are the ones we create. I don't like this one."

"Well, it's not your call," Brooke sneered.

Wendy fumed and flung open the door.

"Where are you going?"

Wendy glared at her.

"I'm breaking a rule."

She marched across the lot to Devon. He trembled in a puddle of his own bloody vomit. She knelt. He wasn't a small guy. His blond hair was streaked with the evidence of his sickness.

"Devon?" He opened one bloodshot eye. "Let me help you. Can you stand?"

"I don't know," he whispered raggedly.

"Well, try."

From the corner of her eye, she saw them coming. Asa in the lead, with Juan on his heels, and at least seven others adorned in masks. They halted several yards back. She ignored them and concentrated on getting Devon to his feet.

"You're not taking him anywhere."

She stopped, a tense anger pinching her. Devon fell back with a moan, and she stood. Asa's eyes were stern.

"You can't do this, Wendy. He knew the rules. And now you've risked getting infected."

"No."

Determined, she marched over to Asa.

"Look. My sister threw up all over me seconds before she died. It got in my eyes, my mouth. That was yesterday." Tears welled, but she didn't avert her eyes. "I'm not sick. And you." She jabbed an accusing finger into his chest. "You were there with your family. A slaughterhouse, you said? And you're not sick. None of us are." Her eyes swept across the others. "We're the only ones who can help the sick die with some dignity. I would have wanted that for my mom. For my sister. And Devon's mama would want that for him."

The group stood in utter silence. And Juan raised his gun, and shot Devon in the head.

Wendy jumped, covering her ears as the report of the gun echoed off the building. In shock, she turned. Devon's body slumped, a bloody, quiet lump on the broken asphalt.

Nobody moved. Juan spoke.

"We should have done that to begin with when he wouldn't leave." He holstered his gun and looked at Asa. "You know it. I know it. We all know it. We all agreed."

He cast his eyes over Devon and made a sign of the cross.

"The infected are going to die in horrible ways. I just did him a favor." He gestured with a nod of his head to two members. "Take care of the body."

Wendy covered her face with her hands and spun to flee toward her room.

"Wendy!" Asa caught her by the arm. She yanked out of his grip.

"Don't touch me!" A sob escaped. Asa yanked his mask down.

"I'm sorry, Wendy." He dipped his head to catch her eyes. "We have to do things to protect ourselves. This had to happen."

"No. It didn't." Her lip quivered.

"Look. I understand. What you said was right. It just wasn't smart. And we're all scared."

"You're right," she whispered. Her eyes pierced him. "Devon was scared."

He blinked once. She turned away. There was nothing more to say.

* * *

In the middle of the night, someone else began showing symptoms. Carlos came by pounding on doors to alert everyone to stay inside. Wendy double-checked the lock and climbed back into bed. She buried herself under the covers. Brooke was at the window again.

"It's Lisa," she said quietly.

Wendy wiped at a lone tear. This was a nightmare.

"We're all going to die." Brooke's voice cracked with the words, and she crumpled to the floor, sobbing. "It's only a matter of time."

Wendy slipped out of the bed and knelt to wrap her arms around mean girl, Brooke Applegate. A girl who had never said a word to her in school unless she'd needed help in calculus. A girl who'd spent the majority of her time looking down her nose at everyone else. But tonight, they had something in common: fear. Brooke leaned into the embrace.

The humming of an engine caught Wendy's ears. Lisa must be leaving. She hoped so because she didn't care to see a repeat of Devon's demise. Standing, she peered through the curtains.

Lisa stood near a streetlight, a small suitcase dangling from her fingers. The light was so bright that Wendy saw everything clearly. And the humming engine was not a car. It was an armored truck. It slowly rolled to a stop beside Lisa.

"Who is that?" Wendy asked. Brooke scrambled to her feet.

"Who?" She sniffled and squinted through the window.

The truck was bright white under the light. A diamond-shaped logo graced its side, overlaid with three large, crisp letters. PFD.

"Prep for Doom." Brooke leaned back. "It must be Montgomery."

Their eyes met; Wendy's heartbeat thumped erratically. Without thinking, she pulled the curtain wide.

Chad could be in that truck.

A side door on the truck slid open just as the two preppers on perimeter duty cautiously made their way over to greet it. Simultaneously, Lisa bent over and threw up on her shoes.

A man in a HAZMAT suit appeared in the open doorway of the truck. Lisa straightened, and with a sharp pop, he put a bullet through her brain.

Brooke gasped; Wendy pressed a hand against the cool glass; the two group members halted in shock before they turned and fled toward the lobby. They never made it.

Gunfire suddenly fractured the night. Brooke screamed and ducked beneath the window. Wendy dove for the space between her bed and the wall. They heard shouts, return fire. Wendy curled into a tight ball as the Fourth of July celebration finally arrived in the form of exploding bullets.

Ages later, Asa miraculously arrived at their door unharmed, the butt of his rifle propped against his hip.

"You two okay?"

Wendy climbed to her feet.

"Yeah," Brooke's trembling defied her answer. "Who are those people?"

"I have no idea. But get your things." He eyed Wendy. "We're leaving."

"Leaving?" Wendy panicked. "But…what about Montgomery?"

What about Chad?

"The internet's down," Asa answered. "But we left a note in the lobby. Anybody coming here will know where to go." He smiled weakly. "Don't worry, he'll find us."

Wendy's heart sank, but she grabbed her duffel bag and followed him.

The parking lot was a graveyard that Wendy couldn't stomach. Bile rose in her throat. The fight had ended with four dead men in HAZMAT suits. The group had lost six.

Would this nightmare never end?

The lobby was a mess of broken glass and tattered furniture. Asa's note was taped to a window full of bullet holes. She bit back her tears.

Where are you, Chad?

"What are you going to do with the bodies?" she asked numbly.

Asa's expression turned grim.

"Nothing," he replied. "We can't help the dead. We need to worry about the living, and the motel has been compromised."

Wendy's heart ached. Some of these guys were his friends. She heard pain reflected in his words.

Members hurriedly loaded vehicles with supplies. Brooke dragged her rolling suitcase past. Wendy dug Chad's guitar pick from her pocket.

"Wendy?" Asa took a step. "We need to go."

"Just a minute."

She disappeared into the lobby. Behind the counter, she found a black marker. She quickly scribbled one word across the back of the guitar pick. Asa watched her curiously as she taped the pick securely next to the note. She stepped back with a sigh.

Asa didn't say a word, but he offered his hand. She took it gratefully, and she made a silent promise to herself.

She would survive. She would see Chad again. And she would never stop believing in hope—even in a dying world.

Hope was all she had left.

SIXTEEN: *Where You Hang Your Hat*

by Harlow C. Fallon

Luke stared at the shotgun laying heavy in his hands. He'd discovered it a year ago, hidden in a secret spot in his father's closet. His dad claimed to be a pacifist and believed guns created more problems than they solved, so it didn't make sense that he owned a weapon. Luke had never confessed to his dad that he'd found it or asked why he had it. He meant to, one day, but that day never came.

Things were different now. The world had changed and Luke was alone. It might be a good idea to figure out how to use the gun.

He examined it carefully and discovered it was already loaded. After a search of the top shelf, Luke found a box that held extra shells. He shoved four into his pocket.

Brewer looked at him with questioning eyes from his spot on the floor.

"Want to go for a hike, boy?"

Brewer's tail thumped. He got up and walked over to Luke, pressing against his leg, waiting for a reassuring scratch behind the ears. Luke obliged.

In the kitchen, Luke loaded a backpack with items he'd need for the hike. Shouldering the pack, he grabbed the shotgun and headed out.

It was a warm and humid July morning. Brewer ran ahead, sniffing a dozen important smells, and once, flushing out a rabbit, which skittered away into the bushes. "Stay, Brew," Luke said, and the dog reluctantly obeyed.

The hike up Hawk Hill proved uneventful, and as he walked, Luke's mind wandered back to the day his father called to tell him Ivy had died. She was two years younger but they shared the same birthday. In three weeks he would turn eighteen and Ivy sixteen. She'd always been the outgoing one—pretty, with long dark hair and dark eyes, catching the attention of their wide circle of friends. She never knew a stranger. Luke envied her in that way. He was too quiet, too reserved. They had their share of fights, but a love of the land, animals, and growing things—which their parents had cultivated in them from day one—kept them united. They were a tight unit, their family.

His parents had rushed Ivy to the hospital, but the virus had taken her like it had millions of others. He'd received one phone call from his dad telling him his sister was dead and his mother had fallen ill, then not another word. Were they still alive? Was anyone still alive? Anyone he knew?

Why was *he* still alive? He pondered that. He'd never been sick his whole life, except for a mild case of chickenpox when he was four. When his sister and parents dealt with colds and the occasional flu, Luke sailed right through it all, unaffected. His dad had jokingly called him Super Boy. Maybe he was.

He raked a hand through his long dark hair. Today he needed some answers. He'd been reluctant to go into town, but maybe from the top of Hawk Hill, with the binoculars, he could see if there was any activity in Anchorton. Maybe things were fine there. If so, he'd take the car and drive down into town, stock up on supplies. There'd probably be news about the pandemic; maybe he'd see some of his friends.

Luke followed a well-worn deer path through the trees, one he'd used countless times. He veered off the path twice to check two cabins—the Perrault's place, and a half-mile away, the Ackroyd's. Normally they'd be occupied, being the height of the summer season, but neither of them showed signs of occupation. Maybe those folks were dead too.

By early afternoon they'd made it to the overlook. He took a long drink from his water bottle, then poured some in a bowl for Brewer, who lapped it noisily.

Ahead, the foothills of the Adirondacks spread out like a rumpled green blanket. To the north they swept up to majestic mountains. Little Coin Lake nestled below like a shiny dime on a glittering chain, and next to it lay Anchorton. Luke pulled out his binoculars and searched. Anchorton was a ghost town.

Despair washed over him. He couldn't be the only person left in the world, but it felt that way.

Behind him a twig snapped. Brewer growled. Luke swung around and aimed the shotgun in the direction of the sound. He waited, realizing with dread that he'd left himself in a bad spot, his back to the overlook with no escape, gripping a weapon he had no idea how to use. He prayed it was only a deer.

A man stepped out of the trees, hands raised. He was tall, dark-skinned, with short black hair. He smiled and took a couple steps closer. Brewer lowered his head and growled deep in his throat, hackles raised.

"Hey there," the man said, eyeing the dog. "Didn't mean to startle you."

Luke didn't move. His hands shook. He gripped the gun tighter so it wouldn't show.

"Name's Phil. Phil Janus. You live around here?"

He didn't answer.

Phil took a tentative step but stopped when Brewer growled again. "Hey, I can see you're on the defense." He nodded slowly. "Which is good. You don't know me from Adam. But I'm not going to hurt you. Besides, you've got the gun."

Luke had no idea what to say or do.

Phil stepped closer, his eyes on the shotgun. "You know how to use that thing?"

"Of course I do." Luke's gut twisted in a knot. His finger moved to the trigger.

Phil smiled. "So you can talk."

"Where are you from?" Luke asked warily.

"Albany by way of Staten Island."

"You've come a long way, then," Luke said. He scanned the trees, in case Phil wasn't alone, but saw nothing.

Phil nodded. "Yes, I have."

"What are you doing here?"

"Looking for a place to settle," Phil said with a slight shrug. "Someplace I can be useful."

"No, I mean what are you doing *here*?"

Phil looked around. "Same as you," he said. "I wanted to scope out the area. And, truth be told, I heard you and your dog."

Luke gave him a long look as he pondered the situation. Phil wasn't out for an afternoon stroll, that much he could tell. If he was scoping out the area, maybe it meant he was hiding from someone, or on the run. How long had he been following?

"Why'd you end up here?" Luke asked. "Out in the middle of nowhere?"

Phil's palms turned up and he tilted his head to the side in a quizzical manner. "Surely you know what's going on everywhere."

"I know."

"Then you probably know that it's safer away from the cities and populated areas."

Luke's eyes narrowed as an alarming thought came to him. "Are you infected?"

"If I was, I doubt I'd be standing here," Phil said with a half-grin.

Luke could kick himself for forgetting a bandana to cover his mouth and nose, even though he had no clue if it would help.

"I'm not sick," Phil said, and then gave him a pointed look. "Are you?"

"As fast as it comes on, I don't think so." His mind flashed to his sister, her face pale, her breathing shallow as she lay half-conscious on the couch while he held her hand. The sting of grief made his chest tight and he swallowed hard. "I was exposed…my sister got it…but I didn't."

Phil's eyes softened and he shook his head. "I'm sorry. That's tough."

Luke didn't know if he was trustworthy, but his response seemed genuine. The thought of being alone indefinitely hit him like a fist to the gut. He wanted company, someone he could talk to, who could help him with the chores, who wouldn't make the house feel so empty.

Phil appeared to be in his late forties. He looked strong and fit. His clothes—jeans, t-shirt, and over-shirt with the sleeves rolled up—seemed fairly clean, not worn and dirty like someone who'd been traveling on foot. That bothered him a little.

"Can you work on a farm?" Luke asked.

"I can do just about anything," Phil said with a grin.

He was still wary, but he had to take a chance. He took a deep breath and said, "I'm Luke."

"Nice to meet you, Luke. It'd be great if you'd kindly stop pointing the weapon at me."

He hesitated, then lowered the shotgun. "Have you been to Anchorton?"

"Worked my way past there, yeah." Phil eyed Brewer nervously when the dog stepped closer to sniff his boots.

Luke snapped his fingers, and Brewer returned to his side. Phil seemed relieved. "Anybody left?" Luke asked him.

"Not that I could see. I didn't get too close, though. Is that where you're from?"

Luke shook his head. "I live down the hill."

"The rest of your family okay?"

Luke hesitated a beat. "No."

Phil sighed. "Sorry to hear that. I really am. Anybody need burying?"

"No."

"All right, then," Phil said with a nod. "I'm ready to be put to work."

As they made their way down the hill, Luke staying safely behind Phil, he started thinking about all the projects Phil could help with. By the look of him, he could handle hard work. Then Luke noticed the bulge at Phil's back under his shirt. Luke raised his shotgun. "Hold up."

Phil stopped and turned. His expression remained blank, but Luke could see that he knew.

"You have a gun," Luke said.

Their eyes held for a long, tense moment. Then Phil said, "Yes. I do."

"But you said—"

Phil opened his hands. "Did you really think I'd be unarmed? Or did it occur to you at all?"

Luke remained silent.

"If I wanted to kill you, you'd already be dead," Phil said. "The fact that I haven't pulled my gun should tell you something. And for future reference, it helps if you release the safety before you fire."

Luke's face heated. He hated that his ignorance was so obvious. He lowered the shotgun. "Let's get going."

There was no more conversation until they made it back to the farm.

As they walked past the barn and garden to the house, Phil whistled. "Nice little place. How long you lived here?"

"All my life." Luke climbed the steps to the porch and opened the door, stepping aside so Phil could enter.

"Well, Luke, I work better with food in my stomach," he said as he took in his surroundings. "Got anything to eat?"

* * *

After a meal of sandwiches and fruit, Luke directed Phil outside to the garden, and together they picked beans, cucumbers, squash and tomatoes, what was left of the broccoli, and a half-dozen peppers. Phil talked while they worked, sharing about living on Staten Island before the outbreak. How everything had gone to hell in a hand basket, as he put it, and how the dead lay in the streets, on the sidewalks, in their cars, everywhere. Men had shown up in HAZMAT suits and began collecting the corpses, but when they started rounding up survivors and rumors spread that they were locking down the Island, Phil decided to get out.

"How'd you know where to go?" Luke asked.

"I knew my way around. I slipped out, managed to get across the bridge before it closed and kept going." He shook his head and sighed. "Chaos everywhere. I knew my best bet was to head away from the city. So that's what I did."

"You didn't have family?"

Phil's face was brooding as he dropped a handful of green beans into the basket. "My wife died four years ago. Cancer. Never had any kids."

Luke could see that it was a sensitive subject, so he asked a different question. "What were the roads like?"

"Choked. At least near the city. Couldn't navigate at all. I hoofed it when I could. Took a car when roads opened up. When I got stuck, I started walking again. Finally somewhere around Spring Valley things cleared out more and I was able to drive to Albany."

"All that exposure and you never once caught the virus."

Phil glanced up from his work and gave Luke a measuring gaze, as if looking for some hidden intent in his question. "Some are naturally immune. I figure I'm one of them. Maybe you are too."

He'd suspected it, after what had happened to Ivy. "Was it bad in Albany too?"

Phil nodded and tossed another handful of beans into the basket. "Just like everywhere."

Luke turned his face away and set to work on the weeds. He was glad for the fading light, and hoped Phil didn't notice as he blinked to clear his eyes. It was too much, the thought of so many people dead. How could something like this have happened? And so fast?

"You haven't talked much about your situation," Phil said. "What happened to your family?"

Luke stared at his hands for a long moment. "My sister got sick. It was so quick. One minute she was fine, and the next..." He swallowed and took a breath. "My folks rushed her to the hospital. I waited all night to hear something. The next day my dad called to tell me she'd died. My mom was sick too and they were under quarantine. He said they'd be home as soon as they could. But that was three weeks ago."

Phil remained quiet for a moment. "I'm sorry."

Luke stood up and brushed the dirt from his jeans. "It's getting dark. We should take this stuff inside."

In the kitchen, Phil set to work washing the vegetables and snapping the beans. Luke bagged them and put them in the fridge.

"You seem to know your way around a garden," Luke said.

Phil smiled. "That I do. I grew up on a farm in Texas, then moved to New York. Got married. We always had a little garden. Nothing better than fresh vegetables. These would make great vegetable beef soup."

"We don't eat meat," Luke said.

Phil quirked a brow. "No? Vegetarian? Or vegan?"

"Vegetarian," Luke said. "We eat eggs. Sometimes cheese." He grinned. "I like cheese."

Phil washed the broccoli and handed it to Luke. "Well, you look healthy," he said. "How old are you? Twenty?"

"Seventeen."

Phil's eyes widened. "Now, that's a surprise."

They finished the vegetables and Luke heated water on the stove for tea. "What did you do on Staten Island?" he asked.

"I worked for a home improvement store. Just a jack-of-all-trades. Before that I worked for the government. Took early retirement when my wife got sick."

Luke pulled two mugs from the cupboard. "Sorry about your wife," he said as he poured the tea.

"Thanks. I appreciate that," Phil replied.

He set a mug in front of Phil and sat down at the table. "What sort of government work?"

Phil grinned. "If I told ya, I'd have to kill ya."

Luke frowned and looked away.

"That was a bad joke," Phil said. "I apologize."

An uncomfortable silence settled around them. Luke sipped his tea and for a moment wished he was still alone.

"So where did you go to school?" Phil asked. "Anchorton?"

"Homeschooled."

"Really?"

Luke nodded.

"Your folks religious?"

Luke shrugged. "Not really. I mean, they believe in God and all, but they just didn't believe in religion. My dad says he and my mom are Latter-Day Hippies. We live off the land as much as possible. We believe the land is a gift and we should use it wisely, take from it only what we need and give back to it to keep it healthy."

"That's good," Phil said, nodding. "I like that." He eyed the gun propped next to the door. "So if you're vegetarians, that means your dad doesn't hunt. Why the shotgun?"

"I don't know." He lowered his eyes, feeling the sting of loss, remembering the day he found the weapon, wishing he had his dad here now to finally ask him about it. "I guess it was for emergencies. He never told me he had it. I found it by accident."

"So he never taught you about guns."

Luke figured Phil knew that already. "No," he said quietly.

"You want to learn?"

He looked up, feeling a pulse of excitement, and nodded.

"All right, then," Phil said, "first thing tomorrow morning, we're gonna have school." He looked at Luke and smiled. "Then a little target practice."

* * *

Luke woke to something nudging his shoulder. "Too early, Brew," he mumbled.

"Brew wants you to get up and learn how to shoot."

Luke opened one eye.

Phil stood over him with his arms crossed. "Day's half over."

"What time is it?"

"Five."

Luke groaned. "It's still dark outside."

"Lesson starts inside. By the time we're done, it'll be light enough."

Two hours later, Luke knew he possessed a Remington 870 twelve-gauge shotgun, and after steady drilling by Phil, he understood how the gun worked as well as how to load and fire it. They had a quick breakfast of eggs and toast and then headed outside as the first pink streaks of sunrise brightened the sky.

Shooting at targets turned out to be both exhilarating and terrifying. He stood nervously eyeing the empty canning jars perched on fence posts. Currents of fear and thrill charged through him as he raised the shotgun to his shoulder. The first shot knocked him back and sent the chickens into a squawking frenzy in the coop. Even with cotton wedged in his ears, they still rang. Phil helped him adjust his stance and grip. The second shot shattered the glass jar. Luke let out a whoop and grinned.

"You're getting it," Phil said. "Keep at it."

"I don't have that much ammo left," Luke said.

"Shoot," Phil commanded. "Ammo won't make any difference if you can't shoot the damn weapon, right? We'll find more ammo."

Luke squinted and lined up the sights. "Right." He squeezed the trigger. The jar splintered into the air.

They spent the following week catching up on neglected farm chores, and twice they made trips into town to stock up on supplies. The shock of so many bodies left rotting in cars and on sidewalks forced them to keep the trips short, but they managed to pile the back seat of the Honda Civic with ammo and a few guns from the local gun supply shop. It was important they be well-armed, Phil said, but Luke wondered why they needed so much.

"You never know who might come along," Phil said. "Good or bad—it's a toss-up. Best to be prepared."

Phil insisted on putting Luke through hours of target practice. Every morning after breakfast, they'd head out to the pasture and shoot empty tin cans or bottles.

"I don't see the reason I have to keep doing this," Luke said one morning. "I can shoot now. But there's nobody around. You're the only person I've seen in the past month. So why keep wasting ammo?"

Phil rubbed his face as if Luke's question made him weary. "Things are different now, Luke. The world is different. You've heard the reports. Most of the population is gone and that means those who are left just want to survive at any cost. It means the rules have changed. Priorities have changed. It means you have to change."

Luke glared at Phil. "So you're saying I need to shoot people to survive?"

Phil slowly shook his head. "If you want to survive, you have to be willing to examine yourself. Deep down. You've got to be able to see what's a hindrance and what's a help."

"Like you know all about it," he grumbled.

"I do know. I've been surviving a bit longer than you. I've seen what's out there. I know."

Luke picked up a rock and threw it angrily. How was he supposed to abandon everything he'd been taught to be true? "My father said killing was never the right way to solve anything."

"And I agree. But he had that shotgun hidden away for a reason, didn't he? Just in case? When you're looking down the barrel of a gun held by someone who won't think twice about putting a bullet in your brain, what are you gonna do? Close your eyes and let him?"

Luke didn't reply. He didn't want to think about it anymore.

* * *

One morning, Luke was feeding the chickens when he heard the crunch of gravel on the drive. He looked up just as Phil ran from the barn with Brewer following.

"Get in the house," Phil called. Luke whistled for Brewer. They sprinted inside, locking the door behind them.

Luke drew the pistol holstered on his belt. Phil grabbed the shotgun by the door. Both peered through the window overlooking the porch. The curtains were drawn, but they could see through the narrow slits on each side.

Around the bend, a red pickup approached.

"Looks like we got company," Phil said.

Luke sucked in a breath as alarm pulsed through him. "That's my dad's truck."

Phil laid a hand on Luke's arm. "Hold on." He leaned closer, squinting. "That your dad behind the wheel?"

Luke waited as the truck slowly drew closer. "No. Looks like a man and a woman. I don't recognize them."

Luke tried not to think about the implications of someone else having his father's truck. That meant…so many things, none of them good.

The driver's door opened and a man climbed out. Tall and thin with curly brown hair, he looked like a teenager. Slowly raising his hands, he edged around to the passenger side and opened the door for the woman. She stepped out and stood beside him, swaying slightly, as if she could hardly stand up. He said something to her and she lifted one hand. Her other arm remained wrapped tightly around the man's waist for support.

Slowly, cautiously, the two of them approached the house.

Phil glanced at Luke and said, "I'm going out the back. Keep your eyes open. Look for anything that seems off, got it?"

Luke nodded. He hoped Phil didn't see his hands shaking.

When the couple reached the porch steps, they stopped. He could hear them talking in low voices, and he strained to listen.

"We can't do this," the girl said. "It's not right."

"We have to. You know we do," the man replied. "It's us or him."

"There's got to be another way," she said.

"I don't want to die. Do you?"

Luke decided they'd come close enough. "Best thing you can do is turn around and leave," he called out.

They both jumped, startled by his voice. The man reached into his back pocket. Luke raised his pistol. He'd have to shoot through the glass, but the man was close enough to hit. He was puzzled when the man held up a piece of paper. He couldn't make it out, but it looked like a photo.

"Luke Tomlin?" the man said.

His heart raced. How did this guy know his name?

"I know you don't know me. We met your father—Jason, right? We met him at the hospital. He asked us to find you…gave us your address. And a picture of you…your family." The man leaned forward, extending his arm out to show the picture. Luke could see it now. It was the one taken last year on Easter. His dad had carried a copy in his wallet.

Luke tried to calm his breathing. He had to reason this out, but his head was filled with panicked thoughts. Finally, he said, "Is he dead?"

The man's head dropped a little, and he lowered his arm. "Yeah. I'm sorry."

"How do I know you're telling the truth? You could have taken the picture from his wallet. You stole his truck, didn't you?"

"No…we…" The man shook his head, and the girl gave him an anxious, pleading look. "He gave us his truck. He was worried about you, and he wanted us to find you. He said if we found you alive, to give you a message. He said to tell you, 'keep on living, Super Boy.'"

Luke swallowed hard. Super Boy—only his father would have known that. Could they be telling the truth?

Something still didn't feel right. "What do you want?" Luke asked.

The man glanced around nervously, then stared at the girl, whose face grew pale. His gaze settled on the window, as if trying to figure out Luke's location behind the curtain.

"We want…" he began, then he looked at the girl again. "We want you to get down. There's a man…" He grabbed the girl and pulled her to the ground.

The glass shattered next to Luke's face. He fell back, breathing hard. Pain pierced his face. He touched his cheek. Blood coursed down from the shards embedded in his skin. Someone had tried to shoot him. Who? He carefully crept to the corner of the window and peered out. The two were still on the ground, the man shielding the woman with his body. Luke scanned the area, looking for movement in the trees, but saw nothing.

More shots rang out from behind the house. He spotted Phil darting from tree to tree. Did he see the shooter? Then Luke spotted movement in the woods on the left side of the house. A man sprinted through the trees, heading around the back. From Luke's vantage, he could see that Phil had lost sight of him. That meant the man would be coming around behind Phil, and Phil wouldn't know.

Wincing at the needles of pain in his cheek, he scrambled to his feet and ran to the back door. He got there just as the man darted past the house. Luke slipped out the door and followed, his heart pounding and every nerve on alert. The man wasn't aware of his presence; he'd found his target and was fully focused on Phil hidden behind a tree, his gun aimed in the wrong direction.

The man raised his weapon, Phil in his sights.

"Hey!" Luke yelled.

The man swung around, startled, and fired. The bullet whizzed past Luke's ear.

Luke returned fire.

The man jerked as a red stain blossomed on his chest. He crumpled to the ground. Phil ran toward him. Everything that happened next blurred together. Phil knelt next to the man on the ground, then moved to Luke, asking if he was okay. Luke felt sick. He wanted to cry but knew he couldn't; he had to be strong; he had to be brave. He'd just killed a man. He'd just killed a living human being. How was he ever going to be the same again?

He fell to his knees. His stomach heaved, and he vomited.

"It's okay," Phil whispered. "You saved my life."

Luke wiped his mouth on his shirt with shaking hands and took in deep breaths. Hot and cold currents passed through him as he tried to gain control. "Is he dead?"

"Yeah."

From around the corner of the house, the couple approached cautiously. Phil raised his weapon. "No further," he said.

They stopped. "We're so sorry," the man said to Phil. "We had no choice. He forced us to do this." They both looked over at the man crumpled on the ground.

"Do what?" Phil asked.

"To make you think we needed help. So you'd let your guard down. He's been following you."

Phil's expression turned dark. "Damn."

* * *

His name was Sam and hers was Lindy. They met at the hospital. Lindy had come down with the virus but had recovered. She was still pale and weak, her eyes still slightly bloodshot.

"I took my mom to the hospital," Sam said. "She died that night. They put the whole place under quarantine and I was stuck there. I kept waiting to get sick, but I never did. Everybody was dropping like flies, and pretty soon hardly anyone was left alive. I found Lindy; she'd been there about two weeks. It was a miracle she recovered."

"How did you find my dad?" Luke asked.

"We were on our way out," Sam said, his face grim. "We'd decided to just head in a random direction and try to find someplace safe. Your dad was sitting on the floor in the hallway, leaning against the wall. At first we thought he was dead. But he reached for us, asked us to wait. He told us about you, how worried he was. Said he'd give us his truck if we'd go find you and make sure you were safe."

Luke's chest tightened as he pictured his father dying. "You could have just taken off with the truck. Why didn't you?"

Sam stared at his feet. "I wanted to. But Lindy wouldn't let me. Even though your dad would never have known, Lindy said she believed in keeping promises." He glanced at her and she smiled.

"I wanted him to have hope," Lindy said. "I wanted him to know somebody would find you."

"We found a map, figured out where you lived, and took off," Sam said. "Every town we drove through was a ghost town. No signs of life. Only bodies everywhere."

"Then we got to Anchorton. A man flagged us down," Lindy said. "We were so shocked to see someone alive, we stopped. He seemed so happy to see us. And he seemed nice. A regular guy, you know?"

"Yeah, we were stupid," Sam added.

Phil shook his head as if he understood. "You can't trust anybody anymore. So what happened?"

"We chatted about our situations. He said he was from New York City, had lost everyone, and was hoping to find his friend." Sam's brow drew tight as he spoke. "We told him about trying to find you, Luke. We showed him the picture your dad had given us."

"That's when everything changed," Lindy said. "When he looked at that picture, we could tell he recognized your face."

Luke's pulse charged. "How?"

"He'd been following Phil," Sam said. "He'd seen you two in Anchorton, collecting supplies, and connected the dots. He pulled a gun on us and told us to do what he said or he'd kill us both. He forced us to drive him to your house. Since you were together, he believed he'd find Phil here too."

Luke stared at Phil. "You knew him?"

"Yeah, I knew him," Phil said quietly. "His name's Alfred Beeston. I figured out he was following me somewhere around Albany. I thought I'd lost him."

A dozen questions filled Luke's mind, but Phil had turned moody and withdrawn. Luke knew better than to press for answers.

"We're real sorry all this happened," Sam said. "If you want us to go, we will. We'll even leave the truck. We kept our promise to your dad, just not the way we planned."

"No kidding," Luke said. He touched his cheek again, pulling out a sliver of glass. He glanced at Phil and found him staring back. He knew Phil was waiting for him to give Sam and Lindy an answer. Did he want them to go? He wasn't sure, but reason said they could be of use, and there was strength in numbers.

"You can stay," Luke told them. They both grinned.

"Thanks, man," Sam said. "We'll work hard. You won't regret it."

Phil decided they should burn Alfred's body before they buried it, so there'd be no chance of someone recognizing him, even if they dug him up. Luke and Sam helped load the man on the bed of the truck along with a jug of gasoline, and Phil took off on his own to the back pasture, insisting he'd do the job.

In the days that followed, the four of them fell into a routine. They tended the garden, cared for the chickens, gathered eggs, completed necessary maintenance on the house, barn, and coop, and cooked and cleaned. Twice they made trips into Anchorton. With the pickup truck, they were able to load up with enough supplies to keep them going for a long time. They cleaned out Carlton's Gun and Tackle of all their weapons and ammunition. Phil remarked how fortunate they were that Anchorton was far enough off the beaten path that it hadn't been ransacked much by looters. It was a good thing too, because he expected it would only be a matter of time before they started seeing more people showing up in town and at the farm. Not all of them would be friendly. Every day Phil drilled them in the use of weapons. They practiced until they grew confident in their ability to handle a gun and shoot accurately.

Each night they listened to the radio, hoping for some sort of news. Finally they caught a faint, broken message discussing the potential for survivors in Staten Island.

"Beeston mentioned that place once," Lindy said. She glanced at Sam. "Remember? Maybe we should go there."

Sam nodded. "Yeah. He said something about maybe all of us heading there after he found his friend. That was when we first met him. So it's a real thing."

"You don't want to go to Staten Island," Phil said.

"Why not?" Sam asked. "Maybe it's a new start."

Phil rubbed a hand over his face. "Let me tell you something," he said. "Eight years ago, I worked for a government agency that monitored radical groups. We had our eye on a pharmaceutical corporation called Peter Franklin Donalds. We'd followed leads before that took us nowhere, but we ended up hearing talk of a genetically modified virus, similar to Ebola. They were creating a bioweapon."

"That's what this is?" Luke said. "That's where it came from?"

"I'm pretty sure," Phil replied. "I'd been working for the agency about four years when my wife got cancer. I took early retirement so I could be with her. Right before she died, I got word that PFD had identified us, our little watch group. We had names, see, and now they had ours. About that same time, we discovered that certain members of the government were actually encouraging PFD's work. This was all before the outbreak. At the time, I didn't know what PFD was trying to do."

"So that man, Beeston—" Luke started.

"Yeah, I'm getting to that. After my wife died, I worked odd jobs here and there. I found out that several members of our group had turned up missing. I didn't know how many, or who was left. Then came the outbreak, and it all hit the fan. I decided to get out of town while I had the chance. Chaos makes for a good cover sometimes. I knew who Alfred Beeston was. Never met him, but I knew he was bad news. What I didn't count on was that he'd be coming after me. I figured he was dead like most of the population."

Luke, Sam, and Lindy stared at each other, unbelieving. "So was it the government or PFD looking for you?" Sam asked.

"Don't know, but if PFD really is responsible for this outbreak, it sure makes sense they'd want to eliminate everyone who knew about it. Or, for all I know, maybe Beeston was working on his own. Maybe everyone is gone, and he just wanted to finish what he started."

Lindy shook her head. "But you were retired."

"Doesn't matter. I knew things. *Know* things. Which is why I don't think you should go to Staten Island. PFD is running the place. I don't think it's what they're saying it is."

* * *

A few days later, Luke heard the approach of a vehicle up the drive. He yelled a warning and everyone grabbed their weapons and scrambled quickly to their positions. A black van drove slowly around the bend and stopped well back from the house. Two men got out, both dressed in casual clothes—jeans and shirts.

But what caught Luke's attention was the logo on the side of the vehicle: a gray diamond overlaid with the letters PFD. He turned to Phil and said, "You need to hide."

Phil took it calmly. "I won't hide," he said. "If they've come for me, I'll try to stay out of sight. But I'll fight if that's what it comes to."

Luke nodded and took a deep breath. He slowly opened the door and stepped out onto the porch, his pistol trained on the two. "This is private property," he said with as much bravado as he could muster. "You can turn around and leave."

One of the men held up his hands in a placating gesture. "We don't want trouble. We're just looking for information. We're trying to find a man. Black man. Tall, about fifty. Seen anyone like that?"

"Nope. He's probably dead like everybody else."

"We have reason to believe he's not. He's been recently spotted in this area." The man waited for a response. Luke didn't give it.

"You live here alone?" the man asked.

Luke remained silent. He fired a warning shot at the man's feet. An explosion of dust forced the man to jump back. The second man drew his gun. Luke sent a bullet into his shoulder. The man cried out as his weapon catapulted from his hand.

"I answered your question," Luke said firmly. "Now, turn around and leave."

"I think you need to know what you're up against," said the first man, backing up. "This guy is dangerous."

"That's good to know," Luke said. "If I ever come across his corpse, I'll keep it in mind." He took one step off the porch and aimed for the man's leg. Before he could pull the trigger, both turned and ran for the car. The van circled sharply around, spitting gravel, and sped off in a cloud of dust.

Once they were out of sight, Luke retreated inside and locked the door. He could hardly catch his breath. "They might be hanging around, Phil. Maybe they're waiting for a chance to catch us off guard."

"I don't think so," Phil replied as he stared out the window. "But we'll soon know."

"How did they know to come here?" Lindy asked.

"They're probably checking all the remote residences," said Sam.

"Or Alfred tipped them off," Phil added, his voice grim.

They decided to take shifts and keep watch throughout the night. By early morning, there was no sign of their return. Luke climbed into bed, exhausted. But sleep remained elusive. Once again his thoughts returned to his father, a body left in a hospital hallway. It wasn't right.

Brewer jumped on his bed and curled up beside him, as if he sensed Luke's distress. He nudged into Luke's hand with a whine and waited for Luke to give him a comforting rub behind the ears. The warmth of the dog's body eased the ache from Luke's mind, and he slipped into a restless sleep.

He woke a few hours later to sounds from the kitchen. He heard Phil talking to Brewer in a quiet voice.

"Gonna miss you, boy," Phil said. "You gonna miss me?"

Luke climbed out of bed and found Phil in the kitchen putting supplies into a rucksack. Brewer sat at his feet, tail wagging.

"What are you doing?" Luke asked.

"I've had some time to think," Phil told him. "I'm putting you in danger being here. I don't know how far they'll go to find me. It's not fair to you, or Sam and Lindy. So I'm taking off."

Alarm shot through him. "What? You can't. We need you here."

"You'll do just fine without me."

Luke squared his shoulders. "Then Brew and I are going with you."

Phil looked at him sadly. "I can't be responsible for you, Luke. If I'm putting you in danger by being here, how is it any different if you go with me?"

"Because you need somebody who'll have your back. Two are better than one. Brew's a good first alert. You know that. Sam and Lindy, they can run the farm. And if we get to a point where things settle down, and we feel safe again, we have a place to come back to." He hesitated a beat. "And I've been thinking. I want to find my father. I want to give him a decent burial."

Phil kept his eyes on his task, his brow drawn tight over his eyes. "This is your home," he said as he finished packing. "You shouldn't leave it. And your father…is in a better place."

"It's the people who make it a home. Mine are gone. Home is where you hang your hat. My dad always said that… And it's my birthday."

Phil looked up, surprise on his face. "Your birthday?"

"Yeah. And this is what I wish for. To go with you. And to bury my father."

Phil blew out a long breath. "You know it won't be easy."

"I know," Luke said with a nod.

"You'll need to carry your own weight."

"I will."

Phil held Luke's gaze for a long moment. "All right, then. Let's go have a talk with Sam and Lindy."

SEVENTEEN: *Survival Mode*
by Kate Corcino

They'd been tracking a black plume of smoke all afternoon. A shift in the wind sent it swirling around them, and death came with it. Chad recognized the smell now. The acrid mix of hot metal, burning rubber, and gasoline had twined around burning flesh and the smell of bodies already bloating under the hot New Mexico sun.

It had only been three days since the Fever hit Albuquerque. Before they went off the air, the news had said the disease was man-made. Someone knew their job. The virus didn't take its time. The second wave of dead had fallen as first responders died, too, and the summer heat magnified the odor of corpses in cars. It was thick in his nostrils. His nose and eyes ran.

Is it the smell, Chad? Or is it the sickness?

He killed the engine of the dirt bike. The bike teetered for a moment as a wet, painful cough shook him. He didn't know if the smoke was affecting Annee and Elena the same. He'd be damned if he'd look back at Elena, his little sister's androgynous tag-along. He was still furious with her for what she'd cost them—the bunker, the guns—though honestly he knew he should be just as angry at Annee.

And what about you? You're the one who left the gear behind, aren't you?

Chad gritted his teeth against his own taunting thoughts. He'd left the majority of the guns and ammo behind in the fight to keep Elena and her sick brother out of the bunker. He'd lost that fight. He'd lost the gear, too. He'd been too afraid to go back up after it. What if they figured out how to cycle the locks and kept him from getting back in? By the time he'd made the decision to get Annee out of there and go look for help, a stinking thief had marched in through the unlocked front door and taken the guns.

He shifted the strap holding the guitar case across his back and made sure he still had access to the shoulder holster and the .45 in it. He wiped at his face with his forearm, glancing down to check the color of the fluid on his skin with a dart of fear. Only watery mucus ran from his eyes and nose. It was the smoke, not the virus.

Behind him, the other dirt bike engine sputtered and died. The harsh choking sound of his sister's vomiting filled the silence.

She's getting sicker. He swallowed away the acid burn of bile.

"I can't, Chad." The words were lost to another round of coughing that became violent heaving. When they came again, they were breathy. Weak. "I can't. It's the eyes. All their eyes. We need to go the way Dad planned."

The eyes of the dead stared at them from within cars and from the road around them as they wove through the gaps between them. The eyes—all of them—were red. Elena's older brother's eyes had been the same soon after he died. Hemorrhaging capillaries gave Abel a maddened, almost-zombie appearance, even if it was still him behind the violent red. Had it been just that morning that they'd covered his face and those empty red eyes with a blanket?

It was why his little sister couldn't handle the staring eyes. He didn't blame her. At fifteen, four years younger than him, she was the sweet one, the good girl who had dedicated her life to dance. And disaster prepping, of course. Chad was the one who'd rejected their father's fixation.

"Annee, we've been through this." He still didn't look at her. He knew how much her chest hurt. He was getting better, and his chest still ached. He couldn't bear to see whether or not she was vomiting blood yet. At the end, the blood had poured from Abel, over Chad's hands as he held Elena's brother up so he wouldn't choke on the bright bubbles foaming in his nostrils and throat.

Chad pulled his thoughts back to where they belonged with a ragged breath. *Stay in the moment. Focus on getting through right now.*

"We need to get to the motel as quickly as possible and using the freeway is the way to do that." It didn't matter anymore that the only thing Dad had cared about was his online family of *PrepforDoom.com* believers. It didn't matter that the only thing he'd given hours of his attention to every day was his big plan. Dad was two thousand miles away. He might as well be dead.

His plan was dead, too. It was the first decision Chad made after Abel died. Yeah, they'd go...so he could find help for Annee. But stay off the freeway? The freeway was the fastest way out of the city, and his only concern was getting Annee out and to help.

Getting Annee help...and finding Wendy. Something in his chest squeezed into a hard ball. Why hadn't she answered his calls?

"Not if it means we never make it to the rendezvous."

Chad's gaze snapped to his sister at the answering steel in her words.

There was a wet smear across her lips and cheek where she'd scrubbed away the bile after she'd been sick. Her eyes made his stomach twist. Her light brown eyes, so like his own and so familiar, were huge in her pale face. And they were filled with angry fear.

Like Abel's had been down in the bunker.

After their mother had died, Dad's distraction from those last, long months had turned to obsession. He'd spent her life insurance, and most of the trust she'd left behind, digging a bunker out back. He'd told Chad it was to keep them safe, no matter what happened to the rest of the world. What a load of crap. If he'd given a damn about them, he'd have been the one driving Annee to dance and attending her performances, buying the groceries and making the meals. He'd have been the one holding their family together.

But Chad handled it all while Dad was off playing helicopter hot shot with the Guard or locked in his prepper's dungeon waiting for the end. When it came, he was too far away to help them. And the bunker hadn't saved them, either. When Chad got Dad's email telling them to get in the bunker and stay there, Chad scrambled to unload the guns and ammo from the locked cabinet to take down with them. Annee had her own list of tasks, but instead she'd taken off in the car to get Elena, and look how that had turned out. They'd fought him, and he'd given in to the chaos and fear. Some tough prepper he was. Dad would flip.

Except making Dad proud didn't matter anymore. He was in New York and for all Chad knew he was dead, too. The whole world was dying. But not Chad. He'd beat the virus. Annee would, too. He'd keep his focus where it belonged—his sister, and his decision to leave the contaminated bunker and get her to the meet-up where there'd be people who could help.

When he didn't respond, she insisted, "If we're going to make the rendezvous, we have to go the back way."

He swallowed and looked away from her challenging eyes.

"There was a reason Dad planned the route the way he did," she said, "which you'd know if you'd bothered to pay attention. And I don't have time right now to rehash all of his lessons with you. Not if you want to have a chance of getting to Wendy first."

She knew? Of course she did. They spent so much time together, in the car as he took her to and from lessons, in the kitchen as she studied and he cooked. She'd met Wendy, seen the two of them together. Though Chad didn't share much with anyone else, he'd told his sister about the ring he was saving for.

And now she was using his feelings to get her way.

Why won't you answer your phone, Wendy? His thoughts skittered away. He couldn't go there. Not his green-eyed girl, too. His head turned almost against his will and he stared southeast. He wished he'd told her about the bunker. Maybe she would have come to him. He hadn't heard from her since the world had gone crazy. He knew the bunker was a dead zone for cell signal, but before they'd gone down, why hadn't she answered his calls? Were the lines that overwhelmed?

You know why. The truth of it dropped his chin to his chest. What was it the TV said? More than 80% dead or dying? Chad gritted his teeth. He'd taken the freeway because it got them to help for Annee as fast as possible. It got him to Wendy even faster. Tijeras Canyon was along the way. He'd detour and go find his girlfriend.

Except first they had to get past the twisted wreckage choking both sides of I-25 South ahead. It was the quickest way to I-40 and the meeting point. If it weren't for all the cars jamming the way ahead, if it weren't for the burning wreckage smoldering with dangerous fumes, they'd already be there. The delay ate at him. Was Annee right?

Elena lifted a bottle of water to her mouth and sipped as she straddled the dirt bike that Annee must have dived off to throw up a few feet away. The wind shoving the smoke at them didn't even stir her dark boy-short buzz cut. "Maybe if someone had told his little girlfriend about the bunker, told her to come up there, instead of assuming it was all crap that he'd never be using, we wouldn't have to come up with extra time to make a detour." Her words were low, but not so low that Chad wouldn't hear them. "Maybe we wouldn't have to be in such a hurry."

He flicked a hostile glance at her. Did Elena really have no idea why he was in such a hurry?

"I'm not just hurrying to get to Wendy. The faster we get there, the faster we get Annee help before…" He stopped and swallowed the words, glaring at her.

Before she dies, too?

He spoke again, quickly, and made sure his words were deliberately provocative to cover his fear from his sister. "Maybe if someone hadn't insisted on bringing her sick brother along to contaminate our bunker, you guys could've waited for me there while I got Wendy on my own." It was the truth. The minute Elena had dragged Abel with her, she'd put Chad and Annee at risk. "Your family, including your brother, treated you like crap, but that's okay, let's bring him along and get Annee sick, too."

"I don't give a damn what you think—"

"Stop it!" Annee's chest rose and fell in short, shallow breaths. "Just stop, both of you. You're exactly the same. And you're going to need each other before this is all done. You're going to need each other when *I'm* done, so just—just stop."

"You're gonna make it, Annee, just like Chad. You're gonna get better." Elena's voice was firm, but her face was pale. Maybe she was remembering her own brother.

"I've been sick longer than he was. He didn't—"

"But you're not coughing as bad as I did." Chad shook his head and thinned his lips, talking over her when she tried to tell him how tired she was. "You're going to make it."

"You have to," Elena added. She threw Chad a glance from the corner of one of her wide, up-slanted eyes. "You can't leave me with the tall, skinny, white boy. Without you, we'll kill each other in a day."

He thought she meant it as a joke—maybe—though privately he agreed. But Annee closed her eyes, and the expression on her face told him that the words pained her. Her lips moved in a silent prayer.

His gaze swerved away, as it always did when people prayed around him. Wendy did it, too, sometimes. Oh, she liked to complain about having to go to early services with her mom, and she had questions, too. But when push came to shove, she closed her eyes and started praying when she needed comfort.

It wasn't that it bothered him, exactly. And it wasn't that he didn't believe, either. He did.

He was almost sure he did.

He just had a hard time with faith in general—how did you ever really know if you believed in something you couldn't see? When the world was falling apart, how did you hold on to believing in anything?

Chad didn't know. And seeing his sister in prayer was like a little needle stick to remind him of that failure. Apparently, Elena felt something of the same awkwardness. When he self-consciously darted a glance at her, she was fiddling uncomfortably with a gauge in front of her. *Who'd have thought* that's *what the two of them would have in common?*

"Okay, look, fine, have it your way." The capitulation wasn't to give Annee what she wanted, but to get her to come back to reality. It would be easier if they could all be on the same page. "We'll head back to go up Tramway. Okay?"

Dad's plan used the road that went up and skirted the northeast edge of Albuquerque. Chad didn't see how heading up a road that accessed so many residential areas would cut back on time, but at this point, he didn't care. Anything that got him to Tijeras was better than standing here on I-25 and fighting about it.

After a moment, Annee let a long sigh escape. She opened her eyes, and gave him a peaceful smile. "Okay," she said simply and crossed to perch on the back of Elena's bike again.

He thought she'd let it go at that, but just before he started his bike, she tapped Elena on the shoulder with a mischievous grin. "And you said prayer doesn't work."

He could barely hear the soft words. He exchanged a look with Elena. His fear was reflected back at him in her eyes. *Look at us, bonding over my dying sister.*

"We should go." Elena's face was scared—angry, too, but not at him this time. At the universe.

His engine roared to life. The three of them turned back, just as Annee wanted, and headed for the Tramway exit.

What should have been an hour's trip took them almost three. The road wasn't bad heading up the mountain, but the downslope heading down toward I-40 was backed up with the corpse-filled cars of people who'd been fleeing the city. Not as bad as the freeway, but it slowed their progress enough that the sun was lowering toward the horizon behind them as they exited I-40 and made their way through Tijeras to Wendy's neighborhood.

The town was deserted. They'd seen people at a distance in Albuquerque—singletons and small groups. And later in the afternoon, they'd heard the distant sound of gunshots. They weren't the only survivors moving around in the city. And not all of them just wanted to get out. Tijeras was silent. The buzz of the bikes echoed off the walls of the buildings.

He didn't bother with the driveway at Wendy's house. He drove the dirt bike right up to the front door, cut the engine, and dumped it on its side as he took two quick steps up the walk. He pounded on the door twice, even as he twisted the doorknob and flung the door open.

"Wendy!" He stood in the entry, twisting his head to glance into the little living room and the kitchen. Both were empty. "Mrs. Mitchell?"

It took about fifteen seconds for him to get over the oddness of just charging into his girlfriend's home. Those fifteen seconds of silence made his skin crawl. He took the stairs two at a time, bellowing Wendy's name.

He flew back down the stairs, his heart pounding in his chest. Elena and Annee stood in the doorway. Elena supported Annee's weight.

"She's not here!" Despair made his shout to them end in a choking noise. He twisted away and headed down the hall to the sunroom. "She's not..."

Except someone *was* there. Someone would never be leaving.

A pink-striped comforter was draped over the couch in the sunroom. Splotches of brown soaked through from beneath it.

A roaring filled his ears. His hand shook as it hovered over the comforter, just above the dark stains. He made himself grip the edge and pull it back.

A bloody multi-colored quilt covered the body. With an explosive gasp for air, Chad snatched it back, too.

It was too much. The small, pale face and blonde hair, the formerly green eyes, now ravaged red and staring blankly. Chad felt his belly hollow, the air sucked from him as his body curled down.

"Chad?" Annee's faint voice behind him brought him back.

"It's not her," he gasped. "It's not—it's her sister. Wendy and her mom aren't here."

Elena had lost her big brother. Wendy had lost her little sister.

He turned to his own sister, then. Elena half-carried Annee.

"Her fever's raging." Elena's report was grim. "She's been trying so hard to keep it together for us. But she's just not—she's not doing well. She needs to stop now."

"It's thirty minutes up the road now." His voice sounded empty, even to himself.

"She can't. She won't make it tonight."

Chad stared at his sister's friend. He nodded understanding and crossed the room to help Elena, taking his sister's slight weight and carrying her upstairs to Wendy's mom's room.

The bed was bigger. All three of them could fit. He wasn't leaving his sister tonight, and he was pretty sure he'd have a war on his hands if he tried to make Elena leave her. He'd experienced the full force of Elena's fury outside Dad's bunker. He wasn't in any hurry to repeat it.

Elena got Annee settled. Her hands were gentle, but her face was a terrible combination of remote detachment and horrified numbness.

Her fever's raging.

"Is she going to make it to help tomorrow?" His whispered question sounded plaintive in his own ears.

Elena glanced up. "Help? What help? No one can help with this." She shook her head and made a negative huffing noise. "Help. You're as bad as she is, wanting to believe in a miracle."

Annee opened her eyes. They were glassy. "Not a miracle, Elena. Just believing for believing's sake."

"Yeah?" Elena's brusque voice went gentle again. "And what's the point of that, amiga? What does believing get you when bad things are happening?"

"Believing's not about getting. It's about giving, to the people around you, to the universe. Believing doesn't get you anything. It doesn't mean bad things don't happen. It just makes surviving them…more…"

She drifted off without completing the thought.

"Is she going to make it through the night even?" He was afraid to ask the question, but he had to prepare himself. Why he asked Elena, he didn't know. She was a kid herself who'd just lost her own brother.

She shrugged. "Don't know. Doubt it. Maybe we should try *believing*." The word was laced with venom.

Chad looked away, pretending not to notice the watery tracks tracing down Elena's wide, dusty cheeks. He'd never seen the tough girl cry, not even when Abel died. He'd seen her make plenty of other people cry. But with all that Annee had told him about Elena's troubled family life, he'd honestly thought she'd made herself immune to tears.

"You should eat."

"Not hungry." Elena sat on the other side of the bed.

"Then get some rest," he told her. "I'll keep watch. You sleep. I'll wake you up when I get too tired."

She stared away at the dark sky through the window, then curled up on top of the blanket, close beside Annee.

Chad wandered the house. He forced himself to eat a peanut butter sandwich. He studiously avoided Wendy's room. He couldn't go back in there, empty but so filled with her energy. It was a slap in the face, reminding him of her absence.

Where are you, Wendy?

He pulled out his cell phone and pushed the button to call her cell. Like every other time, it never rang. It just didn't go through. It was the same with texts. The little symbol spun and spun, but the status bar stalled at almost complete. Nothing was getting through. He didn't know why.

Why hadn't he told her about the bunker? If he hadn't been so embarrassed about his father's paranoia, they might all be together. He returned to his sister's side and spent the night listening, softly humming to himself, and checking the rising heat radiating from her skin. Alone with the night, there was nothing to keep his thoughts from turning to Wendy.

They'd been together two years. She'd been a baby when they met, only fourteen. But there was something so calming, so true, in her eyes. She wasn't like the other girls.

She never had been.

Was she safe? Was she sick? Was she even still alive?

He had to get Annee to responsible people who could help her so he could go look for Wendy. He'd figure out how to find her. She couldn't just be gone.

He stared at the outline of his guitar case across the room where he'd set it. Ordinarily, he'd be playing it, strumming as he hummed, writing a song for later.

But the song in his heart wasn't one he wanted to remember. It wasn't one he ever wanted to give words.

His eyes turned down to his sister. And what if he lost them both? Annee wanted him to believe, said it could make surviving it all—what? Easier?

He sighed and checked his sister's temperature again before shaking Elena awake and curling up on the other side of his sister. He wrapped his hand around his pistol beneath the pillow.

Chad woke to sunlight on his face. Someone pushed gently on his side.

"I have to pee."

Chad rolled over. Annee's eyes were wide beside him. She smiled and pushed at his side again.

"I really have to pee. Let me up."

Behind Annee, Elena rolled slightly to face them. Her hand pressed to Annee's forehead.

Annee's eyes were bright, aware—not glassy.

"You're better?"

"Her fever broke." The relief was palpable in Elena's breathed whisper.

Her fever broke. Relief flowed through him. She'd be okay. She was going to get better.

"Did you idiots not hear me?" The breath was still wet in her throat and lungs as she struggled to get someone out of her way. "I. Have. To. Pee."

Chad gave himself another second to revel in the elation of her broken fever before he rolled to his feet and helped her up.

Elena helped Annee to the bathroom and then turned, leaning against the door. Her face, creased by the pillow on one side, was bright and relaxed.

"Her fever broke," she repeated. She grinned at him.

Chad couldn't stop nodding.

"It's—this is good. It's a good thing. I can get you guys to the motel, and then I can find Wendy. I'm going to find her."

Annee was better. It was a sign of things to come.

Chad pulled his boots on, settled his shoulder holster and gun into place, then grabbed their gear from the corner. "I've got to load the bikes. Then I'm going to make you guys breakfast. This time you're both going to eat. Can you get your packs?"

Elena nodded.

He stomped downstairs and straight out the door. He couldn't think about Wendy's sister in the sunroom or Elena's brother in the bunker. His sister was better, and he'd use it to fuel his focus on today's goals. Feed them. Get Annee to the meet. Find Wendy.

He dropped the packs beside the bikes and started reloading them.

He'd just started back up the steps when the whining sound of an engine with a bad fan belt echoed down the street. Chad looked up as a van rolled to a stop at the corner. The driver, wearing some kind of white, hooded contamination suit, stared back at him. The man clearly hesitated before he lifted a radio receiver to the area near his mouth and spoke into it. The van slowly approached. It was nondescript, white, with the letters PFD superimposed over a grey diamond.

The man parked the van, watching Chad through the windshield.

Chad felt uneasy. The shotgun was in the saddlebag a few feet away, a rookie mistake he should have known better than to make. He had the .45, though. His hand itched to reach up and draw it.

The man opened the van door, hopped down, and came around to hover half hidden behind the front of the van. Behind the clear face plate of the suit, he seemed their dad's age.

"You okay?" he called out. "Not sick?"

"Not sick. You?"

The man smiled. "No. We're out looking for survivors." The man's face froze.

Elena and Annee stepped out the door behind Chad. Chad glanced over his shoulder. Elena was helping the still obviously weak Annee, supporting her weight.

"I thought you said you weren't sick?" The man's voice went hard and cold.

"We're not, we recov—"

The man swung up the arm he'd hidden behind the van.

Chad barely registered the man's gun before the bright muzzle flare bloomed with three quick bursts of fire. Chad felt the punch low in his side, heat and pain that knocked the breath from him. He stumbled, feet twisting under him and knees going soft.

He fumbled at the holster with suddenly clumsy fingers, but someone's hand was already there, yanking it free.

"No! No, no, no!"

The raw scream came from behind him with a crack of return gunfire.

His gaze was trained on hands that came back from his side bloody. He lifted his head.

The man fell, crimson spreading violently across the pristine white of the suit.

Chad stared. *What had happened? The man was down. Who had fired?*

"No! No, please. You can't leave me, too! Chad!"

His ears rang. Above the sound, far away and somewhere behind him, Elena screamed. Pressing his hand to his side again, Chad turned. Annee slumped across the stoop, Elena leaning over, the pistol clutched in her hand still.

Red bubbled from Annee's chest, a match to the dead man behind him.

"Chad, please! Help me—she has to—she's better. She has to stay with us. Help me!"

Chad struggled to his feet and lumbered to his sister. As soon as he reached her, Elena grabbed his hands and pressed them to Annee's chest, forcing him to apply pressure. Elena leaped to her feet and raced to the bikes, digging through the saddlebag.

Chad stared at Annee, at her blood washing over his fingers.

Elena threw down the medical kit beside him and hovered over his shoulder. She tried to talk, to give him instructions, but it was just sound—gasps. Tears.

It didn't matter. He could see it in Annee's face. She wasn't struggling, though he could hear the wet gurgles. She stared up at him, eyes lit with fever-free energy.

Her lips moved.

Believe. The thread of sound was no more than a wet exhale, but he knew what she said.

"I don't know how. That's why I have you, Annee. You're the believer. I don't even know how."

A small smile lifted her lips. "You do." She barely managed to voice the words. "You believe in love? You believe in Wendy?"

He leaned in and held her head still, as if that would help. "It's not the same. Believing in a person and believing in…everything."

Don't go, Annee.

"It is. Same decision. Just…bigger."

"I don't know how…" He squeezed his eyes shut and lowered his forehead to hers, not caring about the pain in his side, about the hot-cold acid burn of the torn flesh. He'd pour himself into her to give her the strength to go on. She had to make it. Her fever had broken. That meant she'd live, didn't it?

She was supposed to live.

Eyes squeezed shut, hands tangled in her hair, he waited for her to breathe in again, fuel for her next bossy, breathy comment…for her to tell him how to do it. He waited.

Behind him, a low rasping moan became heavy sobs, and then running footsteps. Three more gunshots rang out, then dull thuds of a flurry of fists and feet falling on the man's body. Elena had been waiting, too, standing just behind him. Now, she raged at the dead man.

How did she know?

Chad slowly lifted his forehead from Annee's and lowered his hands from her hair to her cheeks.

It was her eyes. Elena knew because of her eyes.

Annee's light was gone.

* * *

Elena didn't know how long the two of them huddled in the front yard of that house, together but lost in their own grief. She'd probably still be there, waiting for her own death if Chad hadn't lurched away.

He stood, tottering and pale. A fresh flow of blood quickly soaked his drying shirt and ran down the side of his pants. "I won't leave my sister out in the open. I gotta bury her."

"Okay. But I'm pretty sure I'm not strong enough to bury both of you, so you need to let me help you." The way he and Annee had helped her with Abel's death. She swallowed the whine that threatened to escape from her throat.

Elena had attacked Chad when he'd told her sick Abel couldn't come into the bunker. She'd refused to leave her brother behind, even if he was a jerk to her most of the time. He was her brother. But when his final moments came, she backed away, leaving him with Annee and Chad. She'd stood in the corner, rocking, and simply stared as her brother died.

Chad stared at her now, blank-faced. She wasn't sure he'd understood until he nodded and eased down again. His hand hovered over the wound on his side. "I've got nowhere to bury her." She could hear the shock and despair in his voice. "Should I leave her with Wendy's sister?" He shook his head, his voice weakening, drifting. "Neither of them has to be…alone."

And then she was alone in the yard. He'd passed out.

Elena lifted his shirt to look at the wound. There was a small hole on the lower right side with an exit hole angled out his back. She didn't know anything about wounds, or organs, or internal injuries. She thought that maybe he wouldn't be up and trying to walk, even weakly, if something inside was ruptured. Her main concern then was the bleeding. But how did you apply pressure internally?

He wouldn't like her idea, she was sure, but it was the only thing she could think of. She pulled supplies out of her pack, moving quickly. When she had his wound sealed as best as she could, she went inside to get a blanket.

Elena returned to her friend—her only friend—and knelt next to her. She should say a prayer. Except she didn't believe in all of that. And seriously, if the god that Annee believed in couldn't see that he was getting back the best of all the people he'd sent down, well, no prayer that Elena could come up with would make up for his failure.

She rolled Annee in the blanket and dragged her back into the house. For someone so tiny, it was hard work. When she got to the sunroom, she stopped, gagging at the smell in the still room. She pulled the blankets back and managed to lift Annee up onto the couch, settling her just on top and to the side of Wendy's sister, as if the two girls had fallen asleep together.

Something scraped behind her. Chad was awake. He'd dragged himself inside and now leaned in the doorway to the little room. He slid to the floor and fumbled his guitar onto his lap, glancing up self-consciously. "She liked it when I sang to her."

"I know."

But he didn't sing. He didn't strum. After a long moment of silence, he admitted, "I don't know what to play for her." His voice cracked.

"Yeah." Elena wiped at the sweat pouring down over her forehead. "Well. You could play her favorite song."

Chad's brows rose. "Silent Night? A Christmas carol?"

Elena shrugged. "Why not? It was her favorite."

He took a deep breath and his gaze flickered over the two girls, then swerved away again and up to the window and the cloudless blue summer sky outside.

When he began strumming— his low, deep voice hesitantly starting the words—Elena turned back and arranged the blankets over the girls. She didn't stop fussing, moving the blankets and tucking and re-tucking them around the two girls, until he was done. She couldn't stop, not even when his voice cracked as he sang of sleeping in peace, not even when the tears blurred her vision. She didn't need to see to finish what she was doing for her friend.

She didn't want to see.

Elena walked slowly over to him. "That was...nice. It was pretty, Chad. She'd have liked it."

He lifted his face, frowning. "Elena?" He looked down at his wounds and the stray strings hanging from the wound packing in front and then back to her. "Did you stick tampons inside me?"

"Um. Yeah." She shrugged. "It was all I had to stick in there for pressure. They'll, you know, spread and—"

"I don't even—"

"It was the best I could think of at the time!"

"No. It was smart. I just—Wow."

She nodded and moved on. She had to keep moving on. "I can't spend another night here, but we don't have to go to Moriarty, if you'd rather go look for—for your girlfriend."

"Wendy." He worked his way to his knees and then up to his feet. "No. I've got to get Annee to safety first."

There was a long beat of silence between them.

Elena opened and closed her mouth.

Chad lifted his head, a slow, painful movement. "I meant you. I've got to get you to safety first, then I'll go after Wendy."

She bit her lip and started to argue, but he turned and left, lifting his guitar case gingerly and easing the strap over his head to settle the case across his back. They mounted their bikes and left the dead man where he lay in the street.

It didn't take long to get there, but it didn't stop Elena from worrying that he wouldn't make it. Even with the tampons soaking the blood and applying internal pressure, a halo of fresh red remained on his t-shirt.

When he exited I-40, she pulled up next to him. Ahead, a long, low motel ran along the side of the freeway.

"Is that it?"

He didn't answer. She glanced up in surprise. Fury, disappointment, and grief flowed over his face. She swung her gaze back to the motel.

Now that she looked closer, it was clear that something very bad had happened below.

The parking lot was remarkably clear of vehicles. But that absence just made the numbers of abandoned bodies that much more apparent.

Elena could feel desperation scratching up her belly, trying to escape.

Chad carefully reached back and took out the shotgun, hissing in pain. He tucked it between the taut guitar strap and his chest. "Stay close." He revved the engine and raced off.

Elena swallowed. She didn't want to go down there. She wanted to keep riding, find peace somewhere far away from New Mexico and the grief that grew in its hard, rocky soil. She wanted to go back to Annee and lay down with the two girls and sleep.

She wanted to go back to the life she'd hated before.

She pulled into the lot behind him. The smell wasn't bad—not yet. They hadn't been left out in the sun for long.

Chad walked among the dead. He stopped over a young man. Someone he recognized?

"Is it them?"

He nodded. His throat worked. "Some of them."

"So some got away?"

"Or never made it here," he said, his voice dark. It was filled with the helpless, hopeless self-loathing that made a voice sharp. She recognized it because it was how her own voice sounded half the time.

"Should we check inside?"

"Do you think it'll matter?" Bitterness joined the loathing.

She didn't answer. Stepping over the splashes of blood on the pavement, she made her way to a sidewalk and followed it to an office. Through the window she saw devastation inside—broken glass from the other window and door, bullet holes in the furniture that oozed white stuffing. But it was a square of white paper on a mostly intact window that caught her attention.

She scraped at the tape with her fingers. Chad passed her, heading inside. He stood in the middle of the little lobby for a moment, staring at nothing. He wasn't even curious about what she was doing.

After a moment, he hooked the leg of a thinly cushioned chair with his foot and pulled it to rest beside two others. He eased himself down, draping his legs off the side of the third chair. He leaned back on the other two and closed his eyes.

"They left a note," she told him as she entered the stuffy lobby, her feet crunching across broken glass.

Chad grunted a response.

"It's dated today. We're moving on to R2. Will wait a day if able. It's signed PFD-NM."

No response.

"Chad. That means they're only hours ahead, if we leave now. We could catch them."

Why did she want to catch them? She didn't know these people.

But she didn't like that he'd given up.

He shook his head back and forth on the cushioned seat. "Then I'll be two or three days away from being able to get back to go look for Wendy. Everything's just—nothing is the way it's supposed to be."

"Okay. Well. It's the apocalypse, Chad. What did you expect?" It really *was* the apocalypse. She looked back down at the note in her hand, tossing the little plastic guitar pick that had been taped beside it into the air and catching it. She noticed a word scrawled on the back.

"Is 'dork' a code word for you guys or something?"

His brows knit together. "What?"

"'Dork.' Is that a code word for you internet prepper people?"

Chad opened his eyes to stare at her as if she'd grown another head. "No. Why?"

"'Cause this was taped next to the note. It says DORK." She held up the green plastic pick between her thumb and forefinger so he could see the word, written in marker.

Chad went so utterly still that she wasn't sure he was even breathing. A light flared in his eyes—was it hope?—before a low sob caught in his throat. "Could you bring it to me, please?" His voice was shaking. He held out his arm, hand open.

Elena took two steps and dropped it into his hand.

His fingers curled around it and brought it up to his face. The moment he opened his hand and saw it, his body started shaking.

"It's mine."

She was silent, waiting.

"I gave it to Wendy after camp. We exchanged—it's what I gave her. It's from Wendy."

"Wendy? She was here? How—?"

"I don't know. It doesn't make sense. Except—she must have remembered. About my dad. Or the site. Maybe our friend Billy helped her."

"Smart girl."

He nodded. "She's amazing." He bumped the fist that held the pick against his forehead. "She was here. They were attacked, and they couldn't wait for us."

Elena held up the note. "They're going to R2."

"Rendezvous point two, on the way to the bunker in Kingston. In New York."

"Can we go there? Do you know where it is?"

"I don't know," he admitted. "I hated this stuff. Annee knew the route." He lowered his head, beating the back of it in slow thumps against the seat of the upholstered chair. "I have to remember."

Chad stopped talking. His eyes searched the ceiling. She left him be, settling on the floor to wait. After a long while, his face twisted and he shook his head, lowering his hand to his face.

"Chad." She waited until he lowered his hand and turned to her. Elena nodded at the pick in his hand. "We'll find your Wendy. Can't let a girl that perceptive get away."

His head cocked. "That percep—?" Realization washed over his face. With a wobbly grin, he lifted the pick to flash the word DORK at her. "Dork. It's not about me. It's about us, what we call each other, me and Wendy. 'Cause we can be ourselves, always." He flipped the pick around to stare at the letters written with girlish flair. "It's about trusting each other," his voice became soft and almost hesitant, "and making a decision to believe."

"A decision to believe, huh?"

He nodded slowly.

Elena felt a twisting inside. What would that be like, to have the kind of faith that had led Wendy to leave the pick taped to the door? To believe so absolutely, even as people were dropping all around you, that somehow life would bring you together again?

She didn't know. Before all this had happened, she wouldn't have believed at all. But maybe… Maybe the best way to honor Annee was to believe.

"We can do it. We can find Wendy."

He nodded, sliding the pick into the palm of his hand and curling his fingers around it protectively. After a minute, a smile flitted over his face. "Think we can do it without killing each other?"

She laughed, surprised at how easy the sound burst from a chest still numb with pain and loss. "Yeah, well. We made it a whole day, didn't we? Annee would be shocked."

His lips curved up. "Nah. She believed in us more than either of us ever could."

She felt tears begin to close her throat again, and her eyes flooded. She lifted them to him anyway, knowing that if there was one person on the earth who could feel Annee's loss as she did, it would be the jerk in front of her.

"I loved her, you know." If they were going to keep going together, she needed to be able to say it. He didn't have to like it. But he had to let her be free to claim it, finally.

He was silent for a long moment, his eyes dark in the shadow of the dim room. A quick bloom of familiar fear—rejection, flitting through, as it knew its way—joined the heaviness in her heart.

Then he shifted on his improvised cot. His hand reached to hers, clasped around her knees, as she sat on the floor beside him. She could see the bright guitar pick safe within his curled fingers like a promise he refused to let go. The rough, split skin of his knuckles brushed hers. "I know. I loved her, too."

She nodded. Warmth curled inside her, a tiny, flickering thing. It surprised her. It was a funny thing, acceptance. Not as bright a light as love, it still had enough power to push back the shadows. It had the power to nurse hope back to life.

"You're gonna make it, Chad."

"We're both gonna make it, kid. And we're going to keep her alive." He lifted his hand up to bump it on his chest, above his heart, then lowered it again to her.

Elena smiled. Sometimes even the smallest of lights could hold back the dark. She bumped her knuckles against his gently. "Here's to life then."

"Here's to believing."

EIGHTEEN: *Don't Look Back*

by Kate L. Mary

Major Johnsen already stood at the front of the room when Eve walked into the mess hall. Close to sixty other survivors were gathered around the tables, and throughout the room uniformed soldiers stood sentinel. A reminder that even if society had collapsed, there would be no anarchy inside these fences.

Behind the Major, a handful of officers were lined up, Lieutenant Hicks among them. When his eyes met Eve's, Hicks threw her the same easy smile he always seemed to wear, and Eve found herself returning it. After all the death and grief, the gesture felt foreign on her lips, but Hicks brought it out in her. He was her savior. The one who had brought her back to Charleston Air Force Base, back to safety.

Eve had been on base a week now, although it felt longer. Hicks had been out on a supply run with a few other soldiers, and she'd been wandering around Sam's Club in a trance. She had watched her parents die, then her brother. Seen neighbors lying dead in their front yards. The world had turned into some kind of nightmare she couldn't wake up from. When Hicks had told her there were survivors at the base, she almost didn't believe him. After the horror she'd witnessed, it didn't seem possible. But something about him had stood out among the other soldiers, and it had little to do with the dimple in his left cheek or his rugged good looks. There was a softness in his brown eyes that made Eve believe she could trust him.

She slid into a seat at the back of the room and her gaze landed on Doug, the man who had lost his wife and all but one of his six children. Four-year-old Blake sat at his father's side, his blue eyes shimmering with fears a toddler should never have to face. Looking at him tugged at Eve's heart, bringing her own brother to mind. Cade had been older than Blake when he died, but she could remember him at this age so perfectly that the memory felt like it was going to crush her. She swallowed and turned her eyes away from the small boy before the tears clogging her throat could make their escape, and instead focused on the woman sitting across from her.

Stephanie smiled and reached across the table, patting Eve's hand in a grandmotherly gesture that was almost as painful as the terrified expression in Blake's eyes. The woman was in her sixties, and her hands shook so hard that Eve wondered if she was in the beginning stages of Parkinson's. But she was nice, and having someone who cared—even a stranger—helped loosen that ball of tears.

Major Johnsen cleared his throat, but when Eve turned she found herself caught in one of Captain Tanner's hard glares. He'd been with Hicks when they'd found Eve. Even before he'd spoken, it was clear by the look on his face that he wasn't thrilled about finding more survivors. Of course, he'd had no problem voicing his concerns, letting Eve know what a strain on their resources she was going to be. His tone had been as cold and hard as ice. Tanner didn't agree with how Major Johnsen had chosen to run the place. He probably even thought he could do a better job himself. But as far as Eve was concerned, Major Johnsen was doing a great job. He stood center stage at the dawning of the apocalypse, the leader of this brave new world.

Even though the room was already quiet, Major Johnsen cleared his throat for the second time, releasing Eve from Tanner's cold stare. "Thank you all for coming. For those of you who don't know me, I'm Major Johnsen. I've taken charge, but this isn't a dictatorship. We're in this thing together, and I want to be honest about what's going on. As far as we know, there is no working government at this time, and while we're still trying to collect information about this virus, we believe that more than 75% of the population has been wiped out." He paused for a split second and his eyes went to the floor. "Worldwide."

A buzz swept through the room as people reacted to the Major's announcement. The number hit Eve like a tsunami, and for a few seconds she could hardly breathe. All the questions she'd had before walking into the mess hall evaporated like a drop of water on a hot sidewalk in July. What were they going to do?

The Major didn't pause long enough for the conversation to rise higher than a whisper. "The virus may have run its course," he said, raising his hands to draw the attention his way once again. "But we want to be certain we're still not at risk, which was why you were all given blood tests when you arrived. Charleston Air Force Base is safe, and we want to keep it that way. We want to survive, we want to start over, and we want to keep order. Those are our goals." He paused, allowing his words time to sink in.

Eve found herself once again glancing toward Tanner, curious how the younger man would react. The glare Tanner shot at his commanding officer was so sharp it felt electric. There was something about the younger soldier that made Eve squirm. Something bigger than a few dirty looks or the fact that he didn't want to share their resources.

"Some of you may have heard that we've been in contact with a few other groups spread across the country," Major Johnsen continued. "Those rumors are true. We've located a group out in Boulder, and another in Vegas. Although we aren't liking the intel we've gotten from the Vegas group so far. Then there's this so-called 'safe haven' on Staten Island, run by Peter Franklin Donalds, the corporation. They claim to have it all. Safety and supplies, plus more than enough food to make a go of it. It sounds good, but it's a risk. We're discussing our options at the moment, but we have pilots, jet fuel, and C-17s at our disposal. We can go, join up with one of these other groups, or we can stay." His shoulders drooped like the weight of the decision rested solely on him. "I'm not going to force people to do anything they don't want to do, so this isn't an all or nothing situation. If we decide it's worth it to send a group out, those of us who want to, can go. Those of you who want to stay, are free to."

He looked across the room, pausing to meet the eyes of every person. When his gaze locked with Eve's, the ball of tension in her stomach slowly began to unravel. He seemed to be silently trying to let her know that he was trustworthy. That he'd do his best to bring them through. Eve believed him, as crazy as that sounded.

Once Major Johnsen had looked everyone over, he cleared his throat again. "Now, let's open the floor for discussion."

Someone at the front raised their hand, and the Major nodded. "How many people are in Staten Island?"

"They claim to have several hundred thousand survivors, but they have assured us there's room for more."

"Who's in charge?" someone called.

"I haven't been able to speak to the leader directly. Of course, over the wire like this, I have to take them at their word anyway."

"When would we go?" said a woman up front.

"There is no rush on this and we aren't going to jump into anything. We'll take our time and make a rational decision."

After that the organized information session exploded. People began yelling over each other as the Major tried to relay what little information he had. Belting out questions and opinions and theories that sounded more like B movies than anything that could actually happen. Conspiracy theories about this company and their part in the virus. Crazy things.

"We can't risk it! These people could be luring us up there to steal our supplies!" a man at the table next to Eve yelled, spittle flying from his mouth with each word.

"We need to find more people," a woman across the room responded, her voice so high-pitched that it rose above the others and made Eve cringe.

"There's nothing out there for us—we're better off here."

"We need to find a working government!"

"We have everything we need in Charleston. We'd be idiots to leave!"

The voices soared, making Eve's head pound harder. She couldn't take it anymore. The arguing made her jittery. Nervous.

She got to her feet and stumbled from the room, massaging her temples as she went. The second Eve stepped out into the hot, South Carolina sun, she let out a deep sigh. The humidity was thick, but welcome because it was familiar. So much had changed recently that Eve was willing to embrace anything she recognized, including the heat.

She'd barely made it two steps when the door opened at her back. "Hey!" Eve turned to find Hicks jogging her way. "You okay?"

"Yeah. I just—I couldn't sit through that, you know?" She did her best to keep the tremor out of her voice, but it was impossible. She missed the person she'd been before everything disappeared. Strong and brave. "Everything is bad enough without all the fighting."

Hicks tilted his head as his eyes swept over her like she was a puzzle he was trying to work out. The look made Eve shuffle her feet. She swept her blonde hair back, nervously twisting it around her fingers. Hicks acted like he was trying to read her mind, but everything inside her felt raw and broken. Eve wasn't sure she wanted him to see how messed-up it all was.

"You think we should do it?" he asked, pushing his hat back so he could sweep his hand through his brown hair. "Go up to Staten Island, I mean."

"I don't know, but I know traveling to Staten Island with a bunch of screaming morons sounds horrible." Eve shook her head and her hair swished behind her. "Plus, I think it could be dangerous. We need more information."

"We have a lot of information that Major Johnsen never got to share. Thing is, it could all be bullshit."

"Yeah," Eve said, swallowing when the words almost stuck in her throat. "It's about trust. Can we trust them?"

"I don't know, and I'm afraid we won't know that until we get there." Hicks gave her a sympathetic smile, like he understood the battle going on inside her.

The thought of leaving Charleston had Eve torn. She'd grown up here. Spent summer days at Folly Beach and had fished in the Ashley River with her dad. Every corner of this area was filled with memories of a happy childhood. But it was also where she had watched her family suffer and die. There were so many ghosts in Charleston now... Maybe a change of scenery would be good. She needed to focus on the future and moving forward. To stop looking back.

"What do you want to do?" Eve finally asked.

"Honestly, I'd like to go." Hicks looked away when pain flashed in his eyes. "I'm from Maryland. If my family survived, they could be at this safe zone. It may be the only way I'll ever find out what happened to them."

Eve's stomach clenched. Her family was gone, but at least she knew what happened to them. The uncertainty Hicks had to live with must have been horrible.

"Hicks, I'm so sorry." Without thinking, Eve reached out and wrapped her arms around him. His body was firm and warm against hers, and within seconds Hicks had let out a breath so deep it felt like it had come straight from his soul.

When he pulled away, his eyes were still swimming with pain. "We've all lost." He ran his hand down his face like he was trying to keep his emotions from escaping. "So how's your job going?"

This time, it was Eve's turn to look away. "The cleanup is rough."

She didn't want to talk about hauling dead bodies out of houses. Didn't want to think about dragging herself back to her dorm this afternoon, drenched in sweat and so filthy she felt like she'd never be able to wash off the stink of rotten flesh. It had felt like the rot had penetrated the thin plastic of her HAZMAT suit and seeped into her pores until she thought she would go crazy. When Eve had arrived at the base, she'd promised to pitch in, and in exchange they would provide her with food and shelter. Everyone had to help out, but that didn't make the process any easier.

Hicks put his hand under her chin, tiling her face up and forcing her to meet his eyes. "I'm sorry you have to deal with all that. I know it isn't fun, but it's necessary. Lots of families living on base died in their homes."

"I know," she whispered, mesmerized by the intense way his brown eyes swept over her face. A shiver shot through her when the rough pad of his thumb moved across the underside of her chin. It was as confusing as it was comforting. Having this attractive man in front of her after everything that had changed just didn't seem to fit.

Eve took a step back and Hicks's arm dropped to his side. Her eyes moved to her car, parked only ten feet from where they stood. The desire to escape was so strong, she had a hard time staying where she was. Only she didn't know if she was trying to run from her memories or her feelings for Hicks. Hell, she wasn't even sure *if* she had feelings for Hicks.

Eve backed away, and Hicks frowned. "I have to go," she said, digging her keys out of her pocket. "I'll talk to you later, okay?"

She turned and rushed to her car, thankful Hicks didn't try to stop her.

* * *

The sun had already set when there was a knock on Eve's door, making something inside her jump excitedly. She knew without having to check that it was Hicks. He'd stopped by the last three nights. Even though she'd run out on him earlier, she was glad he'd stopped by. At the time she'd been desperate to be alone, but once she'd gotten back to her room it had felt even more oppressive. She was beginning to wonder if anything would ever feel normal again.

She opened the door to find Hicks leaning against the railing. The smile on his face reminded Eve of someone who had just been told a joke and was still mulling over the punch line. She liked that about him. Her own personality bordered on being too serious at times—especially since the virus—and Hicks's playfulness was a nice contrast.

He had a box of Twinkies tucked under his arm.

"For me?" she asked, pushing the door open wider.

Hicks shoved off the rail and walked into the room, shrugging like it was no big deal. It was a big deal to Eve, though.

"Remembered you liked them," he said, throwing himself on the couch. Acting like he owned the place.

Eve took a seat next to Hicks as he pulled out a snack cake. The plastic crinkled in his hands, a sound that was so familiar it made Eve feel warm and comfortable.

"Thought you'd want to know what we talked about after you left the meeting," Hicks said, passing her a Twinkie.

She smiled as she took the cake. "I do, thank you."

"Nothing concrete yet." He ripped into his Twinkie and took a big bite. His mouth was still full when he said, "Major Johnsen wants to give everyone time to think it over. He's suggested sending a small group out first to make sure everything's okay. We'd have a code set up before the rest of the group heads out, so when we reestablish contact, whoever is left behind will know it's safe."

"Kind of like one if by land and two if by sea?" Eve nibbled on her Twinkie, savoring the delicious sponginess of the little cake.

"Yeah, something like that." Hicks shot her a grin, and Eve returned it. "We could let the people who are anxious to get there go first. Once they confirm the place is good, we send everyone else."

Eve nodded, but all she could think about was Tanner. There was no way someone like him would want to head out and join another group. He wanted to keep it small, so it would be easier for him to control.

"There will still be people who won't want to go," she pointed out.

"We're not going to force them. If they want to stay here and fend for themselves, that's up to them. Major Johnsen has already said this is voluntary."

Eve frowned and Hicks mimicked the gesture, but it seemed subconscious.

"How did Tanner take all this?" Even though they hadn't discussed the other soldier before now, she could tell he didn't like Tanner any more than she did.

"I'm worried there's going to be trouble, which is another reason I wanted to come by." Hicks absent-mindedly twisted his empty Twinkie wrapper between his fingers, and the crinkling got louder by the second. "Tanner has a handful of people who are backing him up. You remember how he was when we found you?" His eyes held Eve's, making her shift on the couch, but she managed to nod. "That's nothing compared to how vocal he is with Major Johnsen. Not only does he not want to take anyone else in, but he wants to implement a pretty strict rationing system."

"What do you think he'll do?" Eve asked, picking at her Twinkie like it had suddenly lost all its appeal.

"Johnsen wants to go. Part of the reason is that he's worried he'll end up with a bullet in his back if he stays here. He plans to offer Tanner half the supplies, but I don't think it will be enough."

"You think Tanner will want it all?"

Hicks finally put his Twinkie wrapper down, his eyes holding hers, and Eve had the urge to lean on him for support. There was something else, too. Something she hadn't expected to feel at the end of the world.

"I think," Hicks said, leaning closer to her, "that we need to be prepared for anything."

He took her hand, and the rough calluses on his palms were comforting against Eve's smooth skin. These were the hands of someone who had worked hard and wasn't afraid to keep doing it. It made him seem strong and capable.

"What are you thinking?" Hicks asked, his eyes searching hers.

"I won't stay with Tanner. He isn't going to look out for the good of the group, and I think he's dangerous." It was on her lips to tell Hicks that she wanted to stay with him, but she bit her tongue. It was too much too soon. They had only known each other for a week, and even though it felt like so much longer, it seemed wrong to form such a strong bond during a catastrophe like this.

Hicks gave her hand a squeeze. "So you'll come?"

"Whenever they're ready to go, I'll be there," Eve said, holding his gaze.

Hicks wrapped his arms around her, pulling her against him. In his arms she felt some of her hesitation and fear melt away. She'd be okay as long as he was with her. She was certain of it.

* * *

Three. That's how many more nights of peace they had inside the walls of Charleston Air Force Base. Deep down, Eve had known it couldn't last. Tensions were rising with each passing day, and every time someone mentioned Staten Island, the arguments became more heated.

It was the soldiers who really worried Eve, though. Major Johnsen had decided to send a party out, and over the next few days half of their supplies were loaded onto a C-17. Tanner hadn't made a move to stop them yet, but it was going to happen, and everyone knew it.

Eve was getting ready to crawl into bed on the third night when someone pounded on her door. Hicks had been busy loading the plane, and she couldn't stop herself from hoping it was him. She'd been lonely without his company, and even though it was late and Hicks coming into her room now would take their relationship to a whole new level, Eve wanted to take that step.

When she opened the door, Hicks rushed in before Eve had a chance to register that it was him. He was panting, and the sound of his heavy breathing set off warning bells in her head.

Hicks slammed the door and grabbed her arm, pulling her toward the bedroom. "We have to go," he said between gasps.

Her heart rate sped up. Thudding in her ears. She almost couldn't concentrate. She forced herself to focus as she pulled her arm out Hicks' grasp and dove for her shoes.

"What's going on?" she asked, shoving her feet into her Sketchers. She tied them so fast the laces would probably have to be cut off later.

"Tanner has his men gathered," Hicks said, crossing the room to the window. "We don't know what they have planned yet, but it can't be good. We don't have much time."

He pulled the curtain aside so he could look out as Eve grabbed the bag she'd packed two nights ago, as well as the family picture sitting on her bedside table. If she lost everything else she could handle it, but she couldn't leave them behind. Not completely.

Within seconds, they were out the bedroom, heading toward the front door. Once there, they paused long enough for Hicks to make sure the coast was clear before rushing out into the moist Charleston night. He grabbed her hand, pulling her toward the stairs. The night was so quiet their footsteps sounded like thunder. When a door opened just behind them, Eve jumped three feet off the ground. A scream stuck in her throat.

Hicks squeezed her hand and shot her a reassuring look. "Sergeant Hayes was alerting others while I came to get you. We're trying to get as many people out as we can."

Eve's hand tightened around his as she glanced over her shoulder to find a handful of people behind them, bags slung over their shoulders and terrified expressions on their faces. Ahead of them, more doors opened, and by the time they ran down the stairs there was a small group of people with Eve and Hicks.

A van sat in the lot ready and waiting, the engine still running. Eve ran for the passenger seat as Hicks climbed behind the wheel, and the other survivors scrambled into the back. The utter silence of the group was more intense than anything Eve had ever experienced.

"Hold on," Hicks said through clenched teeth as he threw the van into gear.

The vehicle lurched forward and Eve's body slammed into the back of her seat. She gripped the canvas strap, the edge digging into her palm as Hicks sped across the base like a NASCAR driver, barely slowing at the turns. The tires thumped over speed bumps and Eve squeezed the seatbelt tighter. When they reached the entrance to the flight line, Hicks sped up.

The C-17 loomed in the distance. Eve leaned forward to get a better look, biting her lip until it threatened to split open. The plane was probably the most beautiful thing she had ever laid eyes on.

When they were still twenty feet away, Hicks slammed on the brakes. The van's tires squealed across the runway and Eve lurched forward so hard the seatbelt locked, tightening against her chest until she was sure it would leave a bruise. Then the van stopped and her body was thrown back, but she barely had time to react before Hicks was throwing the door open, yelling for them to get out.

Eve stumbled out of the van, the rumble of the C-17's engines so loud she covered her ears. A vicious wind swept over the runway, blowing her blonde hair into her face and making it hard for her to see. But even above the roar of the plane, the distant sound of engines could be heard. Hicks grabbed her arm, and as Eve stumbled forward, she glanced over her shoulder long enough to see vehicles racing toward them.

"Go, go, go!" Hicks yelled, pulling her harder.

The C-17's ramp was down at the back of the plane, and Eve gasped for breath as she raced toward it with the other survivors. She'd just set foot on the ramp when the first gunshot cut through the air. Screams broke out, and Hicks pushed her harder, practically shoving her inside. A bullet pinged against the side of the plane. All around her, people screamed as more gunshots rang out.

They'd barely made it into the plane when the ramp's mechanical groan filled the cargo bay. Hicks shoved Eve into one of the seats lining the walls, screaming at her to buckle up as he hurried to the front of the plane. Before the ramp was even all the way up, the C-17 began to move. Eve's hands shook as she latched her belt, trying to block out the sounds of gunfire. Slowly, the aircraft picked up speed, moving them forward faster and faster. With each passing second, Eve was able to relax a little more. When the plane finally left the ground, her stomach lurched with the usual nausea that accompanied takeoff, but she was able to breathe a little easier too. They'd made it.

Around her, the other survivors smiled, and Eve was thrilled to realize that more than just her little group had made it to the plane. At least ten additional people were on board, not including the dozens of soldiers. Stephanie, the grandmotherly woman who had tried to comfort her during the meeting, as well as Doug and four-year-old Blake. The little boy who reminded her so much of her brother Cade that seeing him usually made Eve want to burst into tears. Not this time, though. This time, when Eve looked at little Blake, she was filled with relief.

Now all they had to do was make it to Staten Island.

* * *

The roar of the engines and the wind whipping against the outside of the plane was overwhelming despite the ear plugs the soldiers had handed out after takeoff. Hicks grinned and gave Eve a thumbs up as he went by, heading to the back of the plane. She tried to read his body language, but it was hard with everything else going on. They'd been in the air for over an hour and she knew they had to be getting close.

Hicks paused on his way back, kneeling in front of her. His hand found hers, and he leaned forward, putting his lips close to her ear. "We're going to be landing in about ten minutes!" he yelled over the noise. "Stay close to me and stay alert!"

Eve nodded when he pulled back and his eyes held hers for a brief second before he stood. She watched him climb the stairs to the cockpit, her heart pounding from a combination of fear and excitement.

The sound of the landing gears being lowered rumbled through the cargo bay, and Eve's stomach twisted as the plane began its descent. She gripped the edge of her chair and squeezed her eyes shut, swallowing down the nausea that tried to force its way out like it always did when she flew. The wheels touched down and the entire aircraft shuddered. Eve sucked in a deep breath as her body was jerked to the side in response to the plane's change of momentum. Gradually, the plane slowed until it seemed like they were moving no faster than a car driving down the freeway. Even then, Eve kept a tight hold on her seat.

Soldiers climbed down from the cockpit and started to gear up, putting on armored vests and helmets, gathering weapons. The soldiers who were already in the cargo bay followed their lead. Eve searched the mass of camo for Hicks, but the men were like a giant blob of military preparedness and she couldn't find him. Dread formed inside her, heavy and intense. Almost like she had a boulder resting in her stomach.

The plane turned, then slowed even more. When it finally stopped, Eve and the other survivors stayed where they were, staring at each other like they weren't sure what to do. A few seconds later the engines cut out and silence engulfed the plane. Major Johnsen came down and got busy putting on his own gear. His eyes swept over the survivors like he was taking stock of precious cargo.

When they were geared up and ready, the soldiers headed to the back of the plane, but Major Johnsen stopped to address the survivors. "They're here. We've been talking to them on the radio and everything seems good, but my men and I are going out first. I want all of you to stay where you are until I tell you it's okay. Understand?"

His tone made Eve feel like she was on the way to a firing squad.

She nodded and a few people around her murmured quiet words of acknowledgement, but most looked like they couldn't figure out how they'd gotten into this situation to begin with.

The Major followed his men toward the back, and Eve caught sight of Hicks just as the mechanical groan of the cargo bay door filled the plane. He gave her a reassuring smile, but it didn't reach his eyes.

Once the ramp was down, the men headed out, disappearing into the dark New York night. Eve pulled out her earplugs, hoping to hear something and get an idea of what was going on. Voices floated back, carried on the wind, but she couldn't make out the words. It was like being underwater and trying to listen to the people on the surface as they talked. The tension in her stomach built with each passing second that Hicks was out of sight.

Eve undid her seatbelt and stood, but she'd only taken one step when the man next to her grabbed her arm.

"We're supposed to stay," he hissed.

"Right." She glanced toward the ramp, but couldn't sit back down. Her worry for Hicks was eating at her.

In the darkness, movement caught her eye. Eve held her breath as footsteps pounded up the ramp, and a few seconds later, Major Johnsen came into view. He was frowning, but didn't appear ready to leave. Hicks was with him, and one other soldier Eve didn't know, but no one else. At least twenty of them had gone out, but only three had come back. It didn't look good.

Eve found herself crossing the cargo bay to Hicks. "What's going on?" she hissed.

He pulled her toward the back of the plane, and through the darkness she caught sight of a group of heavily armed men, as well as two buses. They must have been waiting to take them to Staten Island.

"Something feels off—"

Hicks's words were cut off when footsteps pounded behind him. He spun toward the ramp, and his eyebrows shot up. Suddenly, he shoved Eve behind him, putting himself between her and the ramp. Her back was pressed against the wall, making it impossible to see anything over Hicks. The pounding of footsteps got louder. There had to be dozens of men. Eve's heart pounded in perfect synchronization with the footsteps while a cry broke out in the plane. Major Johnsen started yelling, ordering his men forward as another man did the same, only to a different set of soldiers. In front of Eve, Hicks was as stiff as a board. His gun raised, his back pushing her into the wall like he was her only chance for survival.

"Put your weapons down!" Hicks yelled, his voice booming in Eve's ears. "These are civilians. They're only looking for a safe place."

"Lower your weapon, soldier!" someone else replied, his voice deep and strong. Like a bass drum that echoed off the walls of the plane and could be heard even over the cries of Eve's fellow survivors. "You're outnumbered. You came to us and you're going to do things our way. Cooperate, or my men will open fire."

Eve's body shook. The inability to see what was going on made the situation ten times more terrifying. She tried to raise herself up on her toes, but couldn't move with Hicks pressed against her.

"We can talk this out," Major Johnsen said.

The sound of his voice helped ease the cries of the Charleston group, but not all was silent. The soft sobs of Blake cut through Eve, shaking her to the core. Who the hell did these people think they were?

"Nothing to talk about, Major. This is how things are done. You cooperate, or you watch your men get gunned down. It's your choice."

Major Johnsen's sigh was so loud Eve felt like it had penetrated her skull. She clenched her hands into fists, digging her nails into her palms. The Major would give in. He was a good man, and he'd do whatever it took to keep their group safe.

"Lower your guns," Major Johnsen said less than thirty seconds later.

Hicks grunted but did as he was told, kneeling to lay his weapon on the floor.

Finally, Eve was able to get a look at the situation. From where she stood, she could see out into the dark night where the rest of the Charleston soldiers stood, lined up along the bus. Their hands behind them. Probably tied. At least a dozen men with guns stood in front of them, and inside the plane stood more than ten armed men. All dressed in black riot gear.

Their leader was probably seven feet tall and so broad he looked like he would be able to crush a person with just his thumb. He wore a smug smile that said he was used to people doing what he wanted, and the sadistic glint in his eye sent a shiver through Eve. This man was no one to mess with.

"Welcome to New York," he said, his voice booming through the plane. "If everyone does as they're told, this will be quick and painless." He flashed a grin that looked lethal on his face. "For the most part."

"Son of a bitch," Hicks muttered, looking over his shoulder at Eve. "This is going to get ugly. But no matter what happens, stay with me. Understand?"

Eve slipped a shaky hand into his, and Hicks gave it a squeeze just as the huge man started talking again.

"My name is Ramirez, and I'm the head of reconnaissance, which means I go out and find survivors, like you. Our settlement has food and safety and supplies to get us through the rough years ahead. Unfortunately, you won't all be going." He paused, giving his words a moment to sink in.

A low rumble moved through the plane, but it was so quiet that Eve couldn't make out even a single word. The group seemed to take a collective deep breath, almost as if they were bracing themselves for bad news. Little Blake hugged his father, and a teen Eve didn't know burst into tears. Eve's own body tensed in response to Ramirez's words. Who would be excluded? The soldiers because they were a threat? The elderly because they couldn't contribute? The unhealthy because they were a drain on resources?

"Now," Ramirez said, taking a step forward. "We'll have a quick screening process, and those lucky enough to make it through can move to the buses. I want everyone in a single file line!"

He turned without waiting to see if the group would comply. He didn't need to. He was too big and intimidating. His men were armed and ready to follow orders, and it was clear by the way Ramirez carried himself that he would be more than willing to kill every last one of them.

Hicks pulled Eve forward. Already the others had started to line up, meaning Eve and Hicks found themselves at the back of the line.

Eve stood on her toes, studying those in front of her. Her gut twisted when her gaze landed on Stephanie. Now more than ever the older woman's shaking hands stood out. She clenched her hands into fists and pressed her arms to her sides like she was trying to force them to remain still. It didn't work.

"What's going to happen?" Eve whispered, turning to Hicks.

He shook his head and gave her shoulder a squeeze as the line slowly moved forward. "I don't know.

Dread spread through Eve and she took a quick peek at Ramirez. The man stared the Charleston survivors down like he was considering eating them for dinner. "Who do you think they are?"

Hicks moved his face close to hers, lowering his voice. "It's just a feeling I have, but outside they asked a lot of questions. Things we'd already established with our contact at Staten Island. It's possible that someone intercepted our transmission after we left Charleston and decided they'd like a shot at our supplies. Or worse. The best thing we can do at this point is cooperate. If we try anything, they'll kill us."

Eve shuddered and Hicks slipped his arm around her. She had a million questions, but she was afraid to ask them. Afraid to have them answered.

The line moved forward and the group filed out of the plane. At the bottom of the ramp stood Ramirez and two other men. The first asked the survivors questions—their names, ages, health histories—and wrote it all on a clipboard. The second man drew blood, writing the name of each person on the vial and stowing it away before moving on to the next.

Eve watched from her limited vantage point as the first two people were questioned and released, one after the other in quick succession. When it was Stephanie's turn, Eve's body went rigid. Even from a distance, the tremors in the older woman's body were obvious. Stephanie was in the middle of answering questions when one of the men in riot gear grabbed her. She screamed and fought as the man pulled her to the side of the plane. All around Eve people cried out, demanding to know what was going on. Hicks's arm tightened around her shoulders and when Stephanie disappeared from view, Eve tucked her face against Hicks's chest. Less than thirty seconds later, a gunshot broke through the night. Eve's whole body jerked, then all the tension disappeared, leaving her feeling like a wet noodle. Or like she was the one who had been shot.

Silence fell over the group.

"Keep moving!" Ramirez called.

The atmosphere was tense and silent after that. The next four people made it through with no problem, then it was Eve's turn. She stepped forward, shaking so hard her teeth chattered.

The man with the clipboard didn't even look up. "Name."

"Eve Parker." She clenched her hands into fists.

"Age."

Her throat tightened. "Twenty."

"Any surgeries?"

"Just my wisdom teeth." She glanced toward Hicks, who gave her a nod.

"Any illnesses to report?" The man finally looked up, and when he did, Eve trembled even harder. His eyes were cold. "If you lie we'll find out from the blood work. It's better to just be out with it."

"N-none. Well, allergies. That's it."

The man nodded, then went back to scribbling on his clipboard. "Sexually active?"

Eve's face flushed, and she couldn't help looking behind her. The expression on Hicks's face was grim. "Not recently."

"On birth control?"

"No. I mean, I was, but I haven't taken it in a while."

The man didn't even nod as he wrote it down. "You're done."

Eve stepped forward and held out her right arm as the man with the clipboard repeated the same questions to Hicks. The second man tied a tourniquet around her upper arm, then ran an alcohol pad over her veins. She tensed, preparing herself for the needle. It went in so smoothly she barely felt it. The man filled a vial, then swished it around. He set it in the tray with the others. By the time he had taken the tourniquet off her arm, Hicks had stepped forward.

Eve waited, avoiding Ramirez's gaze because she was afraid he'd tell her to move on. She didn't want to move on, not without Hicks. The tension around her was so thick she felt ready to implode. Having someone she trusted made her feel stronger.

When Hicks was done, he laced his fingers through hers and pulled her toward the bus. They'd only taken three steps when sobs broke out behind them. Eve's blood froze in her veins and she stopped moving, but Hicks pulled her toward the buses.

"Keep moving," he said, "don't look back."

Eve kept her eyes forward, but they were so full of tears she couldn't tell how close they were to the bus. When the gunshot cracked through the air, a sob broke out of Eve so hard it felt like she'd been ripped in half. She clung to Hicks, burying her face in his chest.

It wasn't until they had almost made it to the bus that Eve noticed that all the soldiers had been loaded onto one, while the other survivors were on another. Her grip on Hicks tightened and she dug her nails into his side so hard he sucked in a deep breath. Men in riot gear stepped forward to meet them, and she sunk her fingers in deeper. Desperate to hold on.

The man didn't say a word when he grabbed her, ripping her away from Hicks. Eve screamed and fought. Panic swept over her. But he had her around the waist and was dragging her toward the bus while another detained Hicks. Hicks, who was usually so calm, was fighting with everything in him. His eyes were big and round as he watched Eve being dragged away.

Suddenly, another soldier rushed forward. He slammed the butt of his gun into Hicks's skull and his eyes rolled back. Eve screamed when her friend slumped to the ground. She fought harder, desperate to get to him. Her heart was beating so fast she thought it was going to explode. The man holding her huffed and swore as he slammed her into the ground, jerking her hands behind her. Tying them together.

Only ten feet away lay Hicks. Unconscious. A trail of blood running down the side of his head. She was jerked up and dragged away, and by the time she was on the bus, Eve's sobs shook her body so hard she felt like her brain was banging around against the inside of her skull.

The soldier shoved her into a seat mere seconds before the door slammed shut. Then the engine revved to life and the bus lurched forward, taking off into the darkness. Heading into the unknown. Eve twisted in her seat, trying to catch sight of Hicks. He wasn't on the ground anymore and the other bus hadn't moved.

She turned back to find Ramirez standing at the front of the bus, looking them all over like a pirate surveying the spoils of war. When his eyes met Eve's, he grinned. The look sent a shiver shooting through her.

"Don't worry, darling," he said, his smile taking on an evil look. "We're going to take real good care of you.

NINETEEN: *Blood Brother*
by Monica Enderle Pierce

My name is Harman Ferenc Džugi, and this is my apology to the world.

* * *

"A curfew is in effect between the hours of six p.m. and six a.m. until further notice. Only military, medical, and emergency personnel are permitted on the streets during curfew hours. Unauthorized persons will be detained. Anyone exhibiting symptoms of illness will be quarantined."

Tinny and fuzzed, the announcement echoed off the empty brick buildings that faced Third Street, and then was lost in Downing Park's lush trees. But anyone still alive in Newburgh, New York had been hearing the same recording every hour, on the hour, for a week. If they didn't know it by now, they were too dumb to survive much longer.

Harman kept his face down as he waited for the foot patrol and Humvee to pass his hiding spot beneath a trimmed hedge. The thud of the National Guardsmen's boots and the creaking of their gear were uncomfortably close. But he knew how to avoid being noticed. Twenty years of crime and no jail time—it had to be some kind of record.

Two sets of combat boots paused in front of Harman's hiding spot, and he held his breath.

A soldier said, "Man, I wanna smoke." A respirator mask muffled her voice.

"I hear that," her companion said. "I'm sweating like a pig in this damn mask. I hate this thing."

"Yeah? Hate it more than puking and pissing blood?"

He snorted. "Depends. Can I smoke while I puke and piss blood?"

They laughed. Then a snarl from their C.O. sent them off after their company.

Harman exhaled into the grass. Though he was only five-foot-eight and wiry, he hadn't been able to wedge his whole body under the bushes. If the soldiers had bothered to look over the hedge, they'd've spotted him.

The Humvee's rumble faded as the vehicle turned onto Carpenter Avenue and rolled toward the park. Harman scooted out from under the bushes and looked around. A blue-and-pink sunrise promised another warm summer day. People should have been leaving for work, getting ready for school, eating cereal and drinking coffee. But Newburgh's streets were empty, her homes were dark, and only fear moved freely.

Harman cinched his backpack, brushed leaves and dirt from his short, black ponytail, and jogged away from the Guardsmen. He stuck to lawns and weedy medians to muffle his footfalls and gave a wide berth to the corpses he encountered. There were far fewer on the streets now that he was north of the Big Rotten Apple. Either people had fled the area, or they'd stayed home and died.

He was in Newburgh after walking for two-and-a-half days from Newark. It was a distance that was nothing to a man who'd hiked all over South America. As he'd followed Route 9W from New Jersey, he'd kept his eyes and ears open and his Colt pistol at hand. He figured it'd take another day to reach his final destination—Kingston—find his brother, and do what needed to be done.

A heavy pall of smoke tinged the sky reddish brown and stung Harman's nose. Apparently, stealing wasn't enough fun for Newburgh's looters, so they'd set fires. Everything southwest of Broadway was no more than smoldering ash amid the blackened carcasses of buildings. Everywhere else, the damage was hit-or-miss. In the same way that AVHF killed thousands of people yet left some untouched, the looters and vandals burned and robbed some places but left others alone.

Garbled shouts carried from the park followed by the *pow-ping-hiss* of teargas canisters being fired. More shouts then gunfire, and Harman broke into a full run as he crossed South Street and got clear of the park. Dogs barked somewhere off to his left and he kept up the pace. A lot of people had died and left family dogs to fend for themselves. Those that had gotten hungry enough had escaped their yards in search of food. And, to a feral dog pack, Harman looked like lunch.

* * *

The airline attendant for Czech Airlines paused beside Harman and Luca in the dim flight cabin. "Buckle your seatbelts, boys. And welcome to the United States," she said in Slovak. "Once we've landed, I'll escort you off the plane." She crouched beside their seats. "Remember, you're in my custody until I turn you over to your aunt and uncle. Promise to stick with me?" They nodded and she gave them a wide smile. "Great."

After she'd gone, Harman buckled Luca's seatbelt.

"Harman?"

"What?" Harman and his little brother spoke Romani.

"I'm scared."

"I know." Harman put his arm around Luca's shoulders. "But I'll take care of you."

"Do you think the Americans will try to kill us, too?"

They were coming to New York to live with their Uncle Marko and Aunt Julie. Neo-Nazis had set fire to their neighborhood in Hermanovce. Their mother had died saving Luca from their burning house.

"No-no, Luca. They're letting us live with Uncle Marko." Harman stared at the endless lights of New York City as the plane circled to land. "Don't worry. I'm sure it'll be better here than in Slovakia." He pointed out the window. "Ei! Look at that huge city."

"Wow!" Luca gave Harman a tentative smile. "It looks like Christmas in Košice."

Harman smiled back. "Merry Christmas in June, Luca."

* * *

Harman paused at midday in the shadows of a McDonald's. It was the only building on the street that hadn't been gutted by fire, though vandals had busted up the inside. There was a blue Honda Accord in the parking lot, its windows fractured and the headlights smashed.

Across from where he sat eating strawberries, fire had reduced a house to rubble but hadn't burned the detached garage or the green, manicured lawn. The only thing out of place in the front yard was a large plastic sandbox shaped like a turtle.

He and Luca had had one of those when they'd lived with Aunt Julie and Uncle Marko. Their uncle had hated it. The lid was supposed to keep neighborhood cats from pooping in the sand. It worked—when they remembered to put it on. Of course Kevin Rubenecki had made it pointless because he wet his pants every time he came over to play in the sandbox.

Harman laughed. He'd forgotten about Kevin and how that kid and Luca had fought over the Tonka bulldozer. Was the incontinent bastard dead now? That would make Luca smile.

Harman's amusement faded as that thought soured his stomach. He closed the container of strawberries. He'd lost his appetite.

* * *

My brother, Luca Petru Džugi, who works as a virologist for PFD, released AVHF in order to kill most of you.

* * *

Motion to his right caught his eye. Harman glanced up from beneath his brows as he shoved the container into his backpack. The movement came from inside the McDonald's. A young girl appeared behind one of the Plexiglas windows of the PlayPlace climbing structure. She watched him from within a giant, red capsule at the end of a yellow tunnel.

Harman scanned the restaurant. Where were the adults? He didn't want trouble. When he looked back up, the girl was gone. He closed his pack and stood. Best to get outta town.

The child appeared at the bottom of a purple slide. She sat, and he exchanged a steady stare with her for a long moment. She was, maybe, nine? Black cornrows. Filthy, pink pants and an oversized New York Knicks sweatshirt. Enormous brown eyes set in a dark-skinned, gaunt face.

The girl looked up at the climbing tower beside the slide, and then she gave a little nod. Donning a pair of green snow boots, she pushed through an inner door that separated the play area from the rest of the eatery. The girl went to the restaurant's broken side door, stuck her head through where the glass once had been, and pointed across the street.

She said in a loud whisper, "The dogs are coming, mister."

Harman followed her gaze. "Khul," he cursed under his breath. Two dogs—shepherd-types—nosed around the sandbox. Three more dogs emerged from the open garage. He shouldered his pack and slowly backed toward the door.

One of the shepherds stiffened, eyes keen and ears perked. As Harman reached the door, the dog barked, and then growls, baying, and nails scraping asphalt told Harman all he needed to know. He yanked open the shattered door, leaped over broken tables, and reached the play area as the first shepherd got to the restaurant.

The girl shouted, "Shut it! Shut it! Shut the door!"

The dog slammed into the inner door as Harman threw its metal lock.

"Aimee!" the girl cried as she struggled with the lock on a second play area entrance. Harman reached her side and lodged his shoulder against the door as the dogs thudded against it, barking and slobbering on the glass. The lock clicked into its latch.

"Go home!" the little girl ordered, but the pack circled and snarled, snapped at each other, leaped over tables, and foraged behind the front counter.

"You sick, mister?"

It was another child's voice, and Harman followed the weak sound. A teenage girl lay amid a pile of jackets at the top of a climbing tower. Even at a distance, he knew she was dying. Her bloodshot eyes and nosebleed made it all too obvious.

"No. I'm immune." He touched his chest. "My name's Harman."

Beside him, the little girl stuck out her hand. "I'm Sheyna. That's my sister, Aimee."

Harman shook her tiny hand. "Where's your family?" The girls were around the same age that he and Luca had been when they'd come to the U.S.

"Dead," Sheyna answered quietly. "We lived up the street. Momma and Aunt Becca worked here. They died a few days ago, and then some men burned down our house."

The smell of the place struck Harman—not fryer grease but urine and feces, vomit, rotting food, death. He looked around. "Anyone else with you?"

The children had piled their trash in an overflowing bin in a corner. Beside it sat a covered bucket and three industrial-sized rolls of toilet paper—their toilet. Flies buzzed around the area and crawled up the windows. In the main part of the eatery, wrappers, napkins, cups, and trash were strewn everywhere.

"Nuh-uh," Sheyna said. "We hid here while the looters smashed up the place and the dogs ate all the food."

"Hush, Sheyna," Aimee muttered. "You don't havta tell him everything."

Harman sat at one of the cleaner booths. "Don't worry. I'm not going to hurt either of you."

With a groan, Aimee sat up. She wiped blood from her nose with her sleeve and stared at him with dull eyes. Blood-red sweat beaded her upper lip and forehead. "I'm gonna die pretty soon. Probably tonight."

Sheyna picked at a hole in her sweatshirt. "Don't say that."

Aimee continued, her voice emotionless. "Sheyna isn't sick. Can you get her to someplace safe?"

Silence stretched between them, broken only by the muffled sounds of the milling dogs, as Harman considered the girls and the request. The animals were giving up on the restaurant. A few had gone back outside.

A coughing fit—wet and bloody—wracked Aimee's small body and she slid beneath the pile of jackets. She turned on her side and stared at him.

Sheyna kicked off her boots then climbed the PlayPlace tower. She tucked the jackets around her sister, held a cup and straw to her lips, and wiped the red sweat from the girl's face with a white paper napkin.

Harman moved to the tower's first platform and leaned back against its yellow, perforated wall. "My brother wrote to me about a safe bunker in Kingston. That's where I'm heading. I'll take Sheyna with me."

Sheyna's brow furrowed and her chin jutted forward. "Aimee's coming, too."

Her sister shoved her weakly. "You go. I'm dying, just like Momma and Auntie. You can't stay here by yourself. I said I'd take care of you. This is how."

Sheyna crossed her arms. "Then I'm not leaving."

Aimee closed her eyes. "Yes," she whispered. "You are." Her breathing was fast and shallow. "Don't argue, Shey," she muttered. "I hurt too much to fight with you." A trickle of blood oozed from her nose. Another one squeezed from the corner of her left eye and slid into her hair.

Sheyna pulled her knees to her chest and hid her face behind them. "Okay. Sorry." Her answer was muffled.

The last two dogs—big yellow Labradors—slipped out the side door. They trotted across the parking lot and loped up the road after the rest of the meandering pack.

Harman asked, "When are the dogs active?" Best to distract Sheyna and make a plan to leave the next day.

She peered over her knees at him. "Whaddya mean?"

"When do they come out looking for food? Morning and evening?"

Sheyna's face screwed up as she thought, and then she nodded. "Yeah. They sleep in the Wilson's garage when it's hot."

Harman nodded. That made sense. He opened his backpack and pulled out the white plastic container that held the strawberries. He took three then passed it up to Sheyna. "Save some for Aimee."

The little girl nodded. "Thanks," she said around a mouthful of berry.

"Sure." He ate one, even the leaves and stem, and relished its sweetness. He'd found them in a garden box in Ramsey. They'd been an amazing discovery.

Glancing at the trash, Harman frowned. There were a lot of ketchup and mustard packets, crouton wrappers, barbecue sauce and honey mustard cups but not much else. The sisters had consumed little real nutrition. "What do you have to drink?"

"I think there's still ice tea, some Dr. Pepper, and a lotta mango smoothie—that stuff's gross. No more Coke or chocolate milk or Hi-C." Sheyna chomped on another strawberry and added, "No white milk, either; someone stole it. One of the employees, Momma said." She snapped the container shut. "I've been giving Aimee water. There's still a few bottles up here if you want some."

"I'm good, but we'll take them when we go."

Sheyna turned to her sister. "You awake? You wanna strawberry? They're really good."

No answer from Aimee.

Sheyna left the container beside her sister. She picked up a Happy Meal box and crawled into the tube that led into the maze from the tower's top level. Her bare feet thudded and squeaked against the plastic as she made her way back to the red capsule where Harman had first seen her. Muffled sounds carried down the tube; she was playing some kind of make-believe game.

There were two other slides beside the steep purple one. Harman inspected both and chose a blue one. Once he'd climbed to the top, he roamed through a curved tunnel and found a dead end, another windowed bubble like the one Sheyna occupied. Aside from a few old hamburger wrappers, it was empty, so he unrolled his sleeping bag and pulled a clean t-shirt and socks from his backpack.

McDonald's would be home for the next twelve hours.

* * *

"They've succeeded in slow genocide, Harman. Slovakia's wiped out all our kind thanks to forced sterilization, inadequate healthcare, and crappy living conditions."

"The EU—"

"Doesn't care. They never did anything about the fascists who killed

Mámo. And every one of Tsura's lawsuits on behalf of the sterilized women in Šariš was dismissed." Luca's palm smacked his oak dining room table. "But does the U.S. care? Of course not. There's no money to be had in defending a bunch of 'filthy gypsies.'"

Harman sighed. "I'd call the dead and unborn Rom lucky." He stood and stacked plates. "The rainforests are nearly gone, man. And if you think the last three Ebola outbreaks in Africa—and that other virus, whatever it was—have been bad, wait'll you see the viruses coming out of Amazonia. They're nasty bastards, and there's nothing in place to stop some of them." Silverware rattled against china. "It's gotten bad all along the Orinoco, but will anyone listen to me?"

"Of course not. You're just a lazy gypsy who dropped out of school to snort Yopo with the Yanomami."

Harman laughed. "Sell it to them, you mean." He'd ended up in South America to escape the mafia. His habit of skimming funds from the drug money he'd earned for them hadn't been appreciated. And he took a chance every time he returned to the U.S.

Karma stuck her black nose over the table and tried to lick the edge of the plates.

"Ei! Back off, džukel," Luca said to the dog, and she ducked under the table to hunt for crumbs. "You're right about the Orinoco viruses, you know." He stared into his coffee cup. "American and European ambition has doomed this entire planet. All they care about is money."

The dishes clattered as Harman put them in the sink. "I wouldn't say the whole planet. Maybe sixty-five percent of humanity will bite the big one." He returned to his brother's dining room, a blue-and-white dishtowel over his shoulder. "But not me." He shrugged. "My immune system's built like a Sherman tank."

Luca cocked his head as he stood. "How so?"

"The doctors at Tisch flipped out when they checked my blood. They said I've got antibodies for typhoid, yellow fever, malaria,"—he ticked them off on his fingers—"Chagas, Ebola, hepatitis A and B, swine flu, avian flu, smallpox, and a bunch of viruses I've never even heard of." Harman laughed. "Apparently, the Amazon wants me dead."

"Huh. That's interesting." Luca scratched Karma's chin. The dog closed her eyes and sighed. "Can I get a blood sample?"

"I knew you'd ask, weirdo."

* * *

"Harman? You awake?"

"Mm-hmm." Harman stretched and groaned. His shoulders and back were stiff from being curled up in the PlayPlace capsule. Gray light heralded the coming dawn. Sheyna was sitting at the end of the tube. "What's up, kiddo?"

"I think Aimee's dead."

Khul. He pushed out of his sleeping bag and peered into the gloom at the little girl. "You okay?"

She shrugged and gave a jerky nod. "Can we go?"

"Yeah. Well, no. Not until the dogs have hunted. Sorry. We can't outrun them."

"Here." Sheyna reached out and something small rattled as it slid across the tube toward him. "Momma's car is in the parking lot. She said it has a full tank."

Car keys. Harman pocketed them. "Okay. That changes things." He rolled up his sleeping bag. "Do you have stuff you want to bring? Clothes? A toothbrush? Some toys?"

"I got Aimee's Knicks jacket and some dirty clothes. No toothbrush." She held up her Happy Meal box. "My toys are packed."

Harman shoved his things into his green backpack. "Good. Bring the dirty clothes if Aimee didn't touch them. We can find someplace to wash them. Get your stuff now, so we can take off before the dogs come out."

"Okay." Sheyna scooted back along the tube and took one of the slides.

Harman made his way through the colorful maze to the top of the tower. Aimee was cold and not breathing. No pulse. She'd been dead for a few hours, he figured. He did his best to wrap her in the stinking jackets. It seemed so wrong to leave her, but he had no way to bury the girl.

When he reached the bottom of the play structure, his backpack ready to go, Sheyna was waiting with a shopping bag and her toy box. "Did you check Aimee? What if I'm wrong?"

Harman touched the top of her head. "I checked. You're not wrong." He knelt before her, unsure how much comfort she wanted. "I'm sorry, chajorije." The word meant *little girl* in Romani.

Sheyna nodded. She wiped tears from her eyes and cheeks with the palms of her hands, and then her face crumpled. Her mouth opened but no sound escaped, her grief so great she couldn't voice it. Harman swallowed a lump. He hugged her bony little body until she stopped sobbing.

"All right?" he asked, and Sheyna nodded. "Let's get going. I'll take your bag." She gave it up and he said, "Stay close and quiet."

Harman got Sheyna and their things in the car before he went back into the McDonald's. He'd just set the last trash can inside the restaurant on fire when a dog appeared in the doorway of the burned house's garage. Harman kicked over the can and sprinted to the car, praying to every god he could think of as he slid behind the steering wheel.

The Accord started on the first crank. "Yes!" Harman threw the car in gear as the dog pack reached the parking lot.

Sheyna screamed as a tan mutt lunged at her window. Its paws gained purchase on the sill. Its bark fogged the fractured glass. Another dog jumped onto the hood. One hit the front passenger window. Already fragmented, the glass cascaded all over the seat and floorboard, and the dog yelped. But Harman wasn't losing his life or the little girl's to a pack of mongrels. He hit the horn and the accelerator. The dog on the hood tumbled off and the others scattered as the car squealed out of the parking lot and fishtailed onto the deserted main road. Looking in the rearview mirror, Harman saw orange flames, black smoke, and dogs half-heartedly giving chase.

It had been a close call but worth it. Aimee's body wouldn't become dog food.

Once he was back on Route 9W, they sailed along. Sheyna slept in the back, her head on her paper bag. Harman tried to get a radio station but heard only static on FM, and not even the Sunday morning preachers were cajoling and condemning on AM.

Based on Luca's directions Harman figured they had about an hour before they reached Kingston.

* * *

You should know that this was a terrorist act.

Luca blames the world's governments for the out-of-control industrialization that's destroying our planet. He thinks that the only way to save our world is by murdering eighty percent of you and stopping all industry. He's convinced that all governments are corrupt.

* * *

Harman slowed the car to a stop. A black Blazer had collided with a charter bus where Route 9W and Route 299 crossed. The SUV had disintegrated and the bus had broken in half; one section had barrel-rolled into the trees. Metal, plastic, clothing, and body parts were scattered everywhere. Black, oily smoke and orange flames boiled from the other half of the bus where it rested on its side in the middle of the road.

Sheyna stirred on the back seat. "Are we there?" she murmured.

"No. Just stopping at a light. You can sleep."

"Okay." She pulled one of Harman's sweaters up to her chin. "I'm cold and my head hurts."

Damn. "It's probably because this window's busted. Sorry, kiddo." He rolled the car through the intersection, avoiding debris and keeping an eye on the fiery bus. The acrid stench of burning rubber stung his nose. He cleared the intersection and got about twenty feet down the road when he spied movement in the brush just off the side.

A man, bloody, in the grass, waving for help.

Harman stopped the car. *Double damn.* He scanned the area. It could be a trick. He put the Accord in park, turned off the engine, and pulled his pistol from the bottom of his backpack. Sheyna didn't stir as he opened the car door.

"Can you walk, sir?" he called.

"Help me!" Blood matted the man's silver hair and coated the right side of his face, neck, and shoulder. He grabbed fistfuls of grass and pulled his body forward, leaving a red streak behind. A hatchet-sized chunk of black metal jutted from the man's lower back. His light blue polo shirt was turning crimson.

Harman approached, the gun in hand, and his eyes keen for danger. People were predatory and worse than the dog pack he'd left behind. "I asked if you can walk."

"No, dammit! Are you an idiot? My back's broken!"

"You been tested?"

"What? Test— Yes! Negative. Everyone on that bus was negative. We were heading for Staten Island." The man grabbed at the grass. "I've got money. My life savings. I'll pay you to get me there."

Harman considered the man's offer. Did they have medical facilities at the Kingston bunker? And could they fix him if they did? Unlikely. He stepped back toward the open car door.

"For godsake, don't leave me." The man had stopped moving toward Harman. He pressed his face to the grass. "I left my family for this chance. My boys and my wife; they wouldn't come, but I had to try." The man sobbed. "I had to."

Harman grimaced. Would he have done the same thing? He glanced over his shoulder to the car. Sheyna still slept. No. He wouldn't've abandoned his loved ones. He took care of his family, no matter what.

"Your back's not broken, sir. You've got a hunk of SUV in your spine and you're nearly outta blood. Even if I take you with me, you'll die before I reach help. And since I've got a little girl in the back of my car who lost her sister today, I'm not gonna make her watch you kick the bucket, too." He stepped forward again and raised the pistol. "So do you want me to put you out of your misery? Or do you want to take your chances on another car rolling through here before you bleed to death?"

"You bastard. What kind of a choice is that? Get the hell outta here!" The man pulled at the grass and dirt but was too weak to move. "Just go." His face pressed into the grass, again. He grimaced, stiffened, and his body began to jerk as he had a seizure.

Harman crouched, the gun resting across his knee, as he watched the man die. It only took a few minutes, maybe three. Sheyna never stirred in the car. Birds flew overhead. The bus fire crackled and popped. Metal groaned as it warped in the heat. Black smoke marred the blue sky.

* * *

I knew Luca was pissed off, but I didn't know he was a psychopath. He created a doomsday group—Prep for Doom—and set them up in a bunker in Kingston, NY. It's under the old high school on Broadway. But I don't think any of those people know that my brother released AVHF. So when the bunker is raided, please don't hurt them. Especially a little girl named Sheyna and my cousin, Tsura Holomek. I promised Sheyna's dying sister that she'd be safe, and Tsura's a human rights attorney. She's only in the bunker because Luca invited her.

* * *

Harman didn't want to think about the accident. Even though Sheyna slept and the wind in the car drowned his words, he started telling her about Luca.

"My brother, Luca, was the first person in our family to graduate from high school and go to college. I could've but—*man*—I hated school. We're Romani, from Slovakia originally. You've probably never heard of the Romani; most people in the U.S. call us gypsies, though that's actually an insult."

He looked off to the right where the Hudson River flowed. More black, oily smoke rose in a fat column. Was the whole country burning?

"Anyway, we got bullied in Slovakia because we're Romani. And then our mom was killed, so our Uncle Marko brought us to the U.S. when we were, like, your age. And growing up here was pretty cool, but my uncle couldn't afford to send Luca to college, so I decided I'd pay for it. Truth is, Sheyna, I'm not a very good person. I stole cars and stuff and sold drugs for the mafia to help pay for Luca's schooling."

Harman rubbed the back of his neck and looked in the rearview mirror. The girl slept, her head lolling gently with the car's movement and her mouth slack.

"I guess I just figured that if I did bad things to help my brother do good, my crimes would be justified." He shook his head and muttered, "Stupid, I know. But when you grow up in slums where everyone hates you and says you're nothing but a lazy crook, well—it just made sense to me. When I was young."

Harman checked the map as they crossed Rondout Creek and muttered, "Left on Garraghan Drive then right on Broadway." He rotated his shoulders and yawned.

"I was so proud when Luca got his Ph.D. I mean, jeez, that made him a genius in our family. And then he got hired by PFD and ended up leading his own virology team. I thought he was gonna save the world."

Harman turned left and slowed down. He scanned the street and sidewalks, turned onto Broadway, and then circled the block checking addresses. Until—

He found it.

With its high windows and arched, aluminum roof, the hulking, red brick building looked the part of a bunker to Harman. It was attached to a much older building and, if he'd had the time, he would've admired that building's carved, concrete edifice. He liked historical architecture. But he was out of time.

He parked and turned off the engine. Sheyna still didn't stir. Harman sighed. "My brother was supposed to fix people, not destroy them." He gripped the steering wheel and rested his forehead on his knuckles. "*I* was the angry one. *I* was the troublemaker." He glanced at the Colt on the passenger seat and whispered, "Not Luca."

Harman straightened and stared at the brick building then scrubbed his palms over his face and nodded. He cleared his throat and said, "Sheyna, wake up. We're in Kingston." He stashed the Colt in his jacket's inner breast pocket. The car door groaned as he opened it. "C'mon, chajorije."

Sheyna sat up. Her cornrows stuck out at odd angles. She yawned and rubbed her eyes then grimaced and pushed her palm against her temple. "My head still hurts, and I'm thirsty."

Harman pulled open her door. He smoothed down her hair and grunted, surprised. No fever. Her face and scalp were cool. Her eyes weren't bloodshot. "You're probably dehydrated. You've been drinking soda and eating crap for days. There should be some good food in here." Maybe Sheyna wasn't sick. "God knows you need a lot more sleep."

She put on her jacket and grabbed her Happy Meal box. Harman shrugged on his backpack and picked up her paper bag.

Sheyna slipped her hand into his. "I hope they have hotdogs."

Harman grinned at her. "Me, too, Tough Nut."

Her face screwed up. "Why'd you call me that?"

"'Cause you don't crack easily. You ever hear that phrase? 'Tough nut to crack?' That's you."

She stared at him then snorted. "You're weird."

"Takes one to know one." They set off toward the brick building's entrance.

They'd gotten up a flight of concrete stairs when a deep, masculine voice boomed from nowhere.

"Stop!"

The order echoed off the surrounding buildings. Sheyna's grip tightened as she and Harman did as commanded.

"Password?"

Right. The code. Harman fished a piece of paper from his jeans. "HFD0002. Harman Ferenc Džugi."

There was a pause. "What about the girl?"

"She's with me."

"She needs a password."

Harman put his arm around Sheyna's bony shoulders. "She's got no family. I found her in Newburgh. I'm not going to abandon her on the sidewalk."

"Then you can stay out here with her," the disembodied voice said.

Sheyna looked up at Harman, tears in her eyes.

"Fine. You tell Luca that Harman said, 'Thanks for the crappy vacation. I'm going back to Venezuela.' He'll love that."

There was a muttered curse then the voice said, "Wait here."

"Harman?" Sheyna asked.

He rubbed her arm. "Don't worry. I know the guy who runs this joint."

Long minutes passed, and then they were ordered to go around to the Andrew Street side of the structure. Once there, a door clicked open at the top of a set of covered stairs. Inside they faced a long, lit hallway that was enclosed with translucent plastic. The entry door closed behind them and locked with a series of whirs and clicks.

Sheyna clung to Harman's hand and stared, wide-eyed, down the hall as a door at the far end opened and a man in a white HAZMAT suit stalked toward them. His fogged mask hid his face, but what he said as they met in the middle of the hall made his identity clear: "You look like khul, Harman."

"Thanks, phral." Harman used the Romani word for *brother*. He turned to Sheyna. "This is Sheyna. She's uninfected. And she's got no family."

Luca peeled off his mask, mussing his thick, black hair. He sported a neat beard and moustache. "Well, everyone who's not a confirmed carrier or confirmed immune, goes into quarantine." He looked down his nose at the child. "Sorry, kid." He led them further into the bunker. "There are sixteen or seventeen other people in there right now. Three children, I think. That'll be nice, huh? To be with other kids and not my smelly big brother?"

Sheyna stared at him.

Luca shrugged and turned to Harman. "I've got a surprise for you."

* * *

"Don't start that B.S. again, Luca."

"It's not B.S. I see what's happening worldwide every day, Harman. And you've seen it, too. Remember the viruses in Amazonia? All the slash-and-burn exposing jungle and releasing diseases? What about the Yanomami dying from malaria? And now we're seeing rapid mutation among the filoviruses."

"No one's doing it on purpose."

"No?" Luca folded his arms. "Well maybe they should."

Harman stared at his brother. "Jeez, Luca. Go see a shrink before you sprain your brain and end up in a geodesic dome in the middle of Nowheresville eating Spam and canned beans."

Luca laughed. "Hey, nothing wrong with Spam."

* * *

The surprise was their cousin, Tsura. She was helping in the quarantine room.

"Is this your daughter?" she asked in Romani, her eyes wide and her bright smile wider.

Harman shook his head and replied in English, "No. This is Sheyna. I found her in Newburgh." He helped the girl get settled on a cot. "Sheyna, this is my cousin, Tsura. She'll take care of you, and she can't get sick." He met his cousin's dark gaze. "Am I right?"

Tsura nodded. There was terror in those brown eyes. "Right." She sat beside Sheyna and gestured at the Happy Meal box. "Did you bring lunch?"

Sheyna shook her head and opened the box. She pulled out two small plastic ponies, three equally tiny stuffed bears, and a little plastic fairy. "My toys."

"Even better." Tsura smiled and stroked the girl's hand. "Let me get you some food. Do you like Cheerios and bananas?"

Sheyna nodded.

Harman stood. He touched the top of the girl's head. "Get some sleep, too. You'll be in here for a day. I'll make sure Tsura takes care of you, okay?"

"Where are you going?"

"I need to talk to Luca." He crouched to be eye-level with her. "You see he's my baby brother. And now that I've gotten you to a safe place, like I promised, I need to go take care of him." He tugged one of her cornrows and added, "I may not be around much. Okay?"

"Oh. Okay." Then she threw her arms around his neck. Harman returned the hug, relieved to know that he'd done something very right for her. Then Tsura returned with food, and Sheyna snatched up the banana. Harman headed for the door.

"Harman?" Tsura caught up to him in the hall. "You're immune, too?"

He nodded. "Luca made sure of it." Tsura's black hair was streaked with gray; a year ago she'd had none. How much of that had appeared during the last week?

"He's *enjoying* this." She gripped his arm and glanced up and down the empty hall. "He scares me."

Harman squeezed her hand. “I know. That’s why I’m here, Tsura. I’ll take care of Luca, like I always have.” He stepped away from her. “Where can I find him?”

“Down two levels.” She gestured toward a stairway. “Turn left and keep going. His room’s at the end of the building.”

“*Nayis-tuke*.” He thanked her. “Promise you’ll look after Sheyna?”

Tsura nodded. “I will.”

Would her eyes ever lose their haunted look?

* * *

“Hello?”

“Luca, it’s Harman. I got a message that you needed to talk to me right away. You okay?”

“Yeah. Well. Everything’s going to hell, just like I promised it would.”

Harman frowned. “What do you mean?” Luca sounded happy, which didn’t make sense if his life was falling apart.

“I need your help, Harman. I can’t do this without you. I need you to come to Kingston before it’s too late.”

“Too late for what? Tell me what’s going on.” Why had his brother become so strange?

“What’s going on? Don’t you watch the news in the jungle?” Luca laughed. “Just come here and you’ll be fine; I’ve seen to that. I’ve taken care of everything. The people with me will be fine.”

“Luca, I don’t get what you’re talking about. You’re not making sense.”

“Promise me you’ll come to Kingston. I already bought your ticket. You’re flying out of Caracas on a chartered flight.”

“But—”

“Promise, Harman. Brothers take care of each other no matter what, right?”

“Okay, okay. If you need me that much, I’ll come to New York. Where should I meet you?”

Luca gave him an address and a code. “Don’t lose the code. You’ll need it when you get here.”

“Luca, you’re being as clear as mud.”

“Just trust me, Harman.” Luca laughed again. “And Merry Christmas.”

“It’s June.”

"I know."

* * *

Harman knocked on the metal door.

Luca grinned as he opened it and grabbed Harman in a bear hug. "*Mishto avilan.*" He welcomed him.

The room's furnishings were meager—a single bed, a desk, a lamp, a shelf with some reading books. A blue, green, and red Romani flag decorated the wall above the desk, and a laptop displayed a world map. Beside the computer sat a bottle of Double Cross vodka and a set of mismatched glasses.

Luca released Harman. "I didn't know if you'd come."

"I didn't want to, but I said I would. We're family. I can't ignore that, even if you *are* nuts."

Luca laughed; he had their father's laugh, their father's voice. "It's unhealthy to argue and never act, Harman. I realized that ten years ago," he gestured at the map, "and here we are." He poured two drinks.

Harman accepted a glass of vodka. "Yep. Here we are." The map was more red than blue and, as he watched, the world bled more. "You're tracking the outbreak?"

"Of course. Gotta watch my masterpiece do its job." Luca knocked back his shot. "Honestly, I didn't think it'd spread so quickly. Pretty amazing, ei?"

Chills crawled across Harman's scalp and down his spine. "Yeah. Amazing."

Luca eyed him. "Don't look so freaked out. I told you everyone here'll be fine."

Harman looked away, and his gaze settled on the computer once more. "What are the green dots?" His finger hovered over the largest one on the map; it was on New York.

"Confirmed reports of immunity; in case I need to make more vaccine." Luca poured another shot and capped the bottle. "I have the only supply, but it's a limited amount." This time he sipped the vodka. "I'm glad you've decided to see things my way." He nodded toward the door. "Everyone here does."

Harman grunted. "Do they?" Luca was lying; Tsura's fear and caution proved it. He perched on the edge of the desk and crossed his arms. "Do they know you released AVHF, Dr. Death?"

"Funny, phral." Luca snorted. "But you're the one who's been living in an exotic location." He grinned and added, "I bet you've got a secret lair, too." Then he sobered. "Don't make me out to be another Hera Volopoulos."

"Who?"

"She's a James Bond villain; you really should read the books." He gestured toward his bookshelf.

"Yeah, maybe." Harman looked up at the low ceiling. All those trusting people in the bunker, they believed his brother was thinking only of their safety. That always had been Luca's gift, that ability to convince people to follow him blindly. "How'd you get this place?"

"I had help. Preppers will fork over lots of money if you sound like you know what you're talking about and promise to save them from the apocalypse."

Khul.

Luca lifted his shot glass. "To brothers reunited at the end of the world."

Harman raised his glass too, and then downed the shot, welcoming the liquor's heat as it seared his parched throat.

Luca took Harman's glass and put it beside the Double Cross bottle. "We're familia." He turned and gripped Harman's shoulder. "And we take care of each other."

"Yes." Harman caught the back of his brother's head and pressed his forehead to Luca's. He swallowed. "I've come to take care of you." He pulled the pistol from his pocket. "I'm sorry, little brother." As Luca's eyes widened, Harman fired point blank into his chest. Blood splattered Harman's jacket and face. His ears rang. He let go as his brother went to his knees and then slumped to the floor.

Feet pounded overhead. Muffled shouts grew louder.

Harman locked the door. He sat at the computer and pulled up his email account. Ignoring the efforts of the preppers to force Luca's door, he composed a letter that he'd been writing and rewriting in his mind for days.

The doorknob rattled. The frame creaked. Something heavy hit the door.

Harman addressed his email to the CDC's New York office and hit *Send*.

Then he sat back in the chair and raised the gun to his temple.

* * *

But there's hope in that bunker for all of you. Luca stole the AVHF vaccine from PFD's labs before he released the virus. I'm sure the preppers don't know about that either.

I'm not a good person, but I've always taken care of my brother. For a long time that meant dealing meth and robbing people. I've caused a lot of pain over the years, but even I can't accept what Luca's done. And I'll die regretting that I didn't see what was happening and stop him.

So by the time you read this, I'll have taken care of him, and we'll both be dead, punished for our crimes.

For all the suffering my brother and I have caused, I'm sorry.

Regretfully,
Harman Ferenc Džugi

TWENTY: *Martial Law*
by ER Arroyo

Garrison Kane fought the urge to burst through the thin door separating him from one of the most horrific scenes he'd ever encountered in his seventeen years of service. Standing in a rundown apartment, he stared through the peephole into the apartment across the hall. A woman screamed as her husband used a fistful of her hair to drag her away from the open door, through which she'd been trying to escape. He threw her down beside a deceased, bloody toddler with matted hair. Something about kids being involved always crushed Kane.

He threw the deadbolt in the door, still panting from his scuffle in the hall with the same man he was watching now. He looked again and tightened his grip on his gun when he saw the blood-covered, infected man grip a hatchet and threaten his wife. She squalled and fought like crazy to get free of her husband, causing him to lose his grip on his would-be weapon, igniting even more rage on his part. He caught her once more and slammed her body against the wall.

Kane was helpless, his entire body tense as he watched. His job was to protect people. In any other circumstance, he would have intervened. He wanted to now, but there were two problems. Kane pulled away from the door, his gaze traveling across the living room to take in the small frame of problem number one. A boy who stood all of four foot nothing. No mask, uninfected, with an unknown immune status.

Problem number two was on the floor at Kane's feet—his gas mask. Kane had been in the hall on his way to the stairs when the dying man who was now hurting his wife had caught him. He launched a homemade flame weapon at Kane's face, burning through the mask. When Kane realized his mask was compromised, he had broken into the nearest apartment not knowing the child was inside.

See, problems were usually just obstacles, and obstacles came with the territory, but what they amounted to today was simply this: if Kane opened that door and engaged the boy's neighbor again, he risked infecting himself and the boy.

"You did this," the man roared. Kane's new friend squealed in response before sinking into a trembling ball by the window.

"Shhh." Kane brought a finger to his lips.

When Kane returned to the peephole, a bloodshot eye greeted him, followed by a loud thud against the door. "You alive? Still not minding your own business? I'm doin' her a favor, you hear?" the man yelled through the door. "I'll do you one, too! Who else you got in there with you?"

He continued to pound, louder and louder, each time drawing another whimper out of the boy. Kane shimmied two white medical masks from the cargo pocket on his right leg. They weren't ideal but they were his only option.

"If you breach that door I'll open fire. There's a kid in here." He gripped the boy's arm with his right hand and pulled him to his feet, all the while keeping the gun in his left trained on the door.

The man became belligerent, the pounding erratic and intense. At first Kane had thought the man was kicking or beating with his fists until finally a piece of wood splintered around a tiny metal corner. The hatchet. The man was coming in one way or another.

"The window," Kane ordered the now hysterical boy, slipping the white masks on himself and the boy. When the next blow came and cut a lot deeper, Kane fired a warning shot into the wall above the door.

Kane pushed the window open and shoved the little boy onto the fire escape. "Up the stairs," he whispered, pulling the boy's Batman t-shirt up over his mouth and nose for an added layer of protection. Then Kane took things into his own hands. He lit up the door and the surrounding walls with enough rounds to sink a ship.

Kane pushed himself through the window, not waiting for confirmation of his target's death. He scooped up the boy and scaled the fire escape as quickly as he could. "What's your name?" He glanced below several times on his ascent: no sign of the knife-wielder.

"Jagger." The kid's voice was shaky and weak.

"Jagger, you have to be the toughest little kid in the great state of New York. Hang on tight." Kane anticipated the wind atop the building coming off the helicopter and didn't want the boy to lose his grip, but when they neared the final flight of stairs, he realized quickly that he couldn't hear the roar of the blades whipping through the air.

Panic seized him, pushing him even faster toward the roof. When he got there, nothing but plain old shock and awe greeted him. Martin and Rickshaw stood with a handful of survivors where the helicopter should have been.

"Where's Montgomery?" Kane yelled. Both men shook their heads. The bewildered looks on the rescued apartment residents' faces only served to enrage Kane even more. "Where is my chopper? Where is my *co-pilot*?" Kane roared.

"Sir, what happened to your mask?" Martin caught him off guard.

"There was an infected family inside. A man attacked me." Kane tensed when a gust of wind whipped across his burned jaw.

Rickshaw took a step back. "But the intel—"

"The intel was wrong."

Both soldiers shook their heads, and though Kane couldn't see past their masks, he knew they probably thought he was a goner. The kid too.

"I don't think we were exposed," Kane clarified, though he wasn't sure. Siding with caution, he still kept a distance from the others. Not all of them had masks, and most of the ones who did probably had little more protection than a fishing net.

His men, the loyal studs that they were, shook their heads, taking his word for absolute truth. "What are we gonna do, sir?" Martin took a step toward him.

"Don't come any closer. Soon as we get out of here, you're putting us both in quarantine."

Rickshaw cleared his throat. "Yes, sir." He shared another glance with Martin. This situation was crap and they all knew it.

Jagger clung tighter to Kane's neck until he put the child on his feet. "Listen, I don't know how you survived so long or how long you've been alone, but that tells me you're a tough guy and you can take care of yourself. Isn't that right?"

Jagger raised his chin a bit and dried his tears.

"I need you to stay close to me no matter what. If you see anything, tell me so."

The boy nodded even more vigorously. "Y-yes sir," he mumbled.

"What's our plan?" Rickshaw shouted across the rooftop.

Kane glanced down the metal stairs again. "How's the fire escape on the other side?"

"They're shot. They'll only take us down about four flights." The survivors began to murmur.

"We'll have to go this way then." The last place Kane wanted to go was back down that escape. The man who had attacked him could still be down there. Kane hadn't confirmed the kill. "There's an open window on the tenth floor. When you pass it, make sure your faces are covered and you stay alert. Move quickly and quietly. I'll go first. I'll clear the room, then wave you on."

It sounded good in theory. Despite the pain the straps caused against his raw flesh, he checked and adjusted the medical mask. If he'd been infected, he didn't want to breathe on the other survivors as they passed.

"Let's go, kid."

The rusty steps creaked under Kane's weight. As he neared the open window, he paused to listen. Closer still, his heart rate began to pick up. He stopped the kid just outside the window. "Wait here and face the wall." He glanced up the steps to where his men and the survivors waited, scared to come much closer. "When they walk by, make sure you don't look at them, don't turn to face them. If you're sick..." He shook his head, unable to fathom how to relate this kind of concern for others to a child who probably couldn't grasp the concept of anything beyond survival, especially in a situation like this. Kane couldn't blame him for it. This was terrifying.

Kane took a deep breath and knelt by the window, seeing no one inside. He slipped in and set his feet quietly on the carpet as he shouldered his rifle to draw his sidearm from his left hip instead. He moved into the kitchen, checking the cabinets and under the table. In the pantry. In the only bedroom and bathroom in the apartment.

He made his way back to the window. "Clear."

Martin nodded and began guiding the group down the stairs. Kane stayed posted up by the window, pistol trained on the door, head turned away from the window. Who knew if these flu masks even did anything.

The people filed past the window, Kane's every muscle tense from the noise they were making. He wondered if they were even *trying* to be quiet. With as many bullets as Kane had put through that door, anyone could break it down at any moment.

Kane spared a glance over his shoulder. The group was a little more than halfway past. Jagger's eyes seemed focused on Rickshaw's weapon and suddenly he broke out into sobs. Kane reached through the window and pulled the boy close, his eyes apologizing to the people passing by. He even tried not to breathe so as not to spread potentially infected molecules.

Jagger's crying intensified and another cry joined him. Only this one was coming from inside the apartment. Kane whipped his pistol into place and aimed at the heart of the bloody woman from across the hall. She held the dead toddler, limp in her arms. Bloody tears streamed down her face, desperation contorting her features. Her husband lay in a heap by the open doorway behind her.

"Please help us," she moaned. "Help my baby." Her body rocked with deep sobs.

"Don't come any closer. We have survivors just outside." Kane hoped she would listen, but the woman dragged her feet another step closer. "Jagger, turn around." Kane clenched his teeth. He couldn't check whether or not the boy had listened—couldn't take his eyes off the woman and her dead child.

The survivors outside had caught on to what was happening and began to panic, making all kinds of noise, which only sent the woman into more hysterics. "Please help us!" she cried. They moved faster, and so did she. Kane had no choice.

He flipped the safety and pulled the trigger. Twice. He turned and pushed through the window, grabbing the boy. He jogged down the steps after the others, forcing himself to slow down and not get too close.

"Hang in there, buddy." The boy lay his head on Kane's shoulder.

On the ground, the group waited, giving Kane and Jagger a wide berth.

"Where to?" Rickshaw stood ready with his rifle aimed at the ground ahead of him. His eyes were wide with nerves or fear, but his jaw was set and he had a determined look. Kane could always count on him to be resolute. They were on this course and Rickshaw wouldn't question him, wouldn't hesitate, wouldn't relent until these people were brought to safety.

Martin wasn't as solid, though he hadn't gone against Kane in the time they'd been working together. Kane wished, for a moment, that these two had been with him under better circumstances.

They'd met at jump school the week everything started, and he couldn't believe he'd talked them into following him when he went rogue. To help people. They'd settled into the United States Emergency Government Shelter long enough to learn its location and hatch a plan. So far, they'd managed to rescue sixteen civilians, two government officials, and four injured military personnel. They had dropped them off at the entrance, and to their surprise the government shelter had taken them in—to be put through rigorous testing and quarantines, but they'd done what they could. Kane and his men couldn't stop.

Until now, Kane had always known what to do. He always had a plan, thought ahead, and had an easy escape via helicopter. Until now. He couldn't say the words out loud. His pride wouldn't let him. *I don't know what to do.*

He looked around, sweat beading on his forehead. He scanned the buildings around them. He spotted an extended SUV with the door hanging open. He set the boy down and held up a hand signaling the group to wait while he approached the vehicle. He searched for signs of infected people. There didn't appear to be any.

"Any of you know how to hot wire a car?" he asked, not really expecting to be so lucky.

A scruffy guy in the back of the group lifted his hand.

Kane nodded and backed away from the SUV, reuniting with Jagger. While the guy got to work, Kane looked for another vehicle. He couldn't put himself and Jag in the same tight quarters with all those people.

Everyone made their way to the SUV when the engine started to spark and they softly cheered when it finally turned over.

Kane had just laid eyes on a motorcycle when he heard screeching tires a couple of blocks away, followed by a woman's scream. The passengers scrambled into the SUV with Rickshaw at the wheel while Kane checked the ignition on the bike. Keys were in it. He straddled the bike and hoisted Jagger behind him with clear instruction to hold on tightly.

Kane sped toward the sound, slowing to ease around the corner. He stopped when he spotted a wrecked car and a van racing in the opposite direction. He moved closer to the car where the driver was hunched over, fresh blood oozing from a bullet hole in his head.

If he'd had time, Kane would have put the boy somewhere safe first. But he didn't. Instead, he gunned the bike forward after the van. He chased them for three blocks before he gained on them. Someone leaned out the passenger window and opened fire. He twisted his rifle around from his back and returned fire, disabling the shooter, causing him to drop his weapon.

Kane aimed for the back tire on the passenger side. He squeezed the trigger a couple of times before he finally lined up his shot and managed to strike it. The driver began to lose control and Kane took advantage, going after a second tire and soon striking it. Both the van and Kane screeched to a halt. Kane positioned himself on the other side of a car, where he shoved a sobered up Jagger to the ground. "Stay down."

Kane replaced his magazine and aimed at the van, waiting for someone to emerge. After a minute with no movement, he approached slowly. He heard a motor behind him and glanced over his shoulder in time to see his men round the corner from where the SUV waited out of sight. When he turned back, the van's driver, who was dressed in black gear, slipped out with a gun raised. Kane didn't hesitate to take a shot, center mass. He followed with a head shot, just in case the man had a vest under that gear.

Quick footsteps approached Kane, who didn't take his eyes off the van again until Martin and Rickshaw flanked him. "Who are they?" Martin asked, his eyes flitting around for more threats.

Kane made a noise with his mouth to silence his friend and tilted his head to urge them forward alongside him. As they approached the van, they fanned out and peeked into the windows.

Rickshaw reached for the door handle on the van's passenger side. When he swung it open, he reached in and glanced up at Kane. "It's a woman. Alive."

"Armed?" Kane asked, gun still raised.

Rickshaw slung his weapon behind his back, leaning in. He pulled a hood from her head. "Unconscious." He hoisted the woman out of the car and onto his shoulder, toting her to the sidewalk where he set her down. Martin went in behind him and pulled the passenger door open, allowing the body of the first shooter to fall out onto the ground unceremoniously.

Without getting too close, Kane approached Rickshaw. He took note of the woman's wounds: red marks about her neck, a reddened spot on her temple, something that could have been caused by a blunt object. The front of her blouse was setting crooked on her chest, revealing markings from her seatbelt, presumably from the crash moments earlier.

Rickshaw attempted to rouse the woman, but couldn't. He patted his pockets until he found a packet of ammonium carbonate, which he snapped and waved by her nose until her eyes shot open, widening the moment she was able to focus. She scurried away, her left shoe sliding off in the process. Her hair fell haphazardly around her face, the remains of a tight bun a messy pile on the back of her head.

Rickshaw tried to calm her but his words were jumbled and Kane realized Rickshaw's elevated voice wasn't helping. He stepped forward, holding a hand toward the woman. She looked like a wild animal backed into a corner.

"Miss, we're National Guard. I'm Kane and that's Rickshaw. He was just trying to help you. You were in a car accident—"

"I was *taken*," she corrected him.

"Yes ma'am, I was getting to that part. Are you okay?" Kane had to fight the urge to step closer so she could see him better, know that he wasn't a threat.

She pushed herself to her feet, struggling to balance against a light pole. "No. No, I'm not okay." She inched toward her missing shoe and Rickshaw took a step back to accommodate her. She slipped the shoe on.

"We can help you." Kane gestured toward the people now looking on. "We have a small group of survivors we're leading to safety. We're happy to take you in as well, we just…"

Her eyes were locked on the van.

"Do you know those men?" Kane asked her. Movement caught his eye and he glanced up to find Jagger's face peeking over the car where Kane had left him. When their gazes connected, the boy launched out from his hiding place and ran to Kane's side, hiding halfway behind his leg.

"I don't, but…" She shook her head. "I don't know."

Kane didn't buy it. He looked around the area. "We need to get out of here, somewhere safe before whoever those men worked for send more people. Any idea why they were after you?"

She shook her head again but bit her lip while attempting to smooth her hair back. She was lying. "Where are you taking people?"

"It's complicated," Kane explained. "We had a helicopter. We were lifting people to the government's shelter, but one of our own went AWOL with said chopper." He cringed a little, still not wanting to admit defeat. Government ordered or not, this was his mission. The people looking on, terrified for their future, were his mission. The boy hugging tightly to his leg was his mission too. He wasn't sure where they were going to go, but he knew they should hurry.

"I'm Cassandra," she mumbled. "I know a place."

* * *

Cassandra rode shotgun with Rickshaw and the others, giving him directions. When they arrived at the New York offices of the Centers for Disease Control, Kane's eyes widened. The temporary fences had been knocked inward from some sort of crowd that had since dispersed. Bodies lay as evidence all over. Not the kind who had died of infection.

Kane pulled up next to the passenger side of the SUV and glanced over. The woman had her hand over her mouth, her eyes filled with shock, on the brink of tears.

The group pulled their vehicles closer to the building's entrance. Kane and his small unit left all the others at the SUV. An older woman had climbed out to stand with Jagger, not caring if he was infected or not. She attempted to distract him from what was happening. Kane couldn't fathom how the boy was processing all this destruction and death.

Kane pulled open the building's main door, surprised that the glass hadn't been shattered by the bullets that had flown through recently.

It took the three men nearly an hour to clear the entire building, but they secured the survivors in an office after clearing the first floor. When they came down, Cassandra was standing at the door biting her thumbnail.

"Did you find anyone?"

"Just bodies." Kane placed his hand on her shoulder. "I'm sorry, Cassandra."

She tightened her lips and gave a stiff nod.

"I still think this is a good place to set up. We can secure it, create a decontamination room, quarantines in lower floor offices." Kane's mind was racing, creating a checklist of how to make this place safe. "Honestly, our best option is to make sure it doesn't look like we're here at all."

Martin cracked his neck, not making eye contact with Kane. "Good idea to stay here? In light of what went down?"

Kane sighed. "Someone came through and slaughtered these people. What reason would they have to come back?"

"We're assuming these are the same people that tried to snatch the girl, right?"

"Cassie," she interrupted, arms crossed. Suddenly her demeanor changed and she pushed her shoulders back. "I think we should stay. We are equipped for the things you mentioned, and we already have a decon unit."

Rickshaw smiled. "Chief, I'm with you. Put me to work."

"It's settled then. We're staying."

Kane knew it wasn't ideal. What they had been doing up until now had hinged on the fact that they had a helicopter and could get away quickly at any time. He had no idea what prompted Montgomery to take off with the

UH-60. If he'd just bailed, it would have been one thing, because Kane could pilot the chopper. But this guy had taken their only means of extracting survivors.

He didn't know Montgomery very well but he did wonder if his sudden disappearance had something to do with his kids back in New Mexico. Kane didn't have any kids, so he couldn't relate. His mother died in her New York nursing home before Kane could get to her. She was all he'd had in the way of family.

After Kane placed a signal on the roof for Montgomery, Cassandra showed the men to the decontamination gear and how to set it up and implement the protocol. Every member of their group went through decontamination and was placed alone or with family in second floor offices overnight. They'd each taken a canned good from some of the survivors' stashes, which they'd graciously offered.

Kane kept Jagger with him in quarantine. If one was infected, they both were, most likely, so why leave the kid alone?

There had been two casualties through the night, a married couple. They didn't die alone nor very far apart. Everyone had to listen to it, though. The sounds of retching, of sickness. Of moaning in pain, and crying out, emotionally distressed from the impossible task of coming to grips with impending death.

The next day, Cassandra began monitoring the internet, the phone lines, and all of the CDC's incoming communications. She also tried in vain to contact the pilot for her private charter, still hoping to flee the city. She'd inquired about the government shelter Kane had mentioned, but it wasn't an option. It could only be reached by aircraft. They were stuck. There was nowhere else to go.

A week went by with the small group of survivors holed up at the CDC. They brought in other people they'd found on trips searching for food and supplies. The decon and quarantine worked like a charm, which sadly meant more people had died on the second floor. Disposing of the bodies wasn't something anyone looked forward to, but Kane had put Martin in charge of it, along with two young men. They had a routine. No one liked it, but everyone appreciated it.

* * *

"How's it coming?" Kane gripped Rickshaw's shoulder, looking over him to the computer screen where he had logged into the database and satellite feed that they'd been using to scout out survivors. They'd been using it ever since they began doing search and extraction missions post-virus. They had a man inside the U.S. shelter who worked for the CIA before it shut down. He'd been giving them intel, but had quieted down since Kane's unit lost their chopper.

That didn't keep them from logging in and keeping an eye on things.

"What's this?" Cassandra walked up. She'd been scouring the net, too, but it was really just to keep herself busy. She searched forums and news sites, even though most of the posts had been made weeks earlier.

Kane hesitated. Cracked his neck. "It's how we find people." He pointed to the screen showing satellite graphics with blipping red and green dots. He dragged his fingers across the screen. "These are pockets of survivors that we know about. The green dots are places believed to be virus-free."

"I would have thought there would be a whole lot more red by now," she said. "Some should be immune but not this many."

Kane shrugged. "Best we can tell, some people have been able to protect themselves from exposure. More than expected."

"It stands to reason that there are populations all over the world who haven't been exposed. No contact with outsiders." She crossed her arms, index finger on her chin.

Rickshaw zoomed in on the NYC area.

"That's Staten Island," she observed, pointing to the bottom center of the image.

Kane nodded. "It appears to be the most populated location. They've been advertising, though."

"Are you suspicious about it?" Kane got the impression she knew something.

"Peter Franklin Donalds orchestrated it, so, yeah. I'd say so." Kane's jaw tensed and he crossed his arms.

"Isn't there something we can do? Something the *government* can do?" Cassandra appeared to already know the answer to that. She wasn't unfamiliar with government organizations. She straightened her wrinkly shirt, like that would help. She bit her lip again.

Kane lowered his voice. "What are you not saying?"

"It's just…if they had something to do with this—"

"Which you believe they did…" He waited. He could guess what she suspected but wasn't ready to tell her that he knew she was right.

She cleared her throat. “If they did, what use would they have for survivors?”

“They had a contract for the vaccine right? Maybe they’re still attempting to make one.” Kane perched on the edge of the desk, crossing his arms.

“If that were true, it wouldn’t do much good. The virus has already spread worldwide.” She grabbed a nearby chair and sat down.

“The world’s not dead yet. Not by a long shot. Just look at the numbers, look at the maps.” He gestured toward the green and red dots on the computer, even though the green was diminishing. “A small percentage of the world’s population is still a lot of people. They all matter.” In another couple of weeks most would be gone. Kane was saving people by the dozens when the virus was killing by the millions. Nothing within Kane’s power could change that.

A silent moment passed before Cassandra changed the subject. “Are there any other places with that many survivors? Like on Staten Island?”

He cleared his throat. “Not even close. There is a place north a little ways, in Kingston. At least a dozen people. Our guy can’t figure out who these people are, so we’ve been hesitant to approach them. They don’t come and go often, so it seems they’re self-sufficient.”

“Like a bunker.” Rickshaw jumped in.

The sound of a helicopter caught Kane’s attention. He peered out the window and saw a Blackhawk. *His* Blackhawk. He darted up and pressed his fingers to the glass. Normally he kept pretty clear of the windows but this was definitely Montgomery.

Kane took the elevator to the top floor and flew up the final flight of stairs leading onto the roof, with every intention of beating the crap out of the pilot. The whooping sound of air coming off the blades was such a familiar and welcomed sensation that Kane nearly lost his desire to confront the traitor. When the UH-60 landed on the rooftop, directly over Kane’s signal, the engines cut off and Montgomery climbed out, limping over with his hands up, an explanation on his lips.

Kane’s fist nearly connected with Montgomery’s lips too, but three teenagers slipped out of the helicopter, causing Kane to stop mid-movement.

“My kids,” Montgomery pleaded. “I finally got a signal and my kids weren’t where they were supposed to be. They’d left my bunker. I had to go after them.” His eyes watered before he stiffened his upper lip and steadied his resolve. "I lost my daughter."

At his words, the boy behind him grimaced and shot his father a glare that quickly retreated.

Kane rubbed his hand over his face, exhaling deeply. "Montgomery, I..." Montgomery had been so sure his family was safe. Now, Kane didn't know what to say. Couldn't remember what anyone had said to comfort him, or if anyone had even tried. Everything he was coming up with felt phony. The truth was, death sucked and there was no comfort to be had.

Kane's gaze rolled over the kids hiding behind Montgomery. A boy with his arm wrapped around a blond-headed girl, and another teen a couple feet away.

Montgomery introduced them as Chad, Wendy, and Elena. As Kane inspected the trio, Elena tipped her head back and grumbled, "We're fine. Thanks for asking."

Kane ignored the comment. His group had just gained three to their numbers with a helicopter that could only hold eleven passengers. They now had fifteen people to consider besides their chalk of four guardsmen.

Montgomery shifted his weight, unsteady on a newly bum leg. Kane didn't know how he'd come by the injury and at the moment, he didn't care.

Kane asked the most important question there was. "How much fuel?" He knew Montgomery would have had to stop several times for fuel along the way, and who knew when he had stopped last.

Montgomery grimaced and shook his head. "Listen," Montgomery plead. "We're beat up. We're hungry, and we went through hell to get here. Can we just have a minute? And then we can figure out what to do."

A tense moment passed before they made their way inside, and even more tense when they crowded into an elevator.

When the doors dinged open, Cassie was waiting. "You're going to want to see this." Her gaze was fixed on Kane and her whole body was tensed.

Kane stepped out of the elevator first. "What happened?"

She cocked her head toward the cubicle where she'd been working since they arrived at the CDC. Kane turned to the people on the elevator. "Get them some food."

Rickshaw nodded, his face devoid of all the emotions Martin's wore. Kane could always count on Rickshaw to be steady.

At Cassandra's desk, she unlocked the computer screen, turning to

Kane before explaining whatever was on her computer. “I just found an email.” She paused before adding, “from Kingston.”

Kane cocked a brow. “Really?”

He read the message. His jaw went slack, his mind warring with rage and confusion. Not only was Kingston safe and housing uninfected, but it had a sordid coming about.

“Amy. The reporter. She was right about PFD,” Cassandra muttered. “Just not how she thought.”

“It was a terrorist attack. Just like the government said. That’s why they went into hiding.” For a moment, Kane wished this Harman guy hadn’t killed his brother so Kane could do it. All the suffering and death caused at this man’s hands. This twisted nut job. He’d *done* this. On purpose.

“Do you think all the people at Kingston were involved?” Cassandra hesitated to make the accusation, her tone shifting to pure concern.

“The email doesn’t imply they knew.” Kane shrugged, still mulling over the possibilities.

“The email could be a lie. A trap.” Cassie sat back in her chair. She didn’t believe that; Kane knew it.

“I don’t know,” Kane said. “We’ve heard of Prep for Doom. I can’t believe it was all a cover for this Džugi guy’s plans.”

The website, *Prep for Doom*, had sprung up a while back, covering a range of disasters and apocalypses: zombies, pandemics, aliens, climate disasters, nuclear war, and terrorism. Intel said there’d been a bunker secured in New York and before long, similar ones had popped up all over the country. Imitations of the real deal. Of Džugi, apparently.

“Luca Džugi would have the world believe the pharmaceutical company had done this. But it was him. He betrayed them,” Kane said.

“They still created a weaponized virus. And sending an army to secure an entire island on behalf of the company hasn’t exactly helped PFD’s case. So what’s their angle?” Cassandra asked.

“Damage control?” Kane shrugged.

Someone cleared his throat and Kane glanced over his shoulder to find Montgomery. “You mentioned Kingston?” His face was a combination of curiosity and shame.

“What do you know about it?” Kane asked, crossing his arms and turning toward Montgomery. Martin and Rickshaw joined them then, interrupting whatever Montgomery had been about to say.

"What's going on, chief?" Rickshaw rubbed his jaw.

Kane cleared his throat and told them all about the email from Harman Džugi, the terrorist's brother. Rage boiled in Martin's gaze, but even he couldn't bring himself to say anything. Kane's eyes landed on Montgomery. "What do you know about Kingston?" he asked again.

"I'm a member of Prep for Doom. There's a spot for me in that bunker." Montgomery dropped his arms to his sides, as if giving up and welcoming whatever he had coming.

But Kane didn't react. He searched Montgomery's eyes, studied his demeanor. "Do you know Džugi?" Montgomery stared back, jaw slack as he tried to place the name. "Charles. Do you know him?" Kane's pulse quickened as he considered what would have been a far greater betrayal than taking off with a UH-60.

Kane grabbed Montgomery by both shoulders. "Did you know about this? Any of it?" Kane was so close that angry bits of spittle landed on Montgomery's face.

Montgomery's eyes suddenly focused and snapped toward Kane's face, offended. "Of course I didn't. People have been prepping for disasters long before that idiot created Prep for Doom. It was just the newest flavor."

Kane felt his grip tighten and heard his voice raise, both more so than he really intended. "He killed billions of people, Montgomery. *Billions* and counting."

Montgomery's jaw worked as his breathing escalated. He stared down at a spot on the carpet until finally he shook his head. "I had no idea. I never would've…"

Kane forced himself to step back and glanced at Rickshaw, who he didn't realize had been restraining Martin. Cassandra had backed into the corner between the desk and the window, her fingertips pressed to her lips. She didn't meet Kane's eyes.

He turned back to Montgomery. "You're taking us to that bunker."

* * *

Kane somehow convinced Cassie to stay behind. It wasn't an easy sell, but they didn't know what awaited in Kingston, and quite honestly, Kane wanted only soldiers alongside him on this mission—on any mission. Civilians complicated things. Montgomery's leg made him virtually useless on foot, but Kane gave him no choice. He wasn't even sure if he believed Montgomery.

Kane took a car that belonged to someone Cassandra knew from the CDC—they'd found his body when they arrived. The whole drive to Kingston, even during their stop to syphon gas, they barely spoke. Kane had picked up a spare mask from the helicopter and they had all loaded up on ammo.

In Kingston, the men found a place to park behind a yellow Honda with a dead camo-clad man inside. They were a few streets over from the old school building that now housed a bunker created by the founder of the fanatic internet group, Prep for Doom. Luca Džugi had been an employee of Peter Franklin Donalds. But then he sabotaged the company and the rest of the world by releasing a virus for which PFD had been making a vaccine. A virus Kane was convinced they had intentionally made airborne to weaponize. Džugi pulled the trigger but no one's hands were clean.

Kane was turned halfway around in the passenger seat so he could see all three men.

"The message said the brothers were dead, but we are going to assume that's not the case." Kane made eye contact with each man, waiting for them to acknowledge. "Boys, this man created his very own apocalypse. If there are innocents in that bunker, we will do right by them, but we *will* come out with that man's body, one way or another. Understood?"

Each gave a small nod, just enough, their eyes alight, even Montgomery's. This was their job—to protect people. Even if there weren't many left to protect. Kane's thoughts drifted to Cassandra. To Jagger, and the others. They didn't know what they were walking into, but this is what they'd signed up for.

"It's been an honor to serve at the end of the world with the three of you." Kane tipped his chin back, taking a deep breath. "Let's do this."

The men whooped in response, a guttural sound. They secured their masks before slipping out of the car. Approaching the building, they readied their weapons. This wasn't their usual type of gig. They specialized in extractions, the kind with living subjects. This extraction would be much different.

Kane, Martin, and Rickshaw hung back while Montgomery approached, only armed with a concealed sidearm. His limp actually worked in their favor because, at the moment, he looked nothing like a soldier. Save for the mask.

"Stop right there." The voice came from somewhere impossible to distinguish, bouncing off the walls around them. The sun was setting and the dim light didn't help.

Montgomery halted. "My name's on your list," he told the unseen man.

"Password?"

Montgomery rubbed his hand along the thigh of his injured leg. "TFZ9038. Charles Montgomery, from New Mexico."

There was silence for a moment and then, "Come around the side to the stairs."

Montgomery took a few steps that way, his limp suddenly worse than it had been before.

"You're sick?" the voice shot up to a higher pitch, shouting now.

"No, just injured. Just my leg." Montgomery's head shifted around as he tried to spot the speaker.

When Kane noticed the red dot appear on Montgomery's back, he sprang into action, his men falling in right behind. Kane lifted his rifle toward the buildings across the street from the school, scanning windows and rooftops, anywhere a shooter could be hidden.

"Lower your weapons!" the same voice said. Kane detected something in the voice…*fear*? "We'll shoot."

"We're members of the Army National Guard. We're looking for a terrorist named Luca Džugi. Send him out now and we'll have no reason to bother the rest of you." It was to the point and a long shot, but worth taking.

It took too long for the man to respond. "We don't know what you're talking about. We can't help you."

"Do you know who you're protecting?" Kane had finally spotted a security camera. Next to it, a speaker. The man wasn't even outside. "Džugi is responsible for releasing AVHF in New York, knowing full well that there was no cure, and stealing the vaccine from PFD before he did. He endangered everyone, including you."

When no reply came, Kane continued. "We know he's here. His brother sent us a message."

This was getting nowhere. They all knew it. The man was terrified. He had no way of knowing if Kane was telling the truth, or if he meant anyone harm. Kane couldn't stand here and reason with him all day. "We don't want to hurt anyone, but we're coming inside."

Together, the four men moved to the left side of the building. They slowly scaled the covered stairs, guns raised in different directions. Kane was genuinely surprised no one shot at them. He inspected the door for a possible way to break in. But he never got the chance because it clicked open and a small man in a white HAZMAT suit stood, reaching toward Kane's chest to keep him out.

"Please," he begged. "Please just leave us alone. We're safe here. We're just surviving like everyone else."

Kane not-so-gently removed the man's hand, wrenching it behind his back and shoving him into the hallway lined with plastic. "Take me to Džugi."

"You could be infected or carrying contaminants. We have procedures. We have quarantine—" The man's sentence was cut off by Kane's pistol at the base of his skull.

"We'll keep our masks on. Take us inside." Kane had lost his patience, and he didn't like the ugly side of himself that came out when he was challenged. "I'm not asking."

The man's voice thickened. "There are children. Please don't do this; you'll traumatize them. Just please… Put your weapons down and I'll take you wherever you want go."

"To Luca Džugi."

"Fine. Fine, I'll do it." The man fell forward when Kane released him. He proceeded to guide the men through the facility, past the quarantine, down onto lower floors. They passed a common area where a group of shocked people scrambled to their feet, tucking the children behind them and covering their faces with cloth. A dark headed woman placed her hand protectively on the shoulder of a young girl with cornrows. A teenager nearby rose from her seat, stepping closer to a man in casts.

Kane tried to give them all a reassuring smile but he was sure they couldn't see it because of his mask. Probably better this way. The white-clad man led them to a steel door where he stopped. "I think he's dead," the smaller man said morosely. "We couldn't get through the door to confirm it." He touched the cold steel through his white suit. "He was…strange, but I just never would have thought…the things you said."

Kane touched the man's wrist and pulled it gently away. "We have to find out the truth. We have to get in there."

Defeated, the man relented, backing away.

Martin and Rickshaw broke through the door while Kane and Montgomery stood guard. When the door opened, Kane walked through first. He didn't notice any odor through his mask, but it was clear the bodies had begun to decompose. One lay on the floor and one leaned back in the chair. Both killed by gunshot wounds.

Kane sighed deeply, taking in the form of the black-headed man on the floor. The source of it all. The truest evil Kane had ever witnessed, right there in a decomposing heap. A body reduced to nothing.

Kane rolled the chair containing the other brother away from the desk. He tapped the space bar on the computer keyboard, waking the machine from its slumber. Sure enough, there sat Harman's email account. Sending that message was the last thing he'd done before ending his life.

Montgomery stayed at the door while Rickshaw and Martin joined Kane to search the space. They gathered up the dead man's hard drives, his computer gear, all his files. Maybe the information on the vaccine Harman mentioned was stored somewhere within. They could get the information to the government's shelter. Maybe they could turn this around, start helping people. Keep Luca Džugi's legacy from spreading further.

The room was solemn. Kane spoke in simple commands to grab this, grab that.

Maneuvering around Luca's body, Martin knocked a framed flag from the wall—blue, green, and red.

"What's that?" Kane asked, and Martin froze. The spot where the flag had been hanging didn't look quite like the surrounding wall. Kane set down a box and approached. He touched the bricks that didn't seem quite flush with the others, running his fingers over them, pressing on places for movement. He made a fist and slammed the side of it against a seam, a thin layer of mortar shattering on impact.

His eyes widened, and he looked over at Martin who was just as keyed up. Forcing themselves to be careful, they began whittling at the surrounding mortar, releasing brick by brick until a large, hidden cavity had been revealed.

Kane took a deep breath as he pulled out his flashlight and shone it inside, illuminating steel cases with Peter Franklin Donalds insignias. Gently, they pulled the cases out one by one, setting them on the floor. By the time they'd finally gotten them all out, Kane's hands were shaking. He didn't know if this was the virus that had started it all. If it was, everyone in this bunker was at risk.

They transported the cases outside, with the help of the white-suit man. They loaded the cargo and even helped the man dispose of the bodies. In his time in Kingston, he'd been thoroughly convinced that the Prep for Doom members of this bunker were nothing more than survivors. They knew nothing. So he left them to their safety, wishing them the best, and thanking them for their cooperation. He'd got what he came for—Luca Džugi. Maybe even more than that.

Back at the CDC offices, Kane went straight for Cassandra. She'd suited up and met him in the decontamination unit. They locked eyes, their chests rising and falling rapidly. Then Kane opened a case. His brows furrowed as he pulled a vial of yellow liquid from a padded slot.

"What is it?" he said, his voice muffled through dual layers of mask.

Cassandra took the vial from him and inspected it.

"This," she said, eyes wide, "is the vaccine."

THE END

Acknowledgements

First and foremost, Band of Dystopian would like to thank our *Prep For Doom* authors: Laura Albins, Amy Bartelloni, Brea Behn, Casey L. Bond, TK Carter, Kate Corcino, Harlow C. Fallon, Kelsey D. Garmendia, Caroline A. Gill, DelSheree Gladden, John Gregory Hancock, Casey Hays, Kate L. Mary, Jon Messenger, Monica Enderle Pierce, Cameo Renae, Hilary Thompson, Yvonne Ventresca, and Megan White. Working with you all has been a pleasure and we want to thank you so much for the incredible trust you placed in us and in each other over the course of completing this project. It's pretty amazing what we've done, and it's been because of your faith in this book that we pulled it off!

We want to thank Casey L. Bond for giving us the idea to have the short stories exist in the same universe—it sparked the idea that eventually grew into this massive concept for an anthology that reads like a novel. We also want to thank Jon Messenger for not only contributing two stories, but also helping ER Arroyo create the fundamental details upon which the entire book was built. Your help in those early stages was crucial. Thank you!

We want to thank Sara Benedict and the entire team at Your Elemental Solutions for partnering with us on this project, for getting behind our book launch, and for being with us every step of the way.

Thank you Maia Driver for squeezing such a huge project into your schedule for us to get this puppy polished up and ready for the world.

Most importantly, BOD would like to thank all of our Band of Dystopian Authors and Fans group members—past, present, and still to come. You all have turned our small idea into an amazing group of which we could not be prouder. You have kept the wind in our sails with your enthusiasm, support, and friendliness. Onward and upward we go, thanks to all of you.

- ER Arroyo and Cheer Papworth

About Band of Dystopian Authors and Fans

Band of Dystopian (BOD) is a Facebook group, blog, and company dedicated to dystopian, apocalyptic, and post-apocalyptic books. Our mission is to help fans of dystopian fiction find books they will love and help authors of the genre get the word out about their work. Our community of over 2,300 readers and authors has become a supportive, interactive, and insanely fun place to be. We are branching into the publishing world with our first anthology, *Prep For Doom*.

We have over 150 authors in the group, plenty of great conversation, tons of giveaways, and the perfect place for dystopian lovers to find their next great read.

www.facebook.com/groups/bandofdystopian
www.bandofdystopian.com
www.prepfordoom.com

About the Authors

Caroline A. Gill

The Gift (Prologue)

Caroline A. Gill went to school at UCLA and NIU. She married the love of her life. Facing the world with children made her aware of how vulnerable they are. Weaving tales of courage, she tries to find hope. Living near the great California Redwoods, she finds a sense of the finite and infinite touching. The creative world is like that, especially when authors feel inspired.

In July 2015, she will publish her first dystopian novel: *Flying Away*. For a thrill unlike any other, order it at:

www.authorcarolineagill.com

Worlds of magic live right inside our own houses, flights of possibility. Come fly away!

TK Carter

Lethal Inception (Chapter One)

TK Carter is a Southern born-and-bred middle child with all of the complexes that accompany this birth order. She lives in central Missouri and has two children, two dogs, a mortgage, and a dream. She is the author of *Collapse* and *Three Meals to Anarchy*—books one and two in *The Yellow Flag Series*—*Independence*, *The Breakup Mix*, and the short story, "An Afternoon with Aunt Viv."

tkcarter-author.com

Megan White

Siren (Chapter Two)

Megan White is the young adult and new adult author of *The Parish Secrets Trilogy* and *The Supremacy Trilogy*. Raised as a "military brat," she's had the opportunity to live in many locals, but presently resides in the south and loves the hometown she has been adopted into. When not writing, she can be found advocating for human rights, and across-the-board equality on numerous platforms, both online and at the judicial level.

www.facebook.com/AuthorMeganLWhite

Casey L. Bond

Unsafe Haven (Chapter Three)

Casey L. Bond resides in Milton, West Virginia with her husband and their two beautiful daughters. When she's not busy being a domestic goddess and chasing her baby girls, she loves to write young adult and new adult fiction. You can find more information about Bond's books at

www.authorcaseybond.com

Jon Messenger

HAZMAT (Chapter Four)
& CDC (Chapter Ten)

Jon Messenger (Born 1979 in London, England) serves as a United States Army Major in the Medical Service Corps. Jon wrote his first science fiction trilogy in 2008 and has since written and published over 10 novels. The scope of his writing has expanded beyond science fiction to include the new adult and steampunk genres. His books have become Amazon bestsellers, been translated into foreign languages, and have won numerous awards both for content and covers.

www.jonmessengerauthor.com

Cameo Renae

Existing (Chapter Five)

Cameo Renae was born in San Francisco, was raised in Maui, Hawaii, and recently moved with her husband and children to Alaska. She's a daydreamer, a caffeine and peppermint addict, loves to laugh, loves to read, and loves to escape reality. One of her greatest joys is creating fantasy worlds filled with adventure and romance, and sharing them with others. One day she hopes to find her own magic wardrobe, and ride away on her magical unicorn. Until then…she'll keep writing!

www.cameorenae.com

John Gregory Hancock

Trust (Chapter Six)

John Gregory Hancock has been a newspaper graphic designer for several decades. He's lived in so many cities and towns he's lost count.

His visual sense feeds into his writing.

He is a simple storyteller, in the grand human tradition of old men caught spinning yarns at village campfires. His characters tell him what to say, and he chooses only those tales he wants to hear.

Like his character Old Earl, life has shaped and unshaped him.

johngregoryhancock.com

Kelsey D. Garmendia

Roland (Chapter Seven)

Kelsey D. Garmendia, 25, an alumnus of the State University of New York at New Paltz, is originally from Pine Bush, N.Y. She obtained a bachelor's degree in English with a concentration in creative writing. Garmendia is featured in *Confettifall*, *Embodied Effigies*, *Penduline Press*, *The Stonesthrow Review*, *My Unfinished Novel*, *Poydras Review*, and *Midnight Screaming*. She also has four self-published novels: *The Burn Our Houses Down Series* (*Burn Our Houses Down*, *If I Lose*, *Painted Red*) and a stand-alone novel titled *Disenchanted*.

http://kgarmendia.wordpress.com

Amy Bartelloni

Second Chances (Chapter Eight)

Amy Bartelloni is a reader, writer, and coffee addict who lives with her husband, three children, and various animals in the northeastern U.S. When she's not playing mom-taxi, you can find her with her nose in a book or her head in the clouds. A people watcher and science fiction junkie, she still believes dreams can come true. Amy is the author of *The Andromeda Series* with Limitless Publishing, which has been optioned for a TV series or movie. Her next project falls in the sci-fi genre because the possibilities are endless, and she'll never stop asking "what if?"

www.amybartelloni.com

Laura Albins

Nan Tapper (Chapter Nine)

Laura Albins is a British writer living in Suffolk, England. Laura grew up in Birmingham, but has lived and travelled all over, her love of seeing the world only matched by her love of reading. After years of enjoying other people's stories she decided to write some of her own and hasn't stopped since. Her first book, *The Ninth Star*, was published in 2013, followed by the sequel, *Starscape*, and a third installment in the series is due for release in 2015. Laura currently lives in Ipswich with her husband, two kids, and lots and lots of books.

www.lauraalbins.com

Hilary Thompson

Lucky (Chapter Eleven)

Hilary Thompson was born to parents who took many roads less traveled. But she was also a Libra and an independent, willful child, so she has made a habit of taking a few roads on her own. After trying many paths, she retreated back to her first loves of education and writing.

Hilary now teaches high school, writes whenever and wherever she can, and reads as much as her eyes can handle. She tries not to spoil her own independent, willful children or neglect her wonderful soul-mate of a husband. She tends to ignore laundry baskets and dirty dishes.

www.hilarythompsonauthor.com

Brea Behn

Proof Falls Down (Chapter Twelve)

Brea Behn is very passionate about reading and writing in all genres. She began writing at the age of fifteen, when she wrote a memoir for her twin brother. Currently, she writes fiction of several genres, nonfiction, and is building her career as an author and public speaker.

When Brea is not writing, she is reading, usually several books at the same time. She also volunteers at her local humane society, gardens, and homeschools her children.

Brea lives in Wisconsin with her husband and their two children.

www.Breasbooks.com

Yvonne Ventresca

Escape to Orange Blossom (Chapter Thirteen)

Yvonne Ventresca is the author of *Pandemic* (Sky Pony Press, 2014), a young adult novel about an emotionally traumatized teenager struggling to survive a deadly bird flu outbreak. School Library Journal calls *Pandemic* "an engrossing apocalyptic story" and Jim Cobb of *Survival Weekly* says that it "easily ranks in my top 25 favorite disaster novels." Yvonne's other writing credits include two nonfiction books for teens, *Avril Lavigne* (a biography of the singer) and *Publishing* (about careers in the field). Yvonne lives with her family and dogs in New Jersey.

YvonneVentresca.com

DelSheree Gladden

As The Pieces Fell (Chapter Fourteen)

I love books. I love reading them. I love writing them.

Fiction makes it possible to survive reality.

Writing is my escape, and I have escaped to Aztec temples in *The Escaping Fate Series*, into Native American myths in *The Twin Souls Saga*, to a dystopian reality in *The Destroyer Trilogy*, into invisibility in *The Aerling Series*, into wicked desires in *The Someone Wicked This Way Comes Series*, and into sweet romances in *The Date Shark Series*.

DelSheree is a *USA Today* bestselling author and has several new projects for 2015, including *The Ghost Host*!

www.delshereegladden.com

Casey Hays

Edge of a Promise (Chapter Fifteen)

Casey Hays graduated from Eastern New Mexico University in 1995, with a Bachelor of Arts in Literature and Modern and Classical Languages. A former high school English teacher, she launched her writing career with her debut young adult novel, *The Cadence*, in 2012. Her YA dystopian novel, *Breeder*, the first in *The Arrow's Flight Series* won the Kindle Hub Dystopian Book of the Year for 2014. As evidenced by her stories, her Christian faith plays an important role in her life and her writing. Casey Hays resides in New Mexico with her husband of twenty-four years and their two children.

www.whisperingpages.com

Harlow C. Fallon

Where You Hang Your Hat (Chapter Sixteen)

Harlow Fallon grew up in a home where reading was always encouraged. With an artist father and a librarian mother, Harlow's love of literature and art flourished. She cut her teeth on *The Wizard of Oz*, and as a teen discovered the worlds of Ray Bradbury and Frank Herbert. Today, she channels her imagination into her own writing, fueled by the curiosities of the world and the mysteries of the universe. Science fiction and fantasy are her genres of choice. She and her husband have five grown children and have made Michigan their home for the past fifteen years.

www.harlowcfallon.com

Kate Corcino

Survival Mode (Chapter Seventeen)

Kate Corcino makes her home in the southwestern USA, and her desert often appears in her work. She believes in magic, coffee, Starburst candies, genre fiction, descriptive profanity, and cackling over wine with good friends. She also believes in the transformative power of screwing up and second chances. Cheers to works-in-progress of the literary and lifelong variety! She is currently writing the follow-up to *Ignition Point* and *Spark Rising*, the first books in *The Progenitor Saga*, a near-future dystopian adventure series with romantic elements, science, magic, and plenty of action.

www.KateCorcino.com

Kate L. Mary

Don't Look Back (Chapter Eighteen)

Kate L. Mary is a stay-at-home mom of four and Air Force wife. She enjoys writing post-apocalyptic and dystopian fiction, coffee in the morning, and a glass of red wine in the evening. *Broken World*, the first book in her new adult zombie series, was a best seller in post-apocalyptic and dystopian fiction on Amazon for over six months, and the first three books have recently been released on audiobook. Kate currently resides in Oklahoma with her husband and children.

http://KateLMary.com

Monica Enderle Pierce

Blood Brother (Chapter Nineteen)

Monica Enderle Pierce has worked in publishing, advertising, and web development, but her favorite careers have been mother and author. (One of those lets her obliterate things every day.) Her post-apocalyptic book, *Girl Under Glass*, was a 2012 Amazon Breakthrough Novel Award semi-finalist and a sci-fi bestseller. Of her historical, pre-apocalyptic novel, *Famine*, one reviewer wrote: "Jeez. Effing heck. I need more now! Argh!" and "Holy. Wow." Her stories are immersive, detailed, character-driven, and compelling. She has an English degree from UCLA, and lives in Seattle with her husband, her daughter, a transgender fish, a neurotic dog, and two crazy tomcats.

http://stalkingfiction.com

ER Arroyo

Martial Law (Chapter Twenty)

E.R. Arroyo is the author of YA dystopian, *The Sovereign Series*, and co-founder/owner of Band of Dystopian Authors and Fans, a Facebook community, blog, and company that champions dystopian, apocalyptic, and post-apocalyptic fiction. E.R. is passionate about books, music, and her family, and she loves to talk shop with other authors and with her readers.

www.erarroyo.com

Thank you for reading *Prep For Doom*. We encourage you to leave a review with your retailer of choice and Goodreads. If you enjoyed what you read here, check out other works by your favorite *Prep For Doom* authors.

BAND OF DYSTOPIAN

AUTHORS AND FANS

www.bandofdystopian.com

44460716R10220

Made in the USA
Charleston, SC
24 July 2015